CW00945783

Joss was born on the borders of East London and Essex. Leaving Essex behind for Cambridge, she went on to have careers in British diplomacy, as a policy adviser for Oxfam, and along the way gained a doctorate in English Literature from Oxford University. More recently she has written for children and young adults, winning awards in both categories. She has published over fifty novels that have been translated into many languages. She lives in Oxford.

@jossstirling
goldinggateway.com

Also by Joss Stirling

The Jess Bridges Mysteries

Black River

Red House

Grey Stones

Standalones

Don't Trust Me

The Silence

White Horse

JOSS STIRLING

One More Chapter
a division of HarperCollins*Publishers*
The News Building
1 London Bridge Street
London SE1 9GF

www.harpercollins.co.uk

HarperCollins*Publishers*
1st Floor, Watermarque Building, Ringsend Road
Dublin 4, Ireland

This paperback edition 2021

First published in Great Britain in ebook format by
HarperCollins*Publishers* 2020

Copyright © Joss Stirling 2020

Joss Stirling asserts the moral right to
be identified as the author of this work.

A catalogue copy of this book
is available from the British Library.

ISBN: 9780008422615

This novel is entirely a work of fiction.
The names, characters and incidents portrayed in it are
the work of the author's imagination. Any resemblance to
actual persons, living or dead, events or localities is
entirely coincidental.

Set in Birka by Palimpsest Book Production Ltd, Falkirk Stirlingshire

Printed and bound in Great Britain by
CPI Group (UK) Ltd, Croydon CR0 4YY

All rights reserved. No part of this publication may be
reproduced, stored in a retrieval system, or transmitted,
in any form or by any means, electronic, mechanical,
photocopying, recording or otherwise, without the prior
permission of the publishers.

To Caroline Walsh – thank you for many years of working together. You've always been a rock of stability through the ups and downs of the book world – you are much appreciated!

Chapter 1

Leo

Detective Inspector Leo George knew that death was never pretty, but sometimes it had an infernal majesty, like a fallen angel. It opened a fracture in daily life to remind humanity that we were always standing on the edge of an abyss.

The body was stretched out along the back of the White Horse. She rode on the chalk figure cut from the turf three thousand years ago by unknown hands. The hands that put the victim here were equally mysterious, though only the work of a few hours ago. The girl's blank face stared up at the dawn sky. How long had she been here? Were the skies dark when she died? wondered Leo. This was too popular a destination for walkers to allow for a body to be left here during daylight hours without anyone noticing.

Leo wished he could take her away from this awful stage-setting, but that was not the job.

He moved round the victim with as much care as he could, hard though that was to do in the white boiler suit and blue coveralls for his shoes. These made him feel as if he were in some clumsy mascot suit for a grim Disney parade. He paused to take in the scene from a new angle. The blood had trickled downhill so that it stained the chalk like a cut to the horse's neck.

Such a waste of a young life.

The girl's pale skin was now flushed with an unnatural warmth as a finger of light groped in from the east. The sun had just edged over the crest of the Downs, an ancient landscape of trackways and chalk hills. He stood in the dark and silent past while over to the southwest, modern Swindon with its electric lights and wind turbines hummed awake.

The police pathologist, Geraldine Jones, strode down the bank towards Leo. The White Horse lay just off the crest of the hill, best seen from across the valley rather than at close quarters.

'So, what've you got for me, Leo?' She always acted as if Leo laid out the victims for her like a banquet he had specially prepared.

He responded as usual with a calm recitation of the facts. You cannot bring emotion on to a murder site, no matter how you may hate what you see.

'Morning, Gerry. Apologies for the early hour. The body of a young woman, Caucasian, blonde, probably in her late teens or early twenties. Dressed in a white robe fastened at the waist with rope – hemp rather than nylon. Single stab to the heart, done precisely, a small puncture wound so there is little blood splatter but she then bled out. No sign yet of the weapon but we're looking. She is arranged on the chalk-cut horse so she appears to be lying on its back near the neck.'

Geraldine nodded and crossed her arms, taking her first good look. She made a stocky figure in her wellingtons and overalls, auburn hair caught up in a neat coil at the back of her head. You could imagine Geraldine as a vet, birthing calves from labouring cows, or administering shots to a sick elephant. She had chosen instead the life of a pathologist, the last person to care for the dead.

'Are you thinking a ceremonial killing?' she asked. The photographer crouched to get a closeup of the hip where it touched the chalk line. A blood-pattern expert took measurements of the splatter marks.

'Has to be a possibility. The white robe looks handmade. We're a few weeks off Halloween so it's not so likely to be a fancy-dress party or student prank gone wrong.'

'OK, leave her with me. I'll let you know what I find.'

Leo walked away, consigning the dead to the forensic experts. His scene of crime team were already organising a search of the approaches to the White Horse, with particular care being taken around the car park and footpath that led there. The victim wasn't wearing shoes and her feet showed no sign of dirt or abrasion, which meant she didn't walk here like that. She either hiked in, changed, and her belongings were hidden or removed, or she came by car, dead or alive, and was carried. Leo hoped the forensics would be able to tell him.

DS Wong, a young high-flyer in CID, was interviewing the couple who found her. Leo had asked Suyin to do so rather than his other sergeant, Harry Boston, as Harry had already described them as fucking tree-huggers on the strength of the crystals dangling from the driver's mirror. Leo suspected that the unlucky pair had come up here for a spiritual dawn vigil only to find a very different experience awaited them.

From the snatches he overheard, Suyin had the interview well under control so he circled the car park. Their campervan was the only vehicle apart from those belonging to the police and the National Trust warden. Powder blue, it had seen better days, rust eating its way up the wheel arches. Peering through the windows, he could see piles of blankets, sleeping bags, clothes. A reason and a warrant to search it would be welcome but so far the team was taking the witnesses at face value.

Harry busied himself logging the contents of the waste bin into evidence. It would be sorted out in the lab.

'Do we have to do the dog bin too?' he asked, nose wrinkling in disgust. Harry Boston had the bearing and stature of a heavyweight boxer just going to seed but it was wise not to forget he knew how to deliver a punch. Harry was no fan of Leo's promotion above him in rank, protesting that Leo had not served as many years on the streets.

'That's correct, Harry. Bag it all up. There's no sign of a weapon or her belongings so we have to be certain they weren't hidden somewhere here.'

Harry knew this; he was just pushing at Leo, chipping away at his authority. 'Any word on her identity?' he asked, waving on the constable who had the unenvied task of bagging up the dog waste.

'I've asked Missing Persons to run her, but no luck yet. We

will have more chance of finding out who she is when her description goes out on the morning news.'

'Yeah. She looks too well-groomed to be long-term homeless. Someone is going to notice she's not where she should be.' Harry got out a cigarette, saw Leo's look, and put it away again. 'The National Trust wants a word.' He indicated a man wearing a green fleece with the trust's logo, standing miserably by his jeep. The National Trust managed public access to the site which included the chalk figure of the White Horse and the nearby Iron Age hillfort called Uffington Castle. The warden's face was grey and craggy, his hair and beard white; he looked like a Biblical patriarch brought unwillingly to modern times.

'Thanks.' As Leo walked away, the cigarette came out again. Leo had long since decided to pick his battles with Harry. This wasn't one of them. 'Mr Chamberlain? Hello, I'm Inspector George, Thames Valley. I'm the senior officer in charge of this investigation.'

The warden shook hands. He had the calloused grip of a gardener who digs the soil, one of Leo's off-duty tribe. 'Bad business this.' His voice rang deep and resonant, the kind used to introduce trailers of epic films. 'I spend my life chasing off vandals, advertisers, and druids who all want to use this site for their own ends, but this is worse than anything I've seen.' He rubbed a hand over his face. 'Desecration, that's what it is.'

If murder wasn't so wretched, Leo would have enjoyed hearing this modern-day Moses say words like 'desecration'. 'You think the site is holy in some way?'

He looked uncomfortable with the question. 'Not sure I'd go that far, Inspector, but sacred to our island story. It's the first great artwork we know of in England.'

Leo turned to look back up the hill. 'I hadn't thought of it like that.'

'It would have had some practical purpose. A sign to warn off outsiders, maybe? But it is delivered with such minimalist style and flair; artists still struggle to beat it.'

Leo had to agree with him. A horse galloping across the brow of a hill described in five lines. It was the spirit of the horse, not one of the Iron Age's stubby British ponies. It anticipated the arrival of the Arabian horses several millennia later, the same ones that now stocked the racehorse studs thriving close by on the Downs. 'My colleague said you wanted a word. How can I help you?'

'I realise my concerns are petty in the face of that –' his gaze went to the ambulance making its way to the White Horse '– but I just wanted to ask how long you think the site will be closed off to the public?'

That was always the challenge for a murder enquiry: the police were stuck at the moment of death while others pressed for life to go on. 'Shut at least for today, maybe longer, depending on what we find. This site as well as the approaches. I suggest you use the old standby of closed "until further notice". Are you a local man, Mr Chamberlain?' He had responded very quickly to the call, getting here only minutes after Leo.

'Yes. I live in the village just down there.' He pointed into the Vale of the White Horse where lights twinkled. 'My house is on the edge of Kingston Beauchamp, near St Martin's Church.' Leo knew from weekend drives that the villages in the valley were picture-postcard English with thatched houses, stone buildings, slow rivers, and shady old trees.

'Would you say it's a small community where most people know each other?'

He scratched at his beard. 'People are much less friendly than when I first moved to the area. But I know a few of the families.'

'It would be helpful if you would look at a photograph of the victim, in case you recognise her.'

'Oh, I ... I suppose I can do that.' His gaze shifted over Leo's left shoulder as another van pulled in. That would be more scene of crime officers arriving, hopefully with the blood detection dog Leo had requested to sniff out the trail of the murderer leaving the scene.

Leo drew the warden's attention back to the photo. 'I should warn you that this is a photo of the victim. You don't have to do this, but it would be helpful to our enquiries.'

He closed his eyes briefly. 'Oh God. What if I see someone I know?'

'We have no idea at this stage if she is a local but the facts aren't going to change, Mr Chamberlain, whoever you see in the photo.'

'It's just that I've never been very good with that stuff. I chose a quiet life working for the National Trust. You need my older brother – he was the one who went into the army. Yes, you need Roger. He lives in the village too.'

He was trying to push Leo off onto his brother which was

an odd ducking of responsibility for a mature man. Leo would've moved away rather than take a job near a relative who always made him feel like that. Some patterns set in childhood never changed though. 'But he's not here and you are. Will you do it?'

Breathing deeply through his nose, the warden gave a nod. Leo showed him a closeup of the girl's face, one the photographer had taken as soon as there was enough light. He released a breath.

'No, I don't know her, thank God. That fair hair is distinctive, isn't it?' She was almost platinum blonde with pale eyebrows, suggesting that the colour was natural. 'No, I'm fairly certain she's not from one of the village families.'

'Thank you, Mr Chamberlain.'

He drew a hand over his eyes. 'I wish I could unsee it now.'

'Believe me, there are much worse things.' This girl looked almost peaceful in her death. In fact, her perfection might have been what the killer wanted. That was certainly something to add to the report.

'I bet there are.' The warden's smile was friendly now that the ordeal was over and he had done his bit.

'Thank you, Mr Chamberlain. No more questions for the moment. We'll will be in touch if there're any follow-ups.'

'You'll be down in the valley later?' he asked, getting into his jeep.

Leo rested his hand on the door frame to detain him. 'She had to come from somewhere. Please don't talk about the victim to anyone, particularly any details you may have gleaned about how she was found.'

'Don't worry, Inspector. I'm not the kind to run my mouth off.' Leo dropped his hand and the warden started his car. As he drove away, the black Labrador in the passenger seat started barking, lunging at the window to reach Leo, and not with friendly intent.

There came a shout from the footpath that led out of the car park. It went in the opposite direction to the White Horse, along the ancient Ridgeway, heading for the barrow of Wayland's Smithy, a mile southwest.

'Sir, sir, we've found something!'

Chapter 2

Jess

Flicking through a book on paganism, I was accosted by German elves. Their leader, an Orlando Bloom wannabe, addressed me in what I suspected was Elvish.

'Sorry, I don't speak that dialect,' I said. 'You could try me with Vulcan but I don't speak that either.'

This flummoxed them. 'Dwarvish?' the elf lord asked, really trying hard to find something in common.

I tapped my pointed ears and then my fake uptick eyebrows. 'Not an elf – or a dwarf. I'm Spock, or maybe his sister.' I leaned closer and said in a confidential manner, 'You see, I'm not exactly taking this seriously.'

Star Trek cosplay was evidently despised by those who fancy themselves one of the Elder Race. The little flock of elves swivelled away in a flap of grey cloaks.

'Live long and prosper!' I called after them.

This was brilliant. I just loved it here. Michael's promise that the Frankfurt Book Fair would be fun had been fulfilled in spades, or in photon torpedoes, as I should say in my current garb. I was in a huge exhibition centre, one hall of many, surrounded by books and freaky people like me who thought donning a costume was a great way to spend their Saturday. I had a little game going with myself where I tried to identify who was who. I was batting about half and half: some good hits, but many whizzed by me, showing me that I was well behind on all the new series that had been spawned by the growth of streaming services. So far, I had spotted the entire superhero universe, or several universes; enough *Witcher* and *Game of Thrones* characters to stage a battle between them without CGI-ed extras; some steampunk gangs from ... I wasn't sure where; a few Discworld (I thought) refugees; and a motley selection of assassins, aliens, and warrior princesses.

Michael rumbled up in his chair, not avoiding the soft shoe tips of the departing elves in the squash. His 'sorry' did not sound at all sincere. I grinned at seeing him dressed as Captain Kirk in a gold sweater and black trousers, blasting his way through the enemy ships. He did this for me, as his part of our bargain that I come with him to the awards ceremony later today.

'This place is Bedlam!' he growled. 'Has everyone gone mad?'

I kissed him on the cheek in sympathy. 'Everyone was already mad, Michael. I thought you knew?'

He harrumphed but he was smiling now.

'How was your meeting with the publisher?' I asked. We were in front of the display of the shortlisted books for the European non-fiction award that he was up for. 'What's the news?' I knew this meant a lot to him, even though he had been trying to play it down for the last two months since the invitation came through.

'We're meeting for coffee if you want to come. Petra's been promised a place in the top two by the organisers,' he said, scowling now at his competition. Petra was his editor who worked with him on his bestseller, *Type M for Murder*, his book on the psychology of killers. He based this on his research in secure hospitals for the severely mentally disturbed. On the table before us, *Type M* found itself banged up with some strange cellmates. There was the book on modern-day paganism I had been leafing through when the elves arrived, called *Pagan's Progress*. Next to that was a lament to the lost ecosystems of the American west coast, entitled *Last of the Pelicans*. The final contender in this rogue's gallery was a piece on artificial intelligence with the punchy title *You Are F*cked.* Is that the last message we're going to get from computers before they do away with us? I wondered. It started so well with 'Hello, World!', but I suppose it was the logical progression.

Michael was getting jealous as I lingered over the opposition. 'What do you think of them?' he asked.

'I see you aren't alone with the literary pun.'

'Last of the what?'

'Mohicans ... Pelicans. I thought you'd know that since you know everything.' I had decided, now we were redefining our friendship after our breakup, that I had been put in this world to tease Michael. 'I note the dishonourable exception among your foursome. It's taken the "swear at the general public" route that seems so popular at the moment.' Any trip to a bookshop meant being confronted by a wall of asterisked covers, your brain supplying the obvious swear words intended.

'A cliché,' he sniffed. 'Cheap ploy to grab attention.'

I secretly thought it worked but he didn't want to hear that. 'Absolutely. And you should never judge a book by its cover, of course. That's what I'd call my book.'

'You? Write a book?'

We headed for the café where he had arranged to meet Petra. 'Is that so impossible to imagine?'

He wisely pleaded the Fifth.

'Anyway, my book will be called *Don't Judge Me by My Cover*. Good, hey?'

'Too many words. Mine's a black coffee; the lady will have a hot chocolate,' he told the barista.

'Don't you just love that it's cold enough to have hot chocolate again?' I hugged my arms to myself. October had arrived and it was chilly here by the doors to the smoking area. I had a pack in my bag but Michael had been moaning at me to kick the habit. Sometimes we still acted like a couple even though we had theoretically got through that.

'Do you ever stop drinking it?'

He had me there. 'On very hot days.'

'Jessica, you always have a cappuccino in the morning, hot chocolate in the afternoon, white wine in the evening.' He paid for our drinks and I carried them to a table.

'I don't!'

'You do.'

Actually, he might have been right. 'OK, maybe I do. I'm

sure I drink tea too.' I swiped the dirty cups into the bin to clear a space.

'Not in cafés.'

'I'm not paying two quid for hot water and a teabag! I could make that at home for next to nothing.' I moved a stool so he could bring his chair closer. 'Some days, though, I have been known to cut out the hot drinks and just stick to the wine. I'm a purist that way. It's my Drink Wine and Die Young but Happy Diet. I should pitch it to a publisher.'

He snorted in his patrician way. 'You're glossing over the risk of liver disease and alcoholism.'

'Always such a party pooper. Anyway, I'm not being serious.'

'With you, it's sometimes hard to tell.'

'Meow!' I grinned approvingly at his bitchiness. 'Point to you.'

His smile turned more reflective. 'I remember that you did have a phase of drinking green tea.'

That was when I had been with Drew, my ex, who had given me up for the life of a vegan yoga teacher. I didn't think he had struggled much with the exchange, not like I had. He led me to my rebound guy, Jago, who in turn had swum off into the wild blue yonder on his latest documentary project, with fond feelings and no regrets. My record with men was about as good as my communication with German elves.

Petra approached with a gaggle of her publisher friends. I liked Michael's editor. I sensed she was hiding him from a life of chaos under the pretence of ruthless efficiency. There was a slightly desperate look in her grey eyes, and an attitude of feverishly attacking life, that I recognised from the mirror.

She had her red hair in a feathered cut that framed her face, but neatness went out the window when she was stressed and it stuck up like ruffled plumes on a hen.

'Michael, Jess, I've brought some people I think you should meet before this evening. Michael, this is Tanglewood White, author of—'

'Yes, I know, *Pagan's Progress.*' Michael smiled tightly at the fifty-something woman with platinum blonde hair that brushed the nape of her neck. I knew he'd very much prefer not to see his rivals as it was far easier to disparage them from afar. He lifted his hand from his lap to the waiting woman. 'Good to meet you.'

The author made the usual adjustment that people went through when they met Michael. Good-looking guy with glossy auburn hair, seated in a wheelchair, thanks to a close brush with death at the hands of a crazed killer. And what did she see when she looked at me? Smallish blonde bombshell attempting to channel Marilyn Monroe? Only in my most generous dreams.

'I'm so pleased to meet you,' she said. 'I've been wanting to meet you ever since Petra mentioned you both. And you must be Jessica Bridges?'

'Call me Jess.' I shook her hand.

Disconcertingly, she turned her attention to me, rather than the literary star. 'Petra said you live in Oxford and look for missing persons, Jess? I mean, that's what you do for a living?'

'For my sins.' Petra had been introducing me like this to her colleagues because saying I was Michael's definitely-not-his-partner was harder to explain.

'I'm so glad.'

Odd. I glanced at Michael.

'I'm afraid Jessica isn't here to work, Tanglewood,' said Michael.

I wished I were in the right spot to elbow him. 'Not that I ever turn work away.' My bottom line wouldn't allow that.

'Good. Great, in fact.' Tanglewood scrunched up the programme she'd been given, then smoothed it out when she noticed. 'Can we talk after the ceremony?'

'Of course. You've lost someone and you want me to find them?' I asked.

'Oh no. I know exactly where they are.'

I wondered what part of 'I look for missing persons' she wasn't getting. 'Are you sure you need me then?'

'Yes, because she's lost herself and I'm hoping you can help her find her way back. Before it's too late.' She looked quickly over at Petra and the woman who I assumed was Tanglewood's editor. They were ordering generously from the bar for themselves. Don't you just love expense accounts? 'I'm sorry. It's complicated. I'll explain later.'

My mind was now spinning. 'Just one quick question: who is this person to you?'

She clasped her hands to her neck in consternation. 'I should've started with that. Sorry. I'm not thinking straight. It's my daughter. Lisette.'

Chapter 3

Leo

Two members of the search team had found a bundle of material in the hedgerow. Lifting it out carefully, they unrolled it on a plastic sheet spread on the path. It resolved itself into a green cloak and a pair of leather sandals – sturdy Jesus creepers rather than flimsy fashion ones. The female officer held them up in gloved hands.

'No size marked but I'm a six. These are around a four or a five, sir. A woman's shoe – or a child's.'

About the same size as the victim's feet then.

'Good work, Diana. Bag them up for forensics. Tag for blood and DNA.' Leo tried to imagine how they might have come to be there. One possibility was that the girl put them in the hedge herself, tucked out of the way for collection after whatever she expected to happen on the hill concluded. Surely she hadn't expected to die if she walked in? Those who killed her might not even know where she'd left her things. She could have walked the rest of the way on the short downland grass, which would explain why her feet were clean and unmarked.

Alternatively, if they went with the theory that her killer dumped her stuff here, that begged the question why. Why not dispose of it entirely?

He looked down the track to the southwest. If this was a ceremonial killing, then that fact told him that they were going to have to expand the search.

'Harry, are you done with the bins?' Leo called.

'Yes. All bagged and tagged.' His sergeant stubbed out his taunting cigarette.

'Take two officers and head over to Wayland's Smithy by car. Close it off and question anyone you find there. I'll join you shortly. I'll take a team and walk there.'

'You don't want me on a bigger team on the search of the path?' Harry was always so ready to second guess.

'No, our priority is to stop members of the public disturbing any evidence before we have a chance to examine the barrow.'

'You really think there are two sites involved in this?' The DS beckoned a couple of searchers to join him.

Just do your job, Harry, thought Leo. 'It has to be a strong possibility considering the stage-setting of a sacrifice and a second famous prehistoric site so close. I'll contact you if I find anything on the path.'

Leo took with him the two officers who'd found the bundle – he had a much easier rhythm with them. They fanned out across the path. A well-used route, there was little to be made from the footprints in the churned earth, but Leo couldn't rule out more traces of the victim in the bushes and long grass along the fence line. They had to look. On this quick survey, there was nothing to find apart from a depressing number of cans and plastic rubbish. A follow-up team would collect it for examination – one slight good thing to come out of this.

His phone buzzed.

'Good call, Leo,' said Harry. 'There are signs all over the barrow of recent activity. Some kind of religious ceremony by the looks of things. I can see traces of candle wax on the top of the stones, some scratches, and a burnt-out campfire. We'll need SOCOs to go over it with a fine-tooth comb.'

Thank you, Captain Obvious. 'I'll send one of the vans. You didn't go inside the barrow, did you?'

'Don't get your knickers in a twist. Just me and only to check there're no more victims.'

'Did you find anything?'

'No. It's a hell of a creepy place though. We'll need lights but the activity looks like it happened by the entrance.'

'We'll be with you in a few minutes.'

Leo's small search team approached the barrow from the northeast, tracing in reverse the path the victim and killer – or was it killers? – might have taken. Leo had been here several times when walking along the Downs. If the White Horse was about a space dedicated to the sky, Wayland's Smithy was about the earth. A long, low mound, nestled among trees, it was fringed at the southern end by four large standing stones and some smaller ones. Sarsen stones, they were called locally; etymology disputed. It either meant alien, as in 'Saracen' stones, or troublesome, from the Anglo-Saxon *sar-stan*. Leo considered the second more prosaic origin was likely to be correct: the rock that was the bane of any ploughshare. Our ancestors found a use for them and moved them here. The two largest guarded the passageway leading into the barrow, a path almost blocked at two places by shorter sarsens. The doorway itself was a simple construction of two upright stones and one flat stone across the top. He didn't need a professor of archaeology to tell him what those who constructed the tomb had been thinking. As he looked directly into the dark mouth of the barrow, it felt like a womb. Put another way, this was the view a midwife got when delivering a child. *We came from the womb*, thought Leo, *and the barrow reminds us that we return there to Mother Earth.*

The six officers stood in silence before the Wayland's Smithy entrance, taking in the scene. Detective work was about stopping in order to solve puzzles as much as it was activity. They knew that Leo needed quiet to think. In the hush, he noticed a strange ringing in the air and wondered for a moment if his mind was playing tricks.

'Can you hear that?' he asked his team.

Harry smirked. 'Yeah. Put the wind up us when we first heard it. Kyle tracked it down to metal tags on the trees.'

The young officer blushed as he spoke, cursed as he was with the ruddy cheeks of the fair-skinned. 'Yes, sir. I think they're put there by the landowner to mark the beeches for his records.'

But any neopagan rite would have loved the special effects. Leo imagined hearing that at night in the candlelight.

'Are you thinking they started here with whatever it was they were doing, then headed to the horse?' asked Harry.

'If these signs are connected, then yes.' Leo could see them in his mind's eye: a procession, probably lit by flaming torches, excitement. How many had known that a real death was about to happen? Would someone crack and tell them what had taken place here? Or had that atrocity been done by a smaller, select number?

'If they were poncing about here, doing their satanic ritual or whatever, it means we're looking for more than one person involved in the killing.'

'I agree, but what makes you think that?'

Harry waved to the stones. 'There were enough candles here to light a cathedral. It's no laughing matter trying to keep a candle alight outdoors. Tried that for my mother last August – eighty fucking candles on her birthday cake. By the time you get to the last one, the first will have long gone out.'

Thanks to Harry, Leo could see that part now. Acolytes tending the flames while the senior figures in this drama enacted their parts in the centre by the stones. 'Good point.'

'Does it look like a c**t to you?' Harry used a crude word, knowing Leo would have to pull him up on it. It was a war of attrition between them.

'We're on duty, Harry.'

'You don't mind Old Harry's foul language, do you, Liv?' he asked, picking out one of the officers he'd brought with him – the youngest.

She stood to attention, hands behind her back. 'Actually, I do find it offensive, sir.'

That irritated Harry enough that he muttered, 'A cult killing involving a c**t, sorry *womblike* tomb? The press are just going to love this, no matter what you snowflakes think.'

'That's enough, Harry. That language has no place in the Thames Valley Police.' Leo turned to the team. 'And they can dress it up how they like, light as many candles, chant as many prayers, but this is still murder. A girl has lost her life. It's our task to get her justice. Let's do our job.'

Chapter 4

Jess

I sat between Michael and Petra in the Frankfurt Fair auditorium in which the presentation was taking place. This was probably the closest I'd ever come to an Oscar ceremony so I was determined to enjoy it. Sorry to report that the goodie bags weren't up to Hollywood standard: mainly proof copies of books the sponsors wanted to flog and a few bookmarks for things I'd never read. Here was I hoping for at least chocolate.

However, the organisers had spiced up what could've been a tedious hour with presentations on each of the shortlisted books by students from Goethe University. I was amused how each group had interpreted their brief. Michael's book got a tense drama, a reenactment of one of the interviews in his chapter called 'The Psychopath Among Us'. All well and good. The response in the room was electric and my hopes rose. They were then dashed as the book on the pelicans got a nature documentary. Someone, presumably the deep-pocketed publisher, had paid for the team to fly to

Seattle and film in Puget Sound. It was a frighteningly professional job from the media students. The AI doomsday book had attracted the programmers to come up with a computer-generated piece of music in the style of Beethoven, which the makers called 'Ode to Despair'. Very gloomy and Germanic; it didn't win many fans, even if it was a glimpse of our future as slaves of the machine. But my favourite was what they had done for Tanglewood's book; this had been handed over to the students on the Master of Arts programme and they'd come up with an interpretive dance. I kid you not. Five young people – three men and two women, all in black – dancing to a track that sounded like the weird offspring of Enya and Kanye. The performance involved a ram's skull, a wicker man, and something obscure to do with stones. I guessed I'd have to read the book to decode that part. It was all very sexual. As they exited to bemused applause, I decided I would totally vote for that book if I weren't already biased towards Michael's.

Throughout the presentations, Michael looked pained at what he probably considered a vulgar bid for entertainment.

'Be grateful you didn't get the interpretive dance,' I murmured.

'Oh, I am. I definitely am,' he said fervently.

And now the big moment arrived. The trophy sat on a pedestal on the stage: a glass star the size of a dinner plate. Where would anyone put that? Michael had been promised a place in the top two so he could afford to relax a little until the big announcement. First to be presented were the books in the judges' 'Highly Commended' category. These were awarded to *Pagan's Progress* and *You Are F*cked*. The winners didn't get to make a speech. They passed quickly across the stage to receive their certificate, cheque, and little glass star trophy. Applause was polite and barely covered Tanglewood's return to her seat. I gave her a commiserating look, then reached over and squeezed Michael's hand.

'And now, the runner-up in the Frankfurt Non-Fiction Book of the Year is ...' The announcer had seen too many TV programmes where they spin out this moment. She took her time opening the envelope. '*Type M for Murder.*'

Oh dear. I leant over and hugged Michael.

'Fucking pelicans,' he muttered in my ear before pulling away and wheeling himself onto the stage. Over to our right, the publishing team for *Last of the Pelicans* was already celebrating, attracting much of the attention that should have been given to Michael. I stood up and cheered Michael, then added a whistle to draw people back to his progress to the stage. Petra joined me and this shamed those around us to follow suit. At least Michael received his award to a standing ovation. His winner's speech wouldn't be needed though. When he got back to us, medium-sized star trophy on his lap, the pelican guys were already bounding over to pick up their prize as a montage of pelican shots flew on the screen behind them.

'It's a zeitgeist thing,' said Petra in commiseration as the applause echoed around the auditorium. 'It's the environment's moment, what with Greta Thunberg and the fact that we're all going to die if we don't stop climate change.'

'Well, that certainly puts things in sunny perspective, Petra,' I said cheerily. 'So, let me guess, you're a glass-half-full kind of person?'

'It's still very good, Michael. And we're still in with a good chance with the Guardian Readers' Book of the Year,' said Petra, wisely ignoring my sarcasm. 'Keep up the tweeting.'

Michael grimaced. It was exhausting, as he had already told me, finding time to carve out a following for himself in the public arena. He didn't mind kicking off debates but he hated the 'vote for me' aspect of what his publishers wanted him to do. He teased me for my effortless audience of hundreds of thousands for my fake cat lover Instagram account. Well, it wasn't exactly fake as I did like cats, but I kept it so I could follow back other people whom I was pursuing for professional reasons. They were unlikely to suspect CuteCat4567 of anything other than a dubious obsession with hilarious cat antics. Thanks to regular uploads to my account of new videos, I seemed to have become peculiarly popular ... from which I deduced that the internet wanted more kittens, and not politicians, doing funny stuff.

We were both in dire need of a drink by the time the pelican people had done their lap of honour and thanked everyone including their primary school teachers and Susie from the post room. (I might be exaggerating but when have you ever found a list of thanks the least bit interesting when you know none of the people mentioned?) We spilled out into the reception. I cornered an unfortunate German teenager who bore a tray of drinks and took the whole thing from her. She was too shocked to protest. Michael parked up in a corner, I set the tray before us, and we began to make our way through the contents. Petra had vanished. I hoped this wasn't a sign of waning interest from Michael's publisher?

'Jessica, have I ever told you how I like your style?' said Michael, selecting a beer from the array. 'No one else would have the guts to do this even though it's what they all want to do.'

'It's my signature move.' I shifted a crate of leaflets over so I could sit down. The pelican guys didn't need their material advertising their wonderful lives flying round the world to lament the loss of habitat to rising CO2 levels. 'Look at all the trees they're killing,' I said, planting my butt on their collection.

As expected, this invitation to knock the winners cheered Michael up. We agreed that the book should never have been nominated. A European book award given to one about America? Come on. What were they like on the judging panel?

'Kickbacks,' I declared. 'I bet the publisher bribed them.'

Michael knew I was only joking. 'With what?'

'Cash or blow jobs. Maybe both?'

He spluttered into his beer.

'Did that go down the wrong way? I've heard that can be a problem.' I underlined the innuendo with eyebrow wiggling.

'I don't remember you ever having that problem.'

Now it was my turn to cough on my gin and tonic.

Well-oiled with booze, we were sniggering like thirteen-year-olds when Tanglewood found us. I offered her a selection from the diminished drinks on our tray. She grabbed an elderflower cordial. That was fine: neither Michael nor I were going to dilute our alcohol haze with that.

'Bad luck,' I said. 'To both of you. I mean, what did the pelicans do for us, hey? That's what I want to know.'

'You should've won, Michael,' Tanglewood said. 'There's nothing original in that book, and yours has such an interesting story to tell, something we all need to understand as we grapple with the presence of evil in our lives.'

'And yours – I thought they did you a disservice handing it over to a dance troupe,' said Michael, not at all gauging his audience.

'I loved the dance group!' I said indignantly. 'Best bit of the whole evening.'

'I quite liked them too, once I recovered from the surprise.' Tanglewood gave me a little smile. 'My book is about the reinvention of old ideas so it was oddly appropriate.'

'How do you mean? Sorry, I haven't read it yet.'

'I must give you a copy, if you'd like one.'

'I'd totally like that. But go on about reinvention. I'm just about sober enough to listen.'

'Being drunk is definitely an old tradition. We find drinking vessels at all the ceremonial sites. My book's thesis is that modern pagans often latch on to a fragment of an idea that was once embedded in a whole social context. They lift it out and turn it into something that says far more about our time than about anything authentically ancient.'

Most of that went over my head ... and that head was spinning. I attempted a summary and raised my glass. 'So we agree: psychos and pagans are the business, pelicans are pants?'

'How much have you had to drink, Jess?' asked Tanglewood.

I pointed to the empties on the tray. 'Half of those.'

'She's had the wine and spirits; I've had the beer,' said

Michael. 'We are going to have one sick Jessica on our hands tomorrow.'

'So now isn't a good time?' asked Tanglewood.

'Oh God, our conversation!' I tried to slap myself out of my merry daze. It didn't work as I somehow missed my aim and sloshed tonic over myself.

Ah, I see what I did wrong: I didn't put down my glass.

Michael took it out of my hand. 'Yes, I think you'd be better talking to her tomorrow. But in the afternoon. Are you staying on?'

She shook her head. 'I'm on the one-thirty to Heathrow.'

'That's good because so are we. You can talk to Jessica then. I'll make sure she's sober.'

I didn't make a very good poster girl for my business in this state, as Tanglewood had noted. 'Is she any good at what she does?'

Michael paused for a moment. 'Surprisingly, I have to say that she is.'

'Aw, Michael, you say the sweetest things now you're no longer such a dick,' I said, commandeering another tray of drinks.

Chapter 5

Leo

Leo began his enquiries in the valley with the brother of the National Trust warden. Looking him up revealed that the man's full name and rank was Major Roger Horatio Chamberlain, formerly of the Royal Green Jackets. He appeared in many social postings of the local VIP kind: mayoral banquets, political campaigning (for the Lib Dems, surprisingly), and among the racing fraternity. Leo chose the major first, not just because he was interested in seeing this paragon of courage, but also because the major was the chief landowner in these parts. A quick search run by one of the team revealed that Major Chamberlain owned the manor at Kingston Beauchamp and surrounding fields, though he himself lived in the converted manor stable, closer to the centre of the village. That kind of man – privileged, well-connected, a big fish in his own small pool – was bound to be a pain in the neck. He'd have the Chief Constable on speed dial.

Leo drove into the cobbled yard and parked alongside Major Chamberlain's Range Rover. More dogs – this time beagles – ran out to greet him. Tails thrashed his trousers like whips. Gauging their interest to be friendly, he scratched heads as he took in Chamberlain's home. This stable block was built at a time when landowners spent more on the comfort of their horses than they did their own children. Their sons and daughters were sent to spartan public schools; their prized mounts were snugly housed in heated stalls and tended to with zealous care. In the conversion from stable to home, one wing had been kept to show the original wooden divisions, complete with iron mangers and golden horsehead finials to denote the lodgings of the most notable stallions and mares. The other three sides of the court-yard had become a spacious family home. Apart from the lack of a garden, which was a serious drawback, Leo found himself envying the major's deep pockets that could afford this.

'Can I help you?' The superficially friendly question was delivered with icy disdain. The speaker, a woman in her early sixties with ash-blonde hair, a silk Hermès scarf, and quilted jacket, was on her way out if the evidence of the car keys gripped in her hand was anything to go by.

Leo showed her his warrant card. 'Inspector George, Thames Valley CID. Mrs Chamberlain?'

'Yes.'

'Might I have a quick word – and with your husband, if he's here?'

'I've a coffee morning in Burford.'

Leo stood firm. Such privilege pissed him off, but he was good at not letting his emotions show. He'd had years of practice, most of them before joining the police. 'Then I won't take up more time than is absolutely necessary.'

With a toss of her head, she turned on her heel and went back into the house. 'Roger! Roger! The police are here.'

Leo decided she must've meant him to follow her. It was odd that she didn't seem curious as to why he was calling. Normally that was the first question. Had something happened to a loved one? Had there been an accident or a robbery? Perhaps her brother-in-law had already told them to expect a call from the police?

Inside, the house got even better. Their manners might be lacking but Leo couldn't fault their taste. They had left the central wing open so that you could still see all the way down what would once have been the tack room and storage space for carriages. The floor was flagstones with a central aisle of herringbone-laid bricks. Arrangements of furniture separated the room into different spaces for sitting, dining, or watching a large flatscreen. Leo noted that the television was tuned to racing, though the sound was off.

He turned to take it all in. Something was missing. Perhaps it was a little too much like an upscale hotel lounge? It didn't feel lived in, not in the messy sense of a family who was relaxed enough to allow shoes or opened post to lie for a while before being cleared away. This looked like the Chamberlains expected a visit any moment from a photographer to feature it in a glossy magazine.

A man strolled in from the far end, holding a bone-china mug of coffee. Leo could at once see the strong family resemblance to his brother, though Roger Chamberlain was clean-shaven with white hair slicked back from a high forehead.

'Why are you making that racket, Madeleine?' he asked, rather rudely considering there was a stranger present.

She waved her car keys in Leo's direction. 'The police. An Inspector George. He wants a word.'

Leo discounted the idea they would offer him refreshments even though he had been up since the early hours and could do with a coffee. 'Major Chamberlain, Mrs Chamberlain, as you may have heard, there's been a serious incident on White Horse Hill last night. The body of a young woman was discovered there near to dawn. As a result, we are conducting house-to-house enquiries in Kingston Beauchamp today. So far, the victim hasn't been identified and we are asking locals if they know her, either as someone who lives round here or because they may have seen her yesterday as she passed through the village on the way to the hill.' Leo watched them both for a response but got nothing. Not even a 'how did she die?'

'What's this to do with us?' was what the major did ask.

Leo concluded then that if the National Trust brother, Andrew, were an Old Testament prophet, Roger was more like a New Testament Pontius Pilate, ready to wash his hands of any problematic business. 'We are seeking to identify her. We won't know if she connects to you until we know who she is.'

'Connects to us? How could she?' Mrs Chamberlain sounded put out by the very suggestion. Apparently, to be found dead on the White Horse was enough to suggest you weren't one of their type.

'There are many possibilities. She could be the daughter

of one of your neighbours, for example, or someone you recognise from a local shop. I take it you don't have a daughter yourself?'

'Of course we do. Two. Iona, whom I saw just this morning, and Ella.'

'Is Ella here?' If the parents refused to be helpful, perhaps the daughters would be better subjects for his questions.

'Obviously not. She's in South Africa on her gap year.'

And how was Leo supposed to have known that? 'The girl might be one of your daughters' acquaintances, someone you would know by sight.' He was hesitant to show them the same photo he had showed the brother. It sounded very unlikely it was either of their girls – surely the uncle would've identified her? – but he couldn't be certain of that. The warden had just glanced at the image and the girl's eyes were shut.

'Describe her,' rapped out the major, as if Leo were some junior officer reporting to him.

'I have an image I could show you. It's of the body so I will understand if you'd prefer not to see it.'

'Too right I'd prefer not to see it. Had enough of that in the army. Describe her. Distinguishing features and whatnot.'

Leo gave them a brief summary: age, height, likely weight, colouring ...

'Very blonde hair, you say?' interrupted the major, showing his first spark of interest. 'It's not us you want then; it's my tenant at the manor. He surrounds himself with blondes.'

'Awful man,' muttered Madeleine.

'But he pays up on time. That's more than I can say for that friend of yours from Cheltenham.'

Before they launched into a domestic argument, Leo tried to get the interview back on track. 'And what is your tenant's name?'

'On the lease he's down as Terence O'Brien, but in his little commune of nubile beauties, he's known as Father Oak.' Was that an envious glint in the major's eye?

'Father Oak?'

Major Chamberlain snorted. 'Exactly. He's got some New Age scam running, a sort of commune thing. Druidic and Karma Sutra hotchpotch. But as everyone appears above the age of consent and they keep the grounds beautifully, I say "live and let live".'

Madeleine rounded on Leo with her steely glare, standing shoulder to shoulder with her husband. She acted as if the policeman had taken issue with their choice of tenant. 'It's a free country, Inspector.'

That was not a matter that Leo felt he needed to weigh in on. It was a much more complex question than that throwaway comment suggested. He glanced down at the notes he had taken. 'To sum up, you don't know any young women locally with strikingly blonde hair, apart from the ones living in your manor?'

'I wouldn't say we know those women either. We are aware of them,' corrected the major.

'Did either of you notice any strange activity around the village last night? Anyone heading up the hill to either Wayland's Smithy or the White Horse?'

'We played bridge here with the Frazers last night. We didn't go out, did we, Madeleine?'

'Exactly. So we can be of no further use to you. Really, Inspector, I have to go.' Madeleine gave Leo a chilly nod as she passed him on her way to the car.

There was something Leo wanted to look at more closely before he left. He needed just a moment alone. 'Do you have a contact number for your tenant, Major Chamberlain?'

'In my files.' His gaze slid past Leo to latch onto the screen where a race was just lining up in the starting gates, the horses shying and bucking.

'I'd be very grateful if you could dig that out.' Leo gave no sign of moving. If the major wanted to catch that race, his quickest route to doing so was by giving the policeman what he wanted.

With a huff, he gave in. 'One moment then.'

As he disappeared back through the door through which he had entered, Leo moved closer to the grand piano with its collection of family photos in silver frames. The Chamberlains were pictured in variations of the same pose with their two girls, shown at different ages. The older one had dark hair and the younger fair; there appeared to be at least a ten-year age gap between them. The pictures went all the way up from infancy to the early twenties and thirties of the pair. The most recent image showed a smiling young woman in a bridesmaid's dress of gold silk. She stood alongside the dark-haired bride in the doorway of what Leo recognised as the local church, St Martin's. The groom wasn't present for that moment, or if he had been, then he'd been cropped out. The bridesmaid wore a garland of wild flowers woven with corn, giving the impression of being gold all over. Her hair rippled forward over her shoulders. She was quite stunning, even putting her attractive sister in the shade. Unfortunately, she also looked disconcertingly like the victim, though her hair was wavy rather than straight and perhaps a shade darker.

'They're my daughters, Inspector. Ella. Iona.' Roger handed Leo a Post-it with a number written on it. 'That's Iona's wedding earlier this year.'

'You're sure Ella is in South Africa?' Leo asked.

He immediately returned to the defensive. 'Do you think I don't know where my own daughter is?'

'You wouldn't be the first parent to lose track of the whereabouts of their grown-up children.'

'Well, I haven't. Goodbye, Inspector.' And very firmly, he showed Leo to the door.

Leo wasn't going to give up so easily. Something about this couple got under his skin and made him want to dig in his heels. 'Does Iona live locally?' Leo asked on the threshold, thinking that if the father wouldn't answer questions then maybe the oldest daughter would.

'Yes.'

It was like getting blood from a stone. 'And where can I find her?'

'At the vicarage. She's the rector here.'

Leo felt as if he'd missed a step. That hadn't come up in the searches. 'I see.'

For the first time, the major revealed a glimpse of a deeply-buried sense of humour. 'That's what I thought at first. Now I'm used to it. Not that either Madeleine or I are God-botherers ourselves. But if you'd seen Iona at nineteen, you wouldn't have expected her to seek ordination a decade later.'

Naturally, the local vicar was on the list of people to interview. This was all useful stuff. Leo felt a little less resentful of their stiff-necked reception. He gave the most persistent of the beagles another pat as a peace offering.

'Thank you, Major.'

There was no 'good luck with your enquiries' or anything like that. Roger simply shut the door and went back to watch the three o'clock at Newmarket.

They were an odd couple. Leo tried and failed to imagine what growing up in that household had been like. They almost made him thankful for his own dysfunctional mother. At least he had never doubted that she was human.

St Martin's was bathed in the glow of honeyed autumn light as Leo approached the main doors. It was a blocky chalk building with a square tower topped by a pitched grey roof. You could feel the Anglo-Saxon roots here; no fancy Gothic flourishes or Norman excesses. Former parishioners lay in neat rows, many headstones leaning in the same slightly drunken orientation away from the building, like they were straining to look up to the tower. The door was open, so Leo went inside.

'Hello?'

The nave was very narrow, with no side aisles. A cold white light gave it an underwater feel, like he had plunged into the Arctic ocean. On the whitewashed walls were the usual tributes to past squires and ladies, but at the altar end a local artist of not-so-many generations ago had been let loose. Under the influence of the Pre-Raphaelites, they had left a fabulous frieze of red vines with hanging grapes, which stood out starkly against the creamy plaster. The vines curled up either side of the choir towards a painting of two blue-clad angels kneeling above the altar. It was an unexpected jewel. For Leo, this was a little slice of heaven. An urge just to sit down and take it in stole over him. He wished he could let the tendrils curl around him and root him to the spot.

'Magnificent, isn't it?' The rector approached from behind, a pumpkin embraced in her arms to add to the harvest display that was accumulating by the altar. Less polished today than in her wedding photo, she was still an attractive woman with her bob of dark hair and large hazel eyes. Leo imagined they were around the same age, mid-thirties, the see-saw point between youth and middle age. It was odd to think of someone of his own generation being a vicar. He had always pictured priests to be old men in faded cassocks. The Reverend Iona had surprised him a little by wearing denim and a fleece, just like his friends would.

'Iona Chamberlain?'

'Chamberlain-Turner.' She lodged the pumpkin on a pew and offered her hand. 'Couldn't just take my husband's name as it would sound like a boast.'

It took Leo a moment to compute. *I own a Turner*.

'I don't know what my parents were thinking. At least Jimmy isn't a Bucket or a Stamp.' She gestured to a couple of the memorials which were indeed in those names. 'Could be worse.'

Leo chuckled. 'I met your parents earlier. We're making house-to-house enquiries.'

'And you've made your way from the house of Chamberlain to the house of God? Fair enough.' She literally invited Leo to take a pew. 'I suppose this is about the poor girl found up on the Downs. How can I help?' Unlike her mother, this sounded a genuine offer.

'You've heard already?'

'I'm the vicar; of course I've heard.' She smiled slightly. 'First port of call for any trouble.'

'Really?'

'I had my uncle who you met earlier in here in a state, telling me about it but swearing me to secrecy until you've made an official statement. Poor Uncle Andrew, he doesn't deal well with stress.'

'He said he didn't recognise the victim, so I was wondering if you'd be willing to look at a photo of her?' Leo explained that it was postmortem, but that didn't seem to faze her. He supposed that vicars, like policemen, must see a lot of dead people as part of their job consoling the grieving.

'Let's have a look.'

Leo felt he had to say something before she did that. 'I did notice that she bore some resemblance to your sister ... from the family photos.'

'Ella? Oh, Ella's in South Africa.'

'So your parents said.' Leo held out the screen, but watched her face carefully. 'Do you know who she is?'

The shock was instant. 'I ... I ... no, it can't be.' She shook her head and took the phone from him to enlarge the picture so she could see the features in greater detail. 'Oh my God. Ella? No. It has to be someone who looks very like her. The hair's wrong – too short, too straight, too fair.' She was grasping at straws of hope.

'Is there any way of checking if Ella is really in South Africa? Just to rule her out?' Leo asked gently.

Iona rested her head on her arms supported by the pew in front. 'It's just the shock. Sorry, what did you ask? Ella? Oh, no – at least, not easily. She's working at an orphanage way out in the wilds. No phone reception and only intermittent emails.'

Leo's unease grew with each of these admissions. 'Does your sister have any distinguishing features? A scar or a tattoo maybe?'

'Aside from her hair? She has her tramp stamp.' Iona blinked like an owl dragged into daylight. 'Never told our parents. It's vine leaves, like these ones in the sanctuary, but in the shape of angel wings. Designed it herself. She's clever that way. There's a tattoo artist in the next village who does them; it's a kind of cottage industry.'

Leo sent a quick text to the pathologist. 'OK, I'll get that checked out. Can I get someone for you while we wait?'

Having taken her moment, Iona was now rallying. 'It's fine. Just a superficial likeness. Has to be. God, I've been missing her. I'm seeing her everywhere.'

'How long's she been gone?'

'Flew in and out again for my wedding, which was about four months ago. I didn't really see her properly. You know how it is; you don't get to talk to anyone at your own wedding. Too busy.'

He didn't actually know, never having been married. 'And the last message?'

'Two weeks ago. Just the usual "I'm fine, how are you?"'

'Any photos? News about her work?'

Iona shook her head. 'One thing to understand about Ella is that she doesn't like any of us knowing what she's up to. I only know about the tattoo because of the fittings for her bridesmaid's dress.'

Leo got an instant reply back from Gerry.

No tattoo on back. One on shoulder. Heart made of two entwined flowers. Sweet peas.

Some of his tension unwound.

'I've had confirmation. Nothing on the lower back of our victim.'

'Good. I mean, not *good*, obviously. Someone is still dead.'

'I know what you meant.'

'Just had a bad moment there.' Iona braced herself. 'OK, I'm back online. Do you have any more questions for me?'

'I'm afraid so. Were you here last night?'

She grimaced. 'I suppose you have to ask everyone for their alibi, don't you? I was. I began decorating for Harvest Festival with a few of my local ladies. I can give you their names. I find I quite like doing that kind of thing. The artistic challenge of it.'

'What time did you leave the church?'

'About nine. Went straight home.'

'Where's the rectory?'

'It's not the draughty old house next to the church, if that's what you're asking. The church sold that years back. The Frazers live there now. Bankers.' She shrugged, in an accepting way. 'We've a new house in a little development on the edge of the village near the river. Much easier to heat.'

That was on the opposite side of Kingston Beauchamp from the hill.

'How did you get there?'

'Drove. I was ferrying fruit and veg all evening. Normally I'd walk or cycle.'

'Did you notice any unusual traffic, or anything out of place?'

'Nothing out of the ordinary. The pub was busy. It's a popular place. We get a lot of outsiders passing through. I guess that's what she was, poor girl. I was tucked up with my husband by nine-thirty. Neither of us went out again. We're watching a box set about drug lords for relaxation.' She laughed at herself. 'I know; that sounds wrong.'

'Sounds pretty normal to me. Your parents suggested that if I were looking for young, fair-haired women I should try the manor and someone called Father Oak.'

'Terry O'Brien? I suppose that makes sense. He does love to surround himself with girls of that kind.' She now looked sad and weighed down by care – not the result of Leo's questions but something more permanent, he would guess. 'What do you see around here, Inspector?' She gestured to the church.

'Really, I'm not sure ...'

'Please. Humour me.'

'I see a gem of a building, a sense of ages past.'

'That's what visitors expect and it's what they get if they drop in for a few minutes. But the truth is far different if you stay for more than an hour or two. You haven't asked me why I came back to minister here.'

'I assumed to be near your parents?'

She gave a hollow laugh. 'You didn't spend long with them then? No, not that. They would much prefer me to have stayed in Cambridge where I trained. That at least sounded respectable, serving from a distance. They weren't happy when I felt called back here.'

'So what called you?'

'There's a battle here. I saw it as a child.'

'A battle?'

'Against the forces of darkness.'

And he had been liking her so much ... 'Right.'

'You're not a man of faith, Inspector?'

'I'm not much of a joiner. I keep my views to myself.'

'Yes, I can see that.' And Leo felt uncomfortably that she did see him rather too clearly. 'I'm a moderate person. I don't have the fire of a martyr like St Martin.' She smiled self-deprecatingly. 'But I do believe that some people, some places, are given over to evil. Surely as a policeman you must come across that?'

'In the people, yes, maybe. Some killers are sick or inadequate, but some you come across for whom there is no explanation or excuse. But places? No, they're just that: places. Not good or bad unless we make them so.'

'I think I would've agreed if I hadn't lived here all my life. This place is just difficult. St Martin's is the single beacon of light in the village – or I try to make it so. I've got other parishes in my care, other churches, but this one is far and away the most challenging spiritually. It might look like a postcard, but something is wrong here.'

'What kind of wrong?'

She rubbed her face, looking almost sheepish. 'God, I just know that you're going to hate what I say next.'

'Try me. I've just come from a murder scene. I might be more sympathetic than you expect.'

She still feared his scepticism. 'I know it's a lot for a logical person to believe, but there is a spiritual war being waged here. I don't know if it comes from inside a person, or if they open themselves to something out there, but it's real. For the moment, the darkness is winning, and has been for centuries.'

It *was* relevant that he was dealing with a ceremonial killing. There had to be others around who took their twisted version of religion seriously if they were murdering for it. Iona might know something that would help him, names even of people involved in the rituals. 'And do you have a source for this darkness, a name or names?'

'No single source. It's just outside the door – in the people who live here, the woods, the stones and the rivers. It looks very ordinary but this place does extraordinarily wrong things, and makes me very aware of my own failings.' She rose to her feet. 'But, speaking more practically for your purposes, I would say starting with O'Brien would be a good way to go.'

He got up from the pew. 'Thank you. That's most helpful.'

She walked with him to the door, something she doubtless

did for many visitors who crossed this threshold in all stages of hope and despair. 'Mind how you go, Inspector.'

He lifted a hand in acknowledgement as he headed out.

'I mean that sincerely. Watch your back. This isn't a place you can trust.'

He left her in the doorway where she had stood for the wedding photo with her sister. Only now did he notice the wreath of plaited straw with corn dollies hanging over the lintel. The straw girls, held by threads around their necks, swayed in the wind like bells.

Chapter 6

Jess

I hated myself. And I hated – what was it? – Prosecco mixed with gin and tonic. And maybe a martini ... or two?

I knew before I started drinking that I would feel like this the next day, but did that stop me? Did it hell! And now I was paying the piper. I just wished he'd stop blowing his bloody bagpipes in my skull.

Oh no, not pipes. That was the calming 'you're about to take off and possibly crash and die' music airlines think will get us in the right mood for the short play they do on each flight. Why do they like to remind us of all the horrific possibilities? Before they told me, I hadn't been thinking of running for the nearest emergency exit, asphyxiating as the air fails, getting lost at sea with just a little light on my life jacket to show rescuers where I was. Now I could think of nothing else, apart from my throbbing head, that was.

Michael considered my condition amusing. I remembered that I hated him too and told him so.

'No, you don't,' he said, adjusting the window blind for this short flight back to London. 'I got you extra legroom.'

It was the case that, as Michael's plus one, I got to sit next to him on the row at the front. His wheelchair had been stowed in the hold and he had travelled here via a combination of airport golf cart and crutches. I wasn't much help as I'd felt like throwing up during the transfer. I thought the aircrew had me down as a complete waste of space and a failure as a companion – both of which were true.

By the time we were airborne and I'd downed a bottle of water and a couple of painkillers, I was feeling a little more human. Michael noticed.

'Tanglewood is in 8A,' he told me, prodding me with the cheery disaster leaflet from the seat pocket. 'There's an empty seat next to her if you're up for a conversation.'

Oh yes, the lost-but-not-missing daughter. It would at least distract me from the dull pain behind my eyes.

Once the seatbelt light was switched off, I headed down the aisle before the drinks cart could mow me down.

'May I join you?' I asked Tanglewood.

The fat guy (sorry, but it's true) in the aisle seat was none too pleased that I squeezed past him and forced his pudge back onto his side of the armrest. They really should sell seats on width as well as legroom.

'How are you feeling?' asked Tanglewood.

'Like I should've listened to my good angel last night, but it's always the little demon on my other shoulder that seems to have the most fun. She made me do it.'

'You are looking a little pale.'

'Pale and interesting, I hope?'

'Pale and close to vomiting.'

I leant back and closed my eyes. 'Sadly, that's accurate but I can manage if you just tell me what I need to know. I'll listen even if I don't say much.'

The drinks cart caught up with us and Tanglewood ordered a Bloody Mary. 'Can I get you anything, Jess?'

'A tranquilliser gun, loaded for a rhino?' I suggested. Sleep would be good right now.

'I don't think they stock those.'

'Ginger beer then.' I was hoping that would settle my stomach.

Once our drinks were balanced on her tray table, she began her story. I rested my head and tried to concentrate.

'Lisette is my only child. I was last with her two years ago after she graduated. Then, she was twenty-one, bright, passionate about the environment ... a joy to behold. She said she was looking for somewhere to put her energy. I made all of those motherly suggestions – graduate training schemes, working for an environmental charity, even VSO, but none of that was what Lisette White wanted. *No thank you, Mother.* Now she's twenty-three and hates me; she cut off all contact.'

'Is there a Mr White? I mean, Lisette's father? Is he in contact?'

'No, he's never been in the picture. I conceived Lisette through a sperm donor. I was in my late thirties, aware of the biological clock ticking and there was no prospective man in my life so I took matters into my own hands.'

The man next to me grumbled and prodded me with his

elbows as he plugged himself into noise-cancelling headphones. At least now we had privacy.

'Literally your own hands, like with a turkey baster, or via a clinic?' I was a details kind of person.

This shocked a laugh out of her. 'Clinic! A clinic!'

'It's just that you hear of ... OK, never mind. Go on.'

'I believed that Lisette had never felt the lack of a father, that I was enough for her. And my parents were alive then. My own father was an excellent role model.'

I elbowed the fat guy back as I shifted. 'It's OK, Tanglewood, you don't have to justify your choices to me. But if you do want an opinion, that all sounds fine and natural. Well, not exactly natural, but fine. Loads of people grow up in unconventional family settings these days.' I was blithering so I shut up.

Her voice turned wistful. 'Lisette started raising the subject of her biological father when she turned eighteen. She wanted to know if there was any way of tracing the donor. The anonymity law was changed in 2005 but that was too late for her as it wasn't retroactive. It depends on whether the donor chose to lift his anonymity. Last I heard, he hadn't and that sent her into a ... well, a lost state. I think she was looking for some replacement father figure. She ended up joining this peculiar community near Oxford. It's in a village called Kingston Beauchamp. Have you heard of it?'

I shook my head, regretted the movement, then said, 'No, but I've not lived in Oxford long.'

'It's out towards Swindon in the Vale of the White Horse.'

That was undiscovered country to me as I didn't have a car. 'Right, the geoglyph.'

'You actually know what that is? I'm impressed.'

'Earth pictures, like the Nazca monkey in Peru and the Marree man in Australia.'

'That's right. I thought only a few people in my academic area talked about them.'

'I like that stuff and I go down lots of rabbit holes on YouTube. Landing zones for UFOs and all that? The theories are so crazy they make me feel sane.' I'd better change the subject. I was admitting rather too much. 'What kind of community has she joined?'

'They call themselves the Children of the White Horse.'

I pulled a face. 'I hadn't realised your daughter's search for a father had gone quite so bestial.'

Tanglewood gave a sour laugh. 'It's a cult really, or a scam. I can't work out if the leader actually believes what he preaches.'

'It has to be a "he", of course.'

'He calls himself Father Oak.' Her tone was admirably sarcastic. 'He likes beautiful young women. Like my daughter.'

'So you think she's got tangled up – sorry, no pun intended – with some scammy sex cult?'

'Druidic spiritual exploration, according to the website. Lisette told me she thought I'd approve, seeing as how I study these things for a living. I don't approve. This one is rooted in nothing but the ego and earthy imaginings of Father Oak. I can't see a genuine druid recognising any of his beliefs in what that man teaches. Anyone who knows anything about ancient belief systems would laugh at it.'

'You told your daughter this?'

'I did.'

'And let me guess ... she said you didn't understand, that sexy Oakman knew better than you, which means she now knows better than you, and you should stop raining on her druidic parade?'

'Or words to that effect.'

'OK. I get that, but what do you think I can do about it? I would think it's a question of time until she gets fed up with the lifestyle or sees through the guru.'

'Archpriest apparently.'

'Archpriest Oak. Wow. That doesn't sound corny or anything.'

'That's what I hoped for the first eighteen months – that Lisette would see how bogus this all was. But now I'm no longer content to do nothing and let the brainwashing continue. She's not going to come to the realisation on her own. She needs help.'

'What kind of help? Isn't this more Michael's bag, something needing psychological intervention?'

'No, I need a more practical intervention.'

'Like what?'

'I need you to join the cult and persuade her to leave.'

'What?' I opened my eyes with a jolt. Yes, she was still there and I hadn't dropped off to sleep.

'I'll pay you very well for your time. Twenty thousand pounds – that's what I can pull together from my savings. I can't reach her so I've decided that I'll spend every last penny getting her out. Will you help?'

I rubbed my eyes. 'Am I still drunk? You'll pay me twenty thousand pounds to join a sex cult?'

'Ten thousand up front. The other ten if you get her out.'

It was time to be honest. 'For that money you can get someone better. I did work undercover recently on a film set but in very different circumstances. I don't have a lot of experience.'

She counted off the points in my favour on the fingers of her left hand. 'You're experienced with looking for people; you are unknown to my daughter and these cult people; you're highly recommended by Petra; you're young and blonde. Yes, I think I have the right person.'

She could have finished off the finger counts by adding 'strapped for cash' and 'recklessly impulsive'. Many people would run screaming at the idea of joining a sex cult; for me that sounded like a grand idea. In fact, I should've thought of it before.

'OK, I'll take the job.' I gulped down the ginger beer. It was only a dinky can so it didn't take more than a few swallows. If I was going to do this, I was going to have to be on my best form. I needed to kick this hangover to the kerb. 'Wake me when we land.'

Chapter 7

Jess

'You're not doing it.' Michael was steaming as we took the car home from the airport. 'When I sent you to speak to Dr White, I did not expect her to ask you to do something so outrageous!'

'So it's "Dr White" now, is it? Not Tanglewood?' I wondered how much the driver was hearing. Michael hadn't been discreet, blurting out emotive words like 'cult' and 'sexcapades' so I'd bet our chauffeur was taking in every word. I patted Michael's hand. 'Michael, may I remind you that you aren't the boss of me?'

'Have you asked Charles what he thinks?'

Charles Haslam, Michael's friend, was also my doctor and had steered me through some very rough patches in my mental health. 'No, I have not, as we only just got off the plane.' I checked my reflection in the mirror. My blonde hair apparently was something of a calling card for this cult. You either had it naturally or got yours dyed so you could join the White Horse followers.

'I know Charles and he'll agree with me.' Michael actually got out his phone to make the call like he could appeal to VAR, the video assistant referee. 'He'll tell you that you're giving in to your impulses again.'

'No, he wouldn't, because he signed me off. I'm cured, didn't you know?' Michael shook his head. He knew, and I knew, that you can't be cured of what I've got; you're just temporarily stabilised. 'I'm acting rationally and sensibly.'

'Jessica—'

'No, Michael, I am.' I pushed down the hand holding the phone. 'I have a business and, if I do this right, I'll earn a huge chunk of what I need to invest in it properly. I can't continue bumping along hand to mouth. With this kind of money I can get my own place and stop lodging with Cory.'

'I thought you liked Cory?'

'I do, but she has her family and it's a squeeze. I can't run my business professionally from a back bedroom.'

He grunted but he couldn't argue with the truth.

'And how much risk do you think there is in some latter-day flower-power thing? They'll be eating lentils, making love, plaiting garlands. I'll slip in, make friends with Lisette, see how the land lies, and hopefully disillusion one brainwashed daughter.'

'I don't like it.'

'You don't have to. I'm doing it.'

Michael's opposition actually helped. We'd had a rocky five years living together and I had finally learned to enjoy disappointing him. If he had approved, I think I might've had colder feet but, at this moment, they were toasty warm.

'I see you aren't listening,' he grumbled.

'I am. I just don't agree with you.'

'So when are you going to do this?'

'I can't see any point in delaying. I thought I'd hitch over there tomorrow.'

'Hitch?'

'It's not on a bus route and it'll look out of character if I turn up in an Uber. I'm supposed to want to live off-grid.'

'I'll drive you.'

'Oh, Michael, you don't have to do that!'

'I know I don't, but I feel responsible. You would never have met Tanglewood if you hadn't come to keep me company in Frankfurt.'

'But you only asked me to cheer me up after they arrested my dad for stalking. And we both had fun. No favours owed on either side.'

Michael gave a grumpy huff.

'Anyway, she was set on this course of action before she went. I just swam right into her orbit. I think she sees it as confirmation.'

'Confirmation of what?'

'That this was meant to be. She believes in fate.'

'Of course she does. She studies paganism.' We turned into Cory's road where I lived. 'All right. What time do you want to go?'

'There are no official opening hours at the commune. I was thinking of arriving around noon.'

'I'll pick you up at eleven.'

I leant over and pecked him on the cheek. 'Thanks for the Frankfurt trip, Michael. I had a blast.'

He gave me one of his genuine smiles, the sort I used to spend so much time fishing for when we were together. He was much more generous with them now. We were both nicer people when we were apart. 'It was fun, wasn't it?'

'Bloody pelicans,' I said.

'Yes, I mean, what did the pelicans ever do for us?'

'You're parroting me now!' Laughing, I scrambled out and grabbed my carry-on from the boot. 'See you tomorrow, sunshine!'

'Call me if you come to your senses and I'll take you out for a pub lunch instead.'

'Goodbye, Michael.'

The car drove away and I picked up my case. Time to tell my landlady what I was up to.

'A cult? Oh, that's so exciting!' Cory was in many ways Michael's opposite. Whereas he was always preaching caution, Cory found her life much enlivened by my shenanigans. In her mid-thirties and recently divorced, she was looking to find a little sparkle in her life again. As her own had gone flat, she depended on me to provide the fizz. Tucking a lock of her chin-length brown hair back behind an ear, she delved under the grill and returned victorious with only a little smoke. She placed a fish finger on Leah's plate. The three-year-old began carefully to dissect it, taking off the orange bread-crumbs to leave the pallid white interior exposed.

'I think she's going to be a doctor, or a pathologist,' I

predicted, dipping a breadstick into the hummus Cory had put out for us grownups.

Benji frowned at his charred offering. 'Mum, you've burned it.'

On cue, the kitchen smoke alarm started to beep. Knowing my role in this frequent drama, I grabbed a magazine and waved it under the sensor while Cory pumped the backdoor to and fro to dispel the fumes. Our little rescue team was effective in record time and we returned to our places.

'Always good to check the alarm is working,' I told Benji. He continued to scowl. 'How is it that a F I V E-year-old can see through us?' I asked Cory, spelling it out.

'Because we are transparent,' she said. 'Eat up, love. There are children around the world who would be grateful for a meal like that.'

Benji poked his fish finger. I had to say, I was in his camp on the attractiveness of what he'd been served.

'You did not just say that, Cory!' I hissed. 'That's such a terrible old chestnut.'

'But it's true.' Cory was a development expert and assessed international aid programmes for refugees, among other things. She'd just come back from a week in Beirut and had been particularly depressed about the state of the world ever since. I needed to help her lighten up or Benji would be carrying the cares of our pitiful times on his shoulders. I swooped down and stole his blackened fish finger.

'I don't know about poor children but there's a Jessica who wants it!' I gulped it down, carbon and all. 'Yum!'

Benji sniggered. 'Mum! Jess stole my dinner!'

'You can have mine,' I told him, offering him a blob of hummus on the end of a breadstick.

'Yuck!' He batted it away so it fell to the floor.

'OK, kiddo, this is war!' I told him, and handed him a new breadstick. We had a quick fencing match which resulted in yet more crumbs on the tiles as our swords got progressively shorter. Leah watched us with clinical detachment, chewing her fish, while Cory smiled fondly at the mess we were making. As she always said, what were brooms for?

Benji was supplied with a slightly less charred specimen, and soon mealtime was over. The children were sent off to change into their pyjamas, and I helped with the clean-up. After all, I had made most of the mess.

'How long do you think you'll be gone?' Cory asked, switching on the dishwasher.

'A week maybe? Two? It depends how difficult it is to talk some sense into Lisette.'

'Might take longer than that.' Cory filled the kettle as I emptied the crumbs into the food bin. 'Have you ever had anything to do with anyone in a cult?'

'Er, no?'

'I had a friend who got caught up in one once. Took years for him to break away and, to be honest, he's still not a fully functioning member of society even now. He finds how we live so weird.'

'It is, isn't it? Everything is weird when you stop and think about it.'

'True, but it's like driving. If you start to think too much about it, you'll lose the knack and drive into a wall.'

'So we shouldn't think too hard?'

'Exactly. Where is this cult anyway?'

'Very near the White Horse, in a village called Kingston Beauchamp.'

'That's a strange coincidence.' She spooned some decaf into the coffee pot.

'What is?'

'It's been in the news. A girl's body was found up there a day or two ago. I don't think they've identified her yet. I imagine the place will be swarming with police.'

'Oh.' I wondered if my favourite policeman was on that investigation. In the wild swimming case a few months ago, I'd found myself a little intrigued by a certain inspector in Thames Valley CID. I have to admit that I'd been enjoying a few daydreams where I didn't come quietly with him, if you know what I mean.

'I haven't heard that there's any connection with your commune but ...' She called up the story on the BBC local news.

I scanned the piece quickly. 'It'll make slipping in more difficult. They'll be wary of outsiders.'

'You'll have to find a way of earning their trust.'

'Hmm.' I accepted the coffee she'd poured me and added some milk. 'I wonder ...'

Cory smiled indulgently. 'I can see your mind is working overtime.'

'I was just wondering how I can get a foot in the door. I need someone to vouch for me, or some other reason for being there.' An idea came but it would all depend on whether

Michael would play ball. 'How do you think I can best persuade Michael to have a blazing row with me in front of someone from the commune?'

'Give him a back rub?'

That would probably do it but I didn't want to revisit that page in our relationship.

'Any other suggestions?'

'You could offer to do him a favour in return at a time of his choosing.'

'Like feed his cat when he's away? I'd do that anyway.'

'He doesn't have to know.'

'Do you think he'll go for it?'

'Jess, you know the man far better than me. Do you think he'll like having you in his debt?'

'Oh yeah, he'll like that.'

Michael and I took the exit off the A420 to head for the village.

'This is ridiculous,' muttered Michael.

'But you'll do it?'

He grunted, which I interpreted as a 'yes'.

'We just need to find the right person, you get mad at me, and I flounce off to weep.' I finger-combed my hair, having left it loose. A little rinse had taken me a few notches up to almost white blonde. I was hoping this would attract the eye of my target. 'I haven't been this colour since I was five.'

'And this is exactly the kind of idiotic plan a five-year-old would come up with.' He clearly had never met Benji who wouldn't do anything so foolish. He sighed. 'OK, Jessica, where do you want to stage this row of yours?'

'It'll have to be somewhere public. Let's have that pub lunch you mentioned and see who turns up. From the pictures online, the commune people stand out in their white robes. It shouldn't be hard to find one.'

We turned into the car park of the Smithy Arms to find it surprisingly full for a Monday. Some of the cars belonged to the police. What were the chances of meeting someone we knew? Michael advised the police on cases involving psychopathic killers.

We exchanged a look.

'Shall we try something else?' Michael suggested.

'You have an idea?'

'Ring the doorbell.'

'That's your plan?'

'You have to trust me. We can still have our argument, but let's make it hit the right target. The last people you want knowing you're here are the police. They'll blow your cover in two seconds.'

He had a very good point. 'All right, let's ring that bell.'

Chapter 8

Michael

There was something about spending an extended period of time with Jessica that always ended up with him doing something insane. This was no exception, thought Michael. At least this way, taking her right to the front door, he would get to see exactly what she was letting herself in for and, if necessary, he could drag her away if he judged it too dangerous.

They approached Kingston Manor. The gates were wrought iron, supported by stone pillars topped with statues of lions with long curling tails. They each held a shield with the coat of arms of the family who originally built the place. Through the gateway, Michael could see the house at the end of a short tree-fringed drive. A few brown leaves were drifting down in a sombre kind of confetti. The style of architecture appeared to be eighteenth-century neoclassical, fawn stone and balustrade pediment, perfectly symmetrical. The manor was the kind a great lord would have termed a hunting box as it only had one wing and, at a guess, about thirty rooms, but to modern eyes it was palatial.

'Nice place,' said Jessica laconically. 'Being a cult leader must pay well.'

He steered the car to the right so he could reach the intercom.

'Doesn't really go with the whole druid thing, does it? Electronic security? I'd've thought a couple of elves with staves would've been more in the spirit,' she commented.

Only Jessica. 'The manor is rented. I imagine this was put in by the owner.' He buzzed.

They waited.

He buzzed again. This time the intercom crackled. The voice was female. Impatient. 'Yes? If you're a reporter, we're not giving any more interviews.'

'No, I'm a doctor. Dr Harrison from Oxford University. I need to see Mr Oak on a confidential matter. It's urgent ... about a case of mine.'

'Wait one moment.'

Jessica's brows shot up. 'A doctor?' she mouthed.

'Technically I am, a Doctor of Psychology. If the person on the other end makes links to an unspecified urgent medical matter, then that's her affair. And you're my case,' he explained aside.

'*Nut*case?' Jessica sniggered.

The gatekeeper was back. 'All right, Dr Harrison, you can come as far as the entrance and explain your business to Father Oak in person.'

With a smooth movement the gates swung open, first the left, then, after a fraction of a pause, the right.

'Clever,' said Jessica. 'You got us in.'

'Curiosity got us in.'

'Anyone would think you might know something about how the human brain works, *Dr* Harrison.'

'People hate mysteries. If they refused to see me, it would bug them not knowing what I wanted.'

'But you've only got us as far as the hallway.'

'Have a little faith in me, Jessica. I've met this type before.'

'What type?'

Michael raised a brow.

'Oh my God, you think he's a psycho?'

'He'll at least have a narcissistic personality disorder. He's a cult leader – it goes with the territory. Watch your step, Jessica. I mean it.'

'I know, I know. I'm not interested in him. I just want to help Lisette. I'll keep out of his way.'

'Let's hope he doesn't get too interested in you.'

It took Michael a while to get out of his car. Jessica had become quite good at offering just the right amount of help, steadying the wheelchair during transfer but letting him do the brunt of the work.

'You're my much put-upon research assistant, agreed?' he told her. 'Anything I say in there is for effect.' He had already told her this on the drive here but he was worried she would take it to heart. Sometimes home truths leaked out when you were acting angry with someone.

'Got it, captain.'

'Look less ... perky.'

She turned her nervous smile into a sulk. It was unlikely

to stay on her face long because her default setting was cheerful, so they had better hurry up, he surmised.

'I apologise in advance; I'm going to imply you provide more than just note-taking. I want to make him think you're easy.'

She rested her hand lightly on his shoulder. 'Michael, stop fretting. We've got this.'

Of course a house like this didn't come with anything so civilised as a ramp. Jessica went inside to see if she could locate one and returned with two hefty men wearing what Michael would've described as kaftans. Both had bleached hair.

'No ramp, sir, but I did find these nice young men to help,' she said.

The two seized the chair and lifted Michael bodily up the flight of six steps. He felt like he was in some opera scene: Arrival of the King of Sheba.

'Thank you,' he said to his Nubian slaves, not feeling very thankful at all.

They opened the doors and stood either side, making his arrival far more ceremonial than he had intended. He entered, Jessica following a few steps behind. Father Oak – for it had to be the man himself – was waiting on the bottom step of a flight that went straight up behind him. It then split in two before joining the upper floor. The hall was a marble chessboard of white and grey tiles. Ancestor portraits looked down on them, their silks and satins at odds with the plain white cotton worn by the Children of the White Horse.

Seeing that Michael was in a wheelchair, Father Oak relinquished his advantage of the stair and approached, hands out in welcome or blessing. He was in early middle age and could be described as a good-looking man. His black hair was silvered at the temples in distinguished 'trust me' wings. Interesting that he was the only one to have his dark colouration. Another way of separating himself out, Michael supposed. Oak's eyes were an almost hypnotic blue ringed with black, very intense and calculating. He radiated charisma as so many of his kind did.

'Dr Harrison.' Oak's eyes went to Jessica. She had cleverly stood in a patch of sunlight so she was spotlighted. Jessica knew a thing or two about psychology as well, Michael acknowledged.

'This is my ... er ... assistant, Jessica. Jessica, stop daydreaming and do something useful.' He made his tone snappish and overly familiar towards her, acting the part of a misogynistic academic. 'I apologise for arriving unannounced, Mr Oak, but I couldn't think how else to introduce myself. You see, I'm afraid I've lied to you.'

Jessica darted him a distressed look. *Have a bit more faith, love. I know what I'm doing*, thought Michael.

'Really? How ... refreshing that you admit it.' His voice was baritone and mellifluous. Michael could easily see the elements that made him a forceful leader.

'I'm a fellow at Magdalen College. I specialise in unusual psychology. I've recently completed a prize-winning book on the criminal mind, and I'm now turning to the religious. I was wondering if you'd like to be interviewed?'

Oak got out his phone and googled his visitor. 'Congratulations on second prize.'

'Beaten by pelicans,' said Jessica, then giggled in her best bimbo act.

'Jessica!' Michael said sharply.

'Sorry, Dr Harrison.' She pouted her apology.

'Any more lip from you and you can kiss your reference goodbye. I've had quite enough of you already today.' He said this in a furious undertone as if he didn't expect his voice to carry.

She turned away and folded her arms. '*That* wasn't my fault.' She muttered something that sounded like 'you need Viagra for that.'

Amused, Michael cleared his throat, hoping he came across as embarrassed. 'Sorry, Jessica is very unreliable. I've had far better student assistants. Where were we? Oh yes. I want to do a chapter on you and your commune. I find it so interesting that these pagan ideas are springing up again in our post-modern world and would value an opportunity to interview you and your followers to find out what makes you tick.'

Father Oak shook his head sadly. 'I'm sorry, Dr Harrison. I'm flattered but I really don't think our little commune is suited for your project. To understand us you'd have to stay here and live with us, experience our way of life from the inside. Standing apart from us, analysing us, you'll never grasp the truth.'

Michael had expected an answer on these lines. 'I ... er ... can't offer you any money for your time, but you would gain publicity,' he said. Giving up too quickly would look suspicious.

Oak's smile was almost pitying. 'We believe that those who need to be with us are brought here by the path that lies hidden beneath their feet. They don't know it is there until they look back.'

'Oh, wow, that's so true,' said Jessica softly.

'Professional detachment, Miss Bridges. How many times do I …? Oh, never mind. You're never going to learn, are you?' Michael turned his back on her as if giving up. 'So, I can't change your mind, Mr Oak?'

'I'm afraid not.' His gaze cooled.

Michael realised that he and Jessica weren't the only ones playing parts here. He was already fairly certain this man was a con artist rather than self-deluded. He would in truth make a very interesting study. Perhaps the book idea wasn't such a bad one? The psychology of the cult?

'If you change your mind …' Michael tried to hand him a card but Oak didn't move to take it. He put it down on one of the mahogany side tables. 'Thank you for seeing me, albeit briefly. I'll just have to find myself another neopagan commune. Such a shame; you were so convenient for Oxford.'

The leader bowed, hands held to his chest. 'You are always welcome to return, Dr Harrison, if you are ready to come in a more questing spirit.'

At Oak's nod, his two flunkies lifted up Michael's chair and carted him back down the steps, Jessica dragging her feet behind, casting longing looks at Father Oak. Now was the time for their row, while the door stood open.

'Well, that was a bloody waste of my time. I told you to research properly before we approached anyone, Jessica!'

'But I thought they sounded so nice, so loving,' said Jessica in a whine. 'They don't realise you really want to work with them.'

'How can you be so naive? I don't want to work with them; I want to study them.'

'But maybe Father Oak's right? Maybe we can't work on beliefs this way? Maybe we have to go deeper?' She clutched her hands to her breasts, her eyes doe-like. Only he could see the glitter of enjoyment in them.

'Miss Bridges, do you understand the first thing about psychology or am I wasting my time on you?'

She reared back, as if hurt. 'I don't know. You employed me. You saw my references. You said you thought I have promise.'

'To be frank, my dear, I employed you because you were the only applicant who was willing to suck me off to get the job!'

She flinched. It read to their interested audience as if he'd insulted her but he knew that she was really just surprised he had come up with that. It hadn't been so far off their first encounter back at UCL. 'Oh, but I thought you loved me! You told me you did when we ...' she sniffed '... did it together in the Bodleian stacks.'

What a picture that painted. *Concentrate*, Michael told himself. 'Loved you? Miss Bridges, you are a good lay but a shitty assistant.'

She picked up a file of his supposed research and threw it at him. 'I hate you! You're vile! I'm going to report you!'

He took the file in the face, letting the papers flutter to the ground. 'Ah. You attacked me before witnesses. Thank you. That's just what I needed.'

'I'll get you back for this!'

'If you report me, I'll charge you with assault. I think you can consider your contract terminated with immediate effect.' He levered himself into the car, folded and lifted the lightweight chair in after. This took a little too long for the drama but Jessica did a good performance of sobbing and telling him how she hoped his cock would rot off. 'Good luck finding your way back to Oxford from here, sweetheart. I believe there's a bus once a week.' He started the car, reversed, then headed down the drive. In the mirror, he could see one of the flunkies had come down to comfort the sobbing Jessica while the other gathered up the pages. If the man looked, he would find the print-out of a learned article on the subject of religious mania – another reason for Father Oak to hate the prying academic.

One little undercover agent delivered. Michael had to hope that he'd done the right thing.

Chapter 9

Jess

I tried not to worry as Michael drove away. Enjoyable as our little scene was, now I was alone and I had to carry on the make-believe as a solo act. I'd have to dial up the dumb-blondeness. My first decision was to be passive, let them take the lead in to what to do with this snivelling wreck of an assistant.

'Take Miss Bridges into the day room, Brother,' Father Oak told Flunky One. 'She's had a distressing morning. I'll be with you in a moment.' I saw that he wanted to have a quick look at the file I had thrown at Michael.

The hand around my shoulders steered me into a large reception room. The fireplace was dominated by two statues that supported the mantlepiece, both in the shape of devilish-looking satyrs with horns and goat legs – Mr Tumnus's wicked twin brothers. He took me to a rose-pink sofa that had curved legs and wooden arms. It could have been a Chippendale (the furniture maker rather than the dancers).

'Can I get you anything?' he asked. There was a Nordic accent rumbling under his English.

'A glass of water and a new life?' I asked, trying for a brave smile through tears.

'I can manage the first; maybe Father Oak can help with the second?'

He headed to the door.

'Hey, what's your name?' *Please make it Sven.*

'Brother Pine.'

'New names for your life here, am I right?'

He nodded.

'Then I'd be Sister Weeping Willow or something?' I gestured to my tissue. 'Sorry, I'll pull myself together. It's just that I thought ... oh, it doesn't matter what I thought. All men are bastards. Present company excepted.'

Father Oak appeared in the doorway. 'I'm relieved to hear that.'

'Oh!' I made it a little embarrassed squeak. Was that too much?

'Leave us, Brother. I want to have a word with Miss Bridges in private.'

Apparently not.

'Of course, Father.' And just like that, mission to fetch me water cancelled, the Nordic pine walked out.

'Miss Bridges—' Oak took the seat next to me.

'Jessica. Please call me Jessica.'

He smiled patiently, like you do to a child who spoke out of turn. 'Miss Bridges, how may I help you?'

'I ... I don't suppose you have someone who could run me back to Oxford?'

'You have somewhere to go?'

'I ... er ... I suppose not. You see, I was living with Michael ... Dr Harrison, I mean. I guess that's at an end too?'

'It does seem that way. I was impressed, though, that you appeared to understand our way of life far better than the good doctor.'

'He's not good. He's mean!'

Oak chuckled indulgently. I wondered how he didn't see right through me. Did men really buy this big-cupsize-means-small-intelligence thing? I adjusted my best assets to bring them more to his attention. My shirt was unbuttoned to the point where he was getting quite an eyeful.

'You may feel like that now, but you'll see, if you stay with us, that Dr Harrison acts like that because he's trapped in an old and corrupt way of seeing the world.'

'I ... I can stay with you?' I acted as if he was offering me the last lifebelt on a sinking ship.

'I usually sense within seconds of meeting someone whether they are meant to be here. I felt that about you. You might like to experience our novice programme, to see if it would suit you.'

'Novice programme?' *Yes, Father Oak, I'm just a parrot without a crafty thought in my head.*

'It means you would live as part of the community. You would take the first level of vows but you'd be free to walk away at any time if it doesn't work out for you.'

'And how long does this novice programme last?' I bit my lip.

'As long as you feel you need it. Some move on to the second level after three months; some take a year. If you aren't ready to move on after twelve months, I normally suggest that you aren't on the right path and we part ways amicably.'

I hung my head. 'I don't feel like I've ever been on the right path. I can't see the way forward no matter how hard I try.' This was pretty much the truth about my life, actually.

He placed a hand on my bent head. 'Child, you sound so lost. Let me help you.'

'Oh, I am lost, so lost.' I hiccupped a little, hiding my dry eyes in the fall of my hair.

He gathered me to his chest. 'Not anymore. Jessica, you'll find that all of us first arrive here like you have: confused, without purpose, lonely. Here you'll find acceptance, friends, and a purpose. Will you try us?'

'Oh yes. Please let me try.'

'Good girl.' He patted my back. 'So, do you still want me to find you that lift back to Oxford?' He chucked me under the chin.

'Oh no, sir.'

That made him smile. *Yes, you slime ball, I'm pressing your dominator button and you like it.* 'Not "sir". Father Oak. And I'll give you a new name for your novitiate: Sister Poppy – that one is available.'

Ugh. 'Oh wow. Thank you, sir. I mean ... Father Oak.'

'Sister Ivy is in charge of our novices. She'll see to you and explain the rules. I take it you've read our profile on the website so you understand our basic beliefs?'

'You believe in Mother Earth and Father Sky, not literally as gods but as an expression of the balance we should seek in our inner being.' I repeated it like a student who had swotted for her homework assignment. 'You believe that the old ways of the people who once lived in harmony with nature, worshipping in groves and by springs rather than shut up in buildings, that these can teach us how to find a new way of relating to the world.'

'Good. I see you've already absorbed many of the key ideas. In addition to these beliefs, we live in community, sharing our goods, not dressing to distinguish ourselves from one another but to create a sense of family. As a novice, you won't be asked to sign over your personal wealth—'

I laughed. 'Just as well. I'm afraid I only have debts.'

He smiled indulgently. 'Even so, we won't take the small things that mean so much to a person, such as jewellery or photos, but we do ask you to surrender your phone. This is as much for your own health as it is for the community.'

I had to think quickly. 'Oh. But I left it in Dr Harrison's car. That was silly of me!' And it really wasn't sitting in my handbag. No, sir.

'Then that won't be a problem. A clean break with the outside world, that is what we practise here.'

A willowy woman appeared in the doorway. 'Father Oak?'

'Ah. Sister Ivy, perfect timing. Poppy here is ready to be initiated into first order vows and to change.' He turned back to me and kissed me on the brow in what was a very chaste manner. I was beginning to think that this particular sex cult leader was not that into me. 'I'll see you at dinner, Poppy.' He got up and glided out.

There was a small pause as we both admired his impressive butt exiting the room.

'This is all very sudden and unexpected,' I began, shaking my head in disbelief.

'It can be overwhelming at first, but you'll soon adjust.' Ivy smiled benignly, giving me something of a Stepford Wife thrill. 'Please, come with me.'

'Can you show me the loo first? I'm busting.' I needed a moment to remove my phone and stick it down my bra.

'There's one in the changing room where I'm taking you. We encourage newcomers to bathe or shower to signal they are passing from one life to another.'

'Like a baptism?'

She wrinkled her nose at the Christian reference. 'A little, I suppose.'

Finding Lisette was going to be harder than I had imagined if we were all going around with new names dropped on us at random by Father Oak. 'How long have you been here, Ivy?'

'I was the first.' That explained the Stepford glint in her eye. 'I came with the Father when he moved here three years ago. We were in Yorkshire before then.'

That was too long ago and the woman looked a decade too old for Lisette. Still, she might be a good source. 'Why the move?' I picked up my sparkly handbag from where it had fallen by the sofa.

'The Father felt called here.' She gestured through the big windows to the Downs with their magnificent White Horse. 'The energy is very special in this place.'

'Oh yes, I can feel it too.' We crossed the hallway and went down a passageway to the part that once would've been servants' quarters. The paintwork was utilitarian green and the floor was flagstones. At the very end she opened a door onto a communal changing room.

'Please take off all your old things and leave them on the bench. Keep only the essentials from your bag: prescription medicine, glasses if you wear them, that kind of thing ...'

'Cigarettes?' I asked but I feared I knew the answer.

She crossed her hands primly in front of her. 'We would ask you to refrain from smoking while part of our community. We don't pollute our bodies.' She had the manner of an air hostess, calm and unflappable.

So I was about to go cold turkey from cigarettes far faster than I'd expected. Maybe that was just as well as a slow giving up wasn't really my style and I had been wanting to kick the habit. 'OK. I'll try my best.'

Apparently, I was not fervent enough. 'I'm afraid we have punishments for infractions.'

And, just like that, my head went to a very kinky place. 'Really? What kind?'

'Extra kitchen duties, that kind of thing.'

'Oh.'

'You sound disappointed.' Was that a hint of humour?

'I don't mean to— I'm just feeling my way, so to speak.'

She went to a locker and took out a set of folded clothes. 'These are for you. While here, we wear nothing belonging to the outside world. We make our own clothes.'

And the dressmaker had only one pattern: sack.

'How ... er ... inspiring. Wait, everything? Underwear included?'

She nodded. 'There's no point just making a superficial change, is there?'

I disagreed entirely as that was the reason I was here, but I was only thirty minutes into this undercover operation; I couldn't blow it on an argument about knickers. 'Right. Let's get this done.'

I was relieved that she left me to shower, promising to return in ten minutes. I quickly stripped, got wet without much application of soap, just enough to convince her I'd washed away the old life. I towelled dry and quickly sorted through the new clothes. The underpants were closer to what my great-grandmother had worn: drawstring bloomers. Were they having a laugh? They presented a problem as the phone wouldn't stay tucked in there. Why did designers make modern phones so big and heavy? I could have done with one of those little folding designs from the early 2000s. I rooted through the rest of the clothes. Hang on a minute: no bra, just a tank top. My girls were going to be bouncing about unfettered. That was not as fun as it sounded. Without proper support, my back ached after a very short time and it was bloody painful to run or do anything physical without a sports bra. I didn't have time to work out a solution so I finished with the final layer: the sack dress. It fell to an unattractive knee length that reminded me of my school uniform. I remembered that Ivy had hers to the ankle. Maybe that was a novice thing? The skirts got longer, the longer you were here?

Nothing else for it. I tied the rope waistband tight and dropped the phone and charger down so it sat in the hollow by my hip, bound by the rope. I was going to have to find a better hiding place at the first opportunity as they were likely to drop right through when I walked.

I was just folding my clothes in a neat pile when Ivy returned. She beamed at me.

'Well done. So many people try to keep their old underwear and I see you've understood the necessity to put on a complete new skin.'

I folded my arms. 'I'm pretty big up top. Do you make anything for that?' Ivy, I noted, was flat-chested like a ballerina.

'Sister Foxglove has a similar figure. She binds her breasts with cloth and swears it is as good as any bra.' *Oh yeah?* 'I can supply you with some for tomorrow but I'll need to get permission from Father Oak.'

And that was not creepy? 'Thank you. I wouldn't want to break the rules so soon.'

'Excellent. Take a seat and I'll explain what's expected of you as a novice.'

I took a seat obediently on a bench, feeling like I was back in school and the nice games mistress was going to explain exactly why we all needed to go on a hearty cross-country run in the rain, rather than shelter sensibly indoors.

'Novices sleep in a dormitory and unless called away to another work party, you'll spend most of your time with them.'

'How many of us are there?'

'Now? Just two men and two other women. There have been a recent wave of vacancies as novices have moved on.'

'OK.' I wanted to ask if the genders shared the same dormitory but I supposed I'd find out.

'We have a series of bells in the manor. We rise at five-thirty.'

'Oh goody.'

She actually smiled at my tone. Maybe I was getting through to her? 'You'll find you get used to it quickly. We have an hour of meditation, six until seven; breakfast; then morning work until the noon meal. Afternoon work or recreation carries on until five when we have another hour of meditation. Dinner is at six-thirty. We go to bed at ten unless we have a special celebration or starlight ceremony.'

'I like the sound of that.'

'Unfortunately, there aren't any planned this week but maybe soon. There's been a loss locally and we feel we should cleanse the site once it has reopened to the public.'

She must have meant the murder up on the White Horse. 'Are you talking about that poor girl who was dumped up on the hill?'

She gave me a sharp look. 'That was a tragedy. But nothing to do with us.'

I couldn't afford for her to get suspicious on day one. She might think I was some kind of undercover reporter after juicy details on the murder. 'Cleansing ceremony ... that sounds wonderful. Anything else I need to know?'

'So much, but I won't load you down right now. There are some basic house rules that you need to know from the start. I've already mentioned no smoking, but we also don't drink alcohol, we eat mainly what we grow, and sexual relations between community members are banned.'

That was unexpected. 'You don't have sex?'

'Not with other members of the community. Father Oak rightly teaches that it breaks apart the bonds of fellowship to seek this from each other.'

'But you don't leave either?'

'That's right. You thought we were into free love?'

'I guess I hoped you were,' I said with a wry smile.

She squeezed my knee a little too hard. 'You'll understand soon why this is the right way for us. It is all part of our philosophy.'

I'd been expecting a sex-crazed cult and I'd got myself a bunch of nuns and monks. I'd better find Lisette quickly and get out of here before I did something terrible and proved I was not a suitable recruit. 'Great. So where first?'

'I think I'd better show you to your room so you can meet your fellow novices.'

Just what I wanted. I was hoping that Lisette was one of the other two women. Otherwise this might feel like a very long visit.

Chapter 10

Leo

Three days had passed since they found the body on the White Horse and, to Leo's immense frustration, they were no closer to identifying her. You couldn't make headway when you didn't know this most basic of facts. Motive, means, opportunity, the heart of any murder inquiry – all these depended on tracing the victim on her last journey to the hill. Appeals had gone out on national television and online based on an artist's sketch but so far none of the people who claimed to recognise her had checked out. It was as though she'd come into existence on Friday night, only to die by sunrise, like a flower of the evening primrose. Leo's team had run her DNA profile against the police database but found no matches, which meant she and her close family had kept clear of criminal investigations or she was from outside the UK.

The best lead was her clothing. She had been wearing nothing apart from the rope-belted robe. That had been quickly identified by Rev. Iona Chamberlain-Turner as belonging to the community at the manor. However, when interviewed, Terence O'Brien, aka Father Oak, had told Leo that the clothes were indeed very like those his community made but she definitely hadn't been anyone he recognised. He had gone on to say that they had donated old robes to local charity shops and suggested that she might have picked it up there. Leo didn't believe him, but none of the other commune members contradicted his explanation so Leo had had to leave it at that. Surely she had to have come from there? The coincidence was too great. If Leo had had just a little more evidence, something to implicate O'Brien or one of his followers in the murder, he could've argued for a warrant to search the premises. Unfortunately, that had not come to light. The blood dog had lost the trail downhill at the B road in the village so nothing pointed to the commune.

He knew he would have to go back tomorrow and try again, to see if he could find a chink in the armour around that place. It was dangerous to settle too quickly on a chief suspect, but he couldn't shake the notion that there was something they were hiding.

But his own life had to go on despite the ending of the victim's. His superintendent, the formidable Claire Thaxted, who was in overall charge of the murder case, ordered him home after a full debrief on the investigation so far.

'I agree it is disappointing not to have made more progress by now but you'll be no good to anyone, Leo, if you run yourself into the ground. Leave your team to follow up and have a night off. Look at it afresh tomorrow.' Claire always appeared fresh herself, thinking nothing of doing a ten-kilometre run before work. Though ten years older than Leo, she really didn't look it with her sharply cut hair which was highlighted to eliminate the few strands of grey. She claimed they were caused by wrangling for enough budget to cover her division's requirements, not age. Her eyes were usually also grey, like an overcast sky, but just at the moment she didn't seem displeased with Leo and the team; rather, she was resigned to the slow pace of detective work. It helped that, after the initial flurry in the press about the White Horse murder, they'd moved on to a child kidnapping in Surrey and lost interest. Someone else's misery was Thames Valley's gain.

It made Leo ponder the same old question as to why the suffering of some children – usually nice middle-class kids with smiling school photos – garnered so much interest, while there were teenagers going missing daily around the country and no one noticed or cared? Was that the case with this victim? Had she been some runaway or migrant whom nobody noticed? Until she ended up dead.

Now she was Leo's responsibility and he would pay her all the attention he could until he got justice for her.

It was only six when Leo drove up to his house in Iffley, once a village, now part of south Oxford. His home didn't seem much from the front, a 1920s cottage built from Oxford brick (a golden colour, made from the local clay) with red brick courses for accent. It was the kind that had been constructed for canal and railway workers who wanted a bit of land for their family, standing detached in its own plot, with three beds upstairs, two main front rooms on the ground floor, and a kitchen running along the back. Neat but a little boxlike. It was the surviving garden that had sold it to Leo.

He lived out there rather than in the admittedly dark rooms of the house. Today, as was his habit, he barely did more than drop his keys in the bowl by the front door, change into his gardening clothes, and he was out into the garden.

Pushing past the Japanese anemones that overhung the path with their delicate seashell pink flowers, he immediately felt at peace. The garden helped him find his centre after a day of spinning off-kilter. *Put work away*, he told himself, *don't bring it out here*.

His first visit was to his biggest project and also biggest headache: the pond. He was relieved that the five koi carp he had added a week ago were still alive, wisely acting as minions to the granddaddy fish Leo had nicknamed Goldemort, thanks to his habit of killing off all opposition to his rule. They followed behind him like a cult leader's hangers-on, waiting to satisfy his every whim. The bulrushes were taking nicely at the edge of the bog garden that Leo had created last year. Dragonflies had visited the lily pads in large numbers this summer, though they had mostly retired for the evening, leaving the visiting rights to the less welcome gnats and mosquitoes. These had to be tolerated for the sake of other wildlife. Swallows flitted above, scooping up insects. Soon they'd be migrating but for now they kept Leo company until the bats came out at dusk. Nothing needed doing tonight, though he could see scores of jobs that should be tackled on his next day off. He would have to begin ticking off his list before it grew too long, like the lawn. There was grass cutting, weeding, pruning ...

He was not going to think about that now. He was just

going to sit on the log bench he'd made out of a felled elm tree and savour the cold beer in his hand.

His phone buzzed. Couldn't the world give him a moment to himself?

Leo swore softly as he glanced at the screen. Not a call but a reminder. He'd completely forgotten that he'd agreed to a blind date set up by a friend from his college days. Lucia was worried that he was only in his thirties and already turning into a hermit. As she was in Oxford for a conference, she had decided to fix that. Among the people on her panel was a woman she thought 'would be perfect for him'. It was their last night in town and therefore the last chance for them to meet up. His heart was already sinking. He would have to swap a quiet evening in the garden for a wine bar in Summertown? He did want to meet someone eventually but so far his relationships had sunk on the rock of his 'difficult' personality. His reviews were that he was too closed, too silent, too unknowable, according to the opinions of his exes. As there had been three who had lasted more than a year with him, and all had reached the same conclusion, he was beginning to think they might be right.

Understanding him well, Lucia had sent a text.

Don't forget, 8pm. The Wine Café. She's the attractive librarian with red hair. I've told her to look for the tall, dark, handsome stranger who looks like he'd rather be somewhere else. ;)

He wanted to reply that he was unavailable, that work had called him away, but he preferred not to lie to his close friends. Come on, Leo. What could it hurt? Two hours for friendship's sake?

Trying not to sigh, he texted that he had indeed remembered and went back into the house to get changed.

Parking in the shoppers' car park behind the Co-op, Leo was reminded that Jess Bridges lived near here in her off-the-books lodging arrangement with her friend, Cory. He hadn't seen Jess since they closed the wild swimming case but he'd not forgotten her; she was a bundle of chaos and good intentions. Would he bump into her? Her statements had been taken and the CPS was dealing with the case now. It was doubtful that it would get to court because the perpetrator seemed to be criminally insane and probably would be judged unfit to stand.

Figuring out the parking machine took a few moments. Why were simple tasks now made so difficult? Couldn't he just tap his bank card on the machine and get a ticket without entering his registration number and the hours he expected to stay? How did he know? He wanted to press just one hour but that wasn't fair to Linda, his date for the night.

Leo and Linda. No, he couldn't see this working. They sounded like a 70s pop duo.

He walked into the wine bar with the special dread that he associated with blind dates. This wasn't his first. His female friends in particular seemed to regard him as a challenge to set up with the right partner. He already suspected tonight's lady would find him lacking, so why did he even bother? He'd come early to be courteous. She lived in London so was the stranger in town. Leo hoped that if he got to sit down first and adjust to the idea that he had to be sociable, then he'd manage to squeak through this without disappointing Lucia. She told him often that he did have some charm if he remembered to use it ... and to smile. Leo was aware that he didn't smile much. Never had done – not since he was a child, too innocent to know what the world was really like.

He yanked his mind away from those memories. It was best not to be thinking about his miserable teens when about to meet a stranger.

'I believe there's a table reserved in the name of Leo George?' he asked. Lucia had said she'd see to the details for him, giving Leo no excuse to cry off.

'Ah yes. Your guest is already here.' The waitress conducted him over. So much for his politeness of arriving first.

Linda looked up from an academic book she'd been annotating. As promised by Lucia, she was an attractive woman in her mid-thirties, gently waving red hair to her shoulders, earnest expression in her brown eyes. A little mole sat above the corner of her top lip, much as a beauty spot was once placed in the eighteenth century. Natural though hers was, it did indeed draw attention to the fact that she had nice full lips and Leo felt a stir of attraction, a little warming, and cautious hope. She was dressed conservatively in a dark blue suit, making Leo feel a little too informal in his shirt and casual trousers. On leaving the house, he'd ditched the jacket he'd first selected, recalling how previous girlfriends had complained he always looked as though he was about to go to work. Wrong call tonight. How typical for his dating record.

'Oh, Leo. Lovely to meet you. Sorry, I got started without you.' She gestured to the white wine.

'I'm late?'

'No, no. I've only been here a few minutes.'

'What will you have, sir?' asked the waitress.

'Just mineral water – fizzy.' Leo sat down at the seat opposite his date. 'Driving.'

Linda smiled. 'Lucia warned me you were a man of few words.'

Leo realised that he hadn't said that he was pleased to meet her. 'Linda, sorry, I should've said that I'm delighted to meet you. Thank you for coming out tonight.'

She sipped her wine and looked at him with a speculative twinkle in her eye. 'Hardly a hardship. I'm staying just across the road in a pretty mediocre hotel so I've decamped here most nights this week. I nearly qualify as a regular.'

That explained her early arrival. 'Lucia didn't tell me anything about your conference. Have you been giving a paper?'

'Yes. But you wouldn't want to hear about that. All very boring compared to police work.' She slipped her book into her computer bag.

'I'm sure that's not true. Tell me more.'

'I gave a paper on the landscape gardener Capability Brown. I'm writing a biography.'

And now he knew why Lucia thought Linda would be

perfect for him. 'That's much better than police work, believe me. I'm lucky to live so near to Blenheim and Stowe. I've studied his work, in an amateur way.'

Her eyes lit up and his hopes for the evening rose. 'Lucia did say you have a magnificent garden of your own.'

He shrugged, aware that he was a little flustered. *Pull yourself together, Leo. You're a police officer, for crying out loud.* 'Very small scale. I'm sure Lucia made it sound much grander than it is.'

'That's not what she said. She says you've put your heart and soul into that place and, if I was to understand you, I had to get myself an invitation to visit.'

Visiting his garden on first acquaintance was his equivalent of sleeping with someone on a first date. He was not ready to bring her in and gain a new layer of memories that he might not want if – when – this went sour. His garden was the one place he guarded jealously.

Fortunately, the waitress broke the moment by delivering his water. He thought of a polite way of refusing.

'I'd be ashamed to show it to an expert. Tell me, what gardens have you made the closest study of? Which do you think his best?'

They talked happily through the starters and mains about Capability Brown and his philosophy of gardens. His aim was to make them appear like natural landscapes, though they were fiercely planned.

'I sometimes think he's like a clever criminal,' Leo suggested over his salmon on saffron rice.

'Oh? You must explain that!' She sprinkled parmesan on

her spaghetti. 'I wondered when we were going to get to talk about your career.'

He immediately felt regret that he'd ventured the opinion. 'Nothing. It was nothing.'

'No, Leo. You can't go so far, whet my appetite, and then not tell me what you mean.' Linda topped up her glass. She had sunk the best part of the bottle herself; he had only had one glass.

He was going to have to say it now or appear churlish. 'It's just that the best criminal minds are all about making you see their version of the events, and, in fact, they've been working feverishly hard all the while to create an illusion.'

'You mean like the Hatton Garden robbers? The old geezers who dug through a wall so no one would suspect they were stealing from the next-door premises?'

'Yes, but cleverer than that because those guys got caught. I'm thinking more like websites that are so well designed they convince you that they are a legitimate company and take all your savings. Capability Brown would take a piece of parkland, put in a lake and a copse of trees, dig an invisible ha-ha so you wouldn't have to step in cow pats. You'd then look at it and be convinced it was ever thus.'

'Ever thus? Which century do you live in, Leo?' Her tongue loosened by wine, Linda felt able to tease him. Leo was not quite ready for this and only felt his foolishness.

The waitress approached. 'No dessert for me,' said Linda, 'but I will have a decaf coffee.'

'Mint tea,' he said.

'I suppose he did take all the landowners' savings too; his

services did not come cheap. I think your analogy holds up.' She sat back as the waitress cleared their plates.

'Once you see the pattern, you know it's rarely natural – or if it was once natural, you now doubt it.'

'Are we talking Capability Brown or crime?'

'Both.'

The coffee arrived and she stirred hers thoughtfully. 'You know, you talk more than I expected. Lucia told me to expect long embarrassing silences until I could think up another topic.'

Thanks, Lucia. 'I don't think anyone is ever allowed to get a word in around her. She has enough conversation for both of us.'

Linda laughed. 'That's true. She's what my mother would call an old-fashioned busybody. My mum's retired now but she was a teacher. She is very good at reading people. Dad, by contrast, is hopeless. He's an electrical engineer and is far more at home with circuit boards than the odd wiring of people. How about yours? What are your parents like?'

He couldn't believe Lucia hasn't repeated to her all she knew. 'What've you been told?'

Linda had the grace to look a little embarrassed. 'She said that you never talk about your father and that you and your mother lived on a boat for most of your teenage years. That sounds romantic.'

'Sounds, yes.'

'Your mother was a film star?'

'Small-time actress. She'd be thrilled to hear herself described as such.'

'Does she still act?'

'Oh, all the time, but only for herself. You see, my mother landscapes her reality and lives in it. The real world doesn't get a look in.'

'I can't blame her. Sometimes the real world is unbearable.'

Leo thought of his garden, of the swallows and the bats. 'The real world is fine. It's the human one, in which sick people live out their fantasies, that you have to worry about.' His mind went back to the girl on the hillside. That had been someone's fantasy. But whose? It was usually possible to profile a killer from the type of victim they chose, the location, the method and the behaviour after the act. In this case, he had an unknown but presumably vulnerable female victim, a showy location with ancient associations, a surgical strike, and then a successful retreat so the killer seemed to have vanished without trace. But Leo sensed the killer on the edge of the crowd, watching him and what he was doing. They had stepped forward onto the stage of the crime, then gone back into the chorus line. Until he knew why *this* victim, *this* killing, he had no idea if they were likely to strike again. But another question was why wouldn't they? They had got away with this one so far; it would be tempting to solve future problems in the same way.

'Leo?' The sharper note in Linda's voice reminded him that he was supposed to be paying attention to her rather than his work.

'Sorry?'

'I asked how you want to split the bill? I did drink more than you.'

Leo hated the etiquette of moments like this. He wanted to be a gentleman but apparently that could be offensive. 'What would you prefer? I'm happy to pay for the meal. I could be said to be the host as it's my city and my friend who set this up.'

She shook her head. 'I'd feel happier if we split it down the middle.' She waved to the waitress who went off to collect the card machine. 'Lucia was right. We got on well, didn't we?'

Wariness crept upon Leo. 'I had a really nice time.'

'But it was only nice, wasn't it? No spark.' She gestured between them. 'I don't know why, because you, to be frank, are the best-looking guy I've been out with in an age. But I only feel like we could be friends.'

The surge of relief told Leo he agreed. 'I'd like to be friends too.'

'Shall we exchange numbers? Come on a site visit with me sometime. Or we could go to Chelsea together, if you can brave the flower-show crowds? It's not for the faint-hearted.'

'I'd like that.'

'Maybe you'll feel comfortable enough with me to invite me to see your secret garden.' She smiled wistfully.

'I ... that would be good too.' And he realised he wouldn't mind that, now that they were no longer trying the far more taxing negotiation of a relationship.

Bill settled, details swapped, Leo walked Linda back to her hotel and then returned to his car. A detective's brain never really went off duty during a case. The conversation had given him an idea. What if the killing had been managed, Capability

Brown style, to appear naturally to fall one way – a ceremonial killing – when in fact it was something else entirely?

But what that something else was depended on finding out the who and the why. He set his alarm to make an early start for the commune. He wouldn't be leaving the manor until he had some answers.

Chapter 11

Leo

The first time Leo had gone to the manor was on the day the body was discovered. He had brought DS Wong with him and they had both been received with politeness and bland answers, worth precisely nothing. As that had yielded no results, he decided to bring DS Boston with him for the second visit and send Wong to re-interview the Chamberlains. Harry's more combative style might shake loose something where both he and Suyin had failed.

Harry wound down the car window and pressed the intercom to gain admittance. They heard a tentative 'Hello?'

'It's the police, love. Let us in,' he said. The gates swung back. 'How do you want to do this, Leo?'

'I want you to question Terence O'Brien about the events of last Friday. Get him to go through in detail what he and the rest of the community did that day and evening. Let's see if he strays from his initial statement. Pick apart any inconsistencies. Keep him busy.'

Harry waited but Leo said no more. 'Aren't you going to tell me to mind my P&Qs?'

'No.'

'Why?'

'Because last time that slid right off O'Brien's sanctimonious hide. Rub him up the wrong way and see if he has a temper.'

Harry smirked, rolling his head on his bull neck, warming up. 'And what will you be doing while I'm making not-so-nice with the dear leader?'

'I want to take a look around the place and speak to his followers without him breathing down their necks. Last time he provided a room for interviews and I had the distinct feeling everyone believed they could be overheard.'

'He has people spying?'

'Maybe. It's an old house. There could well be concealed passageways and cameras and listening devices that we didn't spot. He claims they're off-grid but that intercom is working, so there must be some electricity somewhere.'

'He keeps his minions on a tight leash?'

'They certainly acted as if they were under surveillance. They were all so careful with their replies, keeping to the script they'd been given.'

'Sounds like they're brainwashed.'

'I'm thinking more ... compliant. Like they want to protect him. So I want to shake them out of that. It would help if we knew who they all really are in real life and not these made-up names they have. Being able to link them to a few criminal convictions or official cautions would mean we could get some of them talking. I'll see if I can get some of them to tell me who they really are.'

'It's bloody ridiculous that we can't make them.' Harry drove up and parked in front of the main doors.

'I said you can be annoying, not illegal, Harry.' Leo watched his colleague's mulish expression with the usual nerves he had when letting Harry loose on the general public. He was an accident waiting to happen – or a referral to the Police Complaints Authority at the very least. Whoever was his commanding officer at that time was going to get it in the neck. 'We can't demand their legal names unless we have cause to think they have committed an offence.'

'They have in my books: an offence to bloody common sense. Look at them, walking around like kids dressed up for a fucking nativity.' Harry gestured to two men walking past in robes that did indeed resemble the gowns thrown together in many primary schools for the angels. 'And what's wrong with dark hair?' He patted his own thinning brown scruff. 'Why do they all have to reach for the bleach bottle?'

'O'Brien has black hair.'

'Well, he's a pervert, isn't he? Likes to surround himself with these blonde bimbos – male and female. Is that his thing, do you think, group orgies of blondies?' He sounded a little too hopeful.

'I really don't know. The locals think the worst but I've not seen any evidence.'

'Worst? I didn't say that. A group of young things at your beck and call, all ready to worship your great oak staff? I'd say that sounds like a wet dream to most men.'

His crudeness did sometimes have an almost Chaucerian ribald wit.

'Try that line on him and see if he's sensitive to criticism or mockery.'

'It'll be my pleasure.'

The acolyte who had met him on the first visit, the one who introduced herself as Sister Ivy, attempted to dissuade Leo from splitting up from Harry. She was clearly torn between chaperoning Harry in his meeting with O'Brien and keeping an eye on the senior officer. In the end, she elected to send a Norwegian man calling himself Brother Pine to keep watch over Leo's movements.

Leo tried to head that off. 'Really, it's all just routine, Sister Ivy. We just want to see if anything new has occurred to anyone since we last interviewed them. I don't need an escort.'

'We'd prefer it if you did,' said Ivy, indicating that this was a line she'd not cross. 'House rules. No unaccompanied strangers.'

Leo didn't want to push in case they started making noises about warrants. 'All right, I'll start with Brother Pine. He can tell me what he remembers while we round up the others.'

Brother Pine did not remember anything new, of course; nor was he willing to part with his real name.

'I began a new life when I moved here,' he said solemnly. 'My past is forgotten.'

Leo quickly scanned him for any telltale signs – track marks, prison or military tattoos, scars – but he was clean as far as the policeman could see. 'It's not forgotten if you want medical treatment, a driver's licence, or to renew your right to remain.'

'I don't want or need any of them,' he said, shutting down that avenue of enquiry.

After similar discussions with those they met in the kitchen and laundry – everything was done by hand without any sign of machines – Leo and his Scandinavian minder headed outside.

'I'd really like to see the gardens. I'm a keen gardener myself.' Perhaps he might be able to get away from Pine there? And so Leo quite deliberately proceeded to bore him into believing him innocuous. He worked to come across as more interested in carnations than crimes by entering into a long conversation with a man tending a border about problems with powdery mildew (they had a bad case on a shrub rose) and another with an older woman on splitting carrots – they agreed that it was probably caused by the sudden downpour last week after a dry spell. Brother Pine began to hang back, his eyes wandering to the house. Excellent. Maybe Leo could actually create space to have a conversation that turned up something relevant and unscripted.

And then he spotted her: a familiar young woman struggling to cut back a beech hedge. Leo decided he had to be seeing things. He had thought of Jess in Summertown the evening before; now he was inserting her into his imagination here. The hedge trimmer probably looked nothing like her. He moved to get another angle on the woman so he could see her face clearly. Hell no. It was definitely her. He drifted in her direction but cleared his throat so he didn't startle her.

She looked up, her eyes widened, and she made frantic 'go away' gestures. No chance of that. Leo knew already that she was impulsive – she'd explained her ADHD to him when they'd worked together over the summer – but this was no place to explore her wilder urges. Leo was all too well aware that he couldn't save everyone but there was one idiotic fool he could get out of this. The trouble was, Brother Pine was following on his heels.

So he approached her as he had all his other encounters. 'Good morning. I don't think we met when I made my enquiries here at the weekend. I'm Inspector George.'

After tensing up, Jess relaxed a little when she realised that he was not about to admit to prior acquaintance. She was simply dressed like everyone here: white tunic, cotton gloves, a straw hat to keep off the rain and sun. This was dangling by its strings to leave her blonde hair uncovered.

'I've only been here since yesterday, Inspector. Nice to meet you. Am I in trouble?'

She would be if she didn't get out of here after his warning. 'Not that I know, miss. I'm just making follow-up enquiries. I thought I'd enjoy this lovely garden at the same time.'

'It's only lovely because we all spend so much time out here. It's bloody hard work. Hi, Brother Pine.' She gave a friendly wave to Leo's Norwegian minder. 'Do all the new recruits get the difficult jobs?'

'Trimming the hedge is not a difficult job,' Pine demurred.

Leo reached across and took her secateurs from her. 'But these are blunt. You need an electric hedge trimmer to do this properly.'

'We don't use machinery,' she said primly, amusement dancing in her eyes. 'We are at one with nature.'

Leo almost laughed. 'And you'll soon learn that nature's a complete bitch. She'll beat you every time if you go at her with no more than a pair of dull scissors.' He snipped a twig, taking it back to the old growth. 'You'll also need a ladder to reach the top.'

'A ladder?' She put her hand to her mouth as if she'd never heard of such an invention. 'Brother Pine, where can I find a ladder?'

'I'm sure it would be too heavy for you to carry out here on your own.' He snipped another twig.

'Oh. Brother Pine, would you be so kind as to fetch me a ladder? I really don't want to disappoint you all on the first task I've been given.' She looked up at the hedge towering above her and then at Pine, like a brave climber about to ascend the Matterhorn. And yes, she even bit her plump lower lip. That was when Leo knew for certain that there was no saving required here; the reckless woman was on a job.

Brother Pine, however, was suckered in by the helpless damsel routine. 'I'll fetch the ladder. Stay here.'

Leo was not sure who Pine was including in the order but he had no intention of obeying the Nordic guard. As soon as he was out of sight, Leo turned to Jess.

'Is there somewhere we can talk without too many people watching?'

'Follow me.' Grabbing a canvas sack of clippings, she took him to the composting area. It had that heavy damp smell of rot that reminded him of the mortuary and it was under the shelter of some dark trees. Funereal in its vibe, it was not an inviting place to linger, but it was as private as they were likely to get.

'I'm on a job.'

'I'm investigating the body on White Horse Hill.'

They both spoke at once. Leo gestured to her to go first.

'OK: headlines. I've just been to Frankfurt Book Fair with Michael. One of the authors there has a daughter in this community. I'm trying to locate her but everyone gets a new name so I'm a bit stuck. Actually, can you do me a favour?' She shoved her hand down her front. 'I'm out of juice and I'm not supposed to have this anyway.' She handed him her phone and charger, still warm from her body. 'I need more photos of my target if I'm to identify her. I've sent a message but the phone died before I got a reply.'

He tucked the phone in his pocket. 'I can do that, but how will I get it back to you? Can you leave?'

She shrugged. 'It's not a prison. We can go into the village if we want.'

He scanned his memory of the village quickly for a place she couldn't miss and wouldn't be seen. 'I'll ask the rector at the church if I can put it under the altar cloth. She's nice and I think she's reliable. It'll be safer than being seen with me. What's the name of your missing person?' Leo was really hoping that Jess was unable to find her only because there were too many candidates here and not because she was already dead.

'Lisette White. Her mum is Tanglewood White. She's written a book on neopagan cults, ironically.'

Or maybe not? Was that the link? He was going to have to show another person the photo of someone who might possibly be a loved one, wasn't he? 'When were they last in contact?'

'Over a year ago. Lisette came here and cut off all communication. I understand why now. They're contact Nazis.'

As she talked, it occurred to Leo that he'd just landed on the kind of source he'd hoped for: an insider. 'Can you explain?'

'Father Oak makes us all hand in our phones and personal possessions on arrival. We're allowed to keep jewellery and photos, but anything that could be a ticket out of here – phones, money, and so on – is taken away. You get them back if you decide to leave, but not until then. At least, that's what he said would happen.' From the worry that now crossed her face, she'd worked out why he was here. 'That body ... do you think it's one of them?' She flicked her fingers to the manor.

'When I was here last, everyone swore they didn't know the girl, but she was found wearing one of the robes used here. Like yours, but without the loose trousers.'

'When inside we novices wear knee-length tunics, men and women. I've not seen so many knobbly knees since my schooldays. What length was hers?'

'To the knee.'

'Then she's a novice – or she was wearing a novice tunic. If you've taken the full vows you get to wear a robe to your ankle. Whoopee.'

Theo recalled the description of the personal effects found on or near the victim. 'Do you wear handmade sandals?'

'Some do, but not me. I asked to keep my own shoes and

they let me for now. Their own cobbler can't keep pace with the community's needs. He's got a waiting list.'

'She had handmade shoes, so that suggests she'd climbed to the top of that list while here. How long's the wait?'

'A few weeks. Just my luck to get to the top when December hits. Sandals in winter? They have to be crazy. Actually, strike that. I *know* they're crazy.'

'You think you'll be here that long, until December?'

'God, I hope not.' She hugged herself. 'The money's good, but these guys, they're so tight.'

'Tight?' That wasn't a word Leo had been expecting.

'No smoking, no drinking, no sex.'

'No sex?' And he was immediately thinking of ways to rectify that omission. *Keep it professional, for God's sake, Leo.*

'Yeah. I mean, what's a good cult without an orgy or two? I suppose it's a relief because I was going to have to think up an excuse not to get it on with someone I didn't fancy.' She darted a look at him. 'And as Michael and I rather sold me as a slut as part of our act to get me in the door, that would've been hard to explain.'

'How—?'

She grinned. 'Ask Michael. Time's short. Any more questions?'

'Yes, many. Do you wear green cloaks?'

'Not that I've seen, but I've only been here a day. Was your girl wearing a bra?'

'No.'

'Was she flat-chested?'

'No, but not big either.'

'A, B cup?'

'I'm not an expert on such things.'

'Poor baby.' She pouted and Leo wondered if she was thinking what he was thinking ... He was half certain that the attraction went two ways. Then again, he wasn't as good at reading women as he was crime scenes. 'Imagine you're in a coffee shop. Would her breasts fill a regular or a grande if this were a coffee order?'

And that was one of the reasons Leo liked her: her quirky way of thinking. 'Regular?'

'OK, then I can't help you there. Those of us with bigger than average breasts bind our chests. I mean, I might've been tempted to join the Children of the White Horse until I heard that.' Her tone was laden with sarcasm. 'It's completely mental. I've been sent back to the Dark Ages, wrapping myself in bandages like Mulan, all on the whim of a guy calling himself Father Oak.'

'His real name is Terence O'Brien.'

'Terence? Terry?' She sniggered. 'I can see now why he changed it. Not exactly a name to strike fear and wonder into your heart, is it? I'm Sister Poppy, by the way, if you need to ask for me. Anything else?'

'Do many of the followers have tattoos, ones with interlinked flowers or foliage?'

'I don't know. I haven't exactly got naked with them.'

'Would you keep that it in mind?'

'In case I do get naked with them? Inspector, what are you suggesting? That I break the rules?'

'That you might see something by accident, or when someone is changing.'

'You want me to be a Peeping Tomasina?'

It was happening again, this surge of energy he got when he talked to her. She made him feel like he had been running on a flat battery and had just plugged into a power source. 'I don't want you to endanger yourself in any way, but I'm wondering if it's something they do here. The style of the tattoo on the body was unusual and very organic. It would fit the ethos of this place.'

'Oh, look out, Sven is back. I bet he'd like to give me a tattoo – on my forehead – saying something like "pest" in Norwegian.'

Leo turned round to see his minder approaching with a stepladder balanced nonchalantly on one shoulder. 'He's called Sven? Sven what?'

'It's just a nickname. I don't know anyone's real names, I told you. That's what makes this all so slow. Hey, Brother Pine, thank you so much for getting me the ladder. The inspector here was just helping me with the cuttings.' She emptied the sack and shook it out. 'He's so strong and knows such a lot about gardens. He's a real garden guru.' She fluttered her eyelashes at Leo, doing a good impression of one of the bimbos Harry suspected filled the place.

'It turns out that Sister Poppy is new so she wasn't here at the weekend,' Leo told his minder, which he was sure Pine already knew. 'Anybody else in the garden for me to talk to?'

'I saw Brother Maple near the icehouse,' said Jess helpfully.

'Icehouse?'

'We're not going to the icehouse,' growled Pine.

'Whyever not?' cooed Jess. 'Inspector, it was built by the original owners of the house and is still in use. No electricity, so we have to keep things cool somehow. But us novices aren't allowed there. Too dangerous apparently. I just think it's full of vintage wine and cheese and they don't want us raiding the stores for midnight feasts. Isn't that so, Brother Pine?'

He looked scandalised, not understanding that she was teasing. 'No, it is not so, Sister Poppy. It is old, it is dark, and it has steep steps. I will send someone for Brother Maple. I have a message from Father Oak. He says you should see everyone back at the house.'

So the leader was now reining Leo in. 'Nice meeting you, Sister Poppy,' Leo said, giving Jess a casual wave. 'Don't forget: cut to where the new bud will form in spring and that hedge will flourish.' Leo didn't want to leave her there but he forced himself to walk away. 'Take care.' He hoped she understood the warning. He didn't know if the killer had come from the commune but he was becoming increasingly convinced that the victim had. So why was everyone denying that they even knew her?

Chapter 12

Jess

It had been a shock meeting Inspector George in the garden. My memory of his face had gone fuzzy over the months since I last saw him, becoming a cliché of the square-jawed, soulful-eyed combo found in the IMDB photos of most leading men (I did a lot of random web searches). I thought reality was bound to disappoint but, nope, I hadn't been fooling myself; he really did look that good, the Henry Golding of Thames Valley. He was not perfect (perfect is so off-putting, like an android). Happily, his nose was perhaps a little too long and there was a scar cutting across his left eyebrow. He also seemed oddly at home as he snipped away at the hedge, smiling at me as he gave me pointers on good pruning habits. The man knows his hedges. It made me wonder what else he knew.

OK, mind, stop imagining him whispering huskily to you as you roll around on grass clippings. That is really not helpful right now.

The inspector asked me to sniff out any links between this

commune and the murder victim. Focused on my own goal, I hadn't yet given much thought to there being a connection. No one had mentioned the killing other than in the most general terms of shock and sorrow, as you would expect from a community close to a murder. Silence would've been suspect and they weren't that, chatting about it at meals, speculating as to how it could have happened and how someone had got hold of one of their robes. None were missing, according to the laundry team, but then how did they know? The robes all looked the same to me.

Laundry, cooking, cleaning, gardening: so far everything they did seemed tame. Nothing signalled a place with a dark secret. I had almost crawled out of my skin during morning meditation. Everyone knew how hard it had been for me to stay still in the library where the session was held. The noise of my fidgeting would have broadcast that I wasn't achieving Nirvana or whatever it was they were aiming for. I was constitutionally unable to sit still. That was why Father Oak, aka Terry, had sent me out to prune the hedge. He said that I would begin to see things more clearly if I got rid of some of my excess energy. I had a Year Six teacher who'd thought the same and would send me off to litter-pick in the school playground. She'd had a year to curb me; I didn't reckon Terry would have any more success than she did.

God, I'm regressing. Living in a place with strict rules was making me act like a naughty child. Show me a rulebook of things not to do and I see it as an excellent list of suggestions of what to try next.

I was going to have to get out this afternoon or I might just jump Sven to test the whole 'no sex' thing.

'Ivy, is it OK if I have a look around the village?' I asked the novice director after a bread and soup lunch. All the food here came in medieval colours of white, brown, and green. Not a single peppy E number to entice and slowly kill us thanks to its carcinogenic properties. Live long and miserable.

She was distracted by a batch of invoices she was entering into the accounts on the single laptop owned by the community. I wondered, if I got a chance to have a look through, what other information might be on that. I should try later, maybe at night? Another question was where she charged the computer. The sockets I'd tried in the main house were all disconnected, doubtless to deter phone-rule flouters like me.

She briefly looked up and smiled, her expression unfocused. 'Of course you may go out. You worked hard all morning and I believe you have some free time?'

'Yes, I'm not expected in the dining room until six to set the tables.'

'Then that's fine. Just remember, we keep ourselves apart from the locals but we are always polite. And unfortunately there may be others taking an interest in us – reporters and such like – since the incident on the hill at the weekend. Don't speak to anyone. Walk away.'

I tapped my forehead. 'Got it. Walk away.'

'Or, if they persist, just tell them the truth: you weren't even here then.'

'No problem.'

She was looking at a spreadsheet now, squinting a little at

the text. I couldn't quite make out the figures but there seemed to be inputs for expenditure of food and utilities, nothing to interest the inspector. 'Do you want someone to guide you? I can see if anyone else is free?'

'I'll be fine. Kingston Beauchamp doesn't seem like it's a big place.'

'True. I think you'll struggle to occupy yourself for more than an hour.'

With a sense of relief, I headed for the front door, grabbing one of the loose linen jackets we were issued for colder days. It came with big square pockets. I stuffed mine with a head-scarf so I could wrap my phone in it on my return.

I escaped the manor grounds. So much goodness was wearing. It was fun pretending to be someone else but it didn't stop me wanting to kick my airhead self for being quite so inane. Goodness made me want to shag, swear, and smoke, because none of them were approved behaviour. Trying to walk off my jitters, I strode down the lane to the centre of the village. Blink and you'd pass it. There was a Co-op with a pub opposite and a village cross with a painted sign that showed the White Horse on the hill above and Morris dancers. It was a really happening place. Heading north, the road crossed the valley to join the main road to Swindon; heading south, it went uphill to the Downs and petered out. There were two intersections in that direction: one with the old Icknield Way, now a B road, and another above on the footpath that was the Ridgeway. I had read online before coming here that the Icknield Way was thought to be a sheltered drover's road – the Ridgeway for when the valley was too wet. That made them each other's diversionary route, heading in roughly the same direction. Both were thousands of years old. Other roads in the village centre joined little area of cottages with names like 'Old Forge' and 'The Malthouse', or went to the church. I took the lane that rejoiced with admirable simplicity in the name Church Way, to St Martin's. I was hoping the vicar had done as Leo asked and left my mobile for me to collect.

Seeing the church through the lychgate, I found that it was a pretty little building, the kind of model you could build out of cardboard boxes painted white in some primary school project – a shoebox for the nave and a muesli box for the tower. I paused by the gravestones, reading off a few names at random. They all sounded like very old families – Leighs, Shepherds, and Clays – traditional ones who were unlikely now to have any descendants able to afford the pricey country homes (fiercely renovated for comfort) that now dominated the village centre. Working-class descendants might cling on in the new housing at the far edge of the village, but not among the lawyers and retired academics with their roses clambering up to the thatch.

I tried the church door. It opened with a satisfying creak, releasing the smell of damp stone and mouldering hymnals particular to old churches. Someone had gone to town for the harvest festival, piling oversized veg by the altar. To one side was a plastic box for food bank collections – they seemed to get everywhere these days, such was the poverty gap; it had gathered a drift of packets of pasta, tinned beans, and tea. My eye fell on a packet of very-bad-for-you pink wafer biscuits and I was tempted. Luckily for my soul, there was a woman on top of a short stepladder, adjusting the numbers on the board that told you what hymn number was next, and the moment passed.

'Hello?' I called.

She turned and smiled. 'Come on in. Don't mind me. Just getting ready for our mid-week communion service.'

From the glimpse of the dog collar under her fleece I deduced that this was the helpful priest Leo had mentioned. With her grin, she had a friendly *Vicar of Dibley* vibe, though slimmer and only in her mid-thirties. I approached her and held out a hand.

'Hi, I'm Jess Bridges.'

She gave it a firm shake. 'Iona Chamberlain-Turner. Are you Inspector George's friend?'

'That's right.'

'I'm sorry, I've not finished charging your phone yet. It's in the vestry. Can I get you a cuppa while you wait?'

'Please.' I followed her into the vestry, the place where kneelers and chairs came to die, from the evidence stacked in one corner. 'You should put those on a bonfire.'

She snorted as she filled the kettle from a plastic bottle of water and switched it on. 'Don't I wish. The PCC is still looking into appropriate disposal because some of them were bequests. The committee doesn't feel we can just chuck them on a fire and dance around the flames on bonfire night. Personally, if I'd sewed one fifty years ago and knew it had come to the end of its natural life, I'd rejoice to hear that it had enjoyed such a jolly send-off.'

I approved of this woman. I took a seat in the scruffy

armchair she indicated; saggy and feather-filled, it was the perfect home for church mice. I would just have to hope that none were in residence. 'Suggest marshmallow toasting. Or s'mores – they're even better.'

'Something new happen in Kingston Beauchamp? I'd never get it past them.'

'So what's a nice lady like you doing in a place like this?'

She fished two teabags out of a caddy. 'Funny, that's almost exactly what I was going to ask you. Inspector George mentioned you were in the commune looking for someone?'

'A client's daughter. She seems to have got swept up in the Father Oak lifestyle and the mum wants me to talk sense to her. That's actually hilarious if you knew me as no one has ever expected sense from me.'

'Have you found her?' She poured the hot water into the mugs.

'Not yet. We all have these made-up names and I've only seen one old photo of her so I wanted some more shots. Without them, I'm not sure I could make a correct guess before approaching her.'

'Are there really that many young women to make it so difficult? I had no idea. Milk?'

'Please. No sugar. Actually, yes, sugar. I'm feeling a bit too pure with all the wholemeal bread and veg. Thanks. Chri— cripes, that's strong.' I grimaced as I sipped because she'd made the tea builder-strength. 'Going back to your question, there are ten young women living in the commune, a few novices, some second order and a couple who have got into the inner circle.'

Iona took a seat on a swivel chair pulled up in front of a desk. A stack of parish magazines teetered as she made space for her mug. She rescued it with the steadying influence of a dark green volume of *Carols for Choirs* that I recognised from my schooldays. 'I worry about all those young people. Father Oak has always struck me as a very domineering man whenever I've had dealings with him.' She offered me a biscuit from a tin that looked pre-war with pictures of the jubilees of dead kings and queens. The cookies were Waitrose so I risked one.

'Are you asking if he's brainwashing them into doing disreputable things?'

She took a pink wafer biscuit from underneath. Had the good rector been raiding the food bank box? Or maybe she donated them? Either way, she had good taste in bad biscuits. 'I think I am.'

'I wish he was. It's all disappointingly tame. I might have to go back to my client and say that her daughter is living a very safe and dull life and no intervention is required. Sure, the clothes and food suck, but I've not come across anything that takes it into wicked territory. So far it feels like a very innocent experiment of living as close to nature as you can in the twenty-first century.'

'In a mansion? How very humble.'

'Yeah, you've got me there. But we don't have electricity, or phones, and we do everything by hand. Cooking is on bottled gas or over fires.'

Legs crossed, she swung idly to and fro on her swivel chair, a habit I doubted she even noticed. 'I always hated barbecues:

so much build-up for a singed offering. My ex-army father would always bark orders and blame us for failures.'

'Can't say I'm a fan either, but I'm on the gardening team today so I haven't had to test my skills.' I looked around, hoping to spot my phone. 'Do you think it's charged yet?'

'I'll check.' She pulled back a curtain to reveal a multi-socket extension cord. My phone was sitting next to a set of bike lights and a phone, all on charge like little electric piglets nestling up to the teats of a white sow. 'Ninety percent. Almost there.'

'Much as I hate waiting, I'd better wait for a full charge so it lasts as long as possible.' I went to the window and woke it up still plugged in. I had a new message from Tanglewood with attachments. Opening the photos, I swiped through the images she had sent. None of them rang any bells.

'Bad news?' asked Iona.

'Not sure. I think I've met all the commune members now and these photos don't look particularly like anyone I've seen. She may have changed her hair, lost or put on weight, but still you'd think I'd recognise her, wouldn't you? Two years isn't that long and she's very beautiful.'

'She may have left?'

'I guess that's possible. Her communication with her mother broke down so she might not want to get back in touch.'

'Or be too ashamed to admit her mum was right? Nothing is worse than 'fessing up to parents that they were correct all along.'

'Do I hear the bitterness of experience speaking?'

She laughed and threw her hands up in mock despair. 'My parents live in the village. They have plenty of chances to point out just how predictably wrong I am and that Kingston Beauchamp won't change just because I want it to.'

'Parents can be a challenge.'

'Where do yours live? Are you close to them?'

'Mum lives with my sister not far from Cirencester. She's not too bad on the "I told you so" front. And my father, well, he's in prison.'

Iona flushed. 'I'm sorry. I'm usually more tactful.'

'I'm not. Best place for him.'

She adjusted. 'In that case, I'm glad for you and sorry for whatever went before. I meet so many people who have difficult parental experiences. Sadly, you are not alone.'

'But you feel alone when you're going through it. Maybe that's why Father Oak is so effective? He makes you feel part of something, like you never have to be alone again.' And mock them though I did, I already felt the pull of the lifestyle, the sense of belonging somewhere that I lacked in my real life.

'That's kind of what we offer here too.' Her eyes went to the cross on the wall behind me. 'But people think they know what Christianity offers without really looking beyond half-baked memories of nativity plays and old school hymns. They don't bother to consider Christ as an adult.'

I drained my cup. I was worried she was going to invite me to an Alpha course or one of those more modern forms of outreach you saw advertised on city buses. I was omni-spiritual if I was anything, and felt awkward being asked to nail my colours to any particular mast – or spire. 'Thanks for the tea. I'd better take my phone and run.'

'Bring it back any time it needs charging. The church is usually open until five. The key for the vestry is in the watering can by the door – all very high-tech security.'

'Yeah, I can see. You really fool those thieves with your cunning.'

'Actually, it's an invitation: break in if you must and take a few broken chairs with you. Save me the hassle.'

As I was swathing the phone in my headscarf, a man with an impressive beard barged in, obviously in a hurry.

'Iona, I've got to talk to you!' he said, his face red. 'Oh, sorry, I didn't know you had company.'

'Jess is just leaving. Take a seat and I'll be with you. Is it the Trust again or has Dad been on at you about the footpaths?' Iona walked with me to the door. 'My uncle Andrew. He needs a pep talk from time to time. Nice to meet you.'

'And you. See you around.'

She didn't close the door behind me, leaving it open to let the fresh autumn air drive away some of the gloomy damp of the church. Cute little corn dollies bounced and spun over the archway. They were an ancient fertility symbol, weren't they?

'So, Uncle Andrew, what's got you upset this afternoon?' I heard Iona say.

'Oh Iona, I'm in such a pickle. If I don't tell someone, I'll go mad.'

Tempting though it was to eavesdrop, I called on my better nature and left them in peace.

It was an odd life, at thirty-something being a priest in a place where your uncle and parents lived. Didn't feel right somehow because, I mean, what authority would you have with people who remembered you in nappies? Wasn't there something about a prophet not being welcome in her own country?

I wandered back through the village and struggled with myself outside the pub. The police didn't appear to be here this afternoon so I would be safe from being spotted, but I had no money. I calculated the odds of being able to sweet-talk someone into buying me a drink, or bumming a cigarette, without getting caught.

But what if my lapse got back to my fellow Children of the White Horse? I'd only been there a day so I was on thin ice.

Oh God, oh God, despite this, I was going to do it, wasn't I? I wanted to howl at myself but my feet had already crossed the threshold.

Reaching the main bar, I found that I was the object of attention of about fifteen late-lunch drinkers: a posse of walkers, three workmen who had slacked off for the day, and two business men hunched over two halves and a shared packet of crisps that they'd torn open to place between them. I supposed I did look out of place in my white robe. They probably expected a begging bowl next, which was kind of the mission. The barman looked over at me; his gaze was unfriendly, tired with rather bulging eyes like that unfortunate breed the Telescope goldfish. Maybe he just had a thyroid problem? He probably knew I didn't have cash.

Who was most likely to have what I needed? Not the clean-living walkers. The workmen would mock me. I decided that the businessmen needed me most. They were the stressed-out middle-management type. I was their light relief.

I hovered at the stool next to their table. 'Is this taken?'

The guys looked at each other; one was dark complexioned and about my age, the other was a tubby, older pale-skinned man with thinning hair.

'Er, no,' said Tubs.

I sat down rather than move the stool. 'Hope I'm not interrupting anything? Of course I am, but I mean, anything interesting? I'm desperate for a crisp. It called to me from the other side of the bar. May I?' The thing about being so blatant was that people had no idea how to handle you. It nearly always worked for me. 'Cheese and onion? Oh well? It takes all sorts.'

The one with the dark-toned skin and sculptured haircut cut smiled at this. 'That was John's choice. I told him it was a mistake and that we'd taste nothing else all afternoon.'

'That's why I like it,' said John. 'Hi. I'm John Bailey.' We shook hands.

'Hi. Jess. Oops, I mean Sister Poppy. I've only just joined the commune here and, between you and me, not doing that well at the lifestyle. Day Two and I'm gasping for a drink.'

John rolled his eyes. 'OK, I get the hint, Jess. What'll it be?'

'White wine, if that's not too much for you?'

'Get her a packet of ready salted too, then maybe I'll help her eat them,' suggested the other. He gave me a wave from across the table. 'I'm Ray. We're with Centrica.'

'What's that?'

'Energy services and solutions, or in everyday speak, gas and electricity.'

'Cool.' My energy-related conversation was limited.

'And you? What's this commune you mentioned?'

I had to remember to behave in case this got back to Father Oak. I wouldn't put it past him to have his spies in the village. 'It's all very new to me but we're called The Children of the White Horse and we try to live in balance with nature.'

Ray cracked his knuckles, casting round for a possible shared interest. 'Are you vegan? I tried that in January. I stopped when my mate cooked bacon five days into the new year.'

'I don't think we are. I've seen eggs and cheese. But as I said, early days for me.'

John returned with my drink and a packet of crisps which he dropped in front of Ray.

'Jess here was just telling me why she joined a commune,' Ray explained as he opened the packet.

'Really? Why the fuck would you want to do something like that?' John had evidently missed out on tactfulness when the good fairies blessed his cradle.

Because I'm undercover. No, I mustn't blurt out the truth even if these guys had nothing to do with the village and were just passing through. 'I just felt I needed a new direction as my old one had led me into a dead end.'

'Talking about dead ends, you'd better be careful you don't end up like the girl they found on the White Horse. She was one of your lot apparently,' said John.

I shivered at the reminder. 'Who said that?'

'The man behind the bar. The owner. He seems to know everything about everyone round here. Said you were likely to be one of the harem some joker called Father Oak has gathered around him.' John was testing me.

'Oh yes, that's absolutely right. I get to sleep with him once a month on the third Tuesday.'

Ray spluttered on his beer. 'Seriously?'

I grabbed a handful of crisps. 'No! I'm pulling your leg. I've no idea where the rumours come from because we are very restrained; think monks and nuns and you'll get the idea.' I wrinkled my nose. 'That might be one of the reasons I'm not cut out for the life but I'll give it a good go before I decide.'

John winked at Ray. 'Maybe we should get you another drink? Help with the old fortitude for celibacy?'

I toasted him with my glass. 'Thanks, John. I really, really need it.'

Chapter 13

Leo

Such was the lack of progress on this case that Leo was beginning to worry it would be taken away from him. He could feel his authority with his team trickling away like a slow puncture. They had to be wondering how long the superintendent would put up with the fact that he had no suspects, no motive, and no name for the victim. There was no CCTV in the village and nothing relevant from the cameras on the main road. All he had was a body, so he decided to go back to that and see what Gerry could tell him.

The mortuary was hidden in the bowels of a local hospital, a well-kept secret from those embedded on the wards upstairs or stuck in corridors waiting for a vacancy in either place. At least in the mortuary you got a trolley and a place in the cold store. Gerry had been warned that Leo was coming in under pressure so she'd brought the victim out of the fridge and was ready with her report. There was visibly more marbling that had bloomed in the hours after he had first viewed the victim. This happened as the blood settled to the lower extremities and a greenish tinge had set in. When he'd first seen her, she could've almost been asleep; now death had taken firm hold.

'Not much more I can tell you, Leo,' said Gerry almost apologetically. 'We have here a fit young woman with excellent muscle tone and no sign of other injuries, new or old. I'd say she was very healthy, apart from the fact that she's dead.'

The blood had been cleaned away and a T section now marred the perfect skin of the torso. Leo brushed his own sternum, feeling an ache in sympathy. 'No substance abuse? No pregnancies? No old fractures?'

'No, no, and no. One thing I can tell you is that she had exceptionally well-cared for teeth. They have veneers that give them that perfect white appearance, otherwise known as the Hollywood smile.' She lifted the top lip with a spatula so he could see the full effect. 'Costs a fortune. Looks fake to me, but it's growing in popularity.'

'Any way of telling where she had the work done?'

'That's not really my area of expertise. I had one of my dentistry colleagues have a quick look, and he thought it was most likely done in America, but he couldn't give a definitive origin as the technique is spreading.'

'How common would you say it is in people you see?'

'I only see the dead ones, and they're usually old. However, I think you'll find more and more young people going for cosmetic treatment. Thanks to social media, they all know these days that the stars don't roll out of bed looking red-carpet ready.'

Still, the victim was young to be able to afford such an expenditure. That raised the likelihood of her either being very wealthy or from a country where it was more usual for someone of her age. The States was the front runner, considering her age and ethnicity. 'Do you have her DNA sequenced yet?'

'That's expected very soon.'

Leo checked the clock on the wall over the entrance. He'd arranged to call Tanglewood White this morning and would prefer to be somewhere private for that conversation. It was a long shot but he had to ask. Much of police work was about elimination.

'OK, thanks Gerry. I really need that DNA profile. I'm getting nowhere at the moment.'

'I'll send it to you as soon as it comes through. The boss has ordered us to try a private provider to cut costs and I can tell you it is a retrograde step. They don't know the meaning of urgent.'

Leo agreed. Police work was now full of stupid short cuts that created huge delays, excessive paperwork and pointless procedures. Sometimes he felt that crimes were just secondary matters in a service that had become a huge bureaucracy that existed only to feed itself.

Leaving the harsh antiseptic smells of the mortuary behind, Leo found a table in a café in the main hospital concourse from which to make his call.

'Inspector George? I have to say I'm worried that you want to talk to me.' The woman Jess had put him in touch with sounded understandably nervous.

'Dr White? I'm sorry to disturb you. I'm investigating an incident that took place near the commune where your daughter lives, and I just wanted to check that she's not involved.'

'An incident? Like a burglary or an assault?'

'Miss Bridges told me you were away this weekend so you didn't see the news. It's a killing, I'm afraid.'

'And you think my daughter is involved? I can tell you, Inspector, that I may not see eye to eye with Lisette but I've never known her to be violent. She has a temper but it always passes quickly.'

It was interesting that her first instinct was to assume her daughter was suspected of killing rather than being a victim. In Leo's experience, humans preferred to keep the illusion that they had agency, rather than accept the truth, which was that any of us could find ourselves powerless against ill fate. 'It's actually the victim I'm trying to identify.'

There followed a long silence.

'No, no, it can't be her.' Her tone was now almost too calm.

As any police officer would tell you, unfortunately it can.

'Would you be prepared to look at a photo of the victim, for elimination purposes?'

'It won't be her.'

'I have to explore all avenues. The victim's identity remains unknown but she's young, about twenty to twenty-five, blonde hair, and she has a tattoo on her shoulder blade.'

'Lisette doesn't have a tattoo.' Her voice was full of relief.

'But you haven't seen her for two years?' he asked gently.

'She hates needles. She can't have changed so much that she would willingly get one.'

'OK then. That sounds positive. But may I still send you the picture?'

'Do it.' He could hear the resolve in her tone: she'd prefer to know now.

He waited while the file winged its way to her email account. There was a sharp intake of breath, then she released it.

'That's not my daughter, Inspector.'

He was relieved for her but also frustrated as another door closed. 'You're sure?'

'I can see that there is some superficial resemblance to her, perhaps about the eyebrows? But the face shape is wrong and Lisette has a little scar on her collarbone. She came off badly at the ice rink one day.'

And as Gerry had said, the victim had no previous injuries to report. 'Thank you. That must have been distressing no matter how certain you were.'

She laughed nervously. 'Yes, well, I had a flutter or two of doubt but it just isn't her. I'm sorry for whoever it is, naturally.' She cleared her throat. 'Have you interviewed all the people in the commune, Inspector?'

'Between me and my officers, yes, we have.'

'If I send you a picture of my daughter, can you tell me if she's OK?'

'I'm afraid I can't do that, but you've got Jess Bridges on the case. She's in the best position to tell you how your daughter is, when she finds her.'

'My daughter's missing from the manor?'

'Not as far as I know. But perhaps you should talk about this with Miss Bridges?'

'Yes, yes, I'll do that. I'll text her. I sent her more photos so I'm hoping to hear back from her soon.'

'I'm sure you will. Miss Bridges is dedicated to finding answers for you.'

'Of course. I know she is. Sorry if I was asking too much. It's just that I feel so useless.'

'Not at all, but as your daughter is an adult and living there by choice, you can see why I can't track her down for you.'

'I suppose I wouldn't like it if our situations were reversed. And you've got bigger fish to fry.'

'Actually, Dr White, there is something you could help me with, if you don't mind me asking? It's about your subject of expertise.'

'Go ahead.'

'What do you think is the intended message of killing someone at the White Horse, then laying the body out along its back? Does that mean anything to you?'

'How was she murdered?' The cool, professional tone was back.

'Single stab wound to the chest.'

'I'll look into it, but my first thought is that these geoglyphs like the White Horse aren't associated with sacrifices or ceremonial killings as far as we can tell from the archaeological records. We sometimes find horses, and occasionally household members, killed and buried with high status individuals, but that would be at a grave site or a barrow. There are graves further up the hill near Uffington Castle, the Iron Age fort, but not on the horse itself.'

'So what did the horse mean then?'

'Ah, that's the million-dollar question. My colleagues and I spend many hours debating the role the White Horse played in the society that made it, but the most compelling explanation I've heard so far is that it is positioned where it is to be in relationship with the sun at different times of the solar year. In the winter, the sun rolls along the top of the Downs, almost as though it is being carried on the back of the horse. Many Iron Age societies had a belief that the sun was drawn in a chariot across the skies during the day and returned under the earth, sometimes on a ship, ready for the next dawn. There may be a link to those stories, some kind of daily cosmic drama.'

There was poetry in that explanation that Leo preferred to the warden's suggestion that it was a sign advertising the presence of the local tribe. 'So a killing up there doesn't make sense under any pagan belief system you know about?'

'No. Had it taken place at Wayland's Smithy, I could have made an argument about an entrance to the underworld, but not out on the hillside. Of course, it doesn't stop someone inventing a story to justify it with only the merest nod to antiquity.'

'Thank you. That's very helpful.'

'I'll ask my colleagues and let you know if anyone has another view. But before last Saturday I would say that no one associated the White Horse with death.'

Leo drove back to the station turning over the significance of white teeth and white horses in his mind. Stopping by DS Wong's desk on his way to his office, he saw that she had finished entering the latest statements from the neighbours.

'Suyin, I've had a thought. Can you check with the Met to see whether anyone has recently reported a missing North American woman who fits our victim's description?'

Suyin got up and stretched. 'Will do. You think she's a foreigner?'

'Just a possibility, based on the work she's had done to her teeth. It would explain why we're drawing a blank on her identity here in the UK.'

'I'll get right on that. Oh, and the rector of St Martin's called. She wants to see you as soon as you can manage it.'

That was probably to report that Jess had picked up her phone. Leo had asked Iona to let him know. 'Have you got her number?'

Suyin passed him a Post-it. 'This is a bloody frustrating case.'

'They sometimes are. We just have to keep following up our leads. Let me find out if our inside source at the commune has anything to offer.'

Chapter 14

Jess

I arrived back at the manor much drunker and more rumpled than when I'd left. The latter was due to the younger of the two businessmen. Ray had followed me out when I went to the ladies' and we had a brief encounter in the corridor. He initiated it and I only have to confess to a bit of smooching before I remembered where we were and what I was supposed to be doing. I ended things gently. Ray didn't appear to mind, agreeing that a pub corridor was no place for this, not with his colleague and other members of the public likely to stumble upon us. He insisted on leaving me his card so I could call him to arrange a date. He was sweet really. And he'd bought me two glasses of wine so I hoped he wouldn't feel shortchanged when he realised that I had no intention of taking him up on the offer.

It was later than I thought when I arrived in the dining room. Everyone was already sitting in front of their bean stew and I'd missed my turn to lay the tables. Bad Jessica. Heads swivelled in my direction as I made my way through the tables and there was a distinct lull in conversation.

'Sorry, sorry, not used to having no phone. I lost track of the time.' My apology was made to the thirty people in the room but it was Father Oak who replied.

'I have to say that we are very disappointed, Sister Poppy. We share work here. We don't leave others to do it when we don't show up. I expected better of you.'

I pulled what I hoped was a penitent face. 'I completely understand, Father Oak. Give me double duties tomorrow. I'll make up.'

'See me after the meal and we'll discuss your attitude and what an appropriate sanction might be.'

'Absolutely. After the meal. Got you.' I took a seat, trying not to breathe over anyone. Ivy was giving me a searching stare from the far end of the room next to our leader. 'I think I'm in the doghouse,' I whispered to my neighbour.

She edged away.

Maybe it was the cheese and onion she was smelling? I dug into the stew, hoping to absorb the alcohol and disguise the crisps. It was only three glasses (or was it four?) but I had downed them quickly on an empty stomach. Not my best decision of the day.

'So what've I missed?' I asked my tablemates brightly. 'Any more visits from the police?'

The man on my right scowled at me – Brother Maple, who tended the area around the icehouse, keeping away interlopers like me. 'No, thank fuck. Pigs.' East London resonated strongly in his accent. He was one of the oldest with a face like a wet weekend in Margate. A lifestyle of meditation and simplicity hadn't done much for the sweetness of his disposition. Put him in ordinary clothes and stick him behind a black cab steering wheel and he'd be much more at home. In the rain. When there was a Tube strike and the roads were gridlocked. I wondered what had brought him here?

'They still don't know who she is. I wish she hadn't got hold of one of our robes,' added Sister Briar. I had her down as one of my possible Lisettes due to her age, but studying her close-to, she didn't resemble the girl in the photos I'd downloaded. 'If she hadn't worn it, then they wouldn't be bothering us.'

Were they all just pretending not to know her or was it genuine? I glanced around the room, wondering uneasily if I was supping with murderers. The commune did have the air of a community that kept its secrets. 'So how was your day in the absence of police attention?' I chirped, remembering that I was channelling airhead and upbeat Jessica, the rejected squeeze of an up-himself academic.

'I had a lovely time baking bread,' said Briar. 'We're experimenting with sourdough. Do you like it?'

The bread was the best bit of meals here. The bean stew did nothing for me but give me wind. 'Your bread is epic.'

'Oh, thank you.' She beamed at me.

'And you, Brother Maple, how was your day?' God, I sounded like a package-tour guide.

'None of your business,' he grunted, dipping his bread in his bowl.

I almost wanted to cheer him for his terseness. 'Of course. Sorry. I was just making conversation.'

'Then don't.'

Sister Briar leant over and stroked my hand. Oh, hello. 'Don't mind him. He's our resident grumpy old man.'

'Hey, less of the old!' he protested.

The commune didn't run to dessert, apart from the ubiquitous apples that appeared at every meal (they had their own orchard and a bumper harvest). I helped clear the tables and then girded my loins for my interview with Father Oak. I hoped he'd not decided to chuck me out already, though I wouldn't blame him. I was walking proof that he wasn't as good a judge of character as he thought.

I tapped on the door to his room.

'Come in.'

He was sitting cross-legged on a mat in the middle of what had to be the main parlour of the house. The sofas and armchairs had been pushed to the edge, leaving a splendid Persian carpet on display. He managed to sit so his feet were neatly tucked in, soles upwards, like a statue of Buddha.

'Oh, um, hi. I'm here.'

'I can see that. Come and join me.' He gestured to the space opposite him on the carpet. He reminded me a little of a younger Jeremy Irons, with hawkish good looks that pulled you in.

'This is where you discover just how inflexible I am.' I tried to copy him but my feet wouldn't go like that. I settled for primary school-style crossed legs instead. 'Work in progress,' I admitted.

'Exactly. We all are. Let's sit in silence for a while.'

'OK.' I tried to even out my breathing and clear my mind as we had been taught this morning but, as usual, I felt like I had ants crawling up my spine. Thoughts whirled: my job here, the body on the hill, a certain handsome policeman, my precarious financial situation ...

'Poppy, I sense you have trouble relaxing?'

'ADHD makes that hard.'

He let a few more minutes pass. 'I've been looking into your condition to see how we might be able to help you. The articles I've been reading suggest that it can be understood as an evolutionary advantage, making you alert to danger because you find it hard to switch off.'

'So while I'm twitching, I spot the sabre-toothed tiger, while my snoozing fellow cave people get eaten?'

He smiled, his eyes still closed. 'Something like that.'

I liked more than I should how he had turned my difficulty into a positive. Damn, he was good at this. 'Then it's good for predators, bad for meditation?'

'Maybe, but can we harness that energy, turn it into more peaceful paths? That's what I want to ask.'

I don't know. You're the guru. I didn't say that out loud, thankfully. 'If you can help me, I'd be grateful, Father Oak.'

'I do have one idea. It is about redirecting your energy.'

Oh yes? 'What do you mean?'

'Would you like to give it a try?'

That depends, thinks cynical Jessica. 'If you think it's a good idea?' said airhead Jessica.

'Come nearer then.'

Here it comes … the moment he shows his true colours.

'I'm going to give you a back rub, just to calm you down. Would you like that?'

'Oh yes, Father Oak.' Both Airhead Jessica and cynical Jessica were up for a back rub. I scooted nearer.

'Now let your muscles relax.' He came up on his knees behind me. I could feel his breath on my neck. His hands started to knead my shoulders. 'How's that?'

'Spectacular.'

He chuckled softly. 'Have you been drinking, Poppy?'

'I … yes, I have. Just a glass of wine. I met a couple of nice guys in the village and they bought me a drink. Just one.'

His fingers delved into my hair and rubbed my temples. 'But you know that we don't do that – pollute our bodies with alcohol?'

I let my head fall back a little. 'So it's not just a rule for the manor?'

'It's an approach to the whole of our lives, not only the part we show to others in the commune. We don't do one thing in the village and another in the manor.'

'I'm sorry then.' And I meant that sincerely, but not in the way he intended.

His hands drifted lower. He was acting as if this wasn't sexual but I was beginning to feel a little revved from the hands-on treatment. Coming after the unfinished business in the pub, my body craved more than just a massage and he was a nice-looking guy for his age.

'Comfortable?'

'Hmmm. Getting there.'

And then he was undoing the breast band. 'You'll feel much more at ease without this. I would much prefer it if you can do without.'

'I think ... I can do without.' My breath was coming in pants now. He had to know he was turning me on.

'I think we need to work on your obedience, Sister.'

'Oh yes. Yes, obedience.'

His hands were now cupping my breasts, massaging them to ease the pain of being bound all day. I knew exactly where this was going. Was I on board with it? My body was, so I let it send out the signals. My brain was lagging behind, playing catch up, trying to remind me that he was a smarmy hypocrite.

'So beautiful.' He kissed my neck. 'You should never be ashamed of your breasts. Mother Earth gave them to you for your pleasure and to nurture your children.'

'I'm not ... ashamed.' I leant back into him so we could join our lips for a kiss.

He brushed his mouth against mine. 'I don't do this with everyone.'

'I should hope not. Brother Maple doesn't seem the sort to appreciate it.'

He smiled and nipped my neck. 'But I do join with very special girls on very rare occasions – ones who need to expel their energy. You're a special girl, aren't you, Poppy?'

I was drifting, careless of my mission as long as he kept this up. 'I can be. I can be anything you want.'

'If we do this, your energy will be released and you can find equilibrium.'

If he said so. I'd settle for an orgasm. 'Oh yes, Father Oak. Whatever you say.'

My adventure in the cult was looking much more promising as Father Oak lived up to my hopes that he was here for the sex and money. Just as I reached down, intending to take my tunic off over my head, there was a knock at the door.

'Father Oak?' came a voice from outside.

He moved away from me. 'What is it now, Sister Ivy?' His tone was understandably irritated.

'I was wondering if you'd finished with Sister Poppy? I have a task for her.'

I shook my head and mouthed to him that I was not in the least bit finished. He quirked a regretful smile and tucked a lock of my hair behind my ear.

'I'll send her out in a moment.'

'Then I'll wait out here for her.'

Ah, so Sister Ivy knew what went on in Father Oak's study and was doing her bit to keep us to our vows – or him to his at least. As far as she was concerned, I could go jump in the lake. Was she jealous, I wondered? How many restless novices had he had on this carpet? That thought cooled my passion.

'We'll continue our meditation practice another time, Sister Poppy,' he said, mindful now of our eavesdropper. He passed me the breast band which I tied round my waist, letting the ends flutter.

'I look forward to it.' I went to the door and blew him a kiss. 'Thank you. I'm feeling much more settled.'

He resumed the position in which I had found him. 'Anything to help. Goodnight.'

'Goodnight, sir.'

I could hear him chuckling as I closed the door behind me.

Sister Ivy started walking, waiting until there was no chance he could hear us. 'You aren't special, you know,' she hissed.

She had heard that, had she?

'There have been many girls like you, ones he plays with for a while, but it means nothing.'

That was probably accurate. 'I bet they had fun, though. Nothing like an older man who knows his way around a woman's body.'

'You won't last. Carry on like you have today and you'll be gone by the end of next week.'

I hoped so. But not before I'd earned my twenty thousand pounds. 'I didn't throw myself at him, Sister Ivy. He was trying to help me meditate and we got a little friendly. Nothing happened.'

'Remember that. Nothing happened. He doesn't feel anything for you.'

I couldn't tell if she was upset that her guru had clay feet or that I was the one he was dallying with and not her. Or maybe both?

'And if you get in his way again, I'll get rid of you.'

Is that a threat from the good sister? I do believe it was.

How far would she go? An image of the girl on the hill flashed through my mind. A little self-preservation might be in order. 'Understood. You said you had a task?'

'You broke several rules today so I want you to clean the grate in my office. We are starting to lay fires tomorrow now that it's getting colder. I want it to be swept and polished tonight.'

'So this is my punishment?'

'We don't think of it as a punishment but a physical task that gives you the chance to reflect on what you did wrong.'

'It's a punishment.'

Entering her room, I saw that Ivy had already set the bucket with polish, dustpan, and brush on the hearthrug. I'd no idea how to clean a grate properly, not being aware of living a previous life as a Victorian scullery maid, so I did my best while Ivy tapped away on the computer. I worked slowly, humming songs from Disney's *Cinderella* and hoping, if I was annoying enough, she would leave me alone in the room for a few minutes. My opportunity came when Brother Pine interrupted our girl-time to tell her that Brother Maple needed her at the icehouse. I couldn't imagine what business they would have out there in the dark – I was hoping it was for a threesome as they could all do with a bit of de-stressing – but Ivy got up to go with a pinched expression. Nothing so enjoyable in prospect then.

'Haven't you finished yet?' she asked.

'Almost.' I swept some ashes into the dustpan and tipped them in the bucket. 'I like this. It feels so retro.'

At least Brother Pine smiled at my absurd statement.

Ivy was unimpressed. 'Put the bucket back in the butler's pantry when you've finished.'

Please don't put the laptop into sleep mode. Please don't. 'Will do.'

She left and I leapt up to stop the laptop going into hibernation. I refreshed the page. It was open on accounts again. I ran my eye down the descriptions of expenditure: lots of things for the garden, water, rent, council charge, electricity ... I checked the figures paid out. It was hard to tell what was a lot for a place this size so I tried to do it by proportion. Rent was a big chunk but the electricity bill did seem very high for a place that claimed to be living mainly off-grid. Did Father Oak have a secret sauna running twenty-four hours somewhere? I wouldn't put it past him. In fact, I'd happily join him in it. I took a picture with my phone. I was very lucky that Father Oak's wandering hands hadn't come across this illicit device wrapped in a headscarf. I sent the photo to Inspector George and immediately deleted the image. If this got found, I didn't want any evidence left on the phone that I'd been snooping. I'd put the inspector in my contacts as Great Uncle George and hopefully they wouldn't recognise the number.

I'd prefer the phone not to be found at all, but I was rubbish at subterfuge. Best to prepare for the worst.

I minimised the accounts on the laptop to have a quick look at other recently opened files. Both the inspector and I needed to know who everyone really was and I wondered if Ivy had the information? There was no helpful spreadsheet of real names set against made-up ones, but I did see a document on donations. Was that how they referred to property when it was added to the community coffers? I opened a browser, went into my account, and sent myself the file, copying the inspector. I'd look at it after lights out.

Footsteps were heading my way, the slap-slap of sandals

on the tiled floor. I deleted the browsing history, hoping Ivy didn't notice it was gone, and reopened the accounts. The fact that she hadn't shut the machine down on leaving must have meant she was intending to return.

Back to the bucket. Nothing to see here. Just a latter-day Cinderella singing 'Bibbidi-bobbidi-boo' as she cleaned up.

Ivy returned. 'You're still here?'

'Just finished.' I dropped the brush into the bucket. I had to keep her that side of the desk so she didn't notice the laptop hadn't yet gone into sleep mode. 'Where did you say I should put stuff?'

'In the butler's pantry.'

'Where's that?'

'I'm sure I showed you on your orientation tour.'

I smiled hopelessly. 'I think you did but I'm not very good with directions. Don't worry, I'll just ask Father Oak to show me.'

Those were the magic words, not the Disney ones I'd just been singing. 'I'll take it back myself.' She plucked the bucket from my hand. 'You'd better head to bed. There's an early start tomorrow.'

'Yes, Sister Ivy.'

Trying not to smile, I headed upstairs as she took the passage to the butler's pantry.

It was second on the left, by the way.

Chapter 15

Leo

Leo rang the rector but got her voicemail. It was getting late and he could leave it until tomorrow, but he decided instead to drive out to Kingston Beauchamp just to put his mind at rest that Jess had been able to get out of the manor to fetch her phone. Even if Iona was out for the evening and he had to wait for morning to get an answer, there was no harm in going over the site again. He'd not yet seen it in night-time conditions so it might suggest some new ideas of how people had moved from place to place and why nothing had been seen by witnesses.

Putting the reverend's home address into his satnav, Leo found it on the edge of the village. The estate hadn't yet grown into itself; the plots around the houses still looked raw, the hedges anaemic. It took a good few years for shrubs to establish themselves, particularly if you opted for a wildlife-friendly mix of hazel, holly, and ash, as she had done. He knocked on the door and a stranger answered. He was a slim, black male, about five-ten, with a shaved head that shone a little under the porch light. He was wearing sports kit, sweat-stained at the neck and armpits.

'Hello?' he said. 'Can I help you?'

'Sorry to disturb your evening. I'm Detective Inspector George with Thames Valley Police.' Leo held up his warrant card. 'I'm looking for Iona.'

'That's my wife. I'm Jimmy Turner.'

'Your wife left me a message earlier. Is she here?'

'No. I was expecting her back by now but she messaged me that she's gone round to her parents' for some kind of family pow-wow.'

Leo couldn't face chasing her into the chilly company of Major and Mrs Chamberlain. 'Does that happen often?'

'Iona being called away unexpectedly? Yeah, mate, all the time. I only have half, or maybe quarter shares in my wife. She belongs to the village and surrounding parishes.' Turner grimaced. 'I tell her it's like being the pub landlord without the booze.'

His jokey bitterness was not promising for the beginning of many years of this, if the marriage was to last. 'I can see I've called at a bad time, but would you be willing to answer a few questions? I see from my log that none of my colleagues have spoken to you yet.'

Turner flapped the front of his vest where it clung to him, clearly not wild about the idea. 'I had a pig of a day in London and I'm starving.' Leo didn't retreat, waiting him out. 'I suppose you can ask your questions if you don't mind me eating while you do that?'

Turner's words reminded Leo that he'd not had anything

since lunch. He had to hope his stomach wouldn't growl too loudly. 'No problem. I won't keep you long.'

He stood back, resigned to doing his civic duty. 'Come through to the kitchen. If you don't mind waiting, I'll just get changed. I cycled from the station and I know I must reek.'

Leaving Leo at the pine table, he disappeared upstairs. Leo's eyes wandered. It was all very new, no appliance over a couple of years old from the look of it. The fittings weren't hi-spec like her parents had at the stables, but they looked well enough to Leo. His own kitchen hadn't been given half this attention. The brushed-steel fridge in this house had a family organiser pinned to the front that seemed full of committee meetings for Iona and business trips for her husband. There were two palm crosses attached with a magnet from Bethlehem. There was also a candid shot from the wedding, the happy couple laughing with the absent younger sister, Ella. Leo was struck again by her resemblance to the victim. Or was it, as Iona said of herself, that he was seeing echoes everywhere as he couldn't yet put a name to the body?

The shower went on upstairs so Leo wandered to the window and looked out on their back garden. They'd not done much to it, leaving it an expanse of grass. A bird table dominated the lawn. It was a bespoke design, made to look like the tower of St Martin's, a gift maybe from her grateful parishioners. Leo couldn't decide if that was a lovely gesture or an unfortunate reminder that she couldn't get away from work, even at home. It had to lead to thoughts of flocks of people pecking at her and coming for feeding at all hours.

Turner came back in, towelling off his scalp, looking a little more cheerful now he'd had a chance to change. 'Can I get you a drink? Tea, coffee, something stronger?'

'Coffee would be great.'

'I'll make some of the real stuff. Parishioners get instant but I reckon you need the dose of full-on caffeine doing what you do.'

'It certainly requires long hours.'

'Can't believe it myself. The murder, I mean. It's so gutting, to think of such a young life being ended that way, here of all places. Part of the attraction of moving to the village was that it seemed so peaceful – a great place to raise kids eventually.' He filled the kettle and put it on to boil.

'Your wife doesn't see it like that?' Leo prompted.

'What? Oh, you got the dark places talk, did you? Iona tends to dramatise things. Half the priesthood are failed actors, Gawd bless 'em, every one.' At the policeman's blank face, he added: 'Tiny Tim? I'm directing the church production of *A Christmas Carol*, doing my bit to help Iona engage the local community with St Martin's. There were bad feelings about the casting when I sent out the email last week.'

'How bad?'

'Nothing that would lead to anything serious – ruffled feathers of a privileged flock. Apparently I passed over old hands for new talent. It's like living in a fucking episode of *The Archers*, pardon my French. The wife's got the dog collar, not me.' He then went to the hob to check the contents of a casserole dish. He glanced over his shoulder at Leo. 'Do you want some? There's plenty. It's pheasant and apple. Roger keeps gifting us with his shooting trophies. Our freezer is stacked with them. I cook a batch at the weekend and it keeps us going until mid-week.'

'That's kind of you, but I think I should ask my questions and leave you to the rest of your evening.'

'You don't mind if I get on with this?' He lit the burner under the casserole dish and got out a plate. 'Fire away with the questions while I get this sorted.'

Leo produced a notebook from an inside pocket. 'Perhaps we can start with your full name and what you do for a living?'

'James Dylan Turner. How is what I do relevant?' He put a biscuit tin in front of his guest. 'Unless you're waiting for me to say vicar's husband.' He nudged it towards Leo. 'To have with your coffee.'

'Thanks. I suppose your profession isn't strictly relevant; it just paints a picture for me. What I'm most interested in is whether any of your commuting journeys might have crossed my victim's path. You mentioned cycling home from the station?'

'Yeah, I'm with Benchley Jackson. I work in Swindon most days but today I went to London to head office.'

'Benchley Jackson?' The name was familiar.

'It's a law firm. Mid-sized. I'm a solicitor, dealing with private client matters, trusts, wills and so on. But wasn't your victim found on Saturday morning? I don't commute to work on weekends so I wouldn't have seen her.'

'We think she died on Friday night. We're looking at what people saw who were returning to the village that evening.'

'Oh, right. I get you. Friday?' He snagged a biscuit. 'Yeah,

Friday. I must've cycled back around seven. It was a rare night when Iona wasn't too busy. We grabbed a quick bite, she went out to do something at the church, but she was back by nine, and we watched TV together.'

And this was all pretty much what the rector had said. 'What route do you take from Swindon? Main road or the B road? And were you cycling?'

'Yes, cycling on the B road.' He added a little hot water to the casserole and stirred. 'I'd better tell you in case you think I'm hiding something: I lost my licence three years ago. I was an idiot and got caught over the limit. I've had to discover the joy of cycling to get around but Iona reminds me it's good for me. Penance for being an idiot.'

'So would you say that you know the area well?'

'Back routes, short cuts, yeah, I know them. Part of that B road lies on the old Icknield Way. I wish they'd make it a designated cycle route. Some of the drivers don't take much care overtaking me, even in my hi-vis kit. It pisses me off.'

'You've had a few near misses?'

'It's still much safer than dicing with death by lorry on the A420.'

'Did you see anything out of the ordinary that night?'

'I remember seeing some of the commune people heading up to Wayland's Smithy when I passed. They were taking the track up the hill. We said hello but I didn't stop. That's not unusual. They hold regular gatherings up on the Downs – sessions they called "starlight ceremonies". Iona even went to one once at the invitation of Father Oak. I think he was trying to improve relations with the villagers which had reached a low ebb. She said it was pretty tame. Candles, chanting, drinking some home brew. I think she was disappointed it wasn't more risqué.'

'Risqué?'

'Locals claim they get up to all sorts, but she saw no wicker men or nudity.' He laughed. 'She'd've been so embarrassed if there had been. Really not her thing. Maybe they only behaved because she was there? According to the village gossip, aka Bob the landlord, those things can get quite spicy.'

'Did you tell her you saw the procession?' Leo wondered why Iona hadn't mentioned it in her statement.

He wrinkled his nose in thought, deep lines appearing between his brows. 'Don't think I did. It's not in the same direction as the White Horse so it didn't occur to me.'

'You said you didn't find it odd to see them, so how usual is it? Regular, like a church service?'

'I guess I see them about once a fortnight? And it's not really a procession. They wander up there in twos and threes. I think they wait for the moon to rise but I'm not sure what time that was on Friday.'

'I can check that. And did you see anyone answering the description of my victim?'

'Yeah, of course. But don't get too excited. Half the girls at that place look like that and, in the twilight in their cloaks, it's very hard to tell them apart.'

'Cloaks? What kind?'

'Green velvet ones. They only wear them for the ceremonies as far as I've noticed. I guess it can get cold in their white robes. They don't look very thick. I did see one daft chick without one. Reminded me of those girls you see lining up for clubs in little bits of nothing dresses – crazy. I'm going to be a terrible killjoy dad, as I'm not letting my kids go out like that.'

Leo wondered about that one girl. His victim? Had she already left her cloak in the hedge? 'And they were all heading for the Smithy? No one was going up to the White Horse?'

'Not that way. But you know there's a footpath between the two?'

'Yes, I do. Thanks, that's really helpful.' He stood and put away his notebook.

Jimmy cleared Leo's now empty mug and tucked it in the dishwasher. 'I know I shouldn't ask you about the case, but do you think it's a one-off? I mean, should I be worried about Iona going around on her own?'

He was the first villager to ask that question. 'Mr Turner, I have very little evidence on which to base an answer. As of this moment, I have no reason to think there'll be another killing but, until we know more about this one, I also have no reason to rule it out.'

He gave Leo a wry look. 'That's a very lawyerly answer, Inspector.'

'Policemen, solicitors, the law is our area. We have far more in common than you think.'

Jimmy showed Leo to the door. 'It was nice meeting you, Inspector. Drop in again if you need a coffee. It can be a lonely life as the partner of a parish priest.'

'Something you have in common with the partners of people in my walk of life. Goodnight.'

Leo got back in the car and headed up the hill to the White Horse, imagining a procession of green-clad worshippers walking the footpaths. That had been surprisingly helpful. He'd turned up an eyewitness to their activities of Friday night who was outside the commune. Now he needed to hammer at the statements the police had been given until he found the cracks. They'd be there, he was sure of it.

Chapter 16

Leo

The site was still closed to the public and Leo was pleased to find that the guard officers were on the alert. They immediately approached his vehicle as he pulled into the car park and demanded to see his ID. When they discovered who he was, they apologised. Leo told them not to apologise for doing their job.

'All quiet?' he asked.

'Yes, sir. We only had a few visitors who failed to read the signs at the bottom of the hill.'

'Ignored it, more like,' said the other.

'A couple of people walked rather than drove in. But no one's made trouble when they've been turned away.'

'Good.' He would have to pull them off soon as they couldn't spare the manpower but he wanted one last look before the public regained access. By the time he reached the slope, the clouds had cleared to reveal the White Horse in the moonlight. Long limbs gleamed in the grey grass. You couldn't tell what it all added up to seeing it at this angle and so close. A heap of bones. Had he just found a metaphor for his investigation? In that case, he should get back to Oxford and see if distance made any sense of this.

He glanced across the tops of the Downs to where the moon loomed on the horizon, shining unusually large and rose-gold in the hazy atmosphere. A harvest moon. Was it on the wane? Gibbous, wasn't that the word? He was conscious of dredging up vocabulary he'd not come across since he'd gone through a phase of reading horror and fantasy in his teens. The word meant 'humped' but he always associated it with 'gibbet', another place of death. So had this gibbous moon been full on Friday night? He took a quick look at his phone. The ceremony had taken place at the full moon, so not really a starlit but a moonlit one.

His phone buzzed, registering a new email from Jess. Just as he went to open it, the mobile rang, the office number flashing up.

'Sir?' It was Suyin. 'We've got a break in the case. We've identified the victim. The tattoo, physical description, everything checks out. You were right: she *is* American. Her full name is Julie Dorchester, twenty-three, from Washington DC. Her parents reported her missing on Sunday. They thought she was enjoying a vacation in England, but she failed to contact them at an agreed time.'

Finally. 'That's excellent work, Sergeant. Have you got a photograph you can send me?'

'It's just come in. Recent. It's a good likeness.'

'Send it out to the team. We'll start canvassing witnesses in the morning. Our first stop will be Kingston Manor. I just had confirmation from a witness that members wear green cloaks like the one we found. Interesting, isn't it, that O'Brien didn't mention that when we told him what we found?'

'He's a slippery customer. But if she's a foreigner on holiday, doesn't that mean she hasn't been living at the commune?'

'And yet she was found wearing their clothes. There has to be a connection, even if we aren't seeing it yet. Did her parents say what she was doing in the UK?'

'According to their missing persons report, Julie was a fan of British culture and spent quite a few holidays over here. She arrived seven days ago. They think she might've had friends locally but, to be honest, there wasn't much detail in their statement. The Americans weren't that worried about Julie as she'd only been out of contact for a few days.'

'Though they filed a report?'

'I think the parents must've been very insistent. And there's another detail that you need to know: Julie worked for the FBI. She had been recruited out of college last year and was on one of their training programmes.'

'It certainly ups the stakes politically.'

'I can't see how this connects with her murder,' said Suyin. 'Surely she's too junior to have any complications that might make the law-enforcement angle relevant?'

'It's too early to rule anything out. But at least now the investigation gets properly underway. We have a name for our victim; that means we can get down to the business of working out why she was killed.'

'How do you want to handle formal notification, sir?'

'I'll call the superintendent. This is going to involve the Home Office and possibly the Foreign Office so will need special handling. I think it's best that Superintendent Thaxted deals with the politics, while we get on with the investigation.' Leo could've added that it was what the top brass got paid for: dealing with the shit as it hit the fan.

'If it were me,' said Suyin, 'and it was my daughter that had been found dead, I'd be on the next plane to Heathrow.'

'Then we should anticipate a visit from the parents. In fact, I'd welcome it. If we still have no clear suspect by the time they arrive, a press conference involving the parents might be exactly what this case needs. I'll suggest it to the Super.'

'Is that everything, sir?'

'I'll come in. Can you put together everything we've got on Julie? I want to know her better.'

'I'll leave the files on your desk if you're not back by the time I leave.'

'Appreciate it. And I appreciate the overtime you're putting in.'

The moon had shrunk in size now that it had climbed higher in the sky. Leo looked down on the spot where they had found her. Julie Dorchester. She had a surname that might come from this area. Had she been searching for her roots? There was a village nearby with an abbey at its heart called Dorchester-on-Thames. It was an ancient site like this, home to the Romans and the Anglo-Saxons and the many people who had found their way to the Vale of the White Horse. Quite a few of them, like Julie, had been incomers who ended their days here. A stone's throw away lay the burial mounds on the top of the hill. Leo wondered whether Julie had simply been here as a tourist, found out about the ceremony at Wayland's Smithy, and joined in to participate in a bit of local colour? If that was the case, then it had been a tragic decision. Somewhere, somehow, on that evening, her path had crossed with someone who had more than moon worship on the agenda for the evening. They wanted to connect to much darker currents from the past: the spilling of blood, sacrifice, and the pretence that violence could bring them closer to whatever god it was that they were worshipping.

The problem with that theory was that it meant the killing, as far as the victim was concerned, was a random event. A piece of monumental bad luck. Another idea was that she had come here to meet someone. That went back to the Capability Brown hypothesis that it only looked like a ceremonial killing but was in fact something else. With that theory at least it meant that he had some hope of finding out who that person was.

There was a lot to think about and he had better get back to Oxford. As he pulled out of the car park, he realised that he hadn't yet read the email from Jessica. He was worried enough about her to look for a convenient spot, pull over, and check the contents.

What he read filled him with alarm. She had really taken

her inside source role to heart and had raided the private files belonging to the commune. *Jess, Jess, what are you doing?* He was sure she had no idea what she was about because she had just presented him with a massive headache. He had no warrant for this material and at the moment no justified cause to call for it. Leo thumped his forehead on the steering wheel, inadvertently beeping the horn. Fortunately, there was no one living near this isolated lay-by to hear. Of course Jess was going to be a loose cannon. He knew her from the wild swimming case and had seen her take insane risks to save other people. She tackled a murderer, after all. And now she was in the middle of his latest investigation firing off in all directions and, if he was not very careful, he might well be hit by her friendly fire as he was hauled up to explain why he was using illegally obtained information.

It was tempting just to delete the email and pretend he'd never received it but she had taken the trouble of getting it for him and it might contain something relevant to the case. It was a dilemma.

Oh, sod it. He'd have a word with her tomorrow but for now he needed to see what she had found.

He soon realised that he needed more than a phone screen to look through the spreadsheets and documents that she had dug out. It was very interesting that she had focused on the financial dealings of the commune rather than sending him information about their practices and beliefs which was what he had been expecting. Her follow-up email explained why. She sounded very pleased with herself.

Pretty cool investigating, hey? As for Father Oak, I can confirm that he's a horny but plausible devil. The Children of the White Horse has to be a very clever scam. You might find answers in how much money they're getting from their donors i.e. the poor suckers who sign up to a life of poverty as Father Oak swans around in a manor and probably has a secret life of luxury hidden away somewhere on site. I'll see if I can find more proof of that.

Horny in what way? An irrational jealousy shivered through him. He had to remind himself that Jess was not his, nor suitable for him if he was serious about his career. At best, he could describe her as a friend and ally, but she was clearly a messy and complicated person, living life in a way rather too reminiscent of his mother's scattershot approach. The upshot of this email, though, was that it looked like he was going to have a very long night at his desk. Fortunately, having a way ahead cleared the exhaustion like a new scent trail for a bloodhound. With a smile to himself, and a little howl at the moon (something he'd never dream of doing if anyone were with him), he started the car and headed back to base.

Chapter 17

Michael

Term had begun again in Oxford and Michael was supposed to be preparing a course of lectures and seeing graduate students. Somehow, though, his thoughts kept returning to Jessica, whom he couldn't help but feel he'd abandoned in the hands of a highly suspect cult leader.

The clouds parted briefly, pouring buttery light on his desk like a golden oil spill. Seen through his office window, the deer herd in the college grounds wandered into view. A haze lay on the river that wound through the gardens so the deer looked as though they were gliding on clouds, then stopped, heads down, in the mist as they grazed. October was a very good month to remember that the city was built on a drained swamp, a fording point for oxen. The turns taken in history were unforeseeable. No traveller passing down the Thames Valley when the White Horse was first made would've dreamed that Oxford would become a place of spires and battlements, libraries and learning, science and arts. Arguably there was a higher average IQ in this square mile than anywhere else in the world, though Cambridge would say otherwise, thought Michael smugly.

And he was aspiring to be one of these famous scholars by consolidating his academic reputation. The idea of writing about cult leaders was beginning to take serious shape in his mind. It would be a logical extension of his expertise, attracting invitations to speak whenever there was a scandal involving a cult or fringe religion. That made sense for the CV but it was also a fascinating question: how did some people manage to persuade others to give up so much to follow them, even to the point of being prepared to die for their cause? He was aware, of course, that this could describe the origins of many major religions, but on the whole these cult leaders stood out as being much more interested in their status among their followers. They were enjoying the power trip, rather than abiding by their own self-denying teachings. It was worth a well-considered academic study and Michael was beginning to research figures who could explain this mentality. It had the popular appeal that would please Petra too when it came to the book. The latter end of the 20th century proved a particularly rich time for these maniacs. They were not restricted to just one culture but, as with many things, America had provided the world with some of the most colourful.

There was the self-proclaimed holy man, the Rev. Jim Jones, who established a cult called The People's Temple in the 50s. At first it had appeared wacky but essentially harmless. The project had unravelled in the 1970s when the authorities started to take an interest in what Jones was doing. Not welcoming oversight, Jones had moved about a thousand followers with him to the Guyanese jungle in 1977, the year of Star Wars, the death of Elvis Presley, and Jimmy Carter's presidency. At a special ceremony, promising that they were going to carry out a revolutionary act, Jones had persuaded or forced hundreds of his followers to drink a cyanide-laced juice. He himself appears not to have fancied the drawn-out pain of a poison death and died from a gunshot wound to his head.

Many of those who died did so unwillingly, seemingly forced by others in the community to take the drink. But from a psychologist's point of view, that in itself was fascinating: how does one man persuade others not only to kill themselves but to kill others – men, women, and children – with whom they had been friends?

He turned to a map of the Oxford area that hung on his wall, and traced the way to Kingston Beauchamp. The cult of the White Horse might seem more benign with its earth worship but Michael had no illusions that O'Brien wouldn't turn nasty should he feel personally threatened by the police investigation, or by Jessica herself. According to the local press, a girl with a possible affiliation to the cult had been murdered on the White Horse so these thoughts of violence were not unwarranted. He would have to urge Jessica to be cautious.

The deer suddenly took off for the far end of the field, following a sign only they understood that now was the time to flee. What was he saying? Jessica? Cautious? That was not possible for her. For his own peace of mind, he was going to have to find a way of checking that she was not getting into anything dangerous – or more dangerous than it already was.

As if his thoughts summoned her, his inbox received an email from Jessica.

Michael,

Father Oak, I'm pleased to say, has lived down to your low expectations. I had a quick ferret around in the accounts and found a record of expenditure and donations, which I attach. I've had a look at these on my phone while hiding in the bathroom (the manor is a mobile-free zone), but I'm worried that my battery is going to run out quickly and there is nowhere to charge it. Would you be a darling and have a quick look to see if there's anything that stands out for you? I'm looking for any connection between these documents and Tanglewood's daughter, Lisette White. Everyone is known by made-up names so I'm having trouble finding out if she is here. Thanks a bunch.

Jessica

PS I am now known as Sister Poppy. I should start a Facebook quiz: what's your cult name? Pick Sister or Brother, then the next plant you see …

That would make him Brother Yucca as he had one by the window. Jessica would like that, thought Michael. Lectures forgotten, he opened up the documents and had a quick scan. Under the donations, there appeared to be a number of regular ones that came from rent on houses and flats belonging to members of the commune. That gave him a place to start. He phoned Tanglewood.

'Tanglewood? Michael Harrison here.'

'Michael? Oh, I was hoping you were Jess.'

'Think of me as her Dr Watson. She asked me to look at some documents she found in the commune. Quick question: does your daughter have a home of her own?'

'Strictly speaking, no, but I did buy her a flat in London when she went to college. She put tenants in because I wouldn't let her sell it while all this nonsense was going on at the commune.'

'What's the address?'

She listed a road in Hammersmith. 'I told her she could always live on the rental income if she was having trouble finding employment.'

The flat appeared on the list Jessica had sent over. 'I think she still is, in a manner of speaking. The rental income is going to the Children of the White Horse. As you own the flat, you could stop that.'

There was a pause as Tanglewood considered this. 'Oh dear. I was hoping she was letting it build up in the bank so she had something to go back to when she left. Yes, I will put a stop to it, if Jess can't persuade her to leave the commune. Maybe they'll decide she's less attractive when she's no longer bringing in the cash?'

'That's a distinct possibility. Jessica is reporting to me that Father Oak is showing his clay feet.'

'I'm not surprised. I've been talking to the police about him, consulting with them on the beliefs of neopagan cults. Have you seen the news this morning?'

'No. What's happened?'

'They've identified the body – an American tourist. I wish they'd found out a little sooner as the inspector I talked to thought yesterday that the victim could be my daughter. I had a nasty moment there. But it's not. It's some other woman's child.'

'Very grim for them.'

'Any parent's worst nightmare.'

Michael ended the call and typed out a quick reply to Jessica, urging her to take care and telling her which line of the spreadsheet proved that Lisette was part of the community. If she was not the body on the hill, and hadn't stopped her donations, then she was still there, wasn't she? He signed it Brother Yucca.

Chapter 18

Leo

Leo was getting to know the victim. Suyin had done an excellent job of pulling together a file on Julie in the few hours she'd had to do her research. He'd stayed in the office until midnight following Julie's journey through the American education system, to university, and finally into the FBI. From the postings Julie made online, she was obsessed with English history. According to her GoodReads profile, her favourite authors were Jane Austen and Hilary Mantel. Julie's visits to England looked like an advertisement for every costume drama made in recent years. A selfie at Chatsworth. On a Cornish beach by a tin mine. At the Tower of London. There was also one of her standing outside the Radcliffe Camera in the centre of Oxford a day before she was killed. Her captions gave frustratingly little away. He didn't know who she was with or whether she was planning to meet anyone. We think everyone is so transparent these days because people post so much online but when you really interrogated a profile, it often came up short. A shop window rather than the stockroom inside. He urgently needed to speak to the parents to find out these details.

The clock warned him to hold fire on that. It was mid-morning here which meant it was the middle of the night in America. Considering Mr and Mrs Dorchester had just heard that their daughter had been murdered, he had better wait until daylight over there before contacting them. It wasn't that he thought they would be asleep – he was sure there were many sleepless nights ahead of them – but he feared to intrude just to ask some questions that could wait a few hours. Besides, he had enough to do today re-interviewing everyone he'd spoken to, armed with the photo of the living Julie Dorchester.

Leo was just about to head out with his team to Kingston Beauchamp when the superintendent came into the incident room in search of him.

'Leo, glad I caught you. I've just received this from the Americans.' She handed him a stack of print-outs. 'It's Julie's personnel file. Some of it is redacted but I had a quick look through.'

Instead of bringing it straight to him. Leo bit back the comment that she was doing his job for him. Claire Thaxted had been an excellent detective in her day and readily admitted that she missed the hands-on aspect of her police work. 'Did you learn anything, ma'am?'

Claire perched on the edge of his desk, settling in for a colleague-to-colleague consultation. 'Such a waste of a promising trainee agent. It seems she was exceptionally bright and was tipped for their fast track programme. On the down side, they also note an independent streak and a tendency to run ahead in the investigations she was given.' So she might have been rash, going into danger without considering her own vulnerability? Leo speculated. Had she been doing some investigating of her own over here? 'Her managers appear to have spent quite a lot of their time reining her in.' She gave him a rueful smile. 'I know what that's like. My best young detectives often want to run before they can walk. They're not all like you, Leo, seasoned, cautious and discreet.'

Leo thought guiltily of the files that Jess had sent him. A cautious officer would not have spent the early hours of this morning combing through those. They made fascinating reading and he was sure there was more to discover. It was a shame he couldn't share them with his team yet, not until he could think of a way of explaining how he got hold of them. The bottom line was that O'Brien's operation was raking in a lot of money from so-called donations. He seemed to be developing something of a property empire with multiple incomes from residences around the country. Leo wondered what exactly the money was being spent on because it wasn't going on the running of the place from the evidence of the spartan life the followers led. Leo would put money on him siphoning some of it off into offshore accounts so that when he'd had enough of pretending to be the inspirational leader, he could vanish and live a life of luxury somewhere away from public attention.

'Any news yet as to whether the Dorchesters are coming to the UK to formally identify the body, ma'am?'

'They have a flight later today so should be with us by tomorrow morning.' She stood up. 'I'll receive them in my office at ten. I'd like you to be there. I think someone from the American consulate in London will be accompanying them.'

'I'll make sure I'm there.'

'They'll want to repatriate their daughter's body as soon as possible. I will attempt to dial down their expectations on that.'

'Thank you. Have you given any more thought to my suggestion of arranging a public appeal?'

'Yes, I think it's a good idea. I don't want the Americans to think we're not doing our utmost. I'll let the consulate know what we're suggesting and they can raise the idea with the Dorchesters. We should hold the conference here, immediately after our meeting. Twelve? We'll hit the lunchtime news if we do it then.'

Her tone suggested she expected him to participate. 'Do you really need me to be there, Superintendent? I think it would be better not to overcrowd the table. The Dorchesters and you would be the best team to field.' He wanted to be out doing the actual investigating rather than feeding the press.

'All right.' She paused at the threshold. 'Talking to the media isn't your strongest suit, is it, Leo? We went over this in your annual review. You'll have to work on that aspect of your performance if you want to earn your promotion to chief inspector.'

Leo knew the brass didn't like his taciturn manner with reporters. He'd not made many friends in the local media – what was left of it. 'I'll try to improve in that area, ma'am.'

'Hmm.' She was sceptical and he didn't think his promotion

would be coming any time soon. 'See that you do. You'd better get back out there. I'd much prefer to be sitting in front of the cameras saying we've made an arrest rather than admitting we have no idea who killed Julie Dorchester.'

The police team met at the pub car park to organise the door-to-door canvas with the new photograph. Leo put Harry Boston in charge of the majority of the follow-ups, leaving the manor for himself. He had asked Suyin to contact all the bed-and-breakfasts and hotels in the area, focusing on Oxford as that was where the last photograph on Julie's social media had been taken. That in itself was a very big task, especially since the advent of Airbnb, so the sergeant wouldn't be available for today's interviews. If Suyin's team found where Julie had stayed, they could make a start on the city's CCTV to see if she had been with anyone.

Shortly before he went into the manor, he received a message from Dr Harrison about her daughter's flat being on the list Jess had found. It was a side issue to Leo's investigation but, now he came to think of it, it did feel a little strange that Jess had been unable to locate Lisette. The commune wasn't that large and he would've thought by now she would have met everybody. If he got a chance, he'd ask her how her search was going. But at least they no longer had to worry that her client's daughter was dead.

'Inspector, this is getting a little boring,' said Father Oak. He had met Leo on the front step, not allowing him entry today.

'Oh, I'm sorry if we're boring you, Mr O'Brien, but I still have the little matter of a murder to solve.'

O'Brien remembered that he was supposed to be a paragon of peace and love and blessed Leo with a forgiving smile. 'Of course, of course. I apologise if I seem ungracious. How can I help you this morning?'

'We now have a photograph and name for our victim.' Leo held up the photograph so he could see it. 'Her name is Julie Dorchester, an American. She was visiting the region on holiday. From the evidence of the clothing in which she was found, we conclude that somehow she got involved in one of your evening ceremonies. Can you explain to me how that might have happened?'

'I have absolutely no idea, Inspector. I don't recognise her. I certainly don't allow outsiders to take part in our ceremonies – they are strictly for the Children of the White Horse only.'

'So you have no explanation to account for why a young woman, who fits the description of many in your community, was found nearby on the same evening that you held an outdoor celebration at Wayland's Smithy?'

O'Brien paused. Leo could see that he was considering a number of different replies. Unfortunately, he came up with the one which was most difficult for Leo to pick apart. 'No.'

'Then I need to ask the other people who live here if they saw her.'

The commune leader folded his arms. 'I'm afraid that isn't convenient today, Inspector. These frequent visits by you and your officers have proved extremely disruptive to the life of the commune and I insist that we are left in peace to regain the harmony I've worked so hard to establish here.'

Leo had been expecting him to come up with some objection. 'Not to worry, Mr O'Brien. We're holding the interviews at the pub in the village. The landlord has offered one of his rooms. Please arrange for members to come and see me this afternoon. I suggest you send them out in groups of two or three and I promise I will process them as quickly as possible so that you can get back to whatever it is you are doing here.' As he turned away, Leo added. 'I do have a full list of everybody who is onsite so it will be easy enough for me to check that I've talked to them all.'

'And if they do not wish to talk to you?' Father Oak called after him.

Leo opened his car door. 'That would be very unfortunate. If you attempt to block my enquiries, I will wonder why and I will have to take a much closer look at your activities.'

'Is that a threat?'

'No, it's a consequence.' He got in and drove away.

Chapter 19

Jess

The inspector's demand that we all went for an interview at the pub during the course of the afternoon had the unexpected benefit that everyone was too distracted to pay much attention to what I was doing. In fact, I was told by Sister Ivy that my presence at a police interview was not required. I intended to ignore this and make sure that I was one of the last that Inspector George saw today. We had a lot to talk about.

I had been put on window cleaning, a job I liked very much because it allowed me to roam the manor with my bucket of vinegar and water, looking out on the outdoor activities as well as spying on the indoor ones. Window cleaner would be a great undercover profession, I decided. The niceness of the people here was beginning to grate. There was definitely something wrong – Ivy was too poisonous, Oak too handsy, and the rest too happy. I couldn't help feeling they were like a family with a pet lamb (me) that they led about on a ribbon when in fact they were fattening me up for the kill. I poked my head in room after room, hoping to find the secret sauna or hot tub that I suspected Father Oak to have hidden somewhere, but he was keeping his secrets. Maybe he had another place somewhere in the grounds? The icehouse was kept a closely guarded secret; I could imagine all sorts of uses for it from the grim to the inspired. A dungeon? A sauna? A huge private stash of Ben & Jerry's? I decided to miss lunch and go for a wander to seek out answers to the commune's mysteries.

I didn't really know the manor very well yet. Behind the house, there was a terrace with steps leading down to what had once been formal gardens. Most of these had been turned into vegetable patches, though the roses remained, perhaps because the hips could be used to make cordial. Our treat on Friday night, apparently, was a glass of rosehip syrup. Woohoo. They really knew how to live it up here. Beyond these productive beds was the beech hedge, the same one that I had been pruning, and after that, the wilder parts of the garden, by which I mean little plantations of trees and shrubberies laced together with gravel paths. There was also a dilapidated folly, built to look like a Roman temple, nestled among a grove of silver birches. There was nothing inside that but pigeon droppings. Beyond the folly, there was a funny kind of ditch that it was very easy to fall into. The outer fields of the estate were given over to pasture for sheep. This rolled up to the foot of White Horse Hill, still grazed by black-faced descendants of ancient flocks. I remembered from my history lessons that mediaeval communities made a killing from selling wool abroad, easily the biggest industry in England at that time.

Any wealth you saw in the shape of old stone houses or churches from that era was paid for in fleeces. The Vale of the White Horse appeared to have been one such area where money was made by wool merchants. There was less money in sheep now. That was probably why Father Oak had turned to fleecing his followers.

Over to the right, hidden amongst trees, and separated from the pasture by a waist-high iron fence, was the icehouse. I wandered in that direction, hoping to avoid Brother Maple, who I had noticed was not my biggest fan. Fortunately, there was no sign of him. The gate opened with a creak and I followed the path to the entrance. This was the furthest I'd got yet without Brother Grumpy Pants heading me off. The icehouse was built by the original owners of the manor and it resembled a huge domed beehive half buried in the ground. Before refrigeration, they would cut ice in winter and stack it in blocks in here. Ice cream and sorbets had become a popular treat for the very rich and a cook could chip off enough flakes to make an impressive display to impress a dinner party. If you didn't know what the building was used for, you might mistake it for a mausoleum. I supposed it was in a way – a memorial to a lost era before home appliances.

Taking the steps down to the sunken entrance, I tried the handle. Locked. I peered through the keyhole but that only gave me a glimpse of light and the smell of green dampness. The light was unexpected. Was this one of the few places in the manor allowed to use electricity? If so, someone had left it on. I'd bet Sister Ivy wouldn't approve.

'What are you doing here?'

I jumped guiltily away from the door and saw Brother Pine, aka Sven, watching me from the top of the steps. 'Being nosy.' No point hiding it.

'Don't be.'

'Is that like rule number 103?' I had forgotten my Scandi friend didn't do sarcasm. 'Sorry. I was just out for a walk and wanted to see it. Tell me not to go somewhere and it usually has the opposite effect.'

'I will walk you back to the manor.'

'No need. I was heading into the village for my interview.'

'But you are not required for an interview.'

'I don't want to be left out. Besides, the policeman is gorgeous. Haven't you noticed?'

He flushed, and my gaydar went off. 'No.'

'Trust me, he is. And it passes the time. I get bored easily. Are you going too?'

'I've just come back. I had nothing to say to him; none of us do.'

I linked my arm with his in a companionable fashion, ignoring the negative vibe he was sending out. *Let's pretend we are friends.* We took the path across the pastures. 'That sounds very mean of you. He's only doing his job.'

'Then he should do it somewhere else. The killer isn't here. We had nothing to do with that girl's death.'

I patted his hand. 'And so we have to show him that.' I steered him away from the icehouse enclosure so he didn't ask further questions about my snooping. 'How long have you been here, Brother Pine?'

'Three years.'

'I've been wondering, has anyone left during that time?'

'Are you thinking of leaving?' He didn't sound upset by the notion.

'Not yet, but I'm finding it hard to settle, as you've probably noticed. So, has anyone left?'

'Yes, but no one has quit after only a few days. Most try it out for much longer.'

'What about recently? Women of my age or younger? Has anyone decided that they had enough?'

'A few.' His pale blue eyes were fixed ahead.

'Can you be more specific?'

'Why?'

'I'm just interested in what they go on to do after they leave, what my own future might look like. Do you keep in contact?'

'No. Once you leave the community, you are no longer one of us.'

'Ouch, that's harsh.'

'It is necessary. Our life demands sacrifice. If you can't deal with that, then the gate is not locked. You are free to go.'

We'd reached the feature he was referencing. The lions had their tails to us, gazing fiercely out at passing cars, spirit brothers to the defiant Sven.

'I'm going through, but I intend to be back. Enjoy your afternoon.' I gave him a perky wave and headed for the village.

The landlord gave me the stink-eye as I entered the pub. I found three other commune members sitting in the public bar. It was like some kind of bizarre doctor's waiting room. In fact, better than most doctors' waiting rooms because there was alcohol on sale. Such a shame I didn't have any money. I sat next to one of the sisters I didn't know very well. I thought she had introduced herself as Sister Rose but I wasn't sure. She rejoiced in a freckly face which clashed with her bleached blonde hair. I'd bet she would have a glorious red mop if she hadn't been caught up in this insanity.

'Have you been waiting long?' I asked.

'Not long.'

That seemed to be the limit of her conversation so I ambled over to the bar, wondering if there was any mercy in the landlord's heart.

'You're that bint who was in here yesterday, aren't you?' He wiped the bar, not that I could see any smears.

'Yes, that was me.'

'What are you doing hanging around with that lot? You don't seem the same sort.'

'You might be on to something. I do find a life of abstinence a tall order. Talking about ordering ...?'

With a wicked smile at me, he filled a pint glass with water and plonked it on the counter in front of me. 'No charge.'

'You're a right charmer, aren't you?'

'That's what all the women say.'

'I'm sure that's not true but you keep on dreaming; it's free, like the water.'

Two police officers came in with a man in plain clothes. I knew the senior man: Detective Sergeant Harry Boston. He'd last seen me near-naked, inadequately wrapped in a newspaper. It's a long story. I had to hope he didn't recognise me with my clothes on.

The three – Harry and the male and female officer – went up to the far end of the bar and I lost my interlocutor to the lure of paying customers. Oh well. I really didn't want to attract Harry's attention. I wasn't sure how much Inspector George had told him and, if he made loud reference to my connection to a previous case he worked on, my three fellow commune members might well be suspicious. Fortunately, the inspector's interviews were moving quickly so they wouldn't be here long. I estimated that each one took only five minutes, probably enough for him to show the photograph of the victim, ask if anyone knew her, and then thank them for their stunning lack of cooperation. I was actually looking forward to seeing him. I wasn't a natural for undercover work and at least with him I wouldn't have to pretend to be something I was not.

The landlord appeared and put a glass in front of me filled with ice and topped with a slice of lemon. 'With the compliments of the gentleman at the end of the bar,' said the landlord.

I glanced over and saw Harry grinning at me. Fearing another joke at my expense, I took a sniff of the glass and discovered it was gin and tonic. I silently asked forgiveness for all the horrible things I had thought about the detective sergeant and raised it in a subtle toast. The tang of the gin was welcome and confirmation that, thankfully, the inspector had thought to brief his team that I might be present. Harry wasn't about to spill the beans.

Life was looking up with a drink in one hand and a seat by a nice log fire. I was beginning to relax. Pubs feel like my natural habitat. Right now, they were better than a back rub. I was in no rush to head back to another medieval supper and a cold dormitory.

Sister Rose approached and tapped my shoulder.

'The inspector will see you now,' she said. 'Is that …?'

'No! Just water.' I curled my hand around the glass defensively. Unless she snatched it from me and took a gulp, Sister Rose had to take my word for it.

She curled her lip in distaste. 'Do you want me to wait for you?'

'No, it's fine. I'll make my own way home.' Home? How odd to hear myself referring to the manor in that way. But it satisfied Sister Rose. She gave me a nod and headed for the door.

I picked up my drink and went to the back room where the inspector was holding his interviews. I was entertained to find that it had a cheaply reproduced fox hunting scene with dogs on the wall behind him. 'Hi, Inspector. Isn't that illegal?'

Inspector George looked up from his notebook to the picture and his face broke into a grin. 'So it is. Do I have to arrest anyone?'

'Not today. Shall I come in?'

'Please do.'

I flopped down into the chair placed opposite his at the desk.

'How was it? Did anyone recognise her?' I pulled the photograph towards me. I hadn't yet seen it close-to but it wasn't a face I knew, though there was a certain resemblance to Lisette now I studied it. I could see why the inspector might have been worried when I first told him I couldn't find her.

'No. Nobody knows her, nobody's seen her. I've drawn a complete blank with your colleagues at the commune.'

'Is that the right term? Colleague?'

'Well, how should I refer to them? I seek your guidance. Fellow acolyte?'

'Worshipper? Brethren? Or my favourite, fellow sheep?'

He chuckled. 'And how is your own search going? I hope you've had more luck than I have?'

I swirled my drink in the glass. 'I'm sorry to say that I've concluded that Lisette White is no longer at the commune.'

'But Dr Harrison told me only this morning that you had discovered that she's still paying into the commune accounts?'

'I know. That's the weird thing. If it were me, and I had had a falling out with them, it's the first thing I would do – cancel the direct debit. And it also doesn't answer the question of where she is now. She's vanished. It would really help if I knew exactly when she left. I've begun to ask questions along those lines, but so far I'm having about as much luck as you at getting straight answers.'

'Are you going to tell Dr White that you can't find her daughter?'

I ran a hand through my hair. 'Oh God, I suppose I'm going to have to, aren't I? Maybe I'll give it another couple of days? Perhaps she's had to go away for some reason and is expected back. I haven't yet got to grips with how the commune behaves. Reading the dynamics, it seems that there is a tight-knit inner circle that includes Father Oak, Sister Ivy, Brother

Maple, and Brother Pine – that's the Nordic God who carried the ladder for me.'

Inspector looked down at his list of interviewees. 'I spoke with all of those earlier this afternoon. They were among my least cooperative.'

'That seems about right. There's something odd about the four of them. Maple doesn't seem a natural recruit for one thing. I can't get the "why" of it.'

'Meaning?'

'Why live like this?' I gestured to my homespun clothes. 'What's their angle?'

'I take it you don't believe in the faith part?'

I shrugged. 'Call me cynical, but no. If it were more fun, I'd understand. I think they have a secret.'

He gave me a sharp look. 'Something they'd kill to hide?'

'Maybe.' I tapped my fingers restlessly.

'Jess, you're living there with no backup. Maybe you should leave?'

I probably should. But there was that little matter of twenty thousand pounds. 'I'm fine. I'll be sensible.'

He got up and led me to the door, fingers brushing my back so briefly I barely felt it. 'Why does that not comfort me?'

Chapter 20

Leo

Interviews concluded for the day, Leo hadn't forgotten that Iona wanted a word with him so he set out to find her. He had no luck tracking her down. She was not at the church and there was no answer at her home address. He even called on her parents but the stables were empty. As the rector was his best source in the village, if she had something to tell him, it was worth spending the extra time locating her. There was one last Chamberlain that he could try so he turned his car in the direction of her uncle Andrew's house.

It was the first time Leo had called on the warden at home. Andrew Chamberlain lived in a detached cottage called Dragonholt on the edge of the village, set in its own orchard. In fact, Leo realised as he approached, it lay on the B road, the Icknield Way, that Iona's husband cycled along to Swindon. This meant that the Children of the White Horse would've walked past this house on Friday night en route to Wayland's Smithy. It would be helpful to find out what Andrew had seen on Friday night.

The house was a whitewashed, double-fronted cottage with a thatched roof. From the plump neatness of the thatch, it seemed the thatcher had re-roofed it recently and left his mark by fashioning a straw dragon for the ridge in a nod to its name. Leo had passed several of these straw flourishes on the thatched cottages of the valley: turkeys, foxes, even a Pied Piper with his string of rats. They had an odd sense of humour around here. He reached for the front doorbell and found that it was a real bell hanging just inside the door on some kind of spring. He could see it swaying to and fro as he pulled on the lever outside. It reminded him of the school bell that clanged to bring children in from the playgrounds. He had gone to a couple of primary schools in villages like this one, never staying long at each one, thanks to his mother's wanderings. Bells had been preferred to whistles. He'd always thought whistles sounded too much like a child's scream.

The first creature to greet Leo was the hysterical black Labrador. It jumped up and thrust its face against the narrow window beside the window. From the smears on the glass, it was clear this wasn't the only time it had reacted like this. This barking made it look fierce, transforming the family-friendly breed into a fearsome guard-dog with yellow fangs. The black dog. That was a mythical creature to go with the dragon and the White Horse. Slow footsteps followed and Leo could hear Andrew telling Brenda to get down. *Brenda*? It would be humiliating to be chased off by a dog called Brenda.

Andrew opened the door, keeping a tight hold of the dog's collar. 'Hello. Sorry about the noise. Brenda, shut up! What can I do for you, Inspector?'

'Mr Chamberlain, just a couple of things. I'm removing my officers from the White Horse tonight and it can reopen to the public. We've got everything we can from the site.'

'That's good news.' Andrew stood blocking Leo's view further into his cottage, keeping the excitable Labrador trapped behind his legs. Brenda still wanted to make unfriendly contact with Leo, the intruder. 'Is there anything else?' He didn't come across as warmly as he had before. Then he had been timid but essentially cooperative. Today, Leo got the distinct impression he would prefer if the policeman went on his way. That, of course, made Leo want to spin out this interview. He was stubborn that way.

'Have you been shown the photograph?'

'Yes, your officers were here earlier.' His fingers drummed on the door jamb. 'I'll tell you what I told them: I've never seen the unfortunate young lady in my life before. It's a ... tragedy.' There was a hitch in his voice and he cleared his throat and blinked.

'I also wanted to ask you about Friday night.'

'What about Friday night?'

'Were you at home?'

'Yes. My social life is very tame.'

'Alone?'

'Yes.' He shuffled. 'I refer you to the tame comment.'

Leo smiled sympathetically. 'Did you notice the people from the commune walking along the road to their starlight celebration?'

'I can't say that I did. I tend to close the curtains and shut out the world in the evenings.'

'So you didn't hear anything, or see anything?'

'No. But I did have Radio Three on rather loud, I'm afraid.'

A policeman's life would be much easier if people were more inquisitive. He got down to the main purpose of his visit. 'And have you by any chance seen your niece?'

'Which one? You mean Iona?'

That was an odd question. Wasn't it agreed that Ella was in South Africa? 'Yes.'

The dog made another bid for freedom. 'Brenda, give over! I think she's in one of her other parishes at a meeting. It's endless meetings with her. We all lose track. You should try calling her.'

'I have tried. I only get her voicemail.'

Giving up on crowd control, Andrew manoeuvred the dog inside and closed the door behind him, so they were both on the doorstep in a dog-free zone. 'That doesn't sound right. You're ringing her mobile?'

'Yes.'

'She always answers promptly when I call.' The implication being that she was avoiding Leo?

'I got a message yesterday that she wants to talk to me.'

'When was that?'

'Late yesterday afternoon.'

'I'm sure it's nothing then. I saw her last night at Roger and Madeleine's. She didn't mention anything.'

'Well, if you see her before I do, then please pass on the message that I tried to return her call.' Leo paused, following his instincts. 'Mr Chamberlain, is everything all right?'

Leo was watching closely so he caught the slight flinch. 'Yes! Why wouldn't it be?'

'Jimmy Turner mentioned that Iona had dashed off to a family pow-wow …?'

'Not a crisis,' Andrew said firmly. 'We were just making plans.'

'Plans for what, if I might ask?'

'Our birthday. Roger and me. We are turning sixty-four next month.' He tugged his beard in what looked like a habitual sign of frustration. 'Madeleine has the terrible idea of throwing us a Beatles-themed party and we were trying to head her off at the pass.'

'So you are twins?'

'Identical. Not that you would know it now.' He shook his head reflectively. 'It was more evident when we were boys. He's the elder, by twenty minutes, and has never let me forget it. Our younger sisters are twins too. Two births, four children for my poor mother. The odds against that must be huge. But it means that birthdays are always a big event for the Chamberlains.'

'I'm glad it wasn't anything serious. I'll leave you to it.'

'Sorry I couldn't be of more help.' He tried the door but the latch had been down when he shut it.

'Are you locked out?'

'No, no. I'll just go round the back. Inspector.' With a nod of dismissal, he took the path under the windows and disappeared down the side to the garden at the rear.

There was something going on here but Leo couldn't put his finger on it. He sensed Andrew was lying but he wasn't sure about what. He contemplated the lavender bushes that lined the path. Andrew had the Hidcote variety that Leo had grown with some success in his own garden. The bees certainly liked it, though it only had a few last surviving flowers this late in the season. He looked back at the house. It was a large place for just one man, even though it was officially a cottage. Roger wasn't the only one with money in this family. A National Trust warden and an army major: neither profession paid that well. Leo wondered what the generation above them had done. He might just have a little dig into their background because there was something not quite on the level about the Chamberlains. And why was Iona avoiding his calls after having been so keen to contact him?

A curtain moved upstairs and he caught a glimpse of a hand pulling it back. Had Andrew dashed into the house to spy on him and check he really had left. Or was he hiding a lover? As he didn't have Andrew down as a ladies' man, Leo wondered if maybe it was Iona hiding out. Maybe there were cracks in the marriage thanks to Jimmy's open frustrations at being wed to the village's vicar and she was having some time away from him? That would explain Andrew's white lie that he hadn't seen her and gave a more plausible reason for an emergency family meeting that didn't include her husband. As Leo couldn't see that Iona's marital situation had any bearing on the case, he'd leave it for now. He had grieving parents to prepare for tomorrow and he wanted to put his notes in order for the briefing.

Getting back into the car, he turned for Oxford. What did he know so far? It was fair to assume that Julie, for whatever reason, had dressed up to blend in with the commune members and joined in their ceremony. Then she'd been separated from the flock – he was thinking of Jess's analogy to sheep here – and had been taken for her own private encounter on the White Horse.

She loved history. Had someone offered to show her the site? He could see how that would lure her away.

But the wound had been made face to face. She'd been standing close to her assailant, possibly in conversation, or at least not scared of them. There were no defensive wounds, which you would expect if someone came at you with a knife.

The cloak and shoes? Had these been hers? Leo could imagine how she could have got hold of a robe easily enough – a bedsheet would do – but according to Jess the sandals were rare items.

Who made the shoes for the commune and would he or she be able to identify them? He couldn't remember anyone owning up to that profession, but as they were all incredibly closed-mouthed about their activities, that was not surprising.

That was something he could ask Jess. If she found out who wore size five sandals, then he might be able to snip off that loose end.

Chapter 21

Jess

My Cinderella-themed stay at the manor was getting a little out of hand. From sweeper of ashes, I had been transformed, thanks to a message from the inspector, into Prince Charming with the task of finding the owner of a size five shoe. He had asked me to do so as long as I didn't put myself in any danger. I couldn't see how I was risking anything. It was perfectly natural for me to make enquiries of the two-person cobbler team who had set up in a garden shed near the kitchens. I'd been hanging around and shirking work in most departments, according to Sister Ivy. It would be odd if I didn't try it out here too.

Sister Rose was one of the cobblers, she of the freckles whom I met down the pub. She was learning her trade from an older man who told me his name was Brother Gorse. So called because he was a prickly bastard, he added.

I thought I'd finally found a friend.

Brother Gorse did not object to my presence in his shed. He claimed to be a veteran of back-to-nature communes, honing his skills at shoemaking at an ashram in India, an unauthorised but well-hidden woodland encampment in Somerset, and finally at Kingston Manor. He claimed that, as he got creakier, he really needed a bed at night and living in a treehouse could get old.

I was watching him work as I made conversation beside the bench. You could not mistake him for anything other than a working man: his hands were as tough as the leather he shaped, there were many scars, and I could see a persistent line of dirt just under his nails. From the oil, he claimed. The nails he kept trimmed short and he told me never to trust a man with long ones. They'd never do a proper day's labour.

'How do you make sure the sandals will fit?' I asked.

The light fell obliquely across his workbench, transporting him back to a sepia past where such handicrafts were the norm. 'I cut a pattern. If we were making closed shoes, the traditional way is to make a dummy foot called a last and fit the leather around that.' He turned out the piece he was cutting. 'Father Oak doesn't believe that's necessary. He thinks we can manage with sandals and, to tell you the truth, it's simpler and cheaper. I'm not complaining. I always leave room so that the owner can wear thick socks.'

I glanced down and saw that he had made himself boots. Sensible man. 'What kind of pattern? I mean, if I wanted some sandals, would you draw around my feet? I have very tickly feet, I should warn you.'

He chuckled at that.

'Can I see your patterns?'

He took out a sole he had already fashioned and checked

the fit, before handing it on to Rose for sewing together with an awl and tough thread. 'You're very interested in all this, aren't you?'

I flicked through the offcuts of leather in a basket on the end of the bench. 'I'm interested in everything. Curiosity is my middle name.'

'Yeah, I can see it suits you.' He slapped lightly at my hand to stop me fiddling with the scraps. 'The patterns are in the cabinet over there. Knock yourself out.'

With that generous invitation, I began to riffle through the files. He had helpfully put them away in size order so it was a simple matter to let my fingers wander to the women's section. There were ten in this pouch, one of the fatter ones. I pulled them out and pretended I was matching them to my feet.

'Don't you mess up my system!' growled Brother Gorse.

'Wouldn't dream of it. Just trying them on for size.'

'And don't think you can sweet-talk me into letting you jump the queue.'

Thank you, Brother Gorse. He had provided me with a cast-iron excuse for my behaviour. I let my bottom lip jut out in chagrin. 'I wouldn't ask you to do that!' I said in a tone that suggested it was exactly what I had been thinking. I took a quick note of the names: Ivy, Rose, Juniper, Rosemary ... and then I came across Poppy. 'Hey, you've got my pattern in here already! The only problem is that I'm a size six'

'That's not you, love. That's the last Sister Poppy. You can't take her place on the waiting list. That's not how it works.' He hammered a hole for a buckle.

'You mean, I'm not unique?'

'I'd say you're certainly that, but Father Oak recirculates the names once someone leaves. He says it keeps things simple and means he doesn't have to think up more native species to use.'

I measured my foot against Poppy's. 'How long has she been gone?'

'She left last week, or maybe at the weekend? I think she had a bit of a falling out with Sister Ivy.'

'Wow, he doesn't let the names grow cold, does he? What did they argue about?'

'You tell me.' His eyes twinkled under bushy brows.

'But I wasn't here.'

'But you're the new Sister Poppy. Sister Poppy is always a very *special* friend to Father Oak.' His sarcasm was sharper than the knife he was using to cut the leather. He glanced at Rose who was apparently absorbed in her task and ignoring us. 'If you stay here, you'll learn that there are rules and there are rules. The one about no sex, well, that's one of the more flexible ones.'

'I'm nothing if not flexible.' I grinned at him.

'Good for you. Have fun with the Father. I hear he's quite skilled.'

'I wouldn't know. Sister Ivy is doing a very good job as a chaperone.'

'Hmm, that one.' He snapped a piece of leather. 'She's a good guard-dog and she's loyal, I'll give her that. Stuck with the Father through thick and thin.'

'Good old clinging Ivy.'

I put the files back where I found them. 'Did the last Sister Poppy look like me too?'

He squinted at me. 'Not really. She was quite a bit younger. Beautiful.'

'Thank you very much.'

'You do well enough, lass, for your age, but I'd put her in her early twenties. Father Oak likes them that young usually. She has a lovely head of hair – down to her waist and wavy, like you see in those old paintings.'

My heart leapt; this was sounding more and more like my missing person.

'Do you think she'll come back?'

'She can't, not now you're in her place, can she?'

'I didn't realise places were rationed?'

'It's one in, one out since we reached Father Oak's target of thirty-five. You're the first new girl we've had since Rose here joined us in the spring.'

'What happened to the last Rose?'

'She decided to retire. She found the lifestyle too hard on her old bones and she had the shock of a diagnosis for cancer. This isn't a good place to be seriously ill. Brother Maple's herbal potions aren't going to help with that. She's gone back to Durham to live with her daughter. Can't imagine that's going well. She was a difficult old baggage, that Rose, more thorns than flowers.'

'Do you get your stuff back when you leave?'

'Not if you've taken all the vows. It becomes part of the community pot when you do that, owned by the Children of the White Horse jointly. Another reason why Rose's daughter wasn't going to greet her with a marching band: Rose sold the family home a while ago and went back with nothing.'

I thought I'd probably extracted as much as I could from him without New Rose becoming suspicious. I dropped a kiss on his head in passing.

'Thanks for chatting to me. I've been feeling very lonely. No one talks here like you do.'

He threw the shoe into the basket of finished items. 'Talks? We all talk.'

'I mean, talks to me like I'm a normal person and not a disappointment. Thank you.' I picked up the sack of windfalls I'd been sent to collect and deliver to the kitchen. I slung it over my shoulder like Santa. 'Ho, ho, ho.'

'Get you gone, you daft woman. Some of us have work to do.' He nodded to the chalkboard that showed the waiting list for sandals to replace those that had worn out. My name was down at the very bottom but now I could see a gap where Poppy might've been wiped out once she left.

I crossed the cobbles to the kitchen door. That had been extremely useful. All size five shoes were accounted for among the women in the commune and my missing person. It appeared that my client's daughter had been here until the weekend and then had quit. Brother Gorse thought it was Ivy's fault, but I had to ask, didn't I, if it wasn't connected to a much more dramatic event that took place at that time? Did she see something? Had she really gone or was she hiding, or being hidden, somewhere in the grounds? I was thinking of both dead and alive possibilities here.

I had to tell the police, but I doubted they'd get permission to search without more evidence. I also owed it to Tanglewood to have a poke around in the places I'd been told not to go. I was remembering the lights on at the icehouse. That would make an excellent prison. It had to be the best place to start.

Chapter 22

Leo

It was difficult facing Mr and Mrs Dorchester's grief. Until someone who loved the victim came into the police station, it was possible to treat the case like a puzzle that needed solving. When confronted by such raw emotion though, that pretence crumbled and Leo was reminded that it was a person who had been killed. Leo never knew what to say to the grieving. Everything felt inadequate.

They were meeting in Superintendent Thaxted's unlovely office in the Kidlington headquarters of the Thames Valley police. It had large windows with a view of the housing estate with its clutter of gardens filled with oversized play equipment. Fortunately, there were no noises of children playing as it was the middle of the school day. That surely would've been too much for grieving parents. A tray of untouched coffee and uneaten biscuits sat between them.

The two Americans, probably fit and young for their age before this news had made them old people overnight, sat opposite him and the superintendent at the conference table.

A young man from the consulate perched at the head, gazing at his hands, looking completely out of his depth. The mother was most like the daughter with her pale colouring and blue eyes. The father was dark, Hispanic perhaps, his hair receding in a widow's peak from his high forehead. They didn't want words of sympathy from him, thought Leo; they wanted an explanation. Why had it been their daughter who had been targeted? Who had done it? When were the police expecting to make an arrest? There were no satisfactory answers to any of these questions as yet. Sometimes there was nothing to say, nothing that made the nightmare any more bearable.

'But I don't understand, Inspector,' said Mrs Dorchester. 'Julie was a levelheaded girl; she had absolutely no interest in new-age religions. She wouldn't have had anything to do with pagan ceremonies.'

Parents often had no idea what really interested their children, not if the children knew they would not approve. 'Your daughter was interested in English history, wasn't she?'

'Why, yes ...'

'We are working on the hypothesis that she saw it as a tourist attraction. Normally those ceremonies are only open to the members of the religious community. It is possible that she got into the procession unobserved.'

'None of this makes sense,' muttered Mr Dorchester.

Leo pressed on. There was nothing else he could do for them but tell them as much as he could. 'It was dark and the location where the ceremony took place was only lit by candlelight. It is completely plausible that no one saw her – and so far no one has said they did.' The clock showed that the morning was passing quickly. He wished he could get up and go back into the field, but he had to get through this interview. 'We are looking through her communications to discover how she knew about it.'

'It would make our job much easier if you would give us permission to read all her emails and other messages,' interjected the superintendent in an appropriately tactful tone.

'And if you know any of her passwords that would also speed up the process.' Leo didn't go on to add that they could get her fingerprint for the passkey from her dead body. That kind of detail was not one you wanted to share with her parents.

'Of course. Julie would want that. She had nothing to hide. She was a lovely, lively girl. She had no enemies – no one would want to harm her.' Mrs Dorchester blew her nose.

'That's very helpful, thank you. And there is nothing so far to say she was targeted in particular,' said Superintendent Thaxted.

'And her career in the FBI,' probed Leo, 'did she ever mention anything connected with that which might've brought her here?'

'Well, no, not that I can recall,' Mrs Dorchester said helplessly.

The official from the consulate sat up at the mention of the FBI. 'I can't see how that's relevant, Inspector.'

'But it's best that nothing is ruled out too soon. We must explore every avenue,' countered Leo. Was there something here that the authorities didn't want him to know? He glanced over at the superintendent. Claire didn't look as if she knew any more than he did. Best not to pursue this with the embassy official present.

'What I most urgently need to know is what brought Julie to this area in particular,' continued Leo. 'I see from her social media postings that she's visited many places around the UK, but this time she came to the Vale of the White Horse. It's not as well-known as many other local places in easy reach of Oxford like Blenheim Palace and Windsor Castle. Did she say anything to you before she left as to why she might've chosen this as her destination?'

Mrs Dorchester took out a fresh tissue from a pack to wipe her eyes. 'Stephen, do you remember what she said? I'm sorry, Inspector, I'm finding it hard to think straight at the moment. I wish I'd asked more. It just seemed like another of her vacations and we would hear all about it when ... she came b-back.'

'No, Margaret, I don't remember.' Mr Dorchester sounded like he was a million miles away. Leo suspected he was on tranquillisers. How else would you get through a trial like this? 'Wasn't it something about a meeting with an old friend? Or a girl that she knew? It certainly wasn't a boy because she knew that you would seize on that.'

'I was always teasing her that she didn't have a steady boyfriend. Don't get me wrong, Inspector, she dated. But there was no one special. She knew it was a joke but I always said I wanted to be a grandmother. And now ...'

'Do you know anyone to whom Julie might've told her plans? Brothers, sisters, close friends?' asked Leo.

'We lost our son to a congenital heart condition two years ago.' Mrs Dorchester gazed at her ragged tissue. 'Marcus.'

Mr Dorchester cleared his throat, too choked to speak.

'I'm so very sorry.' And Gerry had reported the victim to be in perfect health. 'Did your daughter have the same condition?'

'No. We went another way with her.' The mother couldn't take much more of this, Leo felt.

'I'm sorry, I won't ask you many more questions but could you just explain that briefly?'

Mr Dorchester surprised Leo by surfacing enough to reply on his wife's behalf. 'Inspector, you have to understand that my family has a terrible curse. I lost both my brothers to the same condition as Marcus when they were teenagers. I thought I'd escaped. But when Marcus was diagnosed at birth with the same, we knew that I was a carrier. We agreed that our next child wouldn't face the same risk.'

'Julie was conceived thanks to a donor,' said his wife.

'But I loved her exactly as if she were my own natural daughter.'

'I know you did, honey. No one ever doubted it. Julie never doubted it.'

'Didn't she?' He stared at her in anguish.

Leo wasn't sure how diplomatically to follow this up. 'So Julie was aware you weren't her biological father?'

'We never hid it. She was the daughter of my heart.' His gaze was accusatory, as if Leo had said otherwise.

'Did she ever ask who the donor was?'

Mrs Dorchester sighed. 'She did ask but what could I tell her? We got pregnant here, in a clinic in London when Stephen worked at Unilever. But that seems like an age ago. When

Julie was little, she liked the idea that she might have British blood. She liked to pretend she had an English accent, do you remember that, Stephen?'

'Oh yes. It was terrible … terrible.' Tears filled his eyes. 'I just wish I could hear it again for a few minutes.' He reached out and took his wife's hand.

'And her silly snorting laugh. She didn't get that from either of us. I often wondered if that was the donor's or hers uniquely.'

'She was unique, whatever she got from us. She was unique.' Mr Dorchester put his head on the table and sobbed. His wife's tears were falling faster now.

'We'll let you have a minute,' said the superintendent, rising to her feet. Leo followed her out of the room.

They stood for a moment in the corridor, trying to clear their lungs of the emotion that saturated the office like wood smoke.

'It's never easy, Leo,' Claire said.

'No.'

'I'll take it from here. Do you have more questions?'

That was heroic of her. 'None that can't wait.'

'Do you think the donor angle might be relevant?'

'Possibly, as far as it applies to her motive for coming here. If she thought she had British blood, she might've visited as a way of discovering her roots.'

'And an ancient British site like the White Horse might have especially appealed? Yes, I can see that. It's hard not to feel the weight of so many years of history when you stand up there.'

'With your permission, I'll get back out in the field.'

'Of course. Get me more, Leo.'

Leo was grateful to reach the sanctuary of his car. He drove out of the station, taking the cross-country route. It would take longer, but he needed the space to think. The harvested fields with their ploughed earth and occasional flocks of white gulls or black crows (never together) provided a steadying sight. All this carried on even when the world seemed in a constant muddle with no clear purpose. That single tree left by a farmer in the middle of the field seemed to suggest that you should cling on and keep growing. Was that philosophy enough to last a lifetime?

Leo couldn't help but see the parallels between Julie's and his own situation. He had no idea who his father was, other than that he had introduced himself as George, according to his mother. It wasn't more than a one-night stand and the man had no idea he had a son. Left with little else, Leo had used that name as his surname rather than his mother's more notorious one. She hadn't intended to have a child at all but had greeted the accident as the next act in the drama of her life and as a way to gain more attention from the press who were losing interest in this B-list actress. When Leo looked in the mirror, he saw nothing of her. A stranger's face stared back at him with features that hadn't cropped up in anyone from the albums his grandparents had at home. They collected family memorabilia like a bend in the river where the flotsam gathered. His father had probably been Asian, or had had Asian blood, because Leo's eyes were slightly almond shaped and his skin tone darker than his mother's. His hair was also black and dead straight, taking a cut well but needing frequent trims to look neat. He had never seriously looked, had he, into his mother's circle at the time he was conceived? That was strange considering he had become a detective. Was he more interested in the mysteries surrounding others than in his own? Or was he afraid of what he would find if he investigated his own origins? Perhaps it was the knowledge that any discovery would inevitably lead to an anticlimax that put him off? What could happen? He'd knock on a stranger's door and announce himself as the long-lost son. But not long lost – he had never been lost; he'd never been wanted or, at least, never been known to exist. So a mixture of fear and cynicism had stopped his search, but perhaps Julie had been more optimistic? Perhaps she had believed there was some man out there who would be happy to acknowledge her as a biological offspring?

The thought crossed his mind that he'd seen a strong resemblance between the victim and the major's daughter, and Iona had even thought for second it could be her sister when he'd showed her the photo. Was that more than just a fancy?

His phone rang and he answered it on the hands free. 'Yes? George here.'

'Inspector, it's Iona Chamberlain-Turner.'

'Iona! You're a difficult woman to track down.'

'Yes, sorry about that. I understood you were looking for me yesterday? Was it important?'

'Nothing urgent. I got your call and was trying to get hold of you.'

She laughed, but it was a sound without much happiness. 'Phone tag. Happens all the time. I wanted to let you know that the friend of yours – Jess – had picked up her phone. In fact, the reason for calling you now is that she's just brought it back for more charging. Do you have a message for her when she collects it?'

'Just ask her to be careful, though I know she won't listen. Maybe ask her to think twice before she does anything?'

'All right, I'll tell her that.' There came a pause but she didn't ring off.

'Iona, is there something you want to say to me?'

A tractor pulled out in front of him and Leo dabbed on the brakes. Mud flew up from the huge wheels, splattering the road and the front of his car.

'There are some things I cannot tell you because of my duty to my parishioners.'

'OK.'

'But I can ask you to do something for me. Inspector, I think you should run a DNA test on me.'

'But we've identified the victim.'

'Even so, I just think you would find it very useful.'

Leo thought of his nascent suspicions about family links. He might've asked Iona to volunteer a sample to check this out and here she was demanding it of him. 'All right. I'll send an officer to you with a kit. Where are you today?'

'I'll be here at the Mums and Tods Group until noon and then the Golden Oldies session at the church hall this afternoon.'

'Should I ask you why you want this test run?'

'I think not. We can discuss it when you get the results.'

'Will they show that Julie Dorchester was your half-sister?'

She gasped. 'I … I can't say. Run the tests. Please.'

Maybe she didn't know for certain? Maybe she couldn't speak about it without Leo having fair cause to ask questions? Leo saw that the quickest way to getting her to talk was doing as she suggested.

'OK. We'll speak again soon.'

'Yes, I imagine we will.'

Chapter 23

Jess

There was a palpable sense of excitement in the dining room that night. Father Oak had announced that the White Horse was once again open to the public and he intended us to go up there this evening to cleanse it during one of his famous starlight ceremonies. I was imagining people pretending to be trains on roller-skates like the musical but I thought that reference would not be appreciated here.

'What does he mean, "cleanse it"?' I asked Brother Gorse, the shoemaker. I had taken to sitting next to the prickly old man as he was the only one who seemed close to being on the same wavelength as me.

'It means that we're all going to spend far too long out of our beds, traipsing around in the chilly night air, trying to get in touch with Mother Nature. I keep telling Father Oak, I'm far more in touch with nature snuggly wrapped up in bed.'

'Are you sure you're in the right commune?' I teased him. 'You seem to have trouble going along with the current vibe of the place. You need a Sod It I've Had Enough community.' I had a theory that his adherence to this particular commune was far more to do with it being a safe port for him than for any deeply held belief. He agreed with the aim to live in harmony with nature, but that was about it as far as Brother Gorse would go. From his own account, he'd been around for too long to have much faith in anything. His skill was his entry ticket, not his willingness to adhere to a set creed.

'My dear young fool, when you've been in these circles for as long as I have, you know exactly how far you can take your disobedience. I think your problem is that you never had any intention of obeying our rules, did you?'

'It's true, Brother Gorse,' I pulled a long face. 'I have the misfortune of always being a square peg in a round hole. And if it looks like I might be a round peg, I seem to find ways of chipping bits off so I become square after all.' I frowned. 'Hang on, I'm not sure that metaphor quite works. It needs a little polish.'

'I've got one for you then. You're like a stiletto heel on a damp lawn: a mixed blessing.'

'How so?'

'Disaster if you want to get anywhere but good for aerating the soil.'

I burst out into loud laughter, attracting everyone to look at us as we sat at the far end of the room.

Father Oak broke off his conversation with Brother Maple. 'Sister Poppy, would you care to share the joke?'

I grinned. 'Not really, Father Oak. Sorry. It would kind of lose its humour if I tried to tell it again. Maybe it's enough to say that Brother Gorse was teasing me? He finds me shockingly lacking in discipline, as I'm sure you all do. I must be a disappointment to everyone here.' I held out my hands in what I hoped was a winning way.

Father Oak caught my eye and I felt that little tingle of attraction to him, even knowing what I did about him. I have a sad weakness for bad guys, which I know isn't good for me. 'Oh, I think I understood exactly what I was getting when I asked you to stay with us.'

'I'm glad someone did. I am a continual surprise to myself.' We appeared to be talking on two levels here. Did everyone realise? From Brother Gorse's smirk, I thought that maybe they did.

Father Oak waved a hand towards me. 'Sister Poppy, everyone, our newest member. You've probably all met her by now. We must help her make the adjustment to our way of life. In that spirit, we'll introduce you formally to our community tonight during the celebration on the White Horse. We haven't yet had a welcoming ceremony, have we, Sister Ivy? And there's no better place.'

Welcoming? I was rather expecting him to show me the door. Ivy's face betrayed that she for one would prefer to give me a send-off.

'No, we haven't, Father,' said Ivy. 'And Sister Rose too – we haven't officially welcomed her.' Brother Gorse's unassuming assistant looked grateful for being remembered.

'I'm pleased you reminded me. Sister Rose, Sister Poppy, this evening is for you both. We'll meet at eleven in the hall and walk up together.' He got to his feet. 'I'll see you all later.'

'Bring cloaks, everyone,' called Sister Ivy as we all went our separate ways. That woman had missed her vocation: she should've been a particularly bossy nanny.

I hadn't yet seen what it was about this commune that made people want to give it all their money. Or give *him* their money, I suppose I should say. The starlight ceremony might give me the insight I had been lacking.

It was immediately apparent that Father Oak knew a thing or two about stage management. Had he once been an actor, I wondered? We gathered in the hallway dressed in our long velvet cloaks. Mine was green like the other novices. The inner circle – Ivy, Pine, and Maple – wore red. And what was Father Oak wearing when he made his entrance? He wore black, of course. We each fetched a lantern from a side table and lit a candle from a taper Father Oak held out.

'Bless you,' he said to one. Or 'Peace in your heart, Sister Holly.' I'd never seen him more priestlike. When it came to my turn, he varied his performance and took my candle from me to light it himself. He handed me back the candle and murmured, 'You are my light.'

Was he flirting? I very much thought he was, which challenged me to come up with a suitable response.

'Baby, you can light my fire,' I whispered.

He frowned. 'Oh, Sister Poppy, you'll be the death of me,' he murmured, not unappreciatively. He cleared his throat. 'Come, my children, the moon is rising.'

We fell into line behind him and set off in the dark for the hill. The commune broke up into ones and twos, those who took it more seriously walking in solemn silence, those of us who were just enjoying ourselves murmuring to our partners.

'Did the last Sister Poppy like these things?' I asked Brother Gorse as we began a steep climb.

'Why are you so interested in your predecessor?' He handed me his lantern while he pulled on thick gloves.

'I guess it's odd that I am, because I've never met her. Dead man's shoes? Not dead exactly' – God, I hoped not – 'but I feel like I've inherited her place and I'm not sure what to make of the fit.'

'Then, yes, I'll answer you. She loved this stuff. It was her favourite thing we did. I think she took it all very much to heart.'

'And yet she left so suddenly?'

He took back his lantern. 'You're right, that does seem a bit out of character. Poor kid. Maybe she had a lover's quarrel?'

'I thought you said she had a falling out with Ivy?'

'The two go together. Ivy is very defensive when it comes to Father Oak. If Poppy upset him, then Ivy would make life very difficult for her.'

I thought of the grate cleaning. Had Lisette, also known as previous Poppy, simply not been able to take it any more and left like her mother had hoped she would? That would be a bummer as it meant I wouldn't be able to claim my payoff for persuading her to quit. And if she hadn't left? That was far worse. Had they silenced her somehow, not left on the hillside like the first victim, but was there another body to be found? I'd have to hope she got disillusioned and be satisfied with my initial payment.

In fact, maybe it was time I left and just told Leo what I

knew? Lisette wasn't here and I wasn't equipped to handle killers. Mind made up, I decided to pack up and go tomorrow morning.

My thoughts turned from the dead-end of my missing person case to our location. I hadn't yet been to the White Horse and I was surprised by how far it was on foot. Up a hill. Father Oak was really making us work for this. Brother Gorse breathed heavily and clutched his chest. I took the lantern from him again and passed it to Sister Rose.

'Here, take my arm,' I told him. All his joking about wanting to be in bed had not been mere words. He really would've been better staying behind. 'You shouldn't have come.'

'That's not an option. We all agree to turn up at these ceremonies. They are the glue that holds us together, according to the Father.'

'Why? What on earth goes on that makes them so important?'

'You'll see. We have to be all in this together, or not at all.'

I didn't like the sound of that. 'What is this?'

He didn't answer.

'That bad, hey?'

My mind was beginning to go wild, dragging up images from all the horror stories I'd ever heard about cults, ranging from mass suicides to infant sacrifice. Oh my God, had the group actually killed that girl up here last week? Had I been fooling myself that they were nothing more than a weird sect who grew their own beans and wore ugly shoes?

'Does anyone get hurt at these things?' I asked tentatively.

'Not hurt, no.' He wasn't meeting my eyes.

Why did I not find that reassuring. 'So they get ... what?'

'What we all agreed to do.'

'I'm still not following.'

'Live at one with nature.'

Now that seemed to cover a wide range of possibilities.

He squeezed my hand, his rough-skinned fingertips faintly scratchy on mine. 'You're a sweet girl, worrying about an old man like me. You'll be fine. I'll watch your back.'

But the girl had been stabbed from the front, according to the news stories. My back was probably fine. 'Thanks,' I said hoarsely.

We arrived at the car park where the footpath to the White Horse began. The only vehicle was a blue campervan but there was no sign of anyone in it. Father Oak gave it a glance then passed on. As we left the shelter of the hedges, the wind whipped our cloaks around our legs. This landscape seemed scraped clean, like an animal's skin prepared for leather. The grass was short and tough, worn into chalky channels by the passage of many feet. In the distance, slow rolling contours of hill after hill swelled like the flanks of a frozen herd. I felt my bones tingle, not just with the tiredness of my legs after the climb but also with a sense that I was climbing out into a much older world. I was thankful that the unearthly spell was broken from time to time as fellow commune members cursed the stones that got caught in their sandals. Brother Gorse and I, in our sensible closed shoes, were able to walk unimpeded. I noticed that quite a few took off their shoes and walked barefoot on the grass, welcoming the cool, damp soil beneath their toes. I was tempted to join them but I decided that if this gathering turned very weird, and I had to make a run for it, it would be better to do that shod.

We turned off the path to walk the short stretch to the horse's head. At a sign from Father Oak, a few of the men hung back to guard our activities from outsiders. Following some instinct of respect, none of us stepped on the carved figure. Seen at this angle, it appeared like an abstract painting of white curving lines on a greyscale background, like scattered scythe blades. The moon was waning but still gave enough light to make it glow.

'Gather round,' said Father Oak softly. He placed himself with his legs straddling the horse's eye. I recognised that it was an old fertility rite he was tapping into here. Reading up on the White Horse, I'd found out that women in the valley came here to ask for help to get pregnant. I didn't think the custom was supposed to be understood quite so literally as having a stud service offered to you but, of course, my mind went there.

We arranged ourselves in a loose circle so that we encompassed the head. By chance, I came to stand at the place where the head joined the neck and shivered again, a ghostly breeze on my nape.

'Great Horse, carrier of the sun on its journey across the sky, we greet you,' cried Father Oak, his hands raised to the heavens.

'We greet you,' echoed the followers – apart from me who hadn't got the memo that we were supposed to join in.

'You were defiled by the spilling of blood but a week ago. Forgive us.'

'Us' as in humanity, or him personally? I wished Inspector George were here. I didn't want to be a witness to this. It felt like there might be no going back.

'We have come now to cleanse you, calling on the elements of earth, air, water, and fire. Then we will honour you and defy death in a life-giving act.' Father Oak dropped his hands, his gaze finding me in the crowd, stopping my attempt to slide away. 'But first we will welcome our new members so you may see them too. Sister Rose, Sister Poppy, please step forward.'

We glanced at each other and moved together so we stood inside the horse's head.

'We always greet our new members like children new born.' He waited. I wasn't sure of my cue but Sister Rose seemed to know what was expected. She put down her lantern and unfastened her cloak.

New born? Oh, I got it now.

I placed my lantern next to hers and began to strip. It didn't take long but I hoped this wouldn't be a drawn-out ceremony as it was chilly. My nipples were in peaks and not for a nice reason.

Father Oak came forward and took us both by the hand. 'See our sisters, sky clad. Welcome them.' He walked us round the circle and each member muttered a word of welcome. 'Naked we come into the world, so naked we become Children of the White Horse.'

And naked we leave it, I thought, remembering a line from the funeral service.

He brought us back to our places. There had been nothing

sexual in the gesture. He could well have been the male midwife holding us up for the community's approval. He bent and kissed our brows, not touching us but with the lightest brush of his lips.

'Welcome, Sister Rose. Welcome, Sister Poppy.' He stepped back. Rose was gazing at him with adoration. I tried to look similarly lovestruck but in fact I was wondering when I could politely gather up my clothes and get dressed. No time soon, it would seem, as his next order was for everyone to get sky clad. Oh wow, they were really going the whole wacky cult route, weren't they? There were a variety of body shapes on view, enough to keep a life-drawing class busy for a year. At least being joined in my nakedness made this all feel a bit more fun.

I tried not to be too obvious with my observation, but Father Oak turned out not to disappoint in the physique department. He had gone to town on himself, decorating his torso with blue swirls that I realised were elements of the White Horse reproduced on his body. How had he done the ones on his back? I imagined that was Ivy's task. Or Sven's? The Norwegian would love that.

Father Oak knelt and placed a hand on the horse's eye. He rubbed it until some of the white chalk transferred to his palm. 'Come closer, child.' He beckoned me.

I stepped up to him, a little suspicious. Smiling slightly, he daubed my throat with the chalk dust, marking a line down to my navel. From his lingering touch, I could tell he was enjoying this.

'Celebrate life with earth!' he called. As he turned to daub

Rose in the same way, everyone else knelt to get the dust on their hands and trace the same line on their neighbour.

He then took a handful of chalk dust and blew it over our heads. It settled on Rose like a frosting, so I guessed I must also look the same.

'Celebrate life with air!' he ordered.

Again, his followers copied his gesture. Rose gazed at him in rapture but I didn't feel like I was inside this moment, too conscious that I was here on a pretence. All I could think about was how odd we must appear to outsiders. I had to hope no one stumbled across us with a camera. I wasn't sure I wanted an image of this on the news sites. Then I began to worry exactly what kind of 'water' would be involved as I couldn't see any bottles.

Father Oak approached us again. I mentally prepared my escape route. He reached down into the pile of his cloak and brought out a flask. Phew. He poured a little over our heads, letting it run down our bodies until it reached the ground.

'Celebrate life with water!'

The red-cloaked acolytes went around the circle pouring water over each person. Some stood with heads bowed, like this was to be endured. Some threw back their heads, arms wide, like it was something to be embraced.

That left fire. We'd brought lanterns with us so I wasn't worried.

But I should've been.

Father Oak reached into his lantern and took out his candle. 'Hold out your hands,' he instructed us.

Rose held hers out.

I copied but then dropped them to my side in doubt. 'Why?' I asked.

'You will feel the heat of the fire and know that you are alive,' he replied.

Not for the first time, I didn't like the glint in his eyes. He no longer looked like a harmless con artist; he looked to me like someone who enjoyed the pain of others. His gaze went to Rose. 'Watch. See how your sister receives the blessing.' He tipped the candle so that a few drops of wax landed on her palm over her lifeline. She flinched.

'Maybe I'll pass.' I kept my hands behind my back.

'There are no passes here. Hold out your hand.'

I wanted to argue that there were sex clubs where you could find willing partners for this kind of thing, but didn't think that would go down well. I swore under my breath and held out my hand. Dark eyes glittering, he tipped the candle and let a trickle of wax fall to form a pool the size of a ten pence piece. It hurt, but it was bearable. I wanted to brush it away, as you would if wax spilt on you at home, but Rose showed that the deal was to let it grow cold. I kept my hand out, not whimpering, not flinching.

'Celebrate life with fire!' he called and my fellow lemmings all went over the cliff to experience the dubious pleasure of hot wax on their palms. At least they hadn't gone for more delicate parts. Small mercies.

'And now the Great Horse is cleansed. We will celebrate with more life-giving acts and drink to health and wholeness!' said Father Oak. He stooped down to take up his cloak. This was the signal for everyone to take up their clothes. I quickly wrapped myself in mine, hoping the party was over. I had to get out of here.

But we weren't finished. The red-cloaks went around the circle passing out face masks that had a plume of white hair. I turned mine over in my fingers. Children of the White Horse. So was this a mane? Maybe the disguise would help me slip away? The guards couldn't keep tabs on every approach all night, surely?

Brother Gorse found me. 'You might want to go easy on the libation,' he murmured. 'It's fine to sit out.' Putting the mask over his face, he shuffled off to perch on the hillside, wrapped in his cloak, gazing over the valley.

Several wineskins were being passed from hand to hand. After being teetotal in the valley, all the rules were relaxed up here and they were making the most of it. The noise was increasing as the party kicked off. I was feeling less and less at ease as the masks seemed to remove our humanity. I took a gulp when Brother Pine passed me a wineskin with a gesture that said I had to taste it. It had the herbal flavour of home-made wine. It didn't strip the throat but neither would it win any prizes at a wine tasting.

'Thanks.'

'Drink,' he said solemnly, tipping it to my lips again.

This time I only pretended to gulp. Sparkles were already gathering around his head and the world was blurring and turning to wax. The wine was laced with something psychedelic. Couples were forming and heading into the shadows, blobs that came together and parted like the bubbles in a lava lamp. I guessed I now understood what act to celebrate life this had been building up to, and why they all looked forward to starlight ceremonies.

'If I asked you, would you?' I said to Brother Pine, knowing I was safe with him.

'You are not for me. You are not my chosen.'

Ri-ight. 'And how does this behaviour match up with the no sex rule?'

'This is a special time outside of those rules. None of us are exclusive. We can't even be sure who we couple with. This is about community, not about the individual.'

I took the wineskin from him. 'Go find your choice. I wouldn't want you to miss this.'

I carried the drink to Brother Gorse and sat on the grass beside him. 'Want some?'

He sniffed. 'I'm too old for that stuff. I don't like how it makes me feel.'

He had a rather attractive melty face at the moment – but that was just the drink speaking. I contemplated the wineskin.

'Is this an aphrodisiac?'

'Among other things. I used to enjoy it, but now I just can't be bothered. Don't get old, love.'

'I prefer that to the alternative. You know, I thought that if ever I was at a group orgy I'd really go for it.'

'And?'

'I don't feel in the mood. I don't like anyone enough to do what they're doing.' I waved to a couple doing a bit of bare-back riding not far enough away. To my sparkling vision, they were elongating and shrinking, echoing the strange shape of the horse they lay on. 'I'll stick with you.' I lay back and looked at the stars, trying to ignore the grunting and sighing that surrounded us. 'Why doesn't the National Trust stop this?'

'Ask the warden.'

'You mean he ...?'

'Yes, and we have the evidence, but don't tell anyone I told you.'

Blackmail the guy in charge: it was a good strategy. I wondered how many other local people they lured up here and compromised to buy their silence. 'Do you reckon the druids did it up here too?'

'Only the gods know.' He passed me a metal hip flask. 'My own supply. Not drugged.'

'I think I love you.'

'And if I were a younger man, I'd let you show me.'

I giggled and drank a little of the smuggled whisky – not my favourite spirit but I needed it. 'The funny thing is that I was right about this commune after all. I thought it'd be like this, then I swallowed the pious sister act I was sold, and now I find myself in the middle of an outdoor orgy.'

'And is it disappointing to be proved right?'

'No, just puzzling. I thought I'd be more up for this. It all just feels a bit funny.'

'It's harmless. Everyone here is consenting. It does bind the community together. Aye-aye, look lively. Father Oak is heading our way.' Brother Gorse's tone became urgent. 'Do you want him, love?'

'Not really?' I didn't sound certain even to myself.

'Then play along with me.' He threw an arm around shoulders and pulled me to his side.

Father Oak loomed over us. 'Brother Gorse, may I take Sister Poppy from you?'

'You were a bit slow off the mark, young man,' said the shoemaker fiercely. 'She's my chosen for the evening.'

There was a moment of silence. 'Very well.' Oak sounded peeved. 'I wish you joy.' And then he stalked off.

'Lie next to me for a moment,' Brother Gorse said. 'Until he loses interest.'

I stretched out beside him. 'Ruth and Boaz,' I whispered.

'What?'

'Didn't you ever go to Sunday school? I thought it was compulsory for your generation.'

'My parents were communists.'

'Oh. Well then. Bible story. Old guy protecting young woman by casting his cloak over her. Sweet moment in the Old Testament.'

He chuckled into my hair. 'You're not as daft as you make out.'

'Oh, I completely am. Daft sheep in daft sheep's clothing.'

'Give me back my flask, wench.'

'Baa, humbug,' I muttered and passed it back before passing out.

Chapter 24

Michael

Michael woke abruptly. It was one of those rude awakenings that made you feel like you'd just fallen down a flight of stairs and this was particularly unpleasant for him because that exact experience was what had left him paralysed. Taking a second to gather his senses, he groped for his phone.

'Yes?'

'Michael? Oh God.'

'Jessica? You don't sound like yourself. It is you, isn't it?'

'Yes ... no ... kinda is me but I'm not quite here, so maybe not?'

He checked the time. Drunk dialling. It was five in the fucking morning. He'd put up with a lot of crap from Jessica when they were together; he didn't have to have anything to do with it now. 'Fuck, Jessica, do you know what time it is? Are you drunk?'

'No, well, again, not sure. Sorry.' There was a long pause and he could hear wind on the microphone at her end. She was outside. 'I think the drink was spiked with really powerful shit, you know? I don't feel ... right. Everything's kinda melty.'

That was another thing entirely. His alarm rocketed. What had that fucker O'Brien done to her? He remembered the poisoned chalice at Jonestown. 'It's OK, Jessica. It's OK. Where are you? I'll come and fetch you.'

'Really not sure where I am.'

OK, Michael, go back a step. 'Tell me the last thing you remember.'

'Father Oak, aka the smarmy bastard.' She giggled. 'You were so right about him.'

'Jessica ...'

'There was a party ... he held a party-slash-orgy-thing. I was on the hillside with Boaz.' *Who the hell was Boaz?* 'Then I must've wandered off. It's all really vague. My head hurts.'

There was a sob in her voice then and he realised he wasn't going to get any coherent account from her; besides, that wasn't the most urgent thing. Thinking quickly, he came up with a solution.

'Jessica, does your phone have a Find Your Friends app?'

'Er, yes. Think so.'

'Make me one of your friends and I'll use it to find you.'

'But you are my friend, aren't you? We dressed up as *Star Trek* characters together ... or did I dream that?' Her voice had a singsong quality which meant she was drifting.

Michael dug deep for calm. 'Jessica, add me in the app. It should be able to tell you where you are as well, if you look at the map.'

There was silence and some fumbling. 'A big green spot. That's where I am. And the thingy is red.'

'What thingy?'

'Battery thingy.' By some miracle, she must've pressed the right combination of buttons as he saw his phone was now locating her. As she explained, she was indeed in a big green spot, otherwise known as the Downs above Kingston Beauchamp.

'Stay where you are, Jessica. Don't use your phone again but keep it switched on. Have you got that? Keep the phone on.'

'Stay. Phone. Got it. Shit, I feel bad.'

He really wasn't sure that she had got it. 'Why don't you sit down? I won't be long. Wait for me.'

As Michael used the hoist to get himself out of bed, he quickly thought through his options. If she were in the middle of a field somewhere, then he would be hard pressed to reach her in his chair. He needed backup. His first thought was Cory, but that was dismissed as she had small children and no live-in carers. That would delay him. Was there anyone else who would understand what Jessica had been doing without possibly compromising explanations?

Of course there was. And he happened to have the number, thanks to the events of the summer.

'George here.' The policeman's voice was thick with sleep.

'Inspector, it's Michael Harrison. Sorry to wake you so early. I've just had a strange phone call from Jessica.'

'Jessica? Isn't she in Kingston Beauchamp?'

So he knew about that, did he? 'Something's happened. There was some kind of party and she said her drink was spiked.'

George's tone sharpened. He was moving around now, getting dressed by the sounds of it. 'Is she OK?'

'I think so – just disorientated. I'm tracking her by her phone but I don't think I'll be able to reach her where she is.'

'I'll pick you up.' From the sound of a front door slamming, it sounded like the policeman was already on his way in record time.

'Wait a moment, it's easier for me to go in my vehicle.'

'I'll come to you and you can drive. Five minutes. Wait for me.' He rang off.

Michael knew it would take him that long to pull on some trousers and get out to the car. But that didn't stop him resenting the fact that he couldn't spring into action anymore, not like Inspector George. A fine sodding knight in shining armour he made.

He was just backing out of the drive when the inspector pulled up.

'Get in,' Michael said tersely, his mood no more improved by the frustrations he'd just been through. He'd scraped the back of his hand in his hurry.

The inspector climbed into the passenger seat, picking up Michael's phone as he did so.

'She's on this?'

'Her phone's dying but yeah, I have her position. Google maps is no fucking help – just a green square of nothing.'

Michael broke the speed limit down the Botley Road. Normally this would be nose-to-tail traffic jams but not at five-thirty, thank Christ. He swung his car up the slip road to the bypass roundabout and jumped the lights. A single lorry making its stately way around the roundabout honked him but he was already on the A road to Swindon, putting his foot down on the dual carriageway, by the time the vehicle completed its turn. He glanced sideways and saw that his passenger was comparing the phone position to a more detailed map on his own phone.

'Any joy?' asked Michael.

'I think she's at Uffington Castle.'

'The hill fort behind the White Horse?'

'Yes. It's a roughly circular bank and ditch encampment on the highest point of the hill. The interior is about four football pitches in size. Closest point by road is to drive to it on the Ridgeway which runs along the southern edge – not strictly open to vehicles but I'm sure the police will make an exception today,' he said drily.

'I'm not sure my car's undercarriage will grant that exception. If I remember from the old days, it's pretty rutted.'

'Get me as close as you can then and I'll head in from there. I'll fetch her and meet you at the White Horse car park.'

They'd made their arrangements swiftly, having worked as a team before on the wild swimming case, but they still had a half-hour drive ahead of then – twenty minutes if Michael continued to ignore the rules of the road. He was conscious of the many speed cameras. Fuck it: if it meant getting to Jessica five minutes sooner, then he'd take the fine or the frigging speed awareness course.

'So you know about Jessica being at the commune?'

'Yes. I had an unpleasant shock when I found her there, but she's been keeping in touch – helping me understand the internal dynamics of the place. I told her not to do anything risky.'

'Yeah, right.' Michael took some comfort from the fact that when the chips were down, she had rung him rather than Leo George. He let some of his feelings fly away on the next extended stretch of dual carriageway. Try and ignore it as he did, he still had feelings for her and resented the other men in her life.

'We identified the victim; did you see that?' George made no mention of the fact that Michael was trying to break the land speed record.

'I did. An American tourist. Did you establish a link to the commune?'

'Not so far, apart from the fact that she was wearing one of their robes when she died and had probably attended one of their ceremonies. Spiked drink, did Jess say?'

'Yes, that much I did get. Could that have happened to your victim?'

'Nothing showed up in the tests but I found it odd at the time that she had no defensive wounds.'

'So you think she might've been incapacitated?'

'It raises the possibility. When we get Jess to safety, we'll take blood from her and I'll ask the pathologist to look again at our victim and compare the samples. They might be using something that dissipates from the bloodstream quickly. They've got a well-stocked garden and I don't know exactly what's in it.'

'I can ask Tanglewood White if there are any known pagan psychedelics.'

'Thanks. That would help.'

'There are always the old faithfuls: magic mushrooms, opium, if it had reached Britain by then.'

'It has now.'

That was true. This latter-day cult might not adhere too closely to ancient practices, according to Tanglewood. That left the door open to such lovely drugs as Rohypnol and GHB if they produced the desired effects. That last one, if Michael remembered his medical reading correctly, had a particularly short lifetime in the body – four hours in the blood and up to twelve in the urine – making it hard to detect.

'OK, we're almost there. Hang on, Jessica.' He turned off the main road and pushed the speed on the minor roads, trusting to the early hour to keep them safe on the bends. George's knuckles were white on the grab-handle but he said nothing. The policeman had ice in his veins. He rarely showed emotion, something Michael would be interested to probe on another occasion.

Even Michael felt he should slow down as he came to the village. Someone's cat benefited as it got across the street without ending up as roadkill. Jessica would never forgive him if he sacrificed a cat to come to her rescue, he thought wryly. The road up to White Horse and Uffington Castle was also empty, apart from a blue campervan parked in a lay-by. Probably some travellers trying their luck that they wouldn't get moved on despite the clear 'No overnight parking' signs. He passed the car park and carried on up the hill to where the metalled road ended. In the shafts of light just breaking over the hills, he saw that, as expected, the Ridgeway was a churned mess, only passable for a tank, tractor or intrepid four-wheel drive.

'OK, let me out here,' said George, checking the position on the phone and his map a final time. 'She's not moved but if there's any change, ring me.' He got out and slammed the door.

'Yes, boss,' muttered Michael, executing a cautious three-point turn and heading back down the hill.

Chapter 25

Leo

Michael was driving like a man possessed. Leo swallowed his words of caution. He wanted to get there as quickly as the psychologist, but nothing would delay them like a road traffic accident. *Relax, Leo,* he ordered himself. *Stop gripping the handle like it would make any difference in a collision.* Michael had to know the risks and Leo had to let him concentrate rather than argue the merits of obeying the speed limits on blind corners.

As was his practice, when he felt a swell of anxiety or fear, Leo made his face blank. This involved sinking deep inside himself so only the slightest functional part of him remained present with others. This was behaviour learned as a child, and had stood him in good stead as a police officer. No one wanted the authority figure throwing up their hands and shouting, 'We're all going to die!' They wanted control and decision-making – and that was what he normally excelled in.

But Jess Bridges was testing that control.

He leapt out as soon as they reached the top of the metalled road. He growled some instructions to Michael; only after slamming the door did he think he might've come across as a little churlish. Michael was a member of the public, not a man under his command. He'd apologise later. Vaulting a stile, he ran to the Iron Age fort that dominated the hilltop – a double row of grass-covered earth banks in a rough scallop shape.

It should've been easy to find someone on the mound that was known as Uffington Castle, thought Leo. He rang the phone number for her but got no answer. It could be dead by now. The battery might be flat, he corrected, not liking even to think about the possibility of death. The light was growing, shadows were shrinking, and there was no one else around. Trouble was, Leo realised, he was searching for someone who was off her head on psychedelic drugs; she could not be expected to act rationally as a person wanting to make life easy for a search party. She could've taken fright and run, decided the flock of sheep on the next hill held the secrets of the universe, or simply lain down to sleep. At the position he'd marked or her on the map, his heart missed a beat. There was her phone dropped on the grass at the foot of an earthen bank, but no Jess. Had she wandered off? And who knew how far she'd managed to get in the last half hour. Or had someone else got to her first?

'Jess! Jess!' He cupped his hands around his mouth but the words seemed to go no further than a few metres in front of him before dropping limply to the ground. The flat area in the centre of the fortification was very clearly empty – four football fields of nothing, so no need to search there. He climbed to the top of the bank and turned so he had a 360° view of the countryside. Had she got as far as the Ridgeway? Thinking he had spotted something white in the hedge, he ran the hundred metres to pull it out, only to find it was an empty feed sack that looked like it had been there several years. He'd given up his vantage point for this?

A scream to the north of his position pierced the air. It could've been a bird call but his gut told him that it had come from a human. He sprinted as fast as he could towards it.

'Please let her be OK,' he chanted to himself, not sure who or what he was pleading with. 'Please.' Cresting the brow of the hill, he looked down into the steep hollow, called the Manger, that lay below and slightly to the west of the White Horse. It looked from above like a huge upside-down jelly mould with ridged sides and a flat bottom. In the old days, when it came to the Scouring of the White Horse – an occasional fair to restore its brilliancy from encroaching weeds – young men used to risk their necks chasing great rounds of cheese down this slope. Leo couldn't see how they didn't kill themselves doing so; it was treacherous. But now it appeared empty ... No! He'd moved so his gaze could reach to the bottom of one of the gullies. Two bodies were heaped there – white robes and green cloaks, fair-headed. Cursing, Leo called the emergency services.

'I need an ambulance at the Manger, White Horse Hill.'

'What is the nature of your emergency?' asked the call centre voice. Female. Calm.

'Two people. They appear to have fallen. I'm just climbing down to them now.'

'And the Manger, is that a pub?'

'No, a local landmark. Look it up.' He knew he sounded rude but he couldn't do her job as well as his own.

'All right, sir. The ambulance is on its way. Do you require the police?'

'I am the police. Detective Inspector George. I'll call again when I reach them so you can update the paramedics.' Leo pocketed his phone. He could go the long way round and approach from the bottom of the hill, or he could chase the cheese.

Was that movement he saw from one of the bodies?

'Jess, I'm coming!' This was insane. Letting gravity take him, he went over the edge.

Chapter 26

Leo

The world rushed by. Heart pounding, fists pumping, and legs threatening to shoot from under him. The shock of each footfall rang through his bones. He hit the bottom at a flat-out run, knowing that if he tried to brake there would be consequences. Momentum took him past the bodies but, once he'd slowed, he turned back. Jess was lying face down over an older man, one he remembered from the commune. Brother Gorse – a coarsely spoken Londoner who'd seemed amused to be questioned, rather than resentful as so many of the others had been.

Had they both fallen? Had it been Jess's scream he'd heard?

He went over and knelt beside them. The old man was clearly dead, his skin already turning the bluish grey that set in after a few hours. Jess though, she was warm to the touch, thank God. He brushed back her hair and found that she was weeping.

'Jess, it's me, it's Leo. Inspector George.'

Like a child, she transferred herself from Brother Gorse's

chest to Leo's and continued crying. Leo wasn't sure what to do but he thought he could diagnose shock mixed with the confusion of whatever drugs it was that she had taken. She needed to be kept warm. He wrapped the velvet cloak she was wearing more tightly around her.

'It'll be OK. The ambulance is on its way.' One-handed, he pulled out his phone. He saw that he had many missed messages from Michael demanding an update. He'd have to wait. 'Dispatch? DI George here. I think we have one casualty and one shock victim, no apparent injuries. How long until they get here?'

She said something about delays and admitted it would be ten minutes.

'Fuck,' said Leo. 'The nearest access point is on the road to Dragon Hill. Tell them not to go up to the White Horse but stick at the bottom.' He ended the call and rang Michael. 'Found her. She's taken a fall into the Manger.'

'My God, is she all right?'

'Confused, tearful, cold, but yeah, I think she's OK. But Michael, there's another person here. He's dead. I'm going to have to call in my team. Will you look after her? I'll be caught up with the investigation.'

'Of course I'll fucking look after her! I didn't come here to spectate.'

'Yes, sorry.' Shit, he wasn't handling the man right today. 'Come as close as you can. Turn back down the hill and follow the blue lights. The ambulance will be here any moment.'

The last call he made was to his own control room. He was put through to the duty officer, who happened to be

Harry Boston. 'Harry, there's been a development. Get the team down here asap.'

Once Jess had been taken away in the ambulance, Michael following in his car, Leo was left with the victim. He'd already disturbed the scene by not being in protective clothing so it seemed a little late to put it on. Yet that was what procedure required. The old man lay huddled in a foetal ball. Nothing looked broken, though only the postmortem would say this for sure. To all intents and purposes, he could just have fallen here, tripped over the edge in the dark. That might've been Leo's conclusion had he not stood over another body the week before, and had Jess's experience of drugging to take into account. The man might have been unsteady on his legs, but he might also have had help from manmade sources.

And the connection to the earlier killing? Was there some message in youth and old age? One found triumphantly riding the back of the horse like she was taking a trip into the skies, the other huddled beneath the hooves as if he was returning to the womb.

Was he reading too much into this? At least this time he had a witness. Once Jess was sober, he could ask her what she knew.

And if it wasn't an accident, why had the old man been targeted? There was the symbol, of course, but there were other old men in the commune – Brother Maple, for example, who might even be older; it was so hard to tell when you had no real information about any of them. Who was Brother Gorse in real life? Had he fallen foul of the wrong person, a person ready to kill to keep a secret or who felt threatened by him in some way?

And what secret was worth killing for?

Leo left the scene when a doctor arrived to carry out the formalities to declare the man dead. Gerry wasn't available so the postmortem would be held at the mortuary and the scene processed by Leo's officers and a forensic team. A photographer was already taking a comprehensive scan of the site using one of the new 3D imagers Thames Valley had recently acquired. It would enable them to recreate the slope on a computer to calculate if the injuries corresponded with the fall. All that was better left to the scientists. His own time would be well spent waking up the Children of the White Horse and asking his questions before they had an opportunity to fabricate alibis.

He took both DS Boston and Wong with him. He wanted to divide up the thirty or so people quickly and process them while they were still warm from their beds. If they'd all been at the celebration the night before, he anticipated they might have fewer defences prepared.

Harry mashed his finger against the intercom. No answer. Rooks cawed in contempt from the ragged treetops. 'Fuck this,' he muttered.

'Try again,' said Leo, gnawing on his impatience.

There was a hint of static. 'Yes? Who is it?'

'Police. Let us in,' said Harry. The gate began to move.

Suyin overtook Harry's car, which was stopped near the intercom, and sped down the drive.

'What's the play?' she asked tersely, face bare of the usual neat makeup, thanks to the early wake-up call, so that she looked painfully young to Leo as he sat in the passenger seat.

'Get them all into the hallway and make the announcement, then divide them up. I'll take O'Brien, Ivy, Maple and Sven.'

'Who?'

'Sorry, I meant Pine. Jess's nickname for him. Jess identified them as the top team who call the shots here. You process the others. I want anyone who saw anything isolated and questioned, possibly away from this place, if we can arrange that.'

'I'll call the landlord.'

'Yeah, that worked before. Christ, the press are going to be all over this in an hour or so. Make sure you have a discreet way into the pub, maybe by the kitchen door? I don't want photographs of my witnesses in the news.'

'Sir.'

They pulled up by the front steps and strode in without waiting for an invitation. Leo decided that permission was implied by opening the gates and he wanted to be first on the field of battle. He saw an old-fashioned gong beside the entrance.

'Allow me,' said Harry, with a grin. He bashed it enthusiastically.

O'Brien appeared at the head of the stairs in what looked like white pyjamas. 'What the hell is going on?'

'O'Brien, do a roll call, or whatever it is you lot do to summon everyone here,' snapped Leo. 'Then I'll tell you. What's the headcount for a full turnout?'

'That's none of your business.'

'Oh, but it is. Thirty-five, isn't it?' Minus two this morning.

'If he won't call them, then I will.' Harry hit the gong again. It was painful for Leo standing there clear-headed, so it had to be torture for anyone with a hangover.

'That's enough, Sergeant. If that doesn't rouse them, then we'll go up and drag them down here.' He gave O'Brien a steely look.

More members of the community were stumbling in. Some arrived together, half-clothed, others rushed in fully dressed. All looked like they'd partied hard and been put away wet. Leo wondered how many would show traces of drugs in their blood if he took samples now?

'It's all right, everyone,' said Father Oak, trying to take charge. 'The police are just doing this because they aren't making any progress with their case, so they're picking on us because we're a soft target.'

Oh no, he didn't. Leo took his place on the bottom stair, crowding O'Brien so he had to step back. 'O'Brien, take a look around the room. Is anyone missing?'

The man's eyes immediately went to the cluster of novices standing together, marked out by their shorter robes. 'Sister Poppy.'

Leo folded his arms. 'And?'

O'Brien had to think harder this time. 'Brother Gorse is missing. But he's an old man, hard of hearing. I'll send someone to wake him up.'

'I'm afraid that won't be possible. The man you call Brother Gorse was found dead this morning at the foot of the White Horse.'

Several cries of consternation went up; others murmured in alarm.

'Oh my God, that can't be possible! No, I won't believe it,' said O'Brien.

'What you will and won't believe is up to you but it won't change the facts. Now, my officers will be questioning each of you to find out what you saw last night. Wait here until called.' Leo turned away. 'Harry, keep them here and make sure they don't talk to each other. Suyin, you take the novices first – go into the library; I'll see O'Brien in the drawing room.'

'Like a bloody game of Cluedo,' muttered Harry, before turning to the confused people in front of him. 'You heard the inspector. Take a seat. We'll get to you as quickly as possible. No conferring.'

'We need more officers,' said Leo. Even for Harry, this was a large number of people to control. 'I'll wake the superintendent and see what she'll give me. O'Brien, come with me.'

Message sent to his boss, Leo sat in an armchair as O'Brien elected to sit cross-legged on the carpet.

'Is that really necessary?' Leo asked, getting out his notebook. 'This yoga act?'

O'Brien closed his eyes. 'I find it soothing, just as you no doubt find the routine of taking notes steadies you.'

'Fair enough. I'm feeling fairly unsteady this morning as I discovered an old man lying dead at the bottom of a steep slope. I see that you don't look after your flock very well, O'Brien. Did you even know he was missing?'

'And Sister Poppy?'

'Worried about her, are you? Why?'

'Because the last time I saw her she was with Brother Gorse.'

That was an interesting admission. 'She's accounted for,' said Leo, giving no more details. It wasn't his job to answer questions. 'Explain why Brother Gorse was out last night. What were you doing?'

O'Brien rocked slightly. 'We were cleansing the Great Horse.'

'Cleansing? How?'

'We held a starlight ceremony to celebrate life in the aftermath of death.'

'That didn't go very well then, did it? It appears you brought another death to the same spot. Describe this ceremony.'

'It is for Children of the White Horse alone to know.'

'Well, I'm not joining the commune and I need to know so I suggest you change your mind about that.'

His brow furrowed in annoyance. 'All right, but this isn't relevant to anything that went on last night.'

'I'll be the judge of that. The ceremony?'

'We sprinkle our bodies with the four elements: earth, air, water and fire. Then we drink and … er, dance to celebrate.'

'Dance?'

'Yes, we dance together.'

'And did Brother Gorse drink and dance?'

'Yes, with Sister Poppy. She was his chosen partner for the night.'

'What does that mean exactly?'

'They celebrated life together.'

'You're still speaking in riddles.'

O'Brien opened his eyes and glared. 'We had sex, all right,

Inspector? Many times and in many positions. We do what humans have been doing for centuries to celebrate life; we joined together in love.'

Jess and the old man? Leo felt a sickness in the pit of his stomach. Under the influence, had she been raped by Brother Gorse? He couldn't imagine her coupling with him willingly. A new and horrible possibility came to him: had she struggled and was that why they went over the edge together? No, no, that didn't make sense with the timeline. She'd called Michael at dawn and left her phone up on the hillfort. From the coldness of the body, Gorse had been there a while before she joined him at the bottom of the slope.

'I'll need Brother Gorse's real name and last known address so I can notify his family.'

'*We* are his family, Inspector.'

'Don't give me that shit this morning, O'Brien. Name and address or I'll get a warrant to dismantle every last bit of this place until I get my answers.' In fact, he intended to apply for one anyway.

Resentment clear in every line of his body, O'Brien got up and went to a picture of a sea captain on the wall. He lifted it down, revealing a safe. With practised ease, he spun the dial to the right, then the left, then the right again, marking out the combination. It swung open and he reached inside for a notebook. He didn't look at Leo as he made these moves, nor turn around as he read, 'Aaron David Barks, The Treehouse, Tar Steps, Exmoor. I don't know where he came from before that. He lived in an off-grid commune in Somerset before he arrived here. He was a cobbler and a very good one so I suggest you look for his relatives among families in that business, if there's anyone left. He never spoke of blood relations. People rarely do. They come here to get away from all that.'

You never really get away from your family, thought Leo. *You only get extended leave*.

'Do you have the real names of all your people in that book?' asked Leo.

'Yes.'

'And will you give it to me or do I have to get that warrant?'

Hesitating, O'Brien held on to the book.

'What are you hiding, O'Brien? I'm going to find out, you know.'

'Fine, take it. But I expect it back, and I would ask you to respect the privacy of my followers. None of the information in there will give you the answers you seek.'

'Oh really? And how do you know which questions I'm asking?'

'Brother Gorse was an old man. Isn't it clear that he lost his way in the dark and fell?'

'That's clear, is it? I'm pleased you're able to read a crime scene from this distance with no need to carry out a post-mortem. What great powers you have. Will we find traces of drugs in his blood, O'Brien?'

'Drugs? No! Alcohol, probably. We all knew that Brother Gorse liked his scotch. I turned a blind eye to it.'

'And did you turn a blind eye when someone pushed him over last night?'

'No one pushed him. He fell.'

'We'll see. I haven't finished questioning you but please go and get dressed. I'll take Ivy next, or should I say ...' Leo leafed through the book, 'Hailey Robertson?'

O'Brien paled. 'I would rather you didn't let her know that you have that.'

'Oh? Why?' Leo tapped the book on the palm of his hand.

'Because I promised them all anonymity and they'll feel let down by me.'

'And we wouldn't want that, would we?'

'No.' O'Brien sounded humbled for the first time.

Did it really matter which name he used, thought Leo? The real ones were useful for checking up where everyone came from, not for stirring up any more trouble here. A death in this so-called family was enough for this morning.

'I'll not raise it unless it has a bearing on the case,' Leo promised.

O'Brien gave him a nod, surprisingly man-to-man, as if he were a decent human being, and left. 'Sister Ivy, the inspector will see you now. Please give him your full cooperation.'

And pigs might fly, thought Leo.

Chapter 27

Jess

The doctors at the Great Western Hospital in Swindon decided I didn't need admitting. That was good because I wouldn't want to stay in a place that sounded like a steam train but was (disappointingly) a faceless modern building. And I hated hospitals. I'd been telling the medical people myself for an hour that I was fine, arguing that copious amounts of coffee and a hot bath would do the trick, but they insisted on running tests and taking enough blood to satisfy Dracula. They had provided me with scrubs and a blanket as the police had wanted my clothes to be taken in evidence. I was not sorry to see the robe and cloak go. It was highly unlikely that I was going back to the manor, not now. I knew my client's daughter wasn't anywhere I could help her. In fact, I should really ring up Tanglewood and admit that her daughter had left the commune one way or another and it was now a more standard missing person case. The police would be interested, thanks to the killings. The case, as far as I was concerned, had hit a dead end.

A dead end. My brain still cycled through confused memories from last night, disjointed fragments. Had someone killed my friend or had he taken a fall? I remember cuddling up to Brother Gorse but after that it became very blurry. I think I surfaced to find him arguing with someone – I'm not sure who. I thought he might've been telling the person to 'leave her alone', by which I assumed he meant me. Not wanting to find myself next on someone's celebration-of-life list, I stumbled off away from the lanterns and got lost among some confusing hillocks. I think I might've even slept again, but I couldn't swear to it. As the light grew in the east, I gathered enough wits to phone Michael and ask for help. Why him? Possibly because I still had him in my emergency contacts. He wasn't going to let me forget that, was he? Finding myself getting the worse for wear at a pagan orgy. It would confirm everything he'd ever thought about me. And then ... and then ...?

I must've dropped my phone. I didn't have it on me when I was found. Inspector George had been there. Leo. He'd said his name was Leo, hadn't he, when he came to me? How did I remember that when I'd forgotten everything else, like how I got there? I'd not come down the slope but he ran down, the idiot. I can remember seeing him doing it, limbs flailing, and I'd thought he would fall but he didn't. But as for me, I think I must've made it on the road somehow and come in from the bottom of the Manger, drawn by the white robe glimpsed from the hilltop. I'd had no idea it was going to be Brother Gorse. It could've been any of us who stumbled that way in the dark, out of our heads on whatever it was they laced the drink with. And I'd only taken a mouthful.

That was odd. I shouldn't have been so badly affected. Had I drunk more than I thought? Or had I returned to drinking? I really didn't think so. The only thing I do remember gulping was Brother Gorse's scotch. If that had been drugged, I didn't taste anything but the burn of the liquid.

So confusing. I was never going to drink alcohol ever again.

The curtain was pulled back and Michael appeared with the nurse.

'Miss Bridges, you can go now. Dr Harrison here said he'd keep you under observation for twenty-four hours.' She passed me a white bag with a prescription for pain killers. Nothing fancy, just strong paracetamol to help with the stiffness in my limbs and my aching head.

I swung my legs off the side of the bed. 'Thanks. Michael, I'm so sorry to drag you all the way to Swindon.'

He did a nifty swivel to face the exit. 'It's no trouble. My car's just outside.'

'Do you need help?' the nurse asked, seeing me sway on my feet.

I rested my hand on the back of Michael's chair. 'No, I'll be OK if I take it slowly.'

Michael, taking the hint, wheeled at a gentle pace down the corridor.

'Inspector George wants to talk to you as soon as I get you home. Are you OK with that?' asked Michael.

My eyes were still a little weird, producing strange flares around lights. 'God, it's like being in a J. J. Abrams *Star Trek* film,' I muttered, rubbing my face.

'Pardon?'

'Light flares. He always catches them in his films. Once you notice, it's a pretty obvious stylistic tic. Supposed to be all "spacey".' I made an inverted commas gesture and almost lost my balance.

Michael paused by an empty bench. 'Perhaps you'd better sit down, Jessica? I'll get someone to wheel you out.'

'Really, Michael, I'll be fine. I just need a drink.' I saw his expression. 'Of coffee. *Coffee*. Jeez, I don't want alcohol ever again. Or at least, not for twenty-four hours.' I took the seat because it was there. 'God, I could do with a cigarette. Are you going to ring Cory?'

'Why?'

'To tell her to expect the police.'

'Oh. I told the doctors that I would monitor you, and I need to be in my own home so I can move about. Sorry, I should've checked with you first.'

'How could you? I was away with the psychedelic fairies. They have sparkly wings; did you know that? No worries. I think I'd better not be around the kids – bad example right at the moment.' I stood up, finding my feet a little steadier this time. 'Right, I'm good to go. Beam me up, Scotty.'

We made it to the car without me doing a face plant, and I must've fallen asleep again because the next thing I remembered was arriving at Michael's house.

'Uh-oh. Bad idea. I haven't got any clothes here,' I said as I walked in. 'Hello, Colette.' She wound round my ankles.

'I'll find you some temporary ones. If you ring Cory I'm sure she'll run some over.'

'Does she know ...?'

'I haven't told her.'

And the police wouldn't either, so she didn't know. Thinking about it, I couldn't cope with our book-club jungle-telegraph system. Fielding all those well-meaning but inquisitive messages from female friends was more than I could cope with. 'I'll make do for today with your stuff. I'll sneak back in when she's at work and the kids are at nursery.'

Michael went into his bedroom to find some suitable clothes. 'Feed the cat, will you? She missed breakfast.'

I looked in the fridge for an open tin. The shelves were nearly empty. He ate mostly at college high table these days. 'You're such a guy,' I said fondly.

He placed a neat pile of T-shirt and tracksuit trousers on the counter. 'Oh? In what way?'

'You're the psychologist.' I opened the fridge again and showed him the row of artisan beers in the door, a couple of nice whites on their side, and an open jar of Gentlemen's Relish. The only normal grocery was a pint of milk.

'It's not as bad as it looks,' he said defensively. 'The real food is in the freezer.'

I laughed as I filled Colette's bowl with kibble. 'Sorry, princess, you'll have to wait for the posh grub but this will tide you over.'

'Coffee?' Michael put on the kettle.

'Yeah, why not.'

'I don't suppose I could persuade you to drink decaf?'

'I don't suppose you could.'

'OK, OK. Actually, I've got this great new gadget that froths milk. I'll make you a cappuccino. Unless you want hot chocolate?'

I smiled as memories of the café in Frankfurt came back. 'I think I'll treat it as officially still morning for me, seeing as how my day hasn't really started yet.'

'Cappuccino it is.'

Michael had improved in his home skills since I lived with him, finding the pods for the coffee maker and using the machine without referring to the instructions. 'I'm afraid I don't have the caramel flavour you used to like.'

'Straight coffee is fine for me.' I took the clothes into the bathroom, eyed the shower, and decided I needed one to warm up properly. Five minutes later, I was feeling much more myself, my hair wrapped in a towel and wearing a pair of Michael's soft grey sweats that I knew he used for his rehab sessions with his physiotherapist. They bagged at my ankles but the drawstring kept them up. The coffee was waiting for me.

Just as I sat down on the sofa, the doorbell rang. Michael checked his phone, which relayed the image of the person on the front step.

'It's DI George. Are you ready to see him?'

'Yes. I want to thank you both for coming for me.'

'I didn't do anything.' He pressed the buzzer to release the front catch. 'He was the one who went running to the rescue.'

'That's not true. You were there for me when I rang and you stayed with me at the hospital. Thanks.' I leant over and kissed his cheek. 'You're dangerously close to being my best friend.'

'Hmm. I suppose I should be grateful for that. I just wish we could've been more.'

It was at that interesting juncture that the inspector interrupted us. Maybe that was for the best because I'd tried to be Michael's partner but found myself much more suited to the role of scatty best friend. We actually liked each other like that whereas, when we shared our lives, we soon found plenty of reasons to fall out of love *and* liking. I wouldn't go there again. It hurt too much and I'd only just picked myself off the floor after a few more failed relationships. Fool me once, shame on you, fool me twice ... Well, you get the picture.

Inspector George – Leo – came in cautiously, like a visitor to a critical care unit. I'd have to put a stop to that. I got up and threw my arms around him. He'd run down a hill to save me and given me permission to call him by his first name; we were beyond formality now. 'Thank you, thank you so much for finding me.'

He returned my hug with a quick tight pressure of the arms, before putting a more professional distance between us.

OK, maybe we weren't.

'Inspector, can I get you a coffee? Or tea?' said Michael, reminding us that he was here.

'Tea would be good,' Leo replied.

'How do you like it?'

'No sugar and a little milk. And please, call me Leo.' He turned back to me. 'How are you feeling, Jess?'

'I'm fine. Really.'

'May I talk with you? Privately?' He glanced over at Michael who was clearly listening in from the kitchen area.

'Oh. OK. But Michael knows everything about me.' *Almost* everything, I have to admit for accuracy's sake.

'You can go through to the guest bedroom,' said Michael.

We walked down the corridor that stretched to the back of his modern house in the canalside development. Michael's bedroom backed on to the small garden plot but he has another halfway along with a view of the side alley that he used as a home office and guest room. It was where I'd got changed after my shower so I hurriedly kicked my abandoned clothes aside. I am not a tidy person.

'Jess, please sit.'

I perched on the side of the guest bed as the inspector took a seat on the desk chair.

'What's this about, Leo?' I loved saying his name. He looked like he was already regretting giving me permission to use it, especially as we'd immediately moved to a room with a bed.

'Jess, I need to ask you something. When I questioned O'Brien, he admitted that the celebrations involved ... er ... sex.'

I clapped my hand to my face. 'God, yes! I was shocked out of my socks. They all went for it like rabbits. And I'd bought the bullshit that they were all celibate.'

'He said he last saw you having, um, relations with Brother Gorse. Is that true?'

'No!'

Leo didn't look convinced. 'You don't need to feel ashamed. You were drugged.'

'Really, no. Brother Gorse was a sweet old man, past all

that. He protected me. We just pretended to be a couple so I didn't have to think up excuses to refuse others.'

'And what did the others make of that?'

'I'm not sure. Look, I'd better tell you what I remember.' I recounted what I could of the events of the night before.

Leo got up and started pacing. 'Gorse was arguing with someone? Was it O'Brien? Did O'Brien come back for you after having been turned away the first time?'

'I genuinely don't know. There's been some light flirting,' *and heavy petting*, 'between Father Oak and me but nothing that went that far. He could've had anyone that night so I can't imagine he'd be that distressed if I wasn't on the menu.'

'And you don't know if the person Barks talked to was male or female?'

'Barks?'

'Brother Gorse's real name was Aaron Barks.'

'Aaron.' I hugged my arms to myself. 'You would've thought with a name like that he would've been more familiar with the Old Testament.'

'Sorry?'

'Nothing. Aaron told me his parents were communists, if that helps. You might find their names and address on the Communist Party list if they give you access. Might lead you to other family members. Or try MI5. They probably kept tabs on everyone who saluted the red flag.'

He smiled at me, giving me that flush of pleasure that comes when you know someone thinks you're clever. 'Good idea. OK, shall we go back out there?'

I nodded. 'Yes. I don't want Michael wondering what we're doing in here.'

He offered a hand to help me up from the bed, then quickly dropped his hold. He seemed ill at ease, conflicted, wanting to protect but stepping back. 'And what are we doing, Jess?'

'I don't know. You tell me when you've worked it out.'

Chapter 28

Leo

It was time to take stock, decided Leo, as he drove home after a very long day. What did he have? Two bodies: one clearly the result of foul play, the other suspicious but by no means certainly a murder. Even if the tests did come back positive for drugs in the old man's system, that still did not rule out him taking the narcotics willingly and falling accidentally to his death. The most suspicious element was the argument Jess overheard and, unless she remembered more, Leo could not use that against a suspect.

Now at his kitchen table, he scrolled through the witness statements his officers had gathered. He already knew the headlines as the last thing that he'd done that day was hold a case review with his team. Suyin's reports appeared to be all on the same theme: yes, most of them remembered seeing Brother Gorse standing with Sister Poppy. And yes, every single one recalled her as she and another new member, Rose, underwent the welcoming ceremony. He now noticed a detail his sergeant hadn't divulged to the flapping ears of the gathered officers. The welcoming ceremony entailed being led around naked.

Leo had to pause here as he read that. Jess hadn't mentioned that to him and he could see why. But she'd been more involved in the sexual games than she'd let on.

Accounts petered out after that. No one remembered seeing either Gorse or Jess after the circle broke up and they selected partners. They wore masks and some seemed genuinely uncertain whom they'd slept with – not that sleeping seemed to be what any of them had done apart from Jess and the victim. If she had told him the truth about that.

But why lie?

OK, that was a distraction. He shouldn't be thinking about Jess's veracity right now. He needed to run the scenario that it was a coincidence that a second death had happened in the same spot as the stabbing. Different means. Taking drugs outdoors in the dark near a steep slope did have the ingredients of an accident waiting to happen. It was possible.

But it seemed likely that Julie had also attended one of these ceremonies just a week ago and also ended up dead. He couldn't get past that. And how to explain Jess's missing person? Where was Lisette White, the previous Sister Poppy, and what had she seen that had so scared her that she quit a place so suddenly, especially when everyone said that she'd seemingly been happy there? Her name had been in O'Brien's notebook but heavily crossed out. That was something to ask him in interview.

Too many questions, too few answers.

Leo then noticed a new message in his inbox which,

thanks to his plans for the day being derailed at dawn, he'd not got to. The results of Iona's DNA test were back, the one she had insisted she take. He opened the file and scanned the contents. She was indisputably the half-sister of Julie Dorchester.

OK, he had to stop and reconsider. Thanks to recent events, he'd been charging down the route that made the commune the centre of the two deaths, but now he had to factor in the confirmation that family ties to the Chamberlains came into play. What did that mean for the Julie Dorchester case? He wasn't buying a coincidence. Mrs Dorchester had been open about using a sperm donor but what were the chances that Julie had just happened to die on her biological father's doorstep? Had Julie come to Kingston Beauchamp to confront her sperm donor and ask for him to acknowledge the paternal relationship? Had something gone wrong, had someone got angry ... angry enough to kill her? He would have to interview the father and the other Chamberlains again, to see if they admitted, given this DNA test as evidence, that she had made contact.

But that left him with two more mysteries: donating was legal, nothing to be ashamed of, and came with no paternal obligations, so if it went to motive, what threat had Julie posed to the family? She couldn't embarrass the donor for doing a public good so they need not hide her existence. What about money as a motive? The legitimate sisters, Ella and Iona, could be affected if the biological father of Julie had a change of heart and wished to change his will, but so far there had been no hint of that. In any case, Iona didn't seem motivated by financial concerns and Ella was out of the country at the time of the murder.

The second mystery, and perhaps most important, was which identical twin was the donor: Roger or Andrew Chamberlain? Did they even know themselves?

Leo felt he was no closer to getting his answers when he went into work early the next morning. The incident room had that tired smell of too many people putting in too many hours for too little result. Rings left by old coffee cups stained the tables and the bins were full of supermarket sandwich wrappers. Leo didn't have a dedicated desk like he might've expected when he started his career fifteen years ago. Big inquiries like this were housed where there was space, sometimes utilising completely different police stations. At times, he felt like a wandering gypsy, setting up his caravan in a different camp. At least it made it harder for the press to track him down for comment. *They seek him here, they seek him there* … The only way you could tell he'd moved in for the duration was the bonsai tree he placed on his desk at the beginning of each case – a Chinese elm with a beautifully twisted trunk about ten centimetres high. He spent a moment contemplating it. It had come to represent him among the team under his command; it was his mascot. Suyin had even found a tiny star to go on top last Christmas when they were on the Khan case. He was impressed that his colleagues and the cleaning staff never mistreated it. No files were dumped on it or and there was no overwatering behind his back. It looked healthy amidst the crisp and biscuit packets. There had to be something deeply ingrained in the British psyche about gardening, even on this miniature scale.

That gave him an idea. He could use expert help. He thumbed through his contacts to find his most recent date.

'Linda, I hope I'm not disturbing you too early?'

'Leo? Gosh, no. But I wasn't expecting you to call.' And her tone suggested it wasn't welcome. She probably feared he was reneging on their 'let's be friends' pact.

Leo smiled grimly. She was trying to warn him off. 'It's about a case I'm working on.'

'Oh?' She sounded interested now, not to mention relieved. That wasn't flattering. 'Don't tell me, you've opened a cold case and Capability Brown is finally going to have to pay for his crimes against the formal garden?'

'Yeah, we're going to throw the book at him. It does touch on one of his schemes. What can you tell me about the estate grounds at Kingston Manor?'

She searched her mental filing system. 'Kingston Manor? Kingston Manor? I've got it – the hunting box, or small manor house, in a village near the White Horse. Elegant and hardly a box, given it has over thirty rooms. Belonged to the Warnfords, didn't it? Sir Harold Warnford was a courtier of some kind, and merchant. That probably meant blood money from slavery, looking at the dates.'

'That's the one.'

'I've not made a study of it in person as the landowner wouldn't give me permission to visit but I've examined the original plans in the archive. It has the biggest icehouse in Europe – quite extraordinary considering the house was only meant as a place to stay when fox hunting, or whatever it was they hunted then. Maybe deer? Lord knows. Anyway, the Warnfords must've anticipated a lot of parties because they made sure they could cold-store enough food and provide ice for an army of sorbet eaters. Brown designed an attractive dome-shaped building in a copse to hide it from the main house, rather like a folly. But it's more of an iceberg than an icehouse.'

'Meaning?'

'There's much more underground than you see from the surface.'

'I don't suppose you have a copy of those plans, do you?'

'I can dig them out for you. Give me a few minutes. What's your email?'

Leo gave her the information. He drew a dome on his notepad surrounded by little elm trees. There was something here, he knew it. Did he have enough to get a warrant to search the place? An Englishman's home was also his castle.

But the commune was only a tenant. What if he asked the major for permission? If he could convince Roger Chamberlain that he had cause to believe a girl might be trapped there, or had fallen in by mistake ...? A responsible landlord would let him look just to eliminate that possibility, wouldn't he? Lisette, aka Sister Poppy, was still worryingly missing; Julie and Aaron were dead; that should be enough for any concerned citizen.

'I hope I've been helpful?' asked Linda tentatively, probably wondering why Leo had gone silent on her.

'Sorry, I was just thinking. You have. Thank you.'

'Helpful to police enquiries always sounds so ominous.' He could hear the smile in her voice now. 'Leo, how about coming up to town in November? There's a lecture series on at the V&A about Victorian cultivators and their connection to the graphic designers of the era that I think you might like.'

'That does sound right up my street. Let's compare diaries.'

'I'll send you the link so you can see which one you fancy. Goodbye.'

Leo ended the call, re-energised now that he had a sense of direction. The first place he was going this morning was back to the stables.

The major, however, wasn't so cooperative with Leo's inquiry as his gardening expert had been. Not because Major Chamberlain was actively blocking access but because he'd had the inconvenient inspiration to go to see the racing at Goodwood and wasn't expected back until the evening.

'Really, Inspector, if you wanted him to be here, you should've rung and made an appointment,' said Mrs Chamberlain.

'Yes, of course, you're right,' said Leo, politeness covering for annoyance. 'I'm sorry for disturbing you.' He'd caught Mrs Chamberlain standing in the hallway in wellingtons with dog leads in hand, but going out or coming in he wasn't sure. The dogs had so much energy it was hard to tell if they'd been walked or not. He fended off a few inquisitive noses and scratched the more obedient heads. 'May I leave a message?'

'What did you want to speak to him about?' She wedged

her heel in the bootjack, which answered the question about coming or going.

'I wanted to talk to him about having a look for a missing person in the grounds of the manor.'

'A missing person? This is the first I've heard of that. I thought you had two bodies; don't tell me you think there's a third?' She levered off the second boot.

He sincerely hoped not. 'It might be connected but even if not, I still want to eliminate the outhouses at the manor from my enquiries.

She lined her empty wellingtons up against the wall and hung up the leads. The dogs subsided, giving Leo a final sniff before heading off to find their beds. How Mrs Chamberlain managed to still look formidable standing there in boot socks, Leo didn't know, but there wasn't an inch of give about her.

'Then it's my husband you want. I have nothing to do with that side of things. Anything else?'

Had her husband had any calls from biological daughters recently? 'Have you had any strangers asking to see him?'

'Other than yourself?'

Touché. 'I mean a young woman.'

'Inspector, I'm not sure I like the implication of what you are saying.'

'No implication, just a question.' This was a prod on an exposed nerve; there was something there.

'Ask my husband. I have things to do.' And with that she shut the door on him.

The Chamberlains really did have a gift for rubbing him up the wrong way. There was only one member of the family that he could bear. He headed for Iona's home, hoping he'd get lucky and find her there and not at one of her endless meetings.

'Inspector, have you come to rescue me?' Iona asked as she answered his knock. Her chin-length hair was held back by a scarf and she was in a casual sweatshirt and jeans.

'You need rescuing?'

'Sermon writing. Not my favourite part of the job. Nobody really likes the sermon. Modern boredom thresholds are so low. Come in.' She led him through to her study where her laptop showed the composition hadn't gone very far. 'Can you believe that one of my predecessors in the eighteenth century published his sermons? I've had a look – all turgid stuff and it would take over an hour just to read one of them out. I couldn't get away with ten minutes of that material. I'm wittering. Take a seat.' She took a pile of papers off an upright chair. 'I heard about that poor man. Such a tragedy. And your friend, is she all right?'

Leo sat down. From here he could see a flock of sparrows mobbing the peanuts she'd put out for them on the back lawn. 'She's safe. Back in Oxford.'

'Just as well. One death is appalling but seems like an isolated event. Two seems ...' She let her words tail off.

'Seems what?'

She rubbed her upper arms briskly. 'Malevolent.'

Perhaps, but he didn't want to go back to the discussion about dark undercurrents. 'Do you know why I'm here?'

She gazed over his head at her cassock hanging on the door behind him. 'I presume the tests are back?'

'Correct. The girl who died shares twenty-five percent of her genes with you. That tells us she almost certainly is your biological half-sister, but I think you knew that. As she was raised in the States, I assume you didn't know she existed until she turned up dead?'

'Maybe not half-sister,' she said flatly.

'Cousin then, related via your uncle who is your father's identical twin. Iona, how did you know what the result would show?'

'Oh, for crying out loud!' Iona suddenly leapt to her feet and banged on the window. Leo saw that the birds had been joined by a very prosperous looking rat. It had managed to climb up the bird table's stem, using its tail to steady itself. Rats were not to be deterred by mere noise. Iona opened the door that led into the garden and threw a tennis ball at it. The sparrows and the rat fled. 'Sorry, that wasn't very St Francis of me, but I can't abide rats.'

She was delaying her answer? Why? 'You should get the council to provide a trap.'

'I'll add that to the bottom of my to-do list.' She flopped back in the chair.

'Iona?' She pursed her lips together. 'Reverend Chamberlain-Turner?'

'That's just it.' She pointed to him. 'You've nailed it. I can't answer this just as Iona. I've been given some information in a confidential setting as a minister to this parish. I can't even tell my nearest and dearest. I need you to work out the links yourself. I've helped you as far as my conscience will allow.'

Leo thought about this for a moment. He felt like an outline was just coming into sight, like a tree looming out of the fog, but he couldn't quite put all the elements together. 'Is anyone in immediate danger?'

'God, no! I'd tell you if I thought that was the case.'

'And you can't tell me who else knew that Julie Dorchester was related to you?'

She shook her head.

'I'll ask your family. You do understand that, don't you?'

'I do. But if you can avoid saying how you made the connection, then I'd be grateful.'

'And what do you feel, Iona – and I'm talking to Iona now, not the priest – about the fact that your relative – sister, cousin, whatever – is dead.'

'Feel?' She pulled the headscarf off and let her hair flop forward. 'I feel ... I feel sad. Not because I felt any familial tie to her though – at least, only in a small part of me. Some strange illogical instinct that does value blood ... But it wouldn't have been a real relationship; we had no shared memories or love for each other. She's not Ella. How could she be that to me? When medical science developed so that someone could selflessly donate part of themselves to allow others the joy of having a child, then it wasn't meant to be a burden on the family they didn't know. Julie would never have been a Chamberlain, nor should she want to be one. It's more than blood; it's history. Doubtless she had her own.'

'She did. Two loving parents, and until two years ago, an older brother. He died young of a congenital heart condition.'

She squeezed the scarf in her fist, an old-fashioned gesture of hand-wringing that somehow suited her. 'That just adds to the sadness, doesn't it? I saw them on the news, the parents. To lose both children – that should never happen to someone. You shouldn't have to bury your own child, but so many have to do so. It would be wrong to pretend it rarely happens. I can think of four or five in my care that have gone through this in the last decade. Such pain. We all know it, even if at a remove. The face in the school photo who doesn't appear in the next class picture. Don't we all have one of those in our past?'

She was right. Leo could remember a boy lost to cancer and a girl who drowned from his own schooldays. He thought of them often, his ghosts.

'Iona, I won't ask you to break the secrets of the confessional, or whatever it is that you Anglicans have.'

'It's not a sacrament, but a promise – and I like to keep my promises to those that trust me.'

'But I will find out what it means that Julie was related to you and, if you are hiding something criminal, even because you feel you should as their priest, that won't protect you.'

'I know.' Her voice seemed to come from far away. 'But that's what I signed up for, Inspector. Life is full of sacrifices.'

Chapter 29

Jess

I woke in the middle of the night several times wondering where I was. It was a breathless terror, finding myself wrapped in the duvet like I'd been swallowed by a snake. My body was still fighting the shitty drugs.

'You're at Michael's,' I reminded myself. But my body was still revved, still on the alert. Nowhere felt safe. The events of the night before became a strange soup of memory. I'd dig in and fish out another image – bodies writhing together on the grass, white masks suddenly looming out of the darkness, a waning moon overhead. Who had Brother Gorse argued with? Had that argument turned nasty and led to his death? Was Father Oak hiding a darker side to his character? An extreme form of 'my way or the highway' when the old man stopped him approaching me?

It didn't help my thoughts that, when I did wake early and begin prowling, I discovered Michael's kitchen counter covered in articles he'd printed out about cult leaders. Jim Jones – a psychopath surely to kill so many? Joseph di Mambro and

Luc Jouret, who in the 1990s set up a deadly doomsday sect in Switzerland, which in itself was bizarre. Suicidal killings in the land of cuckoo clocks and secret bank accounts? Who did that? More importantly, who fell for that?

The vulnerable, the needy, those who wanted someone to tell them what the heck life was about. The usual victims. And the children. The innocents, dragged in by their idiot parents. Hadn't I felt the pull Father Oak exerted over his flock? I'd let him massage my breasts, for heaven's sake. I could hardly claim I was in no danger of falling for a cult.

And who could forget David Koresh and his Waco standoff in 1993 that ended so bloodily? I saved my tears for the little ones, not the adults like me. That madman Koresh thought – or claimed – he was the Messiah. Not much Christlike sacrificing of himself for others and a whole lot of making others suffer.

Why was Michael hip-deep in this stuff?

From his notes, which I, of course, shouldn't have been reading, his interest seemed to be in whether the leaders actually believed in their own message. The more lost in their fantasy they became, the less likely they would listen to arguments for self-preservation when the authorities came knocking.

What did that mean for the Children of the White Horse? England wasn't America, but then I would've said the temperament of the Swiss ran counter to cult behaviour too. I suppose that taught you never to think it couldn't happen to you. I wasn't convinced that Father Oak was a hundred percent inside his own story. I felt like maybe he liked it, had a loose belief in it, but he had retained a sense of humour and understanding of how others saw him. He reminded me of a joy rider who sees a nice car, steals it for the hell of it, and decides to drive it as far as he can get away with it. While he's in it, he's the driver, but he doesn't feel ownership of the model. I couldn't see Father Oak going as far as the Joneses and Koreshes of this world. He wouldn't die for it or kill for it.

God, I hoped not.

At seven, I made myself a bowl of porridge. Michael had to be sleeping in. Restless, I decided to get the phone call to Tanglewood over with.

'Hey, Tanglewood, sorry for ringing so early.'

'You've news?' she asked eagerly.

'Yes, but not everything I hoped I could get you. I've not found Lisette. But I do know more than I did.' I explained about the shoes and how I'd tracked her down as my predecessor. 'I picked up from a few comments that it's likely she was enjoying herself as the leader's lover but she left around the time of Julie Dorchester's death last week. I don't know if that's connected but it's possible that it scared her off.'

'If a death didn't make the scales fall from her eyes, then nothing would.'

'Do you have any idea where she would go? She'd have no ordinary clothes or money if she left suddenly.'

'No, I don't.' Tanglewood was taking deep breaths to calm herself. 'Oh Lord, I'm not sure this leaves me in a better place. At least before you went in, I could fool myself that she was safe, but she's not safe, is she?'

'I'm sorry. I wish I had better news but I had to tell you what I found.'

'Of course you did. I'm not blaming you.'

'I feel I've failed you.'

'But you're not stopping there, are you? You still have to find her.'

'Tanglewood, I really don't know how much more I can do.'

'She went missing from the commune with no money, nothing. The answers are there. You have to go back.' She was desperate, and I felt her pressure through the phone. It was a mother begging for her child, one of the strongest forces on earth. 'Please.'

'It's not that easy. There was another death. A friend of mine fell and died. I found him. They took me to hospital.' I wasn't explaining this very well. 'I'm OK but I'm not sure of my welcome any more.'

'And you have no ideas where she could be, none at all?'

I thought of the icehouse, the mystery of the light when the rest of the manor was dark. 'I've just got one remaining possibility – but it's really not very likely. I do think she's just made herself scarce and will turn up again.' At least, I was almost sure.

'Can't you check it out? Please?' She could hear my reluctance. 'If you do this, I'll pay you in full.'

I had plans for that money. My willpower was pathetic; I was so bloody temptable. I could go this evening. Not as a member of the cult but after dark when there was no one in the gardens. I knew my way about now. All I needed to do was break into the icehouse and check no one was being held captive there, then get out. The risk was minimal. What could they do even if they did find me? I could claim I was just back from hospital. My presence at the icehouse might take a bit more finessing but I could probably come up with some story. Anyway, dressed properly in black clothes, I stood a very good chance of not being seen so none of the other issues need hold me back. My biggest challenge was getting there. I wondered if Cory would lend me her Brompton folding bike?

'OK. I'll give it one last go and then I really think you'll have to get the police to make the running on this.'

'Thank you, thank you. I knew you wouldn't fail me.'

'I probably will but I'll do my very best for one last attempt and then we'll call it a day, OK?'

She didn't reply.

Cory was only too delighted to let me take the bike. She hauled it out of the shed, removing a coil of hose that had been wrapped around it.

'Keep it, please. It's been admonishing me every time I see it, reminding me that I promised myself to cycle when I go up to London with my job.'

'And you haven't taken it on the train?'

'I took one look at the traffic around Paddington and decided I wanted to live more than I wanted to cycle.'

It was her day with the children, and the au pair's day off, but Benji and Leah were both at nursery. We had the house to ourselves.

'So tell me what's it like being in a cult?' She got out an avocado to make us a dip for lunch.

'Surprisingly hard work. Life without electricity and machines sucks.'

'It may surprise you, Jess, but you aren't the first human to realise that. All my refugees would do anything to get away from living without modern conveniences.' Cory was very involved in her work in refugee camps. She tended to bring it home with her.

'Yeah, I know. Welcome to the capitalist society. It isn't mega riches that motivate most of us but the ability to switch on a light when it gets dark.'

'And was the sex good?' She handed me a packet of cream crackers.

I spluttered on my fizzy water. 'Didn't get any.'

'Oh, shame.'

'Could've done, but when the moment arrived, I wasn't in the mood. Public orgies on the hillside turn out not to be my thing.'

'But private ones ...?'

'I'll get back to you on that. Insufficient data.'

She laughed. 'You do that. I'm not surprised you didn't go for it. Sex outdoors when you're trying to avoid being caught by your parents is all very well, but grown-ups have beds for a reason.' She patted her butt.

'I'd say it was the knees that benefitted most. Are we giving too much away about our sexual habits?' I dipped a cracker into the avocado.

'Is there ever anything that is too much between friends?'

I paused to think about it. 'Definitely, yes.'

Cory sighed. 'And that just shows how limited my imagination is.'

I had plenty of time to consider the wisdom of my actions as I sat on the bus to Swindon. This regular service didn't serve the villages so I'd asked the driver to let me off at the nearest turn to the White Horse. I took the seat at the front of the top deck and watched the countryside roll by. It was a sclerotic road, narrowing arteries between stretches of free-flowing dual carriageways. Buildings – garages, pubs, farms – only cropped up intermittently with most of the space given over to grazing and the occasional crop of solar panels. As we approached Swindon, wind turbines appeared on the horizon. It was in the back of my mind that Leo and Michael would not approve if they knew what I was doing. That was why I wouldn't tell them. What they wouldn't understand was that this job meant the difference between having the money to develop my business and having to carry on in a variety of part-time positions. And if I was serious about the business, I couldn't back away from a hunt just because there was a slight chance it would be dangerous. The commune hadn't really felt geared up for violence, had it? That was just my projection when I got scared. They punished bad behaviour with cleaning fireplaces, for heaven's sake! It was too ... too gothic to let imagination run away and invent dungeons and gory retribution. This was the twenty-first century, not the Dark Ages.

But I couldn't shake my deep-seated unease that I was heading into danger.

Think of the money.

Both Michael and Leo had texted to check I was OK. I wrote upbeat replies and switched off the location finder so Michael couldn't track me. Cory had promised to cover for me and also raise the alarm in the unlikely event that I wasn't back on the first bus in the morning. Getting off at the lay-by bus stop, I thanked the driver and then spent five minutes trying to work out how to unfold the Brompton. A serviceman from the nearby army base at Shrivenham pulled over on his motorbike to help. He was cute, but too young for me, sadly.

Thanking him for solving the mystery of the handlebars, I pulled on a black ski hat, mouthpiece folded up so I didn't look like a bank robber, and began my cycle to Kingston Beauchamp. I was a little worried I'd come across the police in the village but Leo told me that he'd gone back to Oxford. The results on Brother Gorse were in but he couldn't tell me what they said.

And that didn't sound ominous?

I checked the pub car park for any signs of the boys and girls in blue. There were no squad cars, though I couldn't exclude the possibility that Leo's colleagues were driving unmarked vehicles. But I had several hours to kill before it got fully dark. I wasn't going to spend them crouched in a ditch somewhere when there was a perfectly good public house available – and this time I had money.

First I did a quick walk-through to check it was all clear. I'd stuffed my hat in my pocket so I just looked like I had a taste for slimming black clothes. I then approached the bar.

'What'll you have, love?' asked the bug-eyed barman, gaze on the pint he was pulling.

'A big glass of your Sauvignon, please.'

He looked up, looked at my face, then at the tenner I held out. 'You jacked it in?'

'Between you and me, I was never really in. I was on a job.' Look at me, the super discreet agent sharing her secrets with the village gossip. My mouth had a mind of its own.

His expression perked up from depressed to morose. He put the beer down in front of his last customer and reached for a wine glass. 'Oh yeah? What kind of job was that?'

I couldn't compound the mistake of my truth-telling by giving him the full story. 'Research into pagan cults, for my MA.' At least that would check out with how I'd been introduced to the commune if my words got back to them.

He put the wine down in front of me. 'I have to say you really commit to your studies.' I tried to hand him the note but he waved it away. 'On the house.'

'*Now* you're generous?'

He grinned. 'I'd say you earned it.'

If I lived nearer this pub and made it my local, I'd say there was a good chance that we might even become friends. I had a soft spot for curmudgeons.

I took my drink to a corner table near the fire and drank a toast in memory of Brother Gorse.

Chapter 30

Leo

It was official: Leo had another suspicious death on his hands. The blood sample from Aaron Barks came back positive for a cocktail of drugs. They had likely been delivered into his bloodstream by the scotch in the flask found on his person. The liquid left in that – there hadn't been much – also tested positive for the mix. Whoever had doctored it – and Leo couldn't rule out that Barks had done this himself – had included a large amount of cannabis oil, along with a psychedelic drug extracted from magic mushrooms that was listed on the report under the more official name psilocybin mushroom. Little wonder that Jess had been knocked sideways by the combination.

There were a few facts Leo could rely on. Everyone had been taking variations of this combination of drugs at the ceremony. Barks had offered Jess his flask, saying it was pure whisky, but it hadn't been. Both had been badly affected by the contents. Jess had wandered away, Barks had wandered to his death – or been encouraged to go over the edge. There were no signs of a struggle and the bruising was consistent with a fall down a steep slope. The actual cause of death had been heart failure, probably from the shock. He'd broken his wrist in the fall but not his neck. A younger, fitter man might well have survived. The coroner was unlikely to be able to make a clear ruling on these facts so Leo would roll it into his ongoing investigation and see if he could gather more to make the events clearer.

Leo flipped through the file on Barks. Now he had the name, it had been easy to pull the record from the police database. He'd also tracked the one surviving sister to an old people's home in Leytonstone. She'd not heard from her brother for years and didn't seem keen on the idea of taking charge of the body for a funeral when it was released. With her help, and with what had made it onto the system from paper records, Leo discovered that Barks had moved around for most of his life and often had minor run-ins with authority. His first drug offence for possession of LSD was recorded in the 60s. It wasn't the right attitude for a policeman but Leo felt a surge of respect of the man to have been part of that mythologised youth culture. He'd probably had long hair and little glasses like John Lennon and made love not war, Leo mused. Not a bad use of youth. His life had never travelled any conventional routes – no bank account or mortgage, just a trail of temporary addresses, usually near political hotspots such as Greenham Common or the Newbury bypass. In the last decade he'd spent most time in Somerset living in an experiment in carbon-neutral living. That was another thing Leo found admirable. Being caught with a pocketful of home-grown marijuana from time to time didn't seem the worst thing a man could do. Would such a man purposely drug a young woman whom he'd promised to protect? Leo thought, on balance, no. That meant Gorse had been duped and his flask tampered with. Many of the commune members had mentioned that he was known for carrying his own supply 'to keep out the cold nights'. Someone might've taken advantage of that habit.

Harry came over and lounged on the corner of his desk. 'Leo, I've been thinking.'

He didn't give the obvious response, just thought it. 'Yes? About what?'

The big sergeant folded his arms. The top button of his shirt was undone, his tie askew. 'We have three main questions: who killed Julie Dorchester, did someone kill the old guy, and where's the missing girl, Lisette White?' The faces of the two dead people were at the top of the incident board, Lisette off to the right with a question mark next to her.

Leo sat back, listening. 'Correct.'

'There's one person who connects two of them: Jessica Bridges.' He took a sharpie and drew a line between them, adding Jess's name. 'I think we should bring her in for questioning. She knows more than she's letting on.' He threw the pen down on the desk and Leo had to catch it before it rolled off.

'What makes you think that?'

'I talked to Suyin. Apparently, the woman was cavorting around in the noddy before she went to share a sideshow with Barks. And she was there at the foot of the hill when you found them both. Doesn't that look suspicious to you?'

'She's explained what she remembers.'

Harry pulled Jess's picture out of the file they kept on commune members and added it to the board with a magnet. 'You haven't put her up there but she just keeps cropping up. At first, I thought she was just one of those troublesome women, sticking their nose in where they're not wanted, but now I think she's in deeper than that. I buy that she went in there undercover, but then matters went further.'

'What do you mean?'

Harry gave a salacious grin. 'Another thing Suyin learned is that all the women who have the name Sister Poppy in the commune are known to be O'Brien's bit of stuff on the side. So she was having it away with O'Brien and the old geezer. They argued over her. O'Brien spiked the drink so he could push the competition off the edge. Murder.' Harry slapped the picture of O'Brien that had already made it onto the board. 'With her testimony, we should nail the bastard with it.'

Leo tried to keep professional detachment but it was hard where Jess was concerned. 'She wasn't sleeping with O'Brien.'

'How do you know that?'

'She told me.'

'The woman lies.'

She did, but everyone did. When Jess lied it was usually to spare someone's feelings or her own embarrassment.

Harry wasn't giving up. 'By her own account, she was one of the last to see Aaron Barks alive. If O'Brien didn't do it, maybe she even helped the old guy over the edge?'

Anger threatened to crack Leo's professional reserve. 'Why? What motive?' he snapped.

'They were both out of their heads. They don't need a motive, just an accident. But we still need to ask.'

'I've asked her and she found him at the bottom of the hill.'

'But from your record of the interview, you didn't ask her under caution. Leo, we've all noticed the way you treat her. If you won't bring her in for questioning, I might have to go to the superintendent to report that I believe your feelings for a suspect are compromising your judgment.' And Harry would just love that. It was doubtful he really suspected Jess; he just wanted to get under Leo's skin and prove to their superiors that the man they had promoted over him had flaws.

'I know what Jess Bridges will say. I've already spoken to her on numerous occasions.' Was Harry right? Were his feelings compromising his judgment?

'Then you don't need to worry about asking her the same questions under caution, do you?'

He was being backed into a corner and they had an audience of other members of his team. 'I'll think about it.'

'Leo, you know it's the right thing to do, even if just to clear her.'

'I don't suspect her of anything.'

'The rest of the team doesn't share your confidence.'

So Harry had been elected to present this argument, had he? Leo noticed his colleagues weren't meeting his eyes while they surreptitiously monitored the discussion.

He made a show of looking at his watch. 'It's past end of shift and this can wait. I'll ask Jess Bridges to come in voluntarily in the morning to be interviewed and make her statement.'

Harry stood up. 'All right. You do that.'

It was past time he put a stop to Harry's disrespectful tone with him. 'All right, *Inspector* George.' He waited.

Harry looked furious, his face flushing. 'May I go now, *Inspector George?*'

'Yeah, you're all dismissed.' He felt betrayed that his team had chosen Harry of all people to broach this subject with him. 'We'll pick this up in the morning.'

His officers trailed out with a variety of farewells and shuffling into coats. Leo waited them out. He didn't feel like he'd won his point with Harry. In fact, he'd probably just made life more difficult for himself in future. Harry was already straining at the limits put on his behaviour. Leo would have to have a word with the superintendent and request that Harry be deployed elsewhere, on the grounds that he didn't take well to Leo's authority. Add to this the fear that Harry had identified Leo's weak spot – Jess – and would push on it with all his might, possibly managing to derail Leo's so far steady career climb.

Fuck.

Leo got out his phone and tried ringing Jess. He didn't want to do this by text. There was no answer. He rang her landline.

'Hi.'

'Cory, it's Leo ... Inspector George. Is Jess there?'

There was a long pause. 'Sorry, I missed that. Benji was yelling something.'

Leo hadn't heard the children, and it was gone eight-thirty. Wouldn't a five-year-old be in bed? 'I asked if Jess was there?'

'I think she turned in early. She's still not a hundred percent. Can I take a message?'

'Ask her to call me. She has my number. It doesn't matter how early.'

'Absolutely. Call Inspector George when she wakes up. Got it. Is that everything?'

'Yes. Thank you.'

Leo slipped the phone back into his jacket. Cory had lied to him but he couldn't call her bluff. How would that look, knocking on the door of a single parent's house with two minors in residence just to check someone was in bed as claimed? With the hand tucked in his pocket, he stroked the phone thoughtfully. Call Michael? Ask him to check the app he'd used to locate her yesterday? That was pushing his authority too far. He could do that as a friend but not as a detective inspector.

He tried ringing her several times before he went to bed. Towards midnight, he finally gave up and sent a text.

It would have to be a message after all.

Jess, please come to Kidlington police station tomorrow at the earliest possible moment you can make it. New evidence has come to light and we have some more questions for you which will be conducted under caution.

He thought of Harry's gleeful tone, hoping to catch Jess out in some wrongdoing.

You may wish to bring a solicitor.

From the flashing ellipsis he could see she was reading it. So, not in bed asleep then – or at least, still picking up her messages. The dots vanished and she didn't reply.

Chapter 31

Jess

I left my getaway vehicle chained up at the pub. Bob, the landlord, had bike racks for the growing tribe of Mamils (middle-aged men in Lycra), who cycled to his pub at the weekend. I then walked out of the village centre towards the manor, pulling on my ski hat as I did so. That gave me a cheap thrill that I was doing something seriously edgy. I wasn't going to try the front gate, not fancying my chances of scaling the two-and-a-half metres to the spiked top, but I thought I could probably get over the estate wall somewhere in the woods. When trees came down and knocked over the high stone wall, it took a while for the landlord to repair it. It was just a question of following the boundary until I found a spot, preferably far out of sight of the road or the house.

My night sight wasn't great but I'd made the decision not to risk a torch. I had a small one in my back pocket for emergencies but relied on the slight wash of moonlight to help out. It got very dark under the trees and I nearly twisted my ankle on several occasions and had my shins ripped at by brambles. The sports leggings I was wearing made for ease of movement but offered little protection.

Note to self: *next time you break in somewhere, wear thicker trousers.*

I finally found what I was looking for: a large tree had come down in one of the storms earlier this autumn and had taken with it the top of the wall. Using a combination of pulling myself up on the fallen trunk and hooking a leg over the stone wall, I managed to make an inelegant entry to the manor grounds. More Johnny English than James Bond was my own verdict. It took me a moment to orientate myself. Looking back through the trees, I could see the foreleg of the White Horse on the hill behind me. That gave me my bearings. I just needed to head straight and I should hit the pasturelands, in the middle of which lay the copse surrounding the icehouse.

The rough ground did not improve inside the walls. I spent many a painful moment untangling myself from brambles. Tanglewood. Whoever had named my client had a strange sense of humour. It was not the most loving name to give a baby.

Finally, I came out of the trees. A sweep of pasture lay before me, grey in the moonlight. I had a rude shock when something about waist-high and black shot past me but then I realised it was only a muntjac that I had disturbed. I knew that Sister Rosemary, one of those in charge of the kitchen garden, waged a long running battle against these persistent little deer, building more and more protections for her most vulnerable seedlings. Nature wasn't so much red in tooth and claw around here as bloody persistent, she'd told me. I felt a bit bad breaking into the commune like this. The members like Sister Rosemary, Sister Briar, and my special friend, Brother Gorse, had been sweet people, none of them wanting to make any trouble or have a negative impact in their passage through life. How many of us could say the same? Was what I was doing ethical? They'd invited me in, given me a home in good faith, and I repaid them like this? The fact that I suspected some of them of not being sincere didn't justify what I was doing.

Remember the money. Remember the mother.

That second thought salved my conscience somewhat and I pressed on.

The icehouse wasn't hard to find. It was marked out by the tall trees that surrounded it like a feathered crown topping a giant bald head. The gate yielded to my touch and I followed the gravel path to the entrance. I remembered from my earlier visit that the door was secured by a padlock. I had raided Cory's toolkit and bought a hammer, chisel and a hacksaw with me, hoping one of them would yield results. I resolved that I really needed to improve my knowledge of how to break in to places if I were to carry on in this career. Were there lessons for that? DIY burglary seminars online? I wouldn't put it past someone to have posted a course on YouTube.

When I reached the icehouse door, I had a quick look around. The copse appeared deserted and was too far from the house for any sound to carry over there. There was no light this time spilling through the cracks in the doorframe but there was still that same damp green smell I'd noticed earlier.

'Lisette? Lisette, are you in there?' I wasn't sure why I was calling out. She could be hiding there or held a prisoner, but if she'd been in here for a whole week, it was very unlikely she would be close enough to the door to answer. And if she'd somehow got trapped in there, would she even still be alive?

OK, I wasn't going to think like that. I put the penlight in my teeth like I'd seen Tom Cruise do in a movie and took out my tools. I looked at the lock. Shit, this wasn't going to be easy was it?

Having tried fruitlessly with the hammer and chisel, in which I'd done nothing but take off a chunk of my own knuckle as I scraped it against the wooden door in a mishit, I resorted to the hacksaw. It took a long while but finally I was through. The drawback of this procedure was that they would know someone had broken in. I just had to hope I'd be long gone before they began investigating and that they didn't call in the police to take fingerprints.

Crap. I should've worn gloves, shouldn't I? I really was an incompetent burglar.

But I'd been here earlier in the week before Pine turned me away. I could claim that I'd left the prints then. I'd just have to be careful not to touch anything once I was inside.

I pushed open the door. I could sense a void in front of me and warm moist air. Taking the penlight, I shone it into the dark interior. I had heard it was large but it was much bigger than I'd expected, going down well beyond the reach of my little beam. But what was most striking was the row upon row of planters on the walls. The entire icehouse was given over to the growing of cannabis plants. Vertical farming – how on trend. That explained a lot. No wonder Brother Maple hadn't wanted me sticking my nose in here, literally my *nose* as the smell was unmistakable now I had the chance to breathe it in. I'd not seen anyone smoking or using marijuana at the commune and no servings of hash brownies, more's the pity. There was too much here for Brother Maple's private use, or even the use of a select few who were in on the secret. The size and scale of this operation suggested that this was being grown to be sold on. A little cottage drug industry on the North Downs ... how homespun and how dangerous for anyone who found out.

I had to remember why I was here. I'd work out what I would do with this information when I was safe but for now I had to confirm that Lisette wasn't hiding out, being kept prisoner, or trapped. Pulling my sweater up to cover my hands, I groped around on the wall and found a light switch and turned it on. The switch lay next to a complicated control pad that appeared to regulate the irrigation system and phases of light and dark for optimum growing conditions. And that cleared up another mystery: the exorbitant electricity bill. It had to have been running out here day and night but, no doubt, they covered their costs by what they got for the product. It was quite neat really and likely very profitable.

The light also revealed that I was standing at the very top of the building. I felt like a pigeon who had landed in the roof of an enormous dovecot. It was disorientating; I had to remind myself I was at ground level. The gardeners got down to the lower reaches via a long ladder that could be moved around the walls from the gallery at the top, like a circular library ladder. At the bottom I could see a heap of sacks and plastic boxes and a winch system. If Lisette, or Lisette's body, was going to be here, that was the place.

Was I going to do this? I could still call Leo and ask him to come and look for me. I had a crime to report after all. I pulled out my phone and saw a message from him and many missed calls. He wanted me for questioning tomorrow morning. Shit. That did not sound friendly. Telling him I'd broken in somewhere didn't seem like it was going to go down well. I was on my own. I had to check for Lisette, then back off and forget I was ever here.

I closed the door to the outside so my presence wasn't so noticeable, making sure it would swing back open. The last thing I wanted was to lock myself in here by mistake. Switching off my torch and shoving it in my pocket, I seized the rungs of the ladder and began climbing down. At least it was good cardio. This whole case had probably improved my fitness and I hadn't felt the craving for a cigarette more than two or three times. I should take that as a victory for my self-control (she was in the relegation zone in my personal qualities football league). League champion for many years in a row was impulsiveness, in case you were wondering – which you probably weren't by now.

I reached the bottom. The strip lights that regulated the growing plants weren't on, just the sixty-watt bulb in the centre of the ceiling, so it was dark down here. There was a person-sized hump under one bale of sacks and my heart began racing. Maybe I hadn't been so fanciful after all? I got out my torch again and made myself pull back the sacks.

A bag of compost. *Suitable for containers and pots*. And potheads, I added.

I felt stupid. I was Catherine Morland expecting dark secrets in the chest at Northanger Abbey and getting a laundry list instead. Jane Austen would be laughing her high-on-weed head off right now if she could've seen me. A giggle escaped at the image. Can you get high on the smell of weed alone?

A gruff curse came from above, then the light went off and the door slammed.

Shit. Or more precisely, I was in deep shit, surrounded by good shit.

But hang on ... I'd busted the lock! Maybe I could get up there before whoever it was locked me in?

I'd never climbed so fast in my life. It helped that it was dark and I couldn't see how dangerous this was. Then my hand flailed in the dark and I realised I'd reached the top. Getting out my penlight, I scurried on hands and knees to the door. I tried to move the lock. It shifted a little but not enough to let me out. I could hear the padlock banging against the wood. The bugger had put the busted lock back on to hold the catch in place – easy to remove from the outside but not when you're stuck in here.

I thumped on the door. 'Hey, let me out. It's Sister Poppy!' I pressed my ear to the panel. Nothing. Then the light went out on the control panel. My captor must've thrown the switch on the fuse for this place. I checked the electric bulb for confirmation. It stayed dark.

Of course it did, because to leave me here with light would've been too kind.

But hey, I had the technology. I pulled out my phone and confidently called up Leo's number. He'd forgive me, I was sure of it, when I showed him what I'd uncovered.

There was no signal. What? I remembered getting a message from him just the other side of this bloody thick door.

The other side, not this side. Apparently, phone bars didn't make it past the several inches of ancient wood to party with me. I scanned all the way around but the No Service message didn't change.

I swore again and slumped by the exit, hands resting on my knees, head forward. Look on the bright side, I thought, I could get high as a kite if I stayed here. No shortage of that.

And take a plunge off this gallery in some crazy phase where I thought I could fly? No thanks.

But someone knew I was here; the door closing hadn't just been tidying up or they wouldn't have cut the electricity. I was sitting on a very valuable commodity; they wouldn't want to leave this to die. I had to assume they'd panicked and were now going to work out how to handle me. Perhaps they'd go and ask for a second opinion from their collaborators? Ivy, Maple, Pine, and Father Oak all had to be in the know, didn't they? They shouldn't worry too much. I'd come quietly and make myself scarce if only they let me out. I wasn't a hero; I was quite prepared to strike some cowardly deal if it meant I got out unharmed. I had no problem being gagged if I got to live.

They'd better come back soon.

Starving to death was so not on my to-do list.

I just had to wait for morning and see what happened then. Cory would at the very least raise the alarm. She knew I was coming back to the manor, though I didn't think I'd mentioned exactly where I was intending to go. The inspector wouldn't give up if he knew I was missing. Nor would Michael.

It would be OK. Wouldn't it?

Chapter 32

Leo

It was ten o'clock and Jess hadn't rung. Leo made himself another cup of bad coffee and tried to avoid Harry. His team had been running the names from O'Brien's book and several of them had come up in police records. John Regan, aka Brother Maple, was from Hackney, a noted home chemist of the *Breaking Bad* kind. Pine, full name Rune Henriksen, had lost his job on a cruise ship when it was discovered that he had a reputation for selling drugs to the passengers. A new theme connected with drugs was emerging and he would very much like to ask Jess about it, not least so as to get Harry off his back about her.

'Come on, come on,' he muttered under his breath, willing his phone to ring.

He'd finished the coffee and still no sign.

She was obviously avoiding him. He knew she had her foibles but he'd thought their relationship had grown to the point where she would understand that his message was serious and she had to deal with it. She could trust him to be fair when she did come in for interview. Hadn't he already proven that to her?

'Where is she then?'

Christ, Harry had followed him into the gents' and taken a spot next to his. Was nothing sacred?

'I assume you're talking about our witness?'

'Suspect.'

'Witness. You may suspect her, but I don't.' He didn't, did he? But if her conscience was clear, why not turn up and answer questions? Leo zipped up his flies and washed his hands. He scrunched the paper towel with more force than necessary and threw it in the bin.

'Leo—'

Leo walked out. Back at his desk, he picked up his phone. No missed calls. No answers to his follow up texts.

Harry stood before him. 'Inspector George, I note that the person of interest has failed to show up for questioning. I'd like it fucking noted in our enquiry log.'

'Note away,' said Leo. 'I'm chasing it up now. Fucking note that too.' Him and Harry ... it just wasn't sustainable. He went out to the corridor looking for a quieter spot where he wouldn't be overheard. Something wasn't right. 'Cory? It's Leo again.'

'Inspector, I'm on the train.'

He could hear that from the chatter in the background and the announcement of signal failure at Reading.

'I'm trying to reach Jess.'

'I know you are. So am I. I'm pleased you rang. I was going to call.'

His sense of foreboding grew stronger. 'What's happened?'

'Look, I might not've been entirely truthful last night. Jess went back to Kingston Beauchamp for her client. She said she had one last place to look for Lisette before she called an end to her hunt. The mother really laid it on thick about how worried she was and Jess is always a pushover when it comes to appeals like that.'

'When were you expecting her back? She wasn't rejoining the commune, was she?' That would explain the missed calls if she'd had to give up her phone again.

'No, she was done with that, and I expected her back first thing this morning. She took a folding bike and cycled from the main road. She hadn't come home by the time I had to leave for work and Maria, my au pair, was instructed to call me the minute she got in. But Maria's said she's not turned up. Look, Inspector, I'm worried.'

That made two of them.

'I feel responsible as I didn't stop Jess going back. In fact, I think I encouraged her. I was treating it all as a bit of an adventure, a joke even, but it doesn't feel so funny this morning.'

'No, it doesn't. OK, leave it with me. I've got a few lines to tug.'

The next call he put in was to Michael.

'Can it wait, Inspector? I'm in the middle of a tutorial.'

'Sorry but no, it can't. Jess went back to Kingston Beauchamp last night and hasn't returned. Can you see if you can locate her?'

'Christ. I have to take this.' Michael was addressing his students. He then came back to Leo. 'She's opted out of the bloody locating app. She left it last night.'

When she went on the jaunt that she knew neither of them would approve of.

'I'd better get over there and see if I can find her.'

'Do you need my help?'

'I think my officers and I are in the best position to search for her, but thanks for the offer.'

'You'll let me know as soon as you find her?'

'I promise.'

Leo ended that call and leant his head against the wall.

'Are you OK, Inspector?' asked Suyin, coming down the corridor to find him.

'I've found out why our witness isn't here. She's gone missing. Went back to look for Lisette White in Kingston Beauchamp and hasn't been seen since last night.'

'Bloody hell.'

'My thought exactly. Gather the troops; we're going to look for her.'

They found the bike easily enough. It was the only Brompton locked up at the pub. The landlord said he'd seen her leave at about eleven. He hadn't known she was the owner of the bike and was contemplating using bolt cutters to remove it if the owner didn't return by lunchtime opening. He promised to hold onto it until they found her.

'She's a reckless one, that Jess, joining a cult just to study it,' he said.

So Jess had lied to him too about why she was there, or only given him a partial truth? 'If she turns up, let me know so I can call off the search.'

'You don't think she'll turn up dead like the others? I

wouldn't want that to happen to her. She's a nice woman, though she'd drive you crazy if you had to live with her. Reminds me of my first wife.'

'I have no reason to think harm has come to her.' Apart from her status as missing. This really was developing into a hell of a day. Leo had to try hard not to show his alarm.

'You'd better get out there and find her before it does.' The landlord waved them off with a promise of a free round if they found her by lunchtime.

The team fanned out, some of the uniforms searching White Horse Hill where the bodies had been discovered. Leo guessed that Jess would go back to the manor to conduct her search so saved that for the majority of the team. She'd never been happy with the idea that Lisette had just upped and left so suddenly. Leaving Harry and Suyin to run interference at the front gate, he took two men and followed the wall to see if he could spot any sign of her getting in secretly. From what she'd said about the lifestyle, she wouldn't rush to go back into the commune to get her answers. Like him, she was probably more interested in what other secrets the manor held.

They traced the wall to a point where a tree had taken part of it down. This would be the easiest place to get in. They were about to attempt it when Leo heard the fast approach of a vehicle.

'Oy, you lot! What do you think you're playing at? Get down from there!' It was Major Chamberlain, leaning out of his Range Rover window, quite red in the face with fury. There then came a screech of the brakes as Roger Chamberlain recognised the would-be trespasser and the uniforms. 'Oh, Inspector, I didn't expect to see you here. What on earth are you doing?'

Leo dropped back to the ground, wiping his hands off on his trouser legs.

'One of the commune members has gone missing.'

'Not another one? What's wrong with them? Too much trouble, no matter how prompt they are with the rent.' As ever the man was startlingly lacking in compassion.

'Actually, I'm pleased I ran into you, Major. I called by yesterday. Did your wife mention it?'

'Oh yes. Bloody good day yesterday. Two winners. Came home five hundred up.'

The major seemed keener to discuss his gambling wins than to find out what had brought Leo to his door.

'I came to talk to you about searching the manor outbuildings for my missing persons. There's two as of this morning: one from last night, but before that, a girl called Lisette White. Both were known in the commune as Sister Poppy.'

'Christ, how confusing. That place is a madhouse.'

'Do you give permission for me to look?'

'Shouldn't you be asking my tenant?'

'But as landlord, don't you have the right to inspect your property?'

'I suppose I do. Hop in then and I'll take you. By the front gate.'

Leo got in the front while his uniformed officers slid into the back. They didn't have to wait for entry as the major had an opener fitted on his car. Leo was in two minds about whether he should use the opportunity presented by this car journey to raise the issue of whether Chamberlain had been contacted by someone claiming to be his biological daughter but decided that there wasn't enough time and he needed the major's cooperation to find Jess. The other part could wait.

They found Harry and Suyin arguing with Sister Ivy on the front steps. She was insisting that Father Oak was not available and in his absence she didn't feel it her place to agree to them searching the premises.

Major Chamberlain slammed his car door and strode resolutely up the steps towards them.

'Sister Ivy, isn't it? I'm Roger Chamberlain and I own this place. If the police say they want to search it, then I say stand back and let them do so. Understood?'

Sister Ivy glanced over her shoulder to where the big Norwegian and another man stood, guarding the doors. Leo could tell that for one mad moment she considered defying them, but then she stood aside.

'Bless you,' she said fiercely as they walked in.

Leo ignored her. 'Search every room. We are looking for any sign of Jess Bridges or Lisette White. Major, could I ask you to show me the outbuildings?'

'All right.' Roger collared the woman as she passed him. 'Sister Ivy, tell Father Oak I'll be wanting a word when he does make himself available. Tell him I think it's time the Children of the White Horse trotted off somewhere else.'

Chapter 33

Jess

It grew slowly colder in the icehouse. Having been designed to keep things frozen, it actually did quite well at achieving the warmth the plants liked, thanks to the insulation. Still, on a chilly October night, with air creeping in through the gaps around the door and no hot lights to top up the warmth, the temperature was dropping. Thankfully, I had decent skin coverage in the form of my coat, jumper and leggings, not like the night on the Downs where I almost froze in my robe and cloak. The smell of fresh cannabis leaves and the damp were probably worse. This would cure me of any hankerings for a spliff in the near future.

I tried sleeping but that didn't work as I had visions of being caught unawares and rolled off the gallery to my death in the bottom of the pit. So I tried singing to pass the time. The acoustics made even my middling voice sound good and I enjoyed myself for a few verses of Queen, mixed up with Billie Eilish tracks. 'Bad Guy' worked well with the percussion of finger clicks, but even a full and nearly word-perfect rendition of 'Bohemian Rhapsody' couldn't lift my spirits after a while. *Let me go.* I was feeling there was definitely a devil put aside for me somewhere in here.

Perhaps I did doze off, because I was woken to full consciousness by the scrape of the door over the flagstones. As quickly as cramped limbs would allow, I scrambled to my feet and backed up as far from the railing as I could. Daylight poured in, hurting my eyes. A man stood silhouetted in the frame.

'Hello?' I shaded my eyes.

He came in without saying anything and closed the door behind him. My alarm levels rocketed.

'Look, I'm sorry I broke in here. You know me; curiosity is my sin. But I'm no blabbermouth. I can leave and forget I ever saw this. I mean, what "this"? All I see is a derelict icehouse, nothing interesting going on here unless you're a spider or a pigeon.' *Or a drug dealer.*

The electric light switched on; they must've restored the power and I hadn't noticed. Father Oak stood looking at me with sadness in his eyes.

'Sister Poppy, this is unfortunate. I do believe I made a mistake bringing you into our little family.'

So we weren't going to mention the illegal cannabis farm then? 'You might be right. Maybe it's best we part ways, no hard feelings.'

'That presents me with a problem.'

'If you think I'll tell anyone about this, then I promise I won't.' Anyone who knew me would know I was notoriously bad at keeping a secret, but it was my best offer.

'It's not so much what you've seen, though that is unfortunate, but what you've not done.'

'Sorry?'

'Didn't you wonder about the arrangement we came to with those who wanted to leave? How we kept our dealings secret?'

'There are rumours already in the village. You didn't keep your secrets very well.'

He dismissed those with a flick of his fingers. 'Rumours yes, but no eyewitness accounts. It can all be put down to malicious gossip.'

I was beginning to worry that there were no firsthand accounts because they got rid of annoying eyewitnesses like Julie Dorchester. 'So what do you do? Kill anyone who might spill the beans?' *Be angry,* I told myself, *not afraid*. But the churning in my stomach and the chill feel to my skin told me my flight-rather-than-fight instinct was winning the upper hand.

'What? No! We're peaceful people.' Oak sounded genuinely offended.

Tell that to Julie's mum and dad. 'Then you'd better explain, because I'm not really following you.'

'That's the point. You never really followed me, did you?' He reached out to cup my face but I moved away which unfortunately took me closer to the edge. 'I told you that we did things together. I told you that no one was exempt from participating in the starlight ceremony.'

I remembered poor Brother Gorse struggling up the hill, even though anyone with any compassion would've allowed him to stay in bed. 'You did mention this. So? I was there, wasn't I? I took part.'

'Not really. My followers don't take part just because the ceremony is good for body, mind, and spirit. If we've all shared ourselves fully with each other, openly, and so all can see, then none can use it against us. We're all equal.'

I sorted through what he was saying. He was talking about the drugged-up sexfest in the open, wasn't he? And I hadn't joined in, thanks to Brother Gorse.

'You blackmail leavers for their silence?'

'I prefer to say that we have images that we use as security against those who want to ruin our happy little family here. We invite those who might cause problems and gather the same information on them.'

So they silenced the villagers by picking off the trouble-makers and compromising them? 'You never said you would record those sessions.'

'I never said we wouldn't.'

'Does everyone know you do that?'

'If they ask to leave, then I show them.'

Worm. 'And did you show the last Sister Poppy what you had on her?'

He was surprised by the direction of my questioning. 'What are you talking about? Sister Poppy – *that* Sister Poppy – was loyal. I don't know what happened to her. Sister Ivy said she had to leave suddenly. I've not given up hope of her returning. She was a lovely girl.'

But he was talking about her in the past tense which really wasn't reassuring. 'You really need to rethink your naming strategy.' I rubbed my face. 'OK, you're worried about me leaving because you don't have any compromising dirt on me. I get that. You've got your druggy orgies and this business to protect. But I'm not the morality police. What you do is between you and whatever ... your god, your conscience; that's your deal. Look, you're right, I didn't come here in good faith but I didn't come to spy on you.' At least not at first. 'I came here to look for Lisette White – previous Sister Poppy to you – but she's obviously not here. That's why I broke in here last night, just to check. It was the last place I hadn't looked. I had no idea what else you had going on and I say good luck to you – very entrepreneurial and very not my business. So I'll go, forget what I saw, and leave you in peace.'

'That's not enough.'

'You have to understand, I go undercover all the time to look for people. I have a professional reputation to maintain ...' This was laying it on a bit thick, but I had to convince him. 'I don't want my face all over the news in a titillating tabloid exposé. It really is in my interest to walk away.'

'But our rules apply to you whatever your motive for joining us.'

'You ... you want something compromising on me?' Was he suggesting what I thought he was suggesting? Just ugh. Did this guy never give up?

He held out a hand. 'Come to my rooms with me, Poppy, and we'll make love. It needn't be a distressing experience. We can drink, and chat, and enjoy our time together.' That was code for get off our heads and roll around naked in front of a camera? No thanks.

He sensed my reluctance. 'Or we could do it here. There's CCTV.' He nodded up to the little device seated in the shadows of the ceiling. That's how they knew I'd broken in.

'Keep going. I'm waiting for the option that I can stomach.' I circled my hand in a keep-on-rolling gesture. I wasn't sure where I got the guts to sass him but I really wasn't going to do it with the sleazebag. I'd reached a limit I hadn't known I possessed.

'Poppy, Poppy ...' He looked mournful now.

'Let's cut the crap. My name's Jessica Bridges. I look for missing people. I don't get it on with slimy men with a Messiah complex.'

'But you enjoyed my touch a few days ago.'

'Yeah, that was before I realised quite what a prick you are. I thought then you were just having fun with a harmless little power trip, but people have died, Terry.'

He flinched as I pulled out his real name and shot him with it. 'I had nothing to do with that.'

'Oh, really? They died on your watch, at your parties.'

I'd tripped some switch in him. With a sudden move, he closed the gap between us and seized my arms. His face was ugly with rage. 'I. Had. Nothing. To do. With that!' He shook me with each spat phrase. 'Get that into your stupid fucking head!'

'Way to convince me! Get your hands off me.' If I were a better private detective, I would've been able to pull some cool martial arts moves to escape his grip, but I was just an ordinary girl with only a hazy memory of self-defence classes. I had, however, watched *Miss Congeniality* many times. I tried the heroine's tip of stamping on his instep and, when that failed, I went for his balls, but he held me too far away, backing me against the rail.

Shit, Sandra Bullock had failed me. She'd made it look so easy.

He pushed me so I was bent over the void, crowding me so my legs were immobilised.

'You really like to drive people to the end of their tether, don't you?' His grip was bruising.

'That's my superpower.' I squirmed. Crap, I was going to die and I was still blurting out stupid stuff!

'All you needed to do was be sensible. I don't want to harm you.'

'Hey, don't make this my fault!'

Oak mashed his hand over my mouth. 'Shut up! Shut up!' He was now pressed against me so I was having trouble breathing. The rail cut into my waist and my feet had left the ground. One firm push from him and I'd be over. I squealed with fury and fear, clinging on to his shirt with both hands. The cotton tore as I arched backwards. The psycho was going to push me to my death.

Chapter 34

Leo

There was no sign of O'Brien inside the house or in any of the outbuildings. Leo and Roger Chamberlain did find a woman weeping as she made sandals – a Sister Rose who said she'd not seen anyone in there all morning, though she'd noticed Father Oak pass the window about fifteen minutes ago on his way into the gardens.

'Where was he going?' asked Leo.

'To the icehouse. That's what lies down that path.' Rose mishit a stud, her nerves showing. 'But we're not allowed there, not us novices. I don't know anything about it.'

Or what she did know, she wasn't going to admit to the police. What had his date, Linda, the garden expert, called the icehouse? The iceberg. Much more underground than appeared on the surface. Leo would bet that Jess's curiosity would lead her there once she'd explored everywhere else, especially if it was off limits.

And O'Brien had gone that way just fifteen minutes ago.

A lot could happen in that time.

'Come on!' His sense of urgency going into overdrive, he gestured to his team to follow him. He began running down the path.

When they reached the wooded enclosure that contained the icehouse, it looked deceptively quiet. Not much to see but a small brick dome rising out of green turf, a thick wooden door set in the front. No, he was wrong; there was a sign of a disturbance as the padlock had been cut off and the latch hung open. The door was ajar.

Leo swore silently. He didn't have time to plot a raid with his colleagues. None of them were wearing protective gear. He turned to Roger Chamberlain, who had kept up with them.

'Am I right in thinking there's only one way in or out?'

'Yes, Inspector. But it's huge inside, goes down at least twenty feet. Careful as you go in that you don't topple over. You won't survive that fall. You think O'Brien is in there?'

'And Jess Bridges. Please, stand back.' Leo signalled to his team to fall in behind him. 'We have a possible hostage situation. I'm going to make our presence known and try and talk O'Brien out. Keep out of sight unless ordered to follow me in.'

Once the team had taken up their positions, Leo pushed on the handle. The door scraped open.

Leo stood in the entrance. It took a moment for his eyes to adjust but what he saw shocked him to the core. O'Brien was holding Jess over the drop Roger had warned him about. 'O'Brien, step away from the edge and put her down!'

Oak didn't do as he was ordered. He dropped his head to Jess's chest and cursed between sobs. 'I fucking hate you.'

Jess's scared eyes shot to Leo but thankfully she didn't speak, rightly fearing anything she said could provoke him into letting go.

Leo wasn't leaving her hanging like that. He reached past O'Brien and pulled Jess back to firm ground.

'Sergeant!' he called.

Suyin entered and took Jess from him to lead her outside. She collapsed by the path, shaking.

With Jess safe, now Leo could deal with O'Brien. He recited the formal words to make an arrest. O'Brien made no move to resist.

'Would you look at this, boss!' crowed Harry, shining a torch on row upon row of plants. 'We have ourselves a drug bust.'

'We do indeed.' Leo handcuffed O'Brien. 'DS Boston, take O'Brien into custody. Make sure they have room for a few more in the cells. DS Wong, arrest the commune members known as Ivy, Pine and Maple.' Leo followed O'Brien out of the icehouse and crouched beside Jess, placing a reassuring hand on her shoulder. 'Jess, is there anyone else you know directly involved in this?'

She shook her head.

'I'll need a statement.'

She nodded.

'I'll come to your home when I've finished here. I take it you were looking for Lisette White. She isn't here?'

She shook her head again.

'OK, that's all for now. I'll have an officer run you home. You're not injured?'

Jess shuddered, but pulled herself together. 'I'm fine, Leo. Just cold. A bit shaken. Thanks.'

'The officer will stay with you, OK?' He helped her to her feet. 'You're a bloody idiot, do you know that?'

She gave him a faint smile. 'But hey, I exposed a drug ring for you.'

He frowned. 'I was going to search here later today in any case. You going missing just made me do so earlier.'

'Oh well.' She thumped his chest lightly. 'Go get the bad guys, Inspector.'

He gave her a quick squeeze of the shoulders. If he hadn't been surrounded by his officers, it might've been a hug. 'I will, Miss Bridges, I will.'

Chapter 35

Leo

O'Brien didn't demand a lawyer as Leo had expected he would. He seemed not to understand how serious the charges he was facing might be. Instead, he sat mutinously in his chair in the interview room and stared past Leo at the wall opposite like a disgruntled child forbidden his sweets.

With Harry Boston as his partner, Leo sat on his side of the table studying their suspect. They had come to Abingdon police station as it had the largest custody suite with available cells but, to be honest, all interview rooms looked the same wherever you were in Thames Valley. There was nothing on the wall to inspire this fixed attention.

'O'Brien, we have you cold on attempted murder,' said Leo. 'We caught you in the act of pushing Jessica Bridges over the railing in the icehouse.'

O'Brien's eyes flicked to Leo. 'I wasn't pushing her over the railing. I was persuading her to keep her mouth shut.'

'So you were threatening her with death to enforce her silence?'

'I'd never kill anyone ever, for any reason. It's against my philosophy.'

'Just answer the question.'

He rolled his shoulders, trying to shake off his fury at the position in which he found himself. 'I was angry, I admit, and my body language might've seemed a little threatening, but I swear to you that I was just reasoning with her.'

'That's the line you're going to take? It's a weak one. We all saw you hold her, feet off the ground over the drop. She'd ripped your shirt trying to save herself so she felt pretty certain the threat was real.' Leo was having to master some anger of his own at that.

'I wasn't going to let go.'

'So what were you going to do?'

He shrugged. 'I don't know. I've never had anyone defy me like that. Probably keep her there until she saw sense.'

'So you admit to false imprisonment?'

He saw the trap of self-incrimination. 'Hey, that's not fair! She broke in. Brother Maple told me we had an intruder. I went to check. I was going to report her to the police as a trespasser. I was within my rights to apprehend and restrain a burglar.'

Leo poured himself a cup of water. He noticed O'Brien's eyes flick towards it. 'Want some?'

O'Brien folded his arms.

'You have to be careful, O'Brien, you keep changing your story. First, you were asking her to keep a secret, then you're saying she was trying to steal from you. Which is it?'

'She broke in. I stopped her.'

'She broke into an illegal cannabis farm. I'm not sure you can prosecute someone for that. She would say she was exposing a crime, not committing one.'

'Then she'd be lying. Anyway, I know nothing about the cannabis. Ask Brother Maple. He's our herbalist. I assumed they were just medicinal plants.'

'That's one popular definition of them, but unfortunately for you they are illegal and your name is on the lease. As tenant, you are the one held responsible.'

He shrugged. 'It's the truth.'

Leo looked back in his file on the leaders of the commune. 'Why did you leave Yorkshire?'

'I was called to Kingston Beauchamp, to be near the White Horse.'

Harry snorted.

'I was!' O'Brien glared at the sergeant.

'And it was nothing to do with Sister Ivy – real name Hailey Robertson – and her arrest for drug dealing? It seems from the records that your little industry started back then in Doncaster.'

'I had nothing to do with that. I helped Ivy turn away from that life.'

'You did nothing of the kind. You just set her up somewhere else where she could run the operation on a larger scale. From the information we've gathered on Maple, also known as John Regan of Hackney, and Pine, Rune Henriksen, dismissed from his job on a cruise ship for selling drugs to the passengers, you gathered quite a little group of experts around you who knew how to sell your product for the highest price.'

'I had nothing to do with that.' O'Brien's fists curled in his lap. 'That was their thing. I ran the commune; they saw to the finances.'

'Don't tell me you claim you didn't know what your underlings were up to?' sneered Harry.

'That's exactly what I'm telling you.'

'Does this guy think we're idiots?'

'Probably.' Leo could hear it in his confident tone that the man had actually told himself that this was a defence. It wouldn't stand up in court. Leo would call it wilful ignorance if he had to give it a name. 'And what about Brother Gorse?'

'What?' O'Brien was puzzled by the pivot. 'He wasn't involved.'

'I don't mean in the drug dealing. I mean, who was it that doctored his flask so he was high as a kite on the night he died?'

The widening of his eyes suggested that this was news to O'Brien. 'I don't know. He didn't usually partake.'

'Partake?' scoffed Harry. 'You mean to say the old guy preferred his whisky unadulterated with your happy shit?'

O'Brien gave a curt nod.

'Please state your answer for the record,' said Leo.

'Brother Gorse didn't like the sensation the rest of us enjoyed on those occasions and preferred to get drunk on scotch.'

Again, this had the ring of truth.

'What did you think when he nabbed your squeeze for the night then?' pushed Harry. 'He'd grabbed himself your chosen fuck buddy, hadn't he? The new flesh on your meat market.'

'You are denigrating something that is good and natural.'

O'Brien sounded almost prim, which was one hell of an irony.

'If it's so good and natural, why do you film it and use that to blackmail anyone who leaves?' asked Leo, remembering what Jess had told the police officer who had accompanied her in the car on the way home.

'That doesn't stop the essential goodness of what we do! There is nothing more natural than making love under the stars!'

'And is everyone willing? Is everyone able to give informed consent while out of their heads?' asked Leo.

'Of course!'

'But you never explained to Jessica Bridges what to expect. If you'd had sex with her that night, that would've been rape. Were you planning to rape her?'

'No! Once she chose Brother Gorse, I left them alone. I respect the rules of our community.'

'But someone else didn't. Someone argued with Gorse for taking her out of the running and not making her go through with it. That same person likely spiked his flask so he was in no fit state to defend her – or to keep his balance. That person might have pushed him over the edge, just as we saw you trying to do to Jess tonight.'

'That wasn't me – on either occasion! Do you have to twist everything I say? I was reasoning with her!'

'You'll have to do better than that, O'Brien. So far, we have plenty of evidence that you are prepared to resort to violence to clear away obstacles to what you want.'

He actually smiled at that, as if he saw the answer that

would vindicate him. 'I can do better than that. The ceremony was recorded; they're always recorded!'

Leo recognised that he'd just hit a goldmine of evidence. 'And that will show what, exactly?'

'That when I saw that Sister Poppy – Jessica – wasn't available, I made love to Sister Rose on the White Horse eye and stayed with her all night. We returned to the manor together and spent the rest of the night in my room. She'll tell you this herself if you ask her.'

Leo wouldn't put much faith in anything a commune member said at this point. 'How much coverage does that filming of yours give of the area?'

'Brother Pine wore the camera. It's a helmet cam concealed in his mask. He was instructed to get footage of everyone.'

'And where is this footage kept?'

'He gives me the SD cards.'

'And where are they?'

'In my safe.'

The story was too easy to prove false for him to be lying. 'O'Brien, you must see that it is in your best interests to give us access to the safe so we can check your alibi. Have you reviewed the footage from the night Aaron Barks – Brother Gorse – died?'

'No. Pine does a good job. I trust him to get what we need.'

'And you have footage of the other ceremonies?'

'Yes.'

'Including the one in which Julie Dorchester died?'

'No.'

'Why didn't you film that one?' He pushed a pen and a piece of paper in front of O'Brien.

'You don't understand, inspector.' O'Brien was writing down the numbers for the safe. 'There's no footage because we held our ceremony at Wayland's Smithy. We've got footage of that. None of us went to the White Horse that night.'

'That's where you're wrong. Someone did because someone killed her there.'

'Well, it wasn't me, nor was it any of my people.'

'We'll see. Interview end.'

Leo stood up and addressed the constable on the door. 'Take Mr O'Brien back to the cells. We're holding him pending charges.' He picked up the slip of paper on which O'Brien had written the combination. 'Get that to the team at the manor.' He passed it to Harry. 'We'll review the footage at HQ so they're to log and bring everything they find there.'

O'Brien was led out by a uniformed officer. He walked defiantly, like a man who expected to be vindicated. What had they missed, wondered Leo? Why was he so confident?

Harry came off the phone from passing on the instructions. 'What are you going to do, Leo?'

'I'm going to interview our witness then brief the superintendent. If I'm not back by the time the SD cards are in evidence, get all available officers to review the footage and start looking for our suspect and for our victims, Julie Dorchester, Jess Bridges, Aaron Barks and Lisette White.'

Harry cracked his knuckles, looking pleased by the task to review what were in effect homemade porn movies. 'Right you are, sir.'

Leo wished he had someone else he could assign the task but Suyin was tied up at the manor. 'Tell Suyin to bring in the other three – Sister Ivy and Brothers Pine and Maple – and start processing them. We have enough to hold them on the strength of O'Brien's testimony.'

'Sir.'

'Don't cock this up, Harry. No clever remarks, no snide comments. Be professional.'

'I'd say the same to you if I didn't think you'd slap me down for it.'

'What?'

'You're running off, aren't you, to see the naked chick when you should be pushing on with the interviews.'

To argue that this was necessary would make it look like Harry had the right to question his procedures. 'Just get the job done, Harry.' And Leo walked out. Jess had some answers he needed, and he'd have to stop treading carefully around her if he wanted the truth.

Chapter 36

Jess

I could hear Benji and Leah out in the garden but I was too tired to join in and tease them as was my usual habit when they got back from school. After I was brought home, the police officer who saw me inside stayed while I had a bath. She said she wanted to see that I was OK and not suffering from any after-effects. When I told her that I was intending to sleep and that I was sure she had better things to do, she reluctantly took off. Apparently, Leo had told her to stay with me, but that was a waste of their resources. They had to have their hands full dealing with their drugs bust and murder cases.

I tried to keep my own word that I'd catch up on the hours of sleep I'd lost the night before, but my mind was still spinning. I discovered that despite lying flat on my back on top of the duvet, covered in a soft blanket throw, sleep was impossible.

I'd almost died. Amongst all the idiotic things I'd done in my life, I don't think I'd ever come so close. I took my indestructibility for granted. I think we all do or we wouldn't venture outdoors. We never think that *this* time we get in a car, board a plane, or cross the street is the last one. The odds fall short for someone else, not us, because *we* are the survivors. It felt almost too much to handle, that ripping away of a certain amount of security that I'd taken for granted. If I didn't process it, I knew it would become a much bigger deal for me, and I'd lose my nerve for this kind of work. God, I might even lose my nerve to do simple things like meet new people or go to new places. I was facing a basic contradiction now between my old self, who had been fine with risks, saw that as her keynote feature, and the new person, who had suddenly been confronted with her own mortality.

I knew one person who would understand what I was facing, so I gave him a call.

'Hey, Michael?'

'Jessica, you're all right? Christ, sweetheart, Leo told me they found you at the manor!'

'You knew I'd gone missing?' I had a guilty memory of turning off the location finder on the app so he wouldn't be able to track me.

'Yes, look, hang on a moment. I'm in the library being given the evil eye by the staff. I need to get somewhere so I can call you back.' And the line went dead.

I remained on my back staring at the ceiling. I was in Cory's spare room, which had an off-white lampshade that I'd meant to change for a while now. Bland-Ikea. I hadn't found the time or the spare cash. I was like that – full of good intentions that never progressed to action. The pictures could do with changing too: white horses galloping across the Camargue seemed rather too apposite at the moment. I'd had my fill of things white and equine.

My phone buzzed on my chest.

'Hey,' I answered.

'Are you really all right? I could come round, or you could come to my house. That would be easier for me.' Michael must've been outside the Bodleian because I could hear the chatter of passing tourists and students, the ringing of bike bells and no cars.

I didn't want to go out again today. 'I'm fine, really.' I didn't mention the tears running from the outside corners of my eyes, into my hair, and onto the pillow. 'Cory's kids are blessedly normal. I won't have time to dwell.'

'Jessica—'

'I know, I know, I should've told someone where I was going.'

'You're missing the point! You should never have gone!'

'I was doing my job.'

'You were taking an insane risk!'

'I can only apologise and say that it didn't feel like it at the time. In and out, no fuss, no muss.'

He snorted. 'You make it sound like a prophylactic.'

I smiled. 'Say it, Michael: call a spade a spade, or, in this case, a condom.' Damn the man, he was cheering me up. When had Michael ever done that before? I'd always been the court jester in our relationship.

'I'm paid to come up with the big words, love.'

'And you do it so well.' My tears had stopped, which was

good as I was sick of them already. And I thought I'd successfully distracted him from the scolding I'd earned. He was showing me another endearing side to his character which I had not suspected existed. That was worth further exploration, but, for now, I had other things I needed to talk to him about. 'Michael, it scared me.'

'What scared you, Jessica?'

'I almost died.'

'What?'

'Leo didn't tell you?'

'Leo most certainly didn't if you almost died!' He was off again, furious that I'd risked myself. 'Jesus. He just said they'd found you locked in the icehouse. He didn't make it sound like that big a deal.'

Leo was being discreet as usual, but he should've known he could tell Michael the truth. The three of us had shared investigations before. 'They found me when O'Brien was trying to push me over a railing into a two-storey drop.'

'I'll come round.'

'No, Michael. Well, yes, of course you may, but I rang you to ask you something.'

'OK.' He sounded wary now. Maybe he sensed what was coming. 'Go ahead then. Ask.'

'How do you cope?'

'Generally, or something specific?'

'How do you cope with almost dying? I mean, I know you've got it far worse than me, but you must have flashbacks, and you must replay the moment you fell down the stairs so many times. How do you shake it off?'

There was a long pause and I would've thought he'd cut me off if I couldn't still hear the people around him.

'You don't,' he said finally.

'Don't what?'

'Don't shake it off. You face it and tell your stupid brain that springs this on you at the worst moments that you *didn't* die. That you got through. That it should be thinking about that and you're not going to give your attacker any more power over you by dwelling on *almost*.'

'So basically you bitch-slap your subconscious?'

He gave a gruff laugh. 'Basically, yes. It works for me. Does that help?'

'Yes, thanks. I'll give it a try.'

'And, as a professional, I should add, it is advisable that you also talk about it, paying doctors like Charles loads of money for therapy. The pain of that in your wallet distracts from the pain of the replay.'

I giggled weakly. 'Yeah, today's going to cost me a fortune.'

'He'll give you a discount. He likes you.'

'He does not. He thinks I drag down your sorry ass.'

'Americanisms now, Jessica? My, your standards are slipping.'

'You're an arse, Michael. An arse.'

I can hear the humour in his voice. 'That's better. You sound more like yourself. Get some rest. Play with Cory's kids. You'll bounce back.'

'Thanks, Michael.'

'Stay safe, Jessica. I mean it!'

I decided to stay in bed. I was safe here. I could remain in my bedroom and pretend I still didn't have a missing person to find, that I'd done my best.

But the problem was that no amount of bitch-slapping would make my conscience shut up. I dialled my client.

'Tanglewood? There've been some developments.'

When Leo called in, I was playing fairy-tale brides with Leah, who was deeply in love with the glittery dresses I'd bought for her dressing-up box, much to Cory's feminist horror. Benji attacked him with a sword, which he fended off with bemused good grace.

'Hey, guys, this is my friend Leo. He's a policeman,' I announced.

This was met with a swoon from Leah and a challenge to walk the plank from Benji.

'What's this, gender stereotype day?' Leo muttered as he greeted me.

'Best to get it out of the system early, I say. Anyway, sword-fighting is for girls in this family.' I grabbed the other sword and had a quick duel with Benji. 'I'm Anne Bonny. Die, you blackguard!'

'And I'm Captain Jack!' declared Benji. 'I kill ten pirates before breakfast.'

'I'm a zombie bride,' said Leah solemnly, 'and I eat brains.'

'Should I be worried?' asked Leo, looking rather awestruck by the bloodthirsty little girl who was pretending to gnaw at his leg.

'All good, healthy fantasies,' I said briskly.

He gently detached the zombie. 'May I have a word?'

'Let's go up to my room. From now until bedtime, the kids have the run of the house. I imagine what we have to discuss is not the stuff zombie brides and pirate captains should overhear.'

In addition to the bed, I also had a desk and chair in my room. I waved him to the swivel seat and I chose the foot of the bed, back against the wall with the Camargue horses rampaging overhead.

'I'll need a statement from you,' he began.

I passed him the account I'd already written. 'Do you want me to read this out?'

'No, I'll have a look.' He leafed through it. 'Do you think O'Brien killed Julie and is responsible for Lisette's disappearance?'

I pinched the top of my nose. My head was hurting – a stress headache. 'I think he might've pushed me over the rail in the icehouse if you hadn't arrived so I suppose he might have lost it with the other women too. Maybe he doesn't like it when women stand up to him?'

'He swears he didn't harm a hair on their heads.'

'Do you believe him?'

'He seems to think he can prove his innocence. There were recordings of the starlight ceremonies. He was practically begging us to watch those to prove that he was nowhere near Brother Gorse, Julie, or I suppose Lisette, though he claims to have no knowledge of her whereabouts. According to him, she just left and might even come back – though her name has been struck out in his book that kept a record of the members of the commune.'

'He said the same to me.' I wanted to lie down but this, despite it being Leo, was still a formal police interview. 'It just all seems a muddle.'

Leo passed me back the account. 'Would you mind signing and dating that?'

'Is it OK?'

'Yes, very thorough. Anyone would think you were familiar with police interviews.' We exchanged a grim smile. He'd interviewed me a couple of times during the wild swimming case which got tangled in the weeds of my own stalker incident. *Thanks, Dad, for that particular joy.* Last call before I went to Frankfurt, Mum had still been trying to argue that his attention to me had just been a clumsy way of getting back in touch. If she testified at the trial, she'd be for the defence. That meant I was avoiding her calls as she infuriated me when the subject came up.

I added my own loopy signature and date. 'There you go.'

He took it and slipped it inside his suit jacket. He was always the best dressed officer at the crime scene, Detective Inspector Leo George. 'Why do you dress like that?' I asked, tiredness making the question slip out.

'This?' He pulled on his cuffs – cufflinks rather than buttons. 'I guess I like to keep up standards, remind myself I'm on the job and that I take it seriously.'

'Can't be good in high-speed foot chases.'

'Funnily enough, there aren't that many of those. I spend most of my time in cars, offices, or police stations, trying to make sense of a heap of conflicting facts and mysteries. Here's one I really want solved. You didn't find Lisette in the icehouse and we didn't find her on the grounds. Where do you think she is?'

I shrugged. 'At this stage, I really have no idea. Has her bank account been used?'

'No activity on her last known number, credit card, or bank account.'

'So she's dead and been dumped somewhere further afield?' I really hoped not, for Tanglewood's sake.

'That's possible, but why? What would be the motive?'

'Protecting a secret? From what I learned in the commune, she was a happy camper, Father Oak's lover. Maybe she found out about the cannabis farm and she moved from asset to become a risk, or, on the fateful night, she inadvertently saw who killed Julie?'

'I prefer that second theory. The long-term residents of the commune like Lisette surely all had a fair idea about what went on in the icehouse. They all protest their innocence too much.'

Of course they did. It took me less than a week to find out. Granted, I was an abnormally curious person, but even someone with only a modicum of inquisitiveness would have eventually sniffed it out by, well, just sniffing. Their happy juice at the starlight ceremonies had to be sourced from somewhere and it would be foolish not to join the dots. I still couldn't make sense of American Julie's presence though. She could have been wearing one of the masks, I supposed, but from what Leo had said about the crime scene, there had only been a robe, no other paraphernalia. Someone had seen through the mask, if she had worn one. And where would she have obtained it? They were customised to fit the Children of the White Horse theme.

'What was Julie doing hanging around the commune, dressing up for one of their events? Did you find out?'

Leo leaned back in the chair. I realised that he too was tired, deeper grooves bracketing the top of his nose and faint lines on his forehead. 'Beyond the idea that she was doing a kind of pagan tourism? The profile we've drawn up on her stresses her interest in British history. She was also a trainee in the FBI but sometimes coloured outside the lines, undertaking her own enquiries. One case she might have taken too far was about herself. It came to light during the investigation that she was closely related to one of the village families, the Chamberlains.'

'She was related to the nice rector?'

'Yes. Iona's parents and her uncle all live in the village.'

'That's a bit too cosy.' But then, my mother lived with my sister and children, so who was I, a glasshouse dweller, to cast stones?

'The thing I haven't worked out is how Julie found out. When I say related, we're talking biological through anonymous sperm donation. To zero in on Kingston Beauchamp and the Chamberlains, she must've cracked whatever secrecy the clinic had around their list of donors and discovered that her father was one or other of the senior Chamberlains.'

'How does that work ... that she wasn't sure?'

'Identical twins.'

'Oh. And how did she find out they existed at all? Mad computer skills?'

'Maybe. She worked for the FBI so if someone wanted to find something out badly enough in a place that isn't exactly guarding state secrets, I imagine she knew how to do it. But we've been looking into this and it appears that she wouldn't even have to try too hard these days. It's getting easier to trace relatives, thanks to the habit people have of uploading their genetic profile to ancestry websites. The FBI used this data to locate a cold case killer in California recently, so I can't see why it can't be turned to finding relatives of your father and homing in on the most likely suspects. You wouldn't need to hack the clinic at all.'

'So if one of the family did the test as a birthday present – hey, Grandad, see how much Neanderthal you have in you – that data is out there for law enforcement to use to find you?'

'That's right. It drives a coach and horses through the privacy laws.'

'Cute metaphor. I guess you read Victorian novels?'

Leo just shook his head at me. I know, I easily digress.

'OK, stick to the point, Bridges.' I slapped my forehead. 'But we'll talk about your novel-reading habits someday, I promise you. Maybe over a drink when all this is over? In your version of events, Julie did some sleuthing, narrowed it down to the Chamberlain twins, came here, maybe to see if she could contact her real father, and did a bit of tourism on the side, which got her killed? So who killed her? That doesn't hang together very well.'

'No, it doesn't. Her genetic hunt for Dad doesn't suggest a motive to me. OK, it might be a shade awkward to have a grown-up daughter arrive on the doorstep, but she had no legal claim on either of the Chamberlains. They'd done nothing against the law in making their sperm available to childless couples. It all just seems ...' He trailed off, lost in his thinking.

'Not enough to push someone to shove a knife in your heart?' I finished his thought for him. I cast my mind back to my first conversation with Tanglewood on the plane. 'I've just remembered something. Lisette is also a result of sperm donation; her mother told me that it had been something they argued over before she cut off contact. She was also looking for her biological daddy, having never known a father.'

Leo laced his hands behind his head and gazed out the window in thought. 'There's something in all this fertility clinic stuff, isn't there? I'm just not sure what. Do you think you could confirm this?'

'I'll check.' I quickly called my client. 'Hey, Tanglewood, I'm sitting with Inspector George trying to think up some more leads. We were wondering if you remembered the name of the clinic that you used when you had Lisette?'

She sounded surprised at this line of enquiry. 'I ... er ... I'm not sure. It was something like Women's Fertility Centre, in Harley Street.'

'Women's Fertility Centre, Harley Street,' I repeated so Leo could hear. 'Thanks.'

'Are you going to tell me why you're asking?' she asked.

'Just an idea. I'll let you know if it leads anywhere. Thanks.'

Leo looked through his contacts. 'I'll check with the Dorchesters. They're staying in London with friends.'

He got up and went to the window for a little privacy. I

gave up on vertical – it's overrated in my opinion – flopped down on the bed and closed my eyes. It was very restful, having him in here. I liked it. He made me feel safe. No, not safe, *settled* was a better word.

The next thing I remembered was a gentle touch on my arm to rouse me. 'Jess, that checked out. They used the same clinic. Thanks.'

I made to get up but he waved me back down. I wished I had the nerve to pull him down to join me. 'You stay there and sleep. I've got things to chase up now.'

'You're going to see the Chamberlains?'

'Yes, I think it's time they admitted which one of them did the deed.'

'At the clinic?' I yawned. 'It's an altruistic act. Go for the one who is most selfless.'

'I think they used to give students money in the form of so-called expenses.'

'Then go for the most money-grabbing one.'

'You're a great help.' He got up. 'Rest. I'll let you know if we get any news on Lisette.'

'I've promised her mother I'd bring Lisette back to her if at all possible.'

'And I'll see if I can help you keep your word.'

Chapter 37

Leo

Leaving Jess to rest, Leo thought long and hard about the best way of getting the Chamberlain twins to admit which one had fathered children anonymously a couple of decades ago. 'Fathered' was perhaps too strong a word as it had never been intended that the donor play more than an initiating role in the child's life. Still, it was a sensitive topic; they'd been promised anonymity and subsequent advances in DNA were threatening to blow holes in that agreement. Soon it would be very difficult for anyone to be altruistic and help others in their struggle for a baby without it coming back to them twenty or so years later in the shape of a child knocking on their door and wanting to know more about her genetic inheritance.

Or his. That could be him if only he knew who his own father was.

That was not what he should be thinking about right now. It was possible that this hunt for a father played into the circumstances surrounding the murder. He needed to find the strongest position on which to set up his attack. Major Chamberlain was unbeatable on his home turf at the stables – as was his brother, come to think of it, with his strangely aggressive Labrador – so Leo decided it was time to bring them both in for interview. Fortunately, the arrest of O'Brien and the discovery of the cannabis farm gave him a legitimate reason for asking some searching questions as to how much the landowner had known, and how much the brother had seen. Surely someone in the village, not known for being short of gossip, had speculated as to what income the commune had and where it came from?

Unless it was a *Whisky Galore* situation with everyone getting a cut for turning a blind eye? Iona had mentioned a widespread darkness in the village: had that been what she meant? Or had she been alluding to the blackmail videos of locals that O'Brien had taken so that his sexual activities would not be reported? Come to think of it, Jimmy Turner had said that Iona herself had been to one of those events and reported a very anodyne version to her husband. Had she also been caught out by the drugged wine and found herself compromised? That was something Leo was going to have to ask her, but very carefully.

Leo decided the best way to approach the topic of fatherhood with the Chamberlain twins was to make it seem as though it was completely aside from the real reason that he had summoned them. To that end, he'd booked out a conference room with refreshments to give the interview an informal air. *Just tying up the loose ends, Major. Nothing to worry about, Warden.* By putting them both together, he hoped he'd shake loose a confession – or denial – either would serve his purpose. He'd not seen them together yet and was interested to find out how their relationship worked.

The brothers were surprised to find each other at Kidlington police station when Leo brought Roger in to join Andrew. That told him they did not share every detail of their lives with each other. Roger arrived second. The younger brother had already made inroads into the plate of biscuits. To prevent them from objecting to being interviewed together, Leo moved swiftly into distraction mode.

'Sit down, please, sit down. I thought it would save time if I brought you both here.'

'Two birds, one stone?' asked Andrew, pouring a tea for his brother without being asked. He handed it to Roger and was not thanked. Either he was the servile one, or they were so close they didn't need verbal communication.

'I'm very pushed for time, so apologies. As you'll have noticed, the case is attracting a lot of media.' Leo poured himself a coffee, acting as if he was just making conversation before getting down to the real business. He gestured with the milk jug to the pile of cuttings he'd left out strategically on the table. 'I want to thank you again, Major, for helping us this morning at the icehouse. If you hadn't acted swiftly and gained me entry to the manor, we might have been too late to rescue Jessica Bridges.'

'Not at all, Inspector. I'm just pleased we were in time to stop that bastard.' Taking Leo's gesture as an invitation, the major glanced through the mixture of nationals, website articles and tabloid pieces. 'I had no idea just what kind of a man he was. Anyway, Andy, I've given the commune their marching orders. They have to clear out by the end of the month. We'll need to start looking for a new tenant. Bloody inconvenience.'

'Roger, what did you do? I hadn't heard that you'd been heroic.' Andrew sat back in his chair and looked up expectantly at his brother. He had crumbs in his beard. Roger pointed to the spot on his chin and Andy brushed them away.

'I'll tell you the full story later, but suffice it to say the inspector was correct to suspect that O'Brien was a fellow of dirty dealings. They'd only just gone and set up some vile drugs cartel thing in the icehouse. Disgraceful! That building is mentioned in Pevsner.'

It amused Leo to note that Roger Chamberlain's objection rested more on the disrespect paid to the ancient building than to the fact that his tenant had been paying his rent with immoral earnings.

'We surprised Terence O'Brien in the act of threatening a woman who had stumbled upon his secret,' Leo said. 'Did I tell you, Major, why she was there?' Leo took a shortbread and sat down next to Andrew, keeping this informal.

'No, you didn't. I did wonder but thought it wasn't my place to intrude. Police business and all that.'

'That's very discreet of you. But it's not a secret. Miss Bridges was there to find a young woman called Lisette White.' He couldn't be sure but he thought he saw Andrew's hand shake as he picked up his cup. 'She used to belong to the commune but went missing.'

'Probably saw sense.' The name washed over Roger with

no effect. 'I'm glad neither of my girls ever fell into any of that stuff, though I suppose you could say Iona with her funny get-up and sacramental duties verges on it.'

'My brother doesn't respect the Church,' said Andrew. 'Not like Iona and me.'

'I blame you for getting her into all that mumbo-jumbo when she was little. Taking her to services and Sunday school. Pah!'

'I distinctly remember you and Madeleine saying you liked the Sunday lie-ins.'

'Yes, well. She could've been a solicitor, or a banker, not a penniless priest with the prospect of more promotions to equally penurious jobs. They don't even get decent homes these days, but matchbox houses on new estates.'

'An odd thing came up in the course of our investigation,' said Leo lightly as if this was just another side fact. 'It seems highly likely that Julie Dorchester, the murder victim, was here to find her father. We're also looking into whether Lisette White was in the area for the same reason.'

'Sired by the same bolter, eh? Men like that should be gelded. Who was it? The villagers should let him know what we think of him.' The major took a chocolate-covered biscuit.

Andrew kept quiet. But he wasn't drinking or eating any more.

'It's nothing like that, Major. Their father didn't know about them. He was a sperm donor over two decades ago and doubtless did so in order to help other childless couples.'

'Oh. I see.' The major looked puzzled.

'In fact, it turns out that one of you was the donor.'

'What!' The major overturned his cup. Tea went over the *Daily Mail*. 'Damn! Sorry.'

Leo grabbed a handful of serviettes to mop up the spillage. 'It would help me understand why Julie was here if I could direct those questions to the man who was her biological father.'

Roger turned to his brother. 'Well, I know it wasn't me. That's just the kind of damn stupid thing you'd do, Andrew. Did you?'

Andrew looked terrified. 'I did. I wanted to help. I didn't think I'd ever get married so it also seemed a way of having my own children. People out there with my genes who'd be thankful for them.'

'You idiot. You had your nieces!'

'But they're yours, Roger. I'm always Uncle Andrew to them.'

'Do you mean to say that the girl you told us about ... the one in your house, is your *daughter*?'

'Yes.'

So that was where Lisette White had been hiding! The glimpse of someone at an upstairs window. The family emergency. It all made sense. Why had he assumed he'd seen Iona? Leo asked himself. Because he hadn't suspected the DNA link to Lisette at that time. And why should he? The odds that the two girls would both come looking for the same donor at the same time were astronomical. Did that suggest they might have been searching together? Might they have organised to come together?

The warden was looking longingly at the door.

'Mr Chamberlain,' said Leo. 'Andrew, no one is accusing

you of anything, but can you just answer a few questions please?'

'Too bloody right he will. I want some answers too,' blustered Roger. 'He came to us asking us to help with a girl who had quit the commune suddenly and didn't want to go back. He asked us not to tell anyone because she had a jealous boyfriend she wanted to get away from.'

'Was that what she said?' asked Leo. 'Had she broken it off with O'Brien and been forced to run?'

Andrew shook his head. 'No, no, that's not it at all. She came to me because she knew I was her father. She'd made contact a few months before and we'd met occasionally, just to get to know each other. Have tea, you know, father-daughter stuff.'

'And you didn't tell me? Andrew!' Roger was aggrieved. Perhaps they *were* the kind of twins who felt closer to each other than anyone else in the world?

'It was nice, and she was mine. I would've told you eventually, Roger. I wasn't happy that she was in the commune but she liked it there. She said she was close to the leader. I think she's in love with him. She even suggested I meet him, like I could give my paternal approval or something.'

Then he dried up. Leo wondered if he would only start on trickier territory with his brother out of the room and was about to suggest that, when Roger was the one to get him going again.

'That's all right, Andy.' He patted his brother's back. 'We all know you're the one in the family with the waif-and-stray syndrome.' He looked to Leo. 'Any bird out of the nest, batch of abandoned kittens, and Andrew would swoop in to save them.'

'She helped me too. Made me see that I'd made a family of sorts, even though I hadn't expected to. I'd always felt so inadequate compared to you and Madeleine, with Ella and Iona, and here I was handed a lovely full-grown daughter who wanted to know me. She loved the fact that I worked for the National Trust. She said it was important work. She loved the White Horse and knew how much it meant to me.'

'You've dedicated a great deal of your professional life to it,' agreed his brother.

'Did either of you know what went on up there at the commune's ceremonies?' asked Leo.

'I steered bloody clear. Andrew said it wasn't for the faint-hearted,' said Roger. 'A lot of new-age waffle, he said.'

'Andrew?'

'I attended once. Some years ago.' He tugged at his collar.

'Did they show you something which meant you were unable to report them?' Leo pressed. 'Some compromising images?'

Andrew looked away. 'Yes. I ... I don't know what came over me. I can't even be sure how old the girl was. I've been so scared. Only Iona understood.'

'What in God's name are you talking about?' spluttered Roger.

Leo stepped in with an explanation. 'O'Brien has been blackmailing locals by getting them in compromising situations while under the influence of the drugged wine they pass round at those ceremonies.'

The major had been putting his own two and two together. 'So that's why Iona told me to lay off of him when I mentioned I wanted rid of him. Not her too! I'll skin him alive!'

'He's in custody and will be charged,' Leo said, trying to keep things calm.

The major pounded the table. 'This will ruin my daughter!'

'None of it was her fault. She – and Andrew – were both unable to give consent. This won't come back on them.'

'You don't know what the press is like.' Roger put his head in his hands. 'I'll kill him.'

'I know this is distressing but we need to understand what happened to Lisette. What changed for her? Why did she leave?' asked Leo.

'I'm not sure. She won't say,' said Andrew in a small voice. 'I do know that she's terrified to see anyone. I've tried to coax her out but she seems to think she's in danger if she's spotted.'

'And this started on the night of the murder?'

'On the morning. She was there when I got back from the hillside, after seeing you that first time in the car park. I thought for a terrible moment when you showed me the picture that it might be her, but it wasn't, and then when I got home she was waiting on the bench in the back garden. I was so relieved. Of course I let her in. I told Iona. She counselled me to give Lisette time and encourage her to talk. Lisette has been with me ever since.'

Leo knew he had to point it out to Andrew as the man hadn't yet made the connection. 'Mr Chamberlain, we haven't run the test for Lisette, but we do know for sure that the girl who was killed that night was your biological daughter because we compared her DNA to a sample from Iona. As the coincidence is too great, I would guess that Lisette and Julie somehow got to know each other and both came here in search of you. Did Lisette mention that?'

Andrew shook his head in disbelief. 'A second daughter? Another child? And she's dead?'

'I'm afraid so. Her parents are in the country to collect her. Julie had a happy life with them in the US. She'd recently started working for the FBI. She loved England, especially this part, but something here killed her.'

'Oh my God. My child. I dismissed her as someone else's sorrow, pleased it wasn't Lisette, but she was mine!'

Roger put his arm around his brother's shoulder. 'You weren't to know, Andy.'

'No one is blaming you for any of this, Mr Chamberlain,' said Leo. You were too late to help her in life; but will you help her now, in death?'

'Of course! Oh, that poor, poor girl!' Andrew took out a handkerchief and mopped his glistening eyes. 'What can I do?'

'I need to talk to Lisette and find out what she knows. It's obviously something vital, or she wouldn't be so scared. Will you take me to her?'

'She'll think I betrayed her!'

'You're not betraying her; you're helping her – like you're helping Julie. If there's someone who might harm Lisette, we need to know who, so we can stop them. Will you help us?'

Andrew was silent.

'Andy, hiding is not the answer,' said his brother with surprising tenderness.

'Really? It's served me so well for years.' He smiled bleakly at his brother. 'All right, Inspector, I'll help. But let me go in first and explain to her. She won't understand if you kick down the door and drag her out in handcuffs.'

'That wasn't what I had in mind but, please, do pave the way for us. The last thing any of us wants is for her to be scared more than she has been already.'

Chapter 38

Jess

I had thought that was it for my fun-packed day of near-death experiences and I was off duty, but then I got a call from Tanglewood at eight o'clock in the evening. I was wrapped in my blanket, deep into a series on Cory's Netflix account, and had to make myself answer the phone. It was so, so tempting to pretend I had already switched off for the night.

'Hey, Tanglewood, everything OK?'

'Yes ... no, God, I hope it will be.' Her voice was bursting with excitement. I sat up, more alert now.

'Glad to hear it, but maybe you could narrow down the possibilities by explaining what you mean?'

'Lisette rang me just now.'

'Oh, Tanglewood, that's brilliant! Is she OK? Where is she?' It was a huge relief to know we weren't going to find Lisette's body in a ditch somewhere.

'She's still in Kingston Beauchamp.'

'What? Where?' How had she escaped being spotted by the police or a neighbour?

'Look, it's all very confusing. From what I understood, she's scared stiff. She wants to come home ... home to me. She doesn't have a car or any means of transport.'

'I suppose not, but surely you can send her a taxi or even just tell the police? They'll be so relieved to find her that they might give her a lift to the nearest station after questioning.'

'That's just it. Lisette doesn't want to talk to the police. She was very clear about that. She wants to get somewhere safe before she talks to them – and that means back with me.'

'But did you tell her that the police on this case are good people? She has nothing to fear. From what I understand, only those most closely involved in running the cannabis farm are going to face prosecution and I don't think your daughter had much to do with it.'

'It's more than that. Lisette is worried for her safety. I think she feels she's under threat for what she knows. Those commune people have really spooked her.'

'But they're in police custody. They can't harm her.'

'I know, but she doesn't believe me. Father Oak looms so large in her mind. Look, Jess, I know she will have to speak to the police but, for the moment, she just wants to get out without talking to anybody. I promised I'd make this possible for her.'

I was beginning to see why she'd rung me. I was the closest person she knew to her daughter and was in the best position to smuggle her away. The problem for me was that I felt I owed it to Leo not to deprive him of a possible key witness. I couldn't obstruct his enquiries.

'Tanglewood, I'm really not sure about this.'

She cut in before I could argue further. 'I know, Jess, but I'll make sure she talks to that nice inspector as soon as she's calmed down. I'm worried that if I don't come through for her on the first thing she's asked from me for two years, she might just run away and I won't hear from her again ... perhaps forever.' That was a persuasive argument: a witness in her mother's custody was far better than one on the run. 'I said I had a friend who lives locally who could pick her up. You can pick her up, can't you?'

'But Tanglewood—'

'Jess, I hired you to get my daughter out of that commune.' Her tone stiffened, became more businesslike. 'We signed a contract to that effect. Don't tell me you're going back on your part of the deal?'

When she put it like that, I wasn't sure I had much of a choice. My first loyalty was to the client in all cases I took. 'OK, I'll ask a friend if I can borrow her car. Where should I go to meet Lisette? Does she have a number that I can ring?'

'She wouldn't tell me where she was calling from, but she said she would make her way to the road leading up to Wayland's Smithy just out of the village. There's a lay-by as you turn in. She'll meet you at eleven o'clock. You won't be seen there. Does that give you enough time to get to the pickup point?'

'Yes. And where does she want me to take her?'

'Well, I live over in East London. Ideally, here. I know it's a bit of a drive but, at that time of night, it shouldn't take more than a few hours.'

'Tanglewood, I'm really not the world's best driver. Can't

we meet somewhere closer? Why don't you drive here? By the time I've gone to Kingston Beauchamp and back, you could get here to pick Lisette up at my home address.'

Tanglewood thought about it for a moment. 'All right. Expect me at yours at around one. And if you get in trouble with the police for this, I'll explain it's my fault.'

The biggest risk was that I couldn't see Leo trusting me afterwards if I drove off with the star witness. 'And you absolutely promise that she'll talk to the police first thing?'

'If I can persuade her.'

'And if not?'

'I'll tell them myself that she's safe with me. I won't mention how she got here.'

That didn't raise my spirits much. I had a feeling I was going to blab it out to Leo next time I saw him, but her excuse might buy me a few more hours in his good books. I've learned to take that when I get the chance. 'OK. It's a deal.'

I wasn't lying when I said I was a poor driver. Cory had experienced me being behind the wheel and she only handed over her keys after I promised her it was a true emergency.

'Drive slowly!' she said. 'Make sure you leave enough room when passing other vehicles.' I'd lost a wing mirror in my one jaunt to Sainsbury's, but, come on, they design the parking bays in supermarket car parks deliberately narrow. Cory's people carrier had had no hope.

Bunny hopping down the road (I'd not driven for a while), I was just getting back into the groove when I hit the ring road. As per instructions, I kept my speed down and tried not to flinch and close my eyes as articulated lorries thundered past me. The gesticulating drivers appeared to be outraged that anyone would go at thirty in a fifty zone.

I was not having fun reacquainting myself with the joys of driving. I fumbled the lights on the country roads, managing at one skilful moment to turn off the headlamps entirely, rather than dip them as I intended. I can tell you it is very dark away from the city. I was lucky I wasn't pulled over by the police for incompetent driving. I missed the turning the first time I drove along the B road that led to the track up to Wayland's Smithy. When I realised what I'd done, I had to drive on some way until I could find a turning place for Cory's family tank. I eventually reached the agreed spot at ten minutes past eleven.

No one was there.

I turned off the engine, leaving just the sidelights on. I tried not to think about men in masks jumping out of the hedges to stab me. An overactive imagination is a curse in lay-bys after nightfall.

I did almost jump out of my skin when there came a fierce tapping on my window. I looked round and saw a young woman wrapped up in a huge parka coat. I wound down the window.

'Lisette? I'm your mum's friend. Get in.'

'You're late,' she hissed.

Charming. Pleased to meet you too. 'I couldn't find the turn.'

'I was worried Mum might not go through with sending someone.' She went around to the passenger side and slid in. I noticed she was wearing wellingtons, pyjama bottoms and a baggy sweater that was several sizes too big. She looked like she'd absconded from the mental hospital, which I suppose was one description of the commune.

To be fair to her, I imagined ten minutes waiting in the bushes must've felt like an eternity. 'Your mum is moving heaven and earth to help you. She's meeting us in Oxford to take you home. Strapped in?' I turned on the engine. Crap, I was now going to have to turn around. I wished I'd done this before she arrived. Was there enough width here in the road? I didn't fancy my chances of going up the hill to find somewhere. There was nothing but the Ridgeway at the top. If we got stuck up there, we'd be really buggered. 'OK, bear with me. I need to turn around.'

I then proceeded to execute something that was more like a thirteen than a three-point turn. The car lurched forward a couple of times when I misjudged the gears. Lisette was looking pained.

'Sorry. I borrowed the car. Not used to driving something this big.' Or driving at all. 'Where've you been for the last week, Lisette? We were all searching for you.'

She cast me a hostile look. 'You were hunting for me? Wait ... are you the police?' She reached for the door release.

'Seriously? Shit.' My bumper scrunched on something. I hoped it was a bush. 'Do I look like the police to you?' And why was she so anxious not to speak to them? What was she hiding?

'No, you don't.' Her hand dropped back to her lap.

'I look for missing people, kind of like a private detective. I even joined the bloody commune hoping to find you.'

Embarrassed by my manoeuvring failure, she was getting the overspill of my temper.

'What? How could you do that?' She was genuinely horrified.

'Quite easily. Just rocked up, showed my cleavage to the right horny guy and I was in. He even gave me your name. Have to say, he's deeply into recycling, isn't he?'

'Father Oak called you Sister Poppy? I don't believe you!'

That was when I realised that whatever had made Lisette leave the commune hadn't included disillusionment.

'Well, he did. He said he missed you, if that's any comfort.'

'He said that?'

There were stars in her eyes still. I had to remind myself she was in her early twenties and a few illusions could be forgiven. It was bloody annoying though.

'He wondered why you left. He hoped you'd be back.'

Tears now brimmed. 'I ... wanted to go back, but I couldn't. Not with what I know.'

'Is this about Julie?'

She nodded tearfully.

'I'm guessing she's your sister, isn't she? Your half-sister?'

Shock registered on her face. 'How do you know that?'

'A DNA test confirmed her relationship to a local family and your mother told me you were looking for your sperm donor. We then found out that your parents used the same clinic at around the same time. Did you and Julie take a test and find out you were half-siblings? Did you both come here to find your father?'

My wheels were spinning – and not metaphorically. I

thought I might've gone too close to the ditch but I didn't want to alarm Lisette when she appeared to be on the point of confiding.

'How long have you known Julie?' I asked.

'A couple of years. You're right. We met on a site that matched people wanting to find biological siblings. You send in a sample and they check against their database. Lots of people do it who don't know who their father is. I mean, you wouldn't want to date your half-brother by mistake, would you? Some clinics allowed donors to give far too much sperm resulting in too many offspring, so it's not a foolish concern. There've been cases.'

'But you found a sister? That was a bit of a win-win!'

'Yeah, we were so excited. Neither of us had a sister, and her brother was really ill. He died shortly after. That was really sad; the family had known he would have a limited life due to his condition, but it was still so painful for them all. She came to see me in London so I could help her grieve. Tracing our father was one of the things we did together to take her mind off her loss. She was really good at that stuff. Knew all the sites, all the tricks. She wanted to go into law enforcement. Had friends already in the FBI. Andrew Chamberlain had uploaded his profile to one of the ancestry websites because he was interested in history and wanted to find out about his forebears. In doing so, he allowed his profile to be shared. Julie found he was a fifty percent match to both of us.'

'And she led you here.'

'Yes. Thanks to her FBI sources, she narrowed the search

down to the right Andrew Chamberlain and we came to Kingston Beauchamp. That's when things went wrong.'

'You found he was a twin?'

'Yeah. That was the biggest surprise of all. Twins. Identical ones mean that genetically you can't tell the father apart unless he wants to own up. We'd come imagining it was Andrew but that threw everything into doubt. We already knew our father had wanted to stay anonymous as he'd turned down our official applications to the clinic to reveal more about himself. So we were at a bit of a loss.'

'In what way?'

'If he wanted to remain anonymous, why had Andrew allowed his profile to be shared on an ancestry website? Had he just not thought anyone would come looking for him that way or did that mean it was Roger who was our father? We stayed in an Airbnb that time to check them out, trying to guess which one it was. It was a special time. We had matching tattoos done.' She showed me her shoulder blade: twined flowers. 'That's us. Peas from the same pod. She had to get me drunk to agree to it; I hate needles. But I did it for her.'

'Sounds like a nice memory.' I revved but we weren't moving.

'Yeah, she was fun ... then. It was during that trip that I discovered the commune. They'd only fairly recently set up at the manor. Funny to think it belonged to our uncle ... or our dad, I didn't know which then. Only worked it out later. I was looking for a reason to stick around to investigate further and this seemed a great place to stay, in the stately home of our ancestors.'

'But you got hooked?'

'Yeah, I was at a loose end and I was attracted by the ethos and decided to stay on. When Julie went back to the US promising to carry on searching for clues as to which Chamberlain had been a donor at the clinic at the right time, I went back to London, sorted out my house, and returned here. It's been an amazing few years.' She turned to look at me. 'Sorry, what was your name again?'

'Jess.'

'Jess, you'd know since you lived there. You must've seen how peaceful life is in the manor.'

'It did seem work hard, play hard.'

She smiled as if that brought back good memories. 'Exactly. They made me feel special. Wanted.'

'Especially Father Oak?'

She rubbed her thighs nervously. 'Well, yes. We have a special link. He helps me get rid of my negative energy.'

'I bet.'

Her expression told me that she'd caught my sour tone. 'The search for my father was no longer so important to me, not like it was to Julie. Though I did make contact with Andrew. He seemed the most approachable and he owned up when I asked him directly.'

'I see. Did you tell Julie?'

'Not then. I was enjoying having him to myself, you know?

'If everything was going so well, why did you leave the commune?'

She suddenly noticed that we weren't moving. 'Are we stuck?'

'Maybe.' I had to come clean. 'Yes, we are. I think my back wheels are in the mud.'

'Then you need to move the steering wheel to and fro to give them more room and then pull out in the highest gear you can manage; that means two or three in a manual like this.'

'You sound like you know what you're doing.'

She shrugged. 'I've been driving vehicles for the community for a few years now. I know the roads round here. Not the first time I've got bogged down.'

'Would you mind taking over then? I'm not used to driving, especially not this car. I learned in a Corsa. If you get us out of the mud, I'll drive us home.'

'OK.'

We got out to switch seats. Lisette studied the situation that I'd got us into. We were pretty much wedged across the road. It reminded me of the disaster of trying to get a new sofa into my last flat. It got stuck on the stairs for a day until my ex could persuade some mates to come and help us lift it.

'Do you think we'll need to call the AA?' I asked.

Lisette shook her head. 'I think I can do it. Stay out here to guide me, OK? I'm worried about that sapling. It's taken a beating already.'

As had Cory's car. Sweet of Lisette to be worried about the wildlife.

The car responded much better to Lisette's touch than it did mine. She was able to edge it forward and go back so that the angle improved and more room for manoeuvre was achieved.

'One more and then I think you'll have done it!' I called.

And then she did the unthinkable. She swung the wheel and floored the accelerator. Speeding away, she left me standing there, gaping at her rear lights.

My missing person had absconded with my borrowed car and seemed intent on going missing again.

The bitch.

I dug out my phone. Tanglewood's number went to voice mail, probably because she was driving. Enough was enough. I couldn't do this to Cory.

'Leo? First thing, I'm really sorry. I want to report a stolen vehicle and, trust me, though it's not your department, you'll really want to hear this.'

Chapter 39

Jess

I knew I was in the doghouse. Why did I always do this with the men I liked? Mess things up so that any potential we had to be something together was squandered?

It had taken Leo only a few minutes to pick me up from my spot in the lay-by. He had been putting the same story together by interviewing the Chamberlain twins and had learned that Lisette had been hiding in Andrew Chamberlain's house for the past week. He had persuaded Andrew to agree that she should be interviewed by the police about what she saw on the night of Julie Dorchester's murder. However, when they arrived at Andrew's cottage, Lisette had already left. Andrew had made the mistake of telling her when he set out for Kidlington that he was going into the police station to answer questions and this had obviously scared her sufficiently to make her bolt. It had been the reason she'd reached out to her mother after so long being out of contact.

'Have you put out an alert for Cory's car?' I asked.

'I have.' Leo's tone was terse. 'But it would help if you could give us more details than "it's the big pale blue one".'

'I can do better than that. I took a picture on my phone as she drove away because I knew I had no clue as to the registration number. The image is blurry but you can make it out.'

Leo now gave me a more sympathetic look. I had clawed back some of my total idiot points from the huge pile in front of him. 'That was quick thinking. I'll pass this on.'

I sat in silence whilst he updated the control room. It was like looking for a needle in a haystack but at least the late hour meant there were relatively few other vehicles on the road. If she went on any of the motorways in the area – drove down to the M4 or up to the M40 – she would probably be caught on camera fairly quickly.

Leo put his car in gear and started driving. His profile looked stern in silhouette. A warrior.

'Where are you taking me?' *Take me back to your castle and ravish me.*

Shut up, idiot brain.

'I'm taking you where you should've been all night. I'm taking you home.' From the pent-up fury in his tone, I could tell his reserve was about to shatter. 'What were you thinking, Jess? Jesus, why didn't you tell me what was happening?'

'I wanted to, but there's this little thing called professional confidentiality.'

He growled at that.

'Look, Tanglewood hired me to return her daughter to her and I was just trying to fulfil my part of that bargain. She promised that she would talk to you as soon as she got her daughter back, even if Lisette was unwilling. We were both worried that Lisette would take off and never be heard from again if we didn't.' And the fact that she drove off in Cory's car suggested we were bang on target with that fear.

'I'm beginning to think that Lisette White is very good at persuading other people to do what she wants rather than what they know they should do.' He flicked the indicator to the right as we joined the main road back to Oxford. 'She's pulled the same trick with Andrew Chamberlain, persuading him to hide her in his house.'

'What is it, do you think, that she's so afraid of? She must've seen from the news by now that O'Brien has been arrested. If she felt that threatened by him, she would've known that he was in police custody. She could've come forward and spoken up about what she saw at no risk to herself.' I thought back over my brief conversation with the girl. 'Mind you, she's still in love with the guy so that might explain why she's so unwilling to talk to the police. She doesn't want to betray her lover.'

Leo drove smoothly, taking the corners so that I barely noticed them. 'It might not have been O'Brien that she had the information on. We've been looking through the footage recovered from the manor and he's right that he's shown in the company of a woman called Sister Rose on the night Aaron Barks died.'

'So what happened?'

'I'm coming to that. The footage of the night of Julie's murder only shows the ceremony at Wayland's Smithy. Unless they destroyed what they had, or changed their practice and didn't film, there is no recording of what happened on the White Horse.'

'You think there was no ceremony there that night?'

'I think a smaller group of people, maybe just two or three, went there. Although their way of life may be alternative, I got no sense from the followers I interviewed that the Children of the White Horse indulge in anything more than back-to-nature living and the occasional free-love fest. Sacrificial murder definitely isn't in the repertoire. Wouldn't you agree?'

'Oh, completely. These are decent people at heart; well, most of them, apart from the druggie lot. Brother Gorse would never have hidden something as serious as a murder. Neither would some of the nicer people, like Sister Briar or Sister Rosemary.'

'So we're left with the mystery as to what threat Julie Dorchester posed that was so serious someone killed her.'

A new idea was taking shape in my mind. I was having to think the unthinkable. 'OK, let's go back to what we do know. Julie Dorchester was in the area because she was interested in the Chamberlains but the person she actually knew and had spoken to before was Lisette White. They had come here together to look for their father two years back. They had both agreed to carry on their investigation separately and keep in touch. But Lisette admitted to me just now that she discovered which of the two was her father just by asking Andrew and that she enjoyed the father-daughter meet-ups without telling Julie.'

'That works. There's no record of any messages between the two, not for the last year that we've checked. We'll have to dig back further to find their first contact, but recently they'd not been in touch, unless it was a phone call that's not registered. Or a letter we've not yet found.'

'So Lisette got herself quite a nice little set-up here: she had the joy of a new father who was interested in getting to know her, and she was happy at the commune being the lover of Terry O'Brien. Maybe she didn't want to share that with Julie? It would've made her less special to admit to Andrew that she was one of two, maybe more, children out there.'

'You think she might've been reluctant to tell Julie who their father was? Do you think they argued about it?'

'Well, I'm wondering who Julie would follow in the middle of the night to a deserted place like the White Horse. If she was a switched-on FBI agent, she wasn't exactly about to wander off there with a man such as Terence O'Brien, or any of the other people in the commune that she didn't know. Why would she? She wasn't interested in the commune especially, but she was interested in what Lisette had to say about their joint search for a father.'

Leo tapped the steering wheel, which I took as a sign that he was excited by my theory. 'Yes, I can see it. Maybe she wondered why she hadn't heard back from Lisette? Perhaps she came to find out what it was that her sister wasn't telling her? Then Lisette brushed her off or refused to see her? It's quite hard to get into the commune unless they want you to, so Julie could've been left outside the gates, frustrated, and Lisette inside. She'd come all this way and her sister wouldn't even see her. That had to raise her suspicions that something was up.'

'And if she hung around long enough, the locals would've told her about the starlight ceremonies. She could've come back in time for one of those. All she had to do was look at the phases of the moon to find out when it would be.' I glanced out the window. The moon was now a sad semi-circle, sagging to the horizon.

Leo nodded. 'She could've infiltrated the Wayland's Smithy ceremony and confronted her sister. That would've been awkward and put Lisette on the spot with witnesses.'

'Yes, Lisette might've said, "Come with me to this other place so we can talk." She really may have meant just to talk but it got out of hand.' I was struck by how smoothly our thoughts dovetailed.

He stole a glance at me, smiling. 'We won't know exactly what went on until we ask her. But it certainly does make sense of her reluctance to talk to us.'

It was nice to be part of his team. 'And the fact that Lisette nicked a car off the good Samaritan who had come to help her.'

'There is that.'

'That's the last time I run to anyone's rescue.'

'Don't let them get in the driving seat next time.'

We hit the city lights at the Peartree roundabout in Oxford and Leo slowed down. The all-night lights of a garage flashed by.

'I don't think that's going to be a problem. No one's going to lend me their car after this.'

'Why exactly did you let her sit there? You didn't say.'

'Um ...'

'Hold that thought.' We'd turned into my road and I saw what had brought his questions to an abrupt end. Cory's car was parked outside her house. 'Is that ...?'

'Yes, the big blue one,' I confirmed. I checked the time on the dashboard. One-thirty. 'She must've come here to meet her mother after all.'

'She ran to her dad first, so I suppose it follows that she tries her mother when that fails. How did she know where to come?'

'I'd had my home address programmed on the satnav.'

He made to get out to verify that the car was empty but I held him back.

'Shall I check first with Tanglewood?' I pulled out my phone and saw I had a number of missed calls from my client.

'Say nothing about this.'

'Duh.' I pressed reply. 'Tanglewood? Where are you?'

'Jess, sorry, I got held up. My friend had the car tonight and I couldn't get it until midnight. I tried to let you know but you didn't pick up. Are you at your house? Are you with Lisette?'

'How close are you?'

'Just left the motorway. Tell Lisette, I'm fifteen minutes away.'

'OK ... er, Tanglewood, I've some bad news.'

'You didn't meet up with her?'

'No, I did, but she took my car. Just drove off in it and left me stranded. I had to call a friend for a lift home.'

Leo nodded, indicating that I should continue.

'She did what? Oh my God, she must be out of her mind with fear, not knowing who to trust!'

'Yeah, maybe. Look, if she rings you, tell her you're still on course to meet her at my house and that I'm not cross that she took the car. I understand her being scared.'

'That's very kind of you.'

'When you get to our street, park up and give me a call. I don't want to disturb Cory and the kids, OK?'

'All right.'

I ended the call. 'We've got fifteen minutes before she arrives. What do you want to do with it?'

'I'm calling this in. But we need to find Lisette obviously. Where do you think she is?' We both peered past the parked cars to the people carrier. 'Hunkered down inside that?'

I swallowed. 'Actually, she might be in the house. The car keys have a front door key on the ring.'

Leo looked up at the kids' bedrooms. 'Fuck.'

Chapter 40

Leo

Parked further up the street, Leo alerted his team to the rapidly evolving situation. They would need backup but that would take time to mobilise at this hour. All the while, he was calculating the best way to ensure the safety of the civilians who had got mixed up in this. First priority: they either had to remove Lisette swiftly from the house, or take Cory and the kids somewhere safe until they knew where the suspect was hidden. But where to take the family? To a neighbour, or maybe to Michael's? Yes, the psychologist was close and Leo could have a squad car drive them there once they were out. Leo didn't want the kids tangled up in this and Michael wouldn't need reams of explanation before he helped in the middle of the night. He sent a quick text to Suyin to wake the man up.

'Do you have a key?' he asked Jess.

She pulled a bunch of keys from her pocket. 'I took my own set out of habit.'

There was a light on in the second window upstairs. 'Is that normally lit?'

'Yes, that's Benji's room. He doesn't like the dark. Oh God, do you think she'll hurt them?'

'Not if we don't escalate this. Focus, Jess. You can't lose it now when you're doing so well. Describe the layout of the house to me upstairs. You're on the top floor, but what about the first floor?'

'Benji, front room on the right; Leah, room on the left; Cory, master bedroom at the back. The only other room on that floor is a bathroom.'

'And on your floor?'

'I'm the attic conversion so the other door at the top of the stairs is a cupboard that leads into the attic. That's where I'd go if I were hiding out.'

'OK.' Leo got out of the car and softly closed his door. It was very quiet in this street, the families all tucked up in bed on a school night. A slammed door would sound like a gunshot. Jess climbed out on her side and took equal care as she closed hers.

What the hell did Jess think she was doing! 'Stay in the car,' he hissed.

'No way. That's my family in there.'

'Jess—'

'Either you waste time arguing or you let me come with you. Who is Leah and Benji going to trust if they're woken in the middle of the night? Me or a guy in a suit they've seen only a couple of times?'

She did have a point. He wished she didn't. 'Stay behind me and do what I say.'

'I love it when you give me orders.' If he couldn't hear the nerves in her voice, Leo would think she wasn't taking this seriously. As it was, he was beginning to see that she used humour to disguise other feelings.

'And I like it most when you actually obey them.'

He slipped the key into the front door and gently turned the Yale lock. The door swung open with only a light brushing on the doormat. The stairs to the upper floors were directly in front of him. He pointed to the bottom step.

'Wait there. Please. I'm going to check the rooms on the ground floor. If she comes down, don't try to stop her. We can pick her up later. The important thing is to make sure nobody is harmed.' He knew his colleagues would be setting up a cordon around the house. They would be coming in silently so as not to alert Lisette to their presence.

'OK.' Jess took up a position partially hidden by coats hanging on the hooks in the entrance, out of sight to anyone casually looking down the stairs from above. Leo swiftly made his way through the lounge and kitchen area. It helped that he knew the house already from his earlier visits; he knew to avoid treading on Lego in the front room or falling over scooters parked in the back passageway. The thought crossed his mind that police training colleges should really set up their house infiltration courses to mimic a child's playroom for maximum challenge. It was bloody near impossible not to make a noise.

The downstairs was clear and the backdoor was locked from the inside. If Lisette was here, she was on the upper floors somewhere. He went back into the hallway and found Jess waiting patiently. Miracles would never cease. He turned to the stairs but she grabbed his sleeve, pulling his ear down to her mouth.

'I think I heard creaking.' She pointed to the ceiling. 'Benji's room.'

As the stairs were plain wood and wouldn't muffle footsteps, Leo slid out of his shoes and began the climb up the stairs. He was aware of Jess following him barefoot, but he couldn't risk the noise it would take to demand she stay below. He just had to trust she wouldn't mess this up. Reaching the top of the landing, he saw the door to Benji's room was ajar. He could just see a woman's hand on the rug by the boy's bed. The mother? He pointed so Jess could see.

'That's her,' she mouthed. 'Lisette.'

He was about to move forward when Jess caught his sleeve again. 'Let me try.'

He shook his head.

'She won't panic if she sees me. She knows I live here and that I arranged for her mother to meet us. If she looks like she's going to do something stupid, I'll grab Benji and get behind you, OK?'

It was worth a try. As far as they knew, she wasn't armed. The suspect was more likely to do something desperate if he went in, and they had the boy to think about. He gave a single nod and reluctantly let her past him.

Jess went to the door and gave a little tap. 'Benji love, it's Jess. You've left your light on.' She was pretending she had no idea Lisette was in there, giving the woman a chance to decide on her response. 'I'll just turn it off, OK? So you can sleep better.' She pushed the door open. 'Oh, if it isn't the car-stealing word beginning with b.' She placed a cocky hand on her hip.

'Jess?' The little boy had woken up. Leo held his breath. This was the crucial moment. How would Lisette handle this? 'Jess, why's there a strange girl in my bedroom?'

'Yeah, I know. That's pants, isn't it? Didn't she read your notice?'

Leo now saw that Benji had a misspelled GIRLS NOT ALOUD sign on his door.

'Why are you here?' persisted Benji.

'This is Lisette. She's my friend come for a sleepover. She needs a bed for the night. Why don't you scoot along to your mum and Leo to tell them we have a visitor, OK?' Clever Jess. Lisette wasn't to know that Cory didn't have a partner and Jess was clearly hoping Benji would remember Leo from earlier.

Leo knew that was his cue to get ready to field the little boy.

'All right.' Benji trotted into the hallway, hair sticking up every which way, wearing pyjamas with robots. 'Hi, Mr Leo. Have you come for a sleepover too?'

Leo held out his hand. 'Yeah. Let's go wake your mother.'

Cory didn't scream when Benji clambered into bed with her. Thank God for parent training. 'Wha's up, love?' she murmured.

'Jess said Leo and her friend have come for a sleepover,' Benji explained seriously.

'Wha—?'

Leo kept his voice down. 'Mrs Reynolds, the girl Jess was

looking for is in the house. It's a long story. She's upset and we want to bring her in for questioning in connection with ...' – he glanced at Benji – '... something she can help us with.'

Cory shook off the sleep and clutched Benji to her. Her body language said she had guessed what Leo meant, but she attempted to keep her voice calm for her son's sake. 'I see. That's nice. A guest.'

'So if you would just take Benji and Leah to Michael Harrison's for the rest of the night ...?' He kept his tone light to match hers. 'He's expecting you. So we have room for the sleepover here.'

'Oh. Oh?' Cory was catching on. 'What fun. A sleepover at one of Jess's friends' houses. Benji, wait here with this nice man while I get your sister.'

Cory grabbed a robe and went into Leah's room. She came back with Leah draped over her shoulder, fast asleep. 'Come, Benji. We're going on an adventure to Michael's house, but we have to be quiet, OK, so as not to wake Jess's guest.'

Benji took her hand, his expression saying he wasn't completely buying this act. 'OK, Mummy. Bye, Mr Leo.'

Leo saw them out onto the landing. He could see a police officer waiting in the hallway downstairs, having entered silently through the open door as he'd requested. He texted instructions to Suyin, waved to Benji as the boy looked back with a worried glance, then turned to the front bedroom once the family had reached the officer.

Cory and the children were safe. Now all he had to worry about was Jess.

Chapter 41

Jess

I sat down cross-legged next to Lisette. She held in her lap a picture from Benji's bedside table that showed him and his sister with their parents behind them.

'Nice family,' Lisette said absently.

'They are.' I decided not to mention the fact that the dad had left for an old flame, leaving his family in the ashes. I wasn't a fan of Cory's ex. 'That was a dick move, taking the car and leaving me stranded.'

She shrugged. 'An impulse. Sorry. Is my mum here yet?'

'Almost. Lisette, what happened?'

'Excuse me?'

'I've got most of it figured out, but I'm not quite sure what made you do it. Couldn't you just tell her to back off and leave you alone? She had a life in the States; she didn't need a dad here when she had a perfectly good one all her life. Just because he didn't give her his genes, it didn't make him any less of a dad.'

Lisette replaced the photo. 'That's what I told her. I told

her she was lucky. She had someone to fill that gap, while I just had a void. But she wanted two dads.'

'So she was greedy?'

Leaning back on a beanbag, Lisette gazed at me. She had stunning looks, long blonde hair, a slim figure, clear blue eyes. In fact, she bore a striking resemblance to Leah's poster of Elsa from *Frozen*. Just as well Leah hadn't seen her or she'd be demanding she play dressing-up-as-a-Disney-princess. But I found something missing in Lisette's eyes, some spark of understanding of her predicament. I began to ask myself if Tanglewood had got it wrong. Her daughter running away hadn't been a rebellion about finding a father or chasing a dream in a new lifestyle; was it possible that Lisette wasn't well? I meant *mentally* unwell. Some conditions tend to manifest in late teens and early twenties. Was this the case with Lisette?

'I don't think Julie was greedy. Anyway, I was going to share. I was going to send her to my father's brother.'

'I don't think that would've worked.'

'But they're identical twins.' Definitely a few screws loose up there.

'He would've denied being her father.'

'Exactly and she would've had to leave eventually.'

OK, I could see that. It would've been cruel to send Julie off to confront a man who had no idea what she wanted from him and why, but I could see that working. The donor had refused to release his details to the clinic so Julie could explain her reception as him continuing this denial. What could she have done about it? Nothing.

'But you didn't do that?'

'No.' She picked up one of Benji's transformers and manipulated the limbs, turning it into a yellow car. 'I remember these.'

'Yeah, the first movie is actually very witty.' I stretched out, attempting to help her relax by pretending that I was. I could hear noises out on the landing and downstairs and I really didn't want her to think about them. 'Did you see it?'

'Not Mum's kind of film.'

'Then you should try the first one sometime. It's bound to be cheap to download by now.'

'That's our culture: cheap plastic toys and cheap plastic movies.' She put the robot down. 'It's going to kill us. The oceans will drown in plastic and we'll drown in the rising oceans; that's poetic justice.'

I put a cushion shaped like a Dalek behind my back and leant on Benji's chest of drawers. I still hadn't mastered the yogic sitting pose. 'I think the commune was on to a good thing, living closer to nature. But I don't think I could hack the life long-term. Is that why you left?'

'No. I could've stayed there for ever.'

'But you left.'

'I left.' She wasn't going to move off this story.

'Was it because you argued with Julie on the White Horse and killed her?'

Her eyelids flickered. There was no shocked denial. Oh yeah, she'd killed her sister. 'I found Julie dead.'

'Oh really? How did you know she would be there? You see, the police found your sandals and cloak in a hedge near the scene.' They had to be hers, didn't they, because nobody but commune members had Brother Gorse's shoes? 'They know you were there that night, that you fled in panic.'

She drew patterns in the shag pile, making shapes. I realised with a chill in my heart that she was sketching out the spine of the White Horse.

'Come on, Lisette, don't you want to just tell the truth for once? It must be so difficult to keep track of all the various lies you've been telling. The truth is so much easier. And I'm just a friend of your mum's. What harm can it possibly do you if you tell me?'

She rubbed her chest in the spot where the knife had gone in.

'OK, I'll take you as far as I can and you go the rest of the way. Julie infiltrated one of the commune's special services, the one at Wayland's Smithy. Correct?'

Lisette nodded.

'That made you angry?'

She bent her legs to her chest and hugged them. 'Yeah, it did. She made fun of us ... being sky clad, joining together. She hid and watched it all. Then, when we were leaving, she came right up to me and said she needed to talk to me.'

'You didn't want anyone to see her in case you got the blame for an outsider being there so you took her along the footpath from the Smithy?'

'And I meant to show her how magnificent the ancient places are without other people around so she'd give what we do at the commune a fair try. Maybe stay for the sunrise. We walked in together barefoot but she giggled the whole time and said I was probably still high. She was spoiling it. When we reached the horse, I meant to have it out with her then go back to the manor by the other path down from the hill. She could've gone back to where she was staying easily enough and got a taxi from the pub car park or whatever.'

'But that didn't happen?'

'No.'

'So what did happen?'

There was a pause. This was my only chance. I could feel the police gathering outside. They wouldn't give me much longer with her but I had to have answers for Tanglewood – and for Julie.

'She barely even looked at the White Horse. And when I tried to explain it to her, she got angry and told me I'd let her down, that I hadn't carried on with the search but had got sidetracked by the commune. She told me that it was a scam and I was stupid to fall for that bullshit. She called it bullshit.' Her tone was wondering.

Bad timing to decide to be the blunt older sister trying to shake some sense into her sibling. 'I see. That must've been hurtful.'

'Yeah. She said she'd seen enough fucking at the starlight ceremony to report us for public indecency, and for using drugs. That she'd blow the whole corrupt operation sky-high if it meant saving me from Father Oak.'

Oh crap. Julie might've been an FBI analyst in the making but she knew very little about analysing her own sister. The girl was in love with the man and her big sister had been threatening to take it all away.

'And you had a knife? Why?'

'To scrape the wax off the sarsen stones, of course. We don't like to leave traces of our presence behind. It's not respectful.'

At least she hadn't brought the knife as part of a premeditated plan.

'And you used it to stab Julie.'

Lisette rubbed her face. 'I don't know. I remember taking it and pointing it at my own heart, saying how she was ripping that out of me if she did it. Then she laughed.'

'She laughed?'

'Told me not to be so melodramatic. I was so angry.'

'And so you stabbed her.'

'Yes. Just once.'

But once was enough. 'And she died?'

'So suddenly. It didn't feel real. She just stopped, her face still full of shock. I think she thought it a joke too. Like the blade should've been one of those fake ones that they use in the theatre. I wish it had been.'

She had lashed out in a moment of madness and ruined her life, as well as taken her sister's. I couldn't help but feel for her. I knew about battling impulses. 'I'm sorry.'

'I didn't mean her to die. I was just so angry.'

'And because you loved her and didn't mean it, you laid her out on the horse.'

'Yeah.' She swiped a wrist across her eyes. 'I don't know if there's an afterlife, but I thought, if there is, she could ride off on the White Horse as the sun rose. That's what I'd want. That's what Father Oak says happens to souls when they leave the body.'

'I'd like that too. You treated her with respect.'

'I did, didn't I?'

'And what about her shoes?'

'She'd carried them in, not wanting to leave them respectfully behind as I did mine. Told me she didn't want to tread on stones in the car park. I took those. They fitted me and I had to run as I saw some people coming for the sunrise.' Meaning, she hadn't thought she had time to go back for her own sandals. My sympathy ebbed. For all her impulsiveness, there had been some calculation there as the best way to cover up what she'd done. And if she really was sorry for Julie's death, she would've stayed and owned up to the deed.

There came a tap on the door. It would be Leo. He'd probably been listening from the other side. He'd have to get this all again in interview but at least now he knew the right questions to ask.

But it wasn't just Leo.

'Lisette? It's Mum, darling. It's time to come out now.'

I had to hand it to Tanglewood. She did an excellent job of keeping her voice level when she must be fighting so many emotions right then.

'Mum?' Lisette came back from the space we'd been in, a place where confidences were possible. She suddenly seemed to realise just how much trouble she was in. 'Mum, I didn't do it!'

'I know, love. We'll get this all sorted out, but you need to come out so we can talk to the police together.'

Lisette turned on me. 'You brought the police?' She pulled a blade from her pocket.

'Leo! She's got a knife!' I pulled the Dalek pillow out from behind me and held it out as a shield. 'Lisette, put that down.'

'You fucking bitch! You betrayed me!'

Her audacity was breathtaking. 'What? You stole my car, you invaded Benji's bedroom, yet somehow *I* betrayed *you*?' Enough of trying to understand her; she had crossed well over all lines.

She let out an inhuman scream and threw herself at me. I fell back on the chest of drawers and knocked a whole tower of Transformers for six. The Dalek got the knife in the sink plunger. I felt a pressure on my chest but then she pulled it back, feathers flying.

Next she went tumbling onto the bed. Leo had grabbed her wrist, twisted her arm so she released the knife, and pushed her away from us both. He now had the knife in his custody.

'Mum!' wailed Lisette, curling up and sobbing.

My moment of sympathy had passed. I was now disgusted as she wept for herself and not her victim. What a pathetic killer. But then, maybe they always were because murder was so often done to avoid actually dealing with a problem. There were so many other things she could have said or done with her sister that didn't involve stabbing her.

'Are you OK, Jess?' Leo pulled an evidence bag from his pocket and dropped the knife into it. 'Did she get you?'

I was about to say no when I looked down. A red stain was spreading across my T-shirt. Then the pain hit me like a late-running train. 'Leo!'

Chapter 42

Leo

Leo had enough to charge Lisette for assault with a deadly weapon on Jess while he waited for the lab to come back with confirmation that the knife was the same one used in Julie Dorchester's murder. She had clammed up on the advice of her mother, but Leo had heard enough while standing outside the bedroom door to be certain he'd got the right person in custody. What he didn't think he had was a double murderer. Lisette had been hiding at Andrew's when the old man had died; Andrew had confirmed that. She had no reason to be involved in tampering with Barks's whisky, nor did she participate in the events of the night he died.

He laid the case out to Superintendent Thaxted.

'So you think she wasn't involved in Barks's death?'

'No. Andrew Chamberlain has given her an alibi for that night. She was asleep in his guest room.'

'Maybe she slipped out and joined the ceremony wearing a mask? Didn't you find one at Andrew Chamberlain's house when you searched it?'

A white mask with a mane on top had been checked in to the evidence room, along with the white tunic Lisette been wearing when she met her sister. While not visible to the naked eye, fine traces of Julie's blood had been detected when held up against the UV black light. 'We think the mask was the one she used on the night of the Julie Dorchester attack, not later. Lisette had no reason to risk being found by going up there.'

'Maybe she wanted to see her lover, O'Brien?'

'But that wouldn't explain killing an old man who had very little to do with her. I can't see any connection.'

'That leaves us with two killers?'

'I'm convinced that the Brother Gorse incident involved one or more other people, but not Lisette.'

'And not O'Brien, from what you've extracted from the recordings?'

'He might've ordered it, but no, he didn't push that man into the Manger.'

Superintendent Thaxted thumbed through the files on the suspects. 'How are we going to make them confess?'

Leo turned his laptop computer round to show her the shadowy outline of a person talking to Brother Gorse. It was cut from the background of a shot that had the distraction of coupling bodies in the foreground, so it hadn't been obvious at first. 'What do you see?'

'A red-robed figure. Just like the other red-robed figures. You can't even tell height or gender from this. You'll have to get something better if we want the CPS to prosecute.'

'And if I said this man here was Brother Maple.' Leo tapped

a person in the middle ground, handing round a flask. The camera had caught his face in profile and it was clearly an older man.

'That still leaves us with two suspects.'

'No, it doesn't, because we're looking at this from the point of view of the one filming it. You can see the edge of the plume fluttering in and out of shot. It's still mounted in a mask.'

Realisation dawned. 'And O'Brien told you Brother Pine took the film. You've got her, Leo.'

'Yes, we have. I might have to walk the CPS through it, but I think we have enough.'

'It would be even better if you got her to admit to it.'

'That's exactly what I'm going to attempt next.'

'You'd better get over to Abingdon then and see if you can get her to tell all. Who are you going to take with you? Harry? He's done well on this case.'

'I was thinking Suyin. And about DS Boston ... he has shown on more than one occasion that he has difficulty working under my command.'

The superintendent closed the file and put it in her out tray. 'He doesn't exactly rejoice to be under mine either. I long ago worked out that I had to accept a certain amount of rough with the smooth with him.'

'I understand, but I think it might be best if you moved him sideways for a while. I don't think I'm the right person to develop him as an officer.'

She folded her hands on the desk in front of her. 'Leo, I think you're exactly the right person. You have all the qualities he lacks: thoroughness, steadiness, awareness, and respect for the rules. And he has some of the things you need: an ability to get on with the lads, a bit of drive and, dare I say, coarseness that makes him seem more like one of the people we serve than a university-educated superior officer.'

'Only if the people we serve were the kind of people who were comfortable hanging out in a 70s comedy club listening to misogynistic, racist jokes.'

'Some of them are. Policing can be brutal. The criminals we deal with respect men like Harry.'

And they don't respect me? thought Leo. 'I'd better get on, ma'am.'

'Think about it, Leo. Consider this a test of your ability to lead.'

Leo couldn't shake the impression that he was being set up to fail. 'Yes, ma'am.'

Sister Ivy, aka Hailey Robertson, had been brought up from the cells and was waiting for them in the interview room. After starting the recording and reading her rights, Leo played the same footage he'd shown his boss.

'The way I see it, Ivy, by process of elimination, that is you, arguing with Brother Gorse.'

She looked away.

'What had he done? Had he trodden on your toes? I believe it was your job to make sure the novices followed the rules, and he was keeping Sister Poppy from joining in. That must've annoyed you.'

Ivy crossed her arms. 'I'm not saying anything.'

'But you've not asked for a lawyer?'

'No, because I have nothing to say. And why have someone just to say that for me when I'm perfectly capable of telling you this myself?'

Leo rubbed his chin. 'Are you keeping silent out of loyalty to Father Oak? You were loyal to him, weren't you, Ivy? The most loyal.'

She stared at the ceiling and hummed something unrecognisable under her breath.

'If you don't tell us the truth, there's a danger he'll go down for this instead of the real culprit. It was his ceremony, after all; he was the one who ordered you to hand out the drugged wine. Do you want him to take the blame?'

Ivy shrugged. Leo exchanged a quick look with Suyin. Ivy was a tougher nut to crack than he'd expected. He'd thought O'Brien would be her weakness.

'OK, let's go back a bit. You were born Hailey Robertson?'

'You can't go back much further than that, can you?' Ivy seemed amused by her own smart-arse comment. Leo was beginning to suspect that this would be the weakness in her position: the desire to seem cleverer than everyone else.

'You completed secondary education but never went to college despite having a place at Manchester University. Why was that?'

'You tell me. You're the one who's been doing your homework.'

'Actually, that was me,' said Suyin. 'I found it interesting that you spent your early twenties in a series of short-term employments in East London. It was also the time when you started getting arrested on minor drugs charges. Was that when you met Terence O'Brien?'

Ivy just smiled.

Leo pulled O'Brien's file towards him. 'No worries, we do have the answer here. No, it wasn't. You didn't meet O'Brien until much later, when you moved to Doncaster. But we do know who else was in London at that time. You met Brother Maple – Phil Seymour. We have you listed as living at the same address. Were you sleeping together?'

'Me? With Phil? You have to be joking.' That idea did provoke her to break her vow of silence. 'He was always way too old for me.'

'But the Met Police had eyes on that property. They raided it in 2010 and found a little cannabis factory in the upstairs rooms, and some poor Vietnamese kid tending to it, but you and Seymour had fled. There's a warrant on you still outstanding for that. They think someone in their force tipped you off.'

Suyin's tone hardened. 'Do you like using slave labour, Ivy?'

'Why? Was he a brother of yours?' she shot back.

Good. They had to keep stoking this temper. 'The Met are waiting to talk to you once we're finished here,' said Leo. 'And you are finished, Ivy. All the way finished. You and O'Brien, you'll never be getting the band back together.' Leo placed before her the latest news articles splashing O'Brien's face over the front pages, calling him the kingpin of the Cotswold drugs cartel – an absurd description if ever there was one.

'Jesus, you people are so stupid! Terry O'Brien isn't in the band; he's just our front man!'

'Like Adam Lambert to your Queen? He looks pretty and sings your tunes?' suggested Suyin with a smirk.

'Exactly like that. He wouldn't know how to run an operation if you walked him through the steps six times. It was ours, not his!'

'*Ours* meaning Seymour and yourself? I'm guessing Brother Pine was a late addition?' Leo asked.

Ivy realised she'd said too much. 'No comment.'

'No, please go on. You don't seem to realise that we don't need you to talk. There's enough here to charge you with conspiracy to murder as well as drug dealing. Your fingerprints are all over the laptop containing the financials. I have to hand it to you, Ivy, you had a very professional attitude to your little business.'

'There's nothing wrong with cannabis. It's legal in many places.'

'But not in England. And to be honest with you, I imagine quite a few jurors might share your lenient attitude to an occasional toke, but not to murder. Brother Gorse had no idea you'd spiked his scotch, had he? You did that so he couldn't interfere with your plans for the new Sister Poppy, his friend. And that's you arguing with him in the video, isn't it? Go on, Ivy. You claim you're the brains behind this operation; at least have the courage to own up to what you did.'

She glared at him, her pride affronted. 'All right, yes, that's me. Arguing, but *just* arguing. We didn't have any compromising images of that new Poppy. I wanted her to get involved.'

'But not with Father Oak? You could've got your footage

if you'd let her have sex with him at the manor. Why did it have to be out on the hillside?'

'It had to be something she'd want to conceal! Two adults having sex in a room is nothing. Naked on a national monument as part of an orgy, well that's something most people would want to hide!'

Leo was amazed that she so readily admitted to blackmail. Thinking to clear herself of murder, perhaps she did not realise the seriousness of the additional charge that would follow as her victims of previous sessions of this date-rape drug scenario were identified? He thought he could crack her further now she was talking.

'But you still didn't want her partner to be Terry O'Brien. That's because you made the fatal error of falling for your fall guy, didn't you? You got jealous, and desperate. You weren't worried about Sister Rose – Terry had shown no special feelings for her – but you didn't want a new Sister Poppy to edge into your cosy relationship with him, did you?'

'No, I did not! And yes, I was relieved when the old one left. You're right; I didn't want that slutty whore to take her place.' She turned to Suyin. 'Why do they always go for that type? Couldn't he see she was nothing but a skank who probably bought her boobs?'

'Maybe O'Brien preferred her to the egotistical kind who would shout at an old man for protecting a woman from rape?' suggested Suyin.

'Fuck you.' They were seeing the real Ivy now ... or should they rather think of her as Hailey Robertson? 'I'm not saying any more.'

'But you should,' said Leo. 'You've admitted to arguing with Brother Gorse, a man who wouldn't hurt a fly by all accounts. How come he ended up dead?'

'The fucking airhead wandered off, didn't she, while we were arguing. Brother Gorse got paranoid about her safety – the drink we use always made him anxious. That's why he didn't like it. But he couldn't be let off drinking it again – Terry was wrong about that – so I made sure he had some in his whisky. It was supposed to keep him away from Poppy but it had the opposite effect. He went off into the dark to find her and, I dunno, fell or something? No one pushed him. Why would we? He was a bloody good cobbler and never caused any trouble.'

Leo believed her. The woman was driven by greed and vanity. She had caused Barks's death by giving him a drink she knew he reacted badly to, thinking he'd be too befuddled to interfere with her plans for Jess. So that was something, possibly even enough for a charge of manslaughter. But as for the idea that someone had actually pushed the man, he had to admit that it was more likely Barks had just fallen in the darkness and no one had noticed. The heart attack had done the rest.

'All right, Ivy—'

'Call me fucking Hailey, would you? I've had enough of that crap.' She kicked off her sandals. 'These things fucking hurt.'

'Hailey. The sergeant here is going to show you a copy of what we've discussed. If you wish to add anything at this point, this is the time to do so. If you agree that the statement is accurate, then please sign and date it. You can call for a lawyer at any time.'

'You're not charging me with murder, are you? That's well out of order.' She half rose in her seat. 'You can't pin that one me.'

'Not at this time. Not unless other evidence comes to light.'

'It won't. I didn't do it. I liked Brother Gorse.' And for the first time the defiance in her tone dimmed to something like regret. 'He was a stand-up man.'

'That's the impression I got.'

'He'd've fucking hated you,' she sneered as Leo exited.

'Yeah. I get that a lot.' He closed the door.

Chapter 43

Jess

I was looking to the door, hoping that Leo would come and see me, but Michael and Cory arrived instead. Of course, I was pleased to see them too.

'Jess? How bad is it?' asked Cory anxiously.

'Can't be too bad because she's sitting up in an ordinary ward,' said Michael bracingly. 'I imagine they'll let you out later today as long as you promise not to throw yourself on any more knives.'

I smiled and accepted his kiss on my cheek. He was using his crutches so stood high enough to reach me on my hospital bed. 'Sit down, Michael.'

'Before I fall down?'

Cory pulled up a chair for him then gave me a gentle hug. 'The kids have done you cards.' She produced two colourful sketches from her tote. One showed me being struck by lightning and the other was a round blob with vaguely placed features. I liked my hands though; they stuck out like chimney-sweep brooms.

I propped them against my water jug. 'What did you tell them?'

'I said your sleepover had got a little out of hand and that you were on the naughty step for a very long time.'

'No really, what did you tell them?'

Cory sat at the end of the bed. 'That's exactly what I told them.'

'I'll get Benji another Dalek pillow.'

'It's OK. I think the Dalek scared him – bad pick on my part. I said he can choose another one at Dunelm.'

'So I did him a favour? I can't see why I deserve the naughty step.'

'Because you got stabbed!'

I scratched my head. 'Erm ...?'

Michael smiled. 'She's just worried about you. We all are. This case has been hard on you.'

'I didn't think it would be so hard to earn my twenty thousand.' I screwed up my nose. 'Oh no! Tanglewood's not going to pay up, isn't she? I got her daughter arrested on suspicion of murder!'

'I haven't talked to her, obviously, but I don't imagine she'll blame you.'

'She probably wishes she'd left everything well alone.'

'But the attack on Julie happened before you got involved. Really, there is no way this is your fault. So tell us, what's the damage?' He gestured to my heart.

'I was saved by the Dalek. Lisette failed to exterminate me.'

'Jess?'

I undid the knot of my hospital gown and pulled it down

so they could see the bandage just below my collar bone. 'She has great aim. If I hadn't used the pillow to deflect it upwards, it might've been a different story. As it is, I've had six stitches and I think my days as a bikini model are over.'

Michael squeezed my hand. 'I'm sorry.'

'Don't be. Someone once told me that you have to concentrate on the fact that you survived and not the fact that you almost died. Don't give your would-be killer the power over you.'

He smiled wryly. 'Sounds like a very wise person.'

'How are the kids, Cory?'

'They're fine.' She produced a bag of grapes. 'Ta-dah! Traditional hospital visiting gift, already washed.' She handed me a piece of kitchen towel.

'You're such a mum.' I took one. The sharp but sweet taste after the bland hospital food told me why these were considered a good idea. 'What's happened to Lisette the Knife?' I shook my head. 'I totally misjudged her. I was feeling sorry for her, can you imagine?'

'I can. You feel sorry for far too many people, Jessica.' That was my Michael: Dr Bear-A-Grudge-And-Enjoy-It Harrison.

'The inspector said she's in custody and they're questioning her even as we speak,' said Cory.

'Actually, it's Tanglewood I feel sorry for,' I mused.

'And the Dorchesters.'

'God, yes. At least, they have each other. Why do we cock up so badly?' I wondered aloud, thinking of Lisette. I did believe she hadn't meant any of this to go so far. I could see something of myself in her lack of impulse control, but at least my go-to move had never been violence.

'Because we're human. There's no one like your own sibling to drive you over the edge,' said Cory.

'I think she might have deeper issues than that. Serious anger-management problems. How are the kids coping?'

'I've not told them. I don't want them scared in their own house and your story of a sleepover was good enough cover.'

'I'm sorry I brought this to your doorstep. You once said I made your life more interesting. I bet you regret that now.'

Cory shook her head. 'As Dr Harrison said, it's actually not your fault and you did everything you could to protect the children and me. And thank you for not bleeding on the carpet.'

'Oh yeah, that was my first consideration.' Leo had grabbed a towel and pressed it to my chest while he called an ambulance. Strange to think that was the most intimate we'd ever been. 'Still want to write about cults, Michael?'

He helped himself to a grape. 'More than ever. It made me wonder how many of these groups hide people with mental illnesses and stop them getting help for a developing condition. I can imagine they attract people of that sort.'

'I think you're on to something. But not everyone in there was crazy. Some seemed to have very rational reasons for being there.'

'Like they could make money from their little drug industry? I understand that four people are charged with that. The commune has collapsed.' Michael sounded pleased to have his cynical instincts proved.

'It's going to be difficult for the others to find new lives. All their money was tied up in that place.'

'I expect they'll move on to the next squat or people's republic. God forbid they actually get a job.'

'Michael here takes the *Telegraph,*' I told Cory.

'Quelle surprise.' Cory was resolutely a *Guardian* reader. 'I would never've guessed. And to think he took in us refugees last night with no questions asked. Thank you, Michael, for stepping in like that. The kids thought it a great adventure. Your house is cool, apparently.'

I thought through what attractions Benji and Leah could possibly have found at Michael's bachelor pad. 'Don't tell me you let them play with your chair?'

Cory sniggered. 'They went to school calling it an electric chair, which doesn't quite give the right impression, but hey ho.'

I could imagine the bemused teachers trying to make sense of that. 'Michael, you are officially my person of the week. Congratulations.' I slapped his hand. 'But that still doesn't mean you can steal all my grapes.'

Chapter 44

Jess

I examined my chest in the mirror. The scar looked ugly: great black stitches holding together red swollen flesh. Benji had said it was cool but to me it seemed like one great buzz-kill if my drinks date with Leo went well tonight.

Not a date, I reminded myself. What had he said? A chance to catch me up on the case.

Oh God. It was a date, wasn't it?

Cory came in with two high-necked blouses for me to choose from. She held them up to me in the mirror. 'So which is it going to be for Inspector Gorgeous? The red sizzle or the light-blue sunny personality?'

The red reminded me too much of the robes worn by Ivy, Maple, and Pine. 'I think the blue.' I slipped into it, keeping my movements restricted so I didn't pull on my stitches.

'So where are you going tonight?'

'Leo—'

Cory clapped her hands to her cheeks. 'Leo! First name terms and everything. You are going to score, girl.'

'Thank you for that running commentary but it's just drinks ...'

'Which leads to just a nightcap, which leads to just come to bed with me and let's play Hide My Truncheon.'

My lips quirked. 'That's not a real game, and he doesn't have a truncheon.'

'Girlfriend, if he hasn't got one, what are you doing with him?'

'Cory ...'

'All right, all right, but I can see a lot of police-related double entendres in your future. What plans do you have?'

'It's drinks. But he suggested we have them in his garden. He has a firepit that he wants to show me.' I held up my hand. 'And do not roll out your garden-related jokes either.'

'I was just going to remark on him being hot enough not to require a firepit.'

'I'll allow that one as it is nothing but the truth.'

'I think it's sweet he wants to show you his garden.'

'It's his passion, I think. At least, that's the impression I got. The invitation really meant a lot to him. It was like he was handing me an invitation to a Buckingham Palace garden party or something.'

'But it's outside; you'll need a jacket or sweater. Hang on, I'll fetch one.'

I checked my watch. He was coming by to collect me at eight, knowing that Cory had vowed never to let me in the family car again. Good call on her part. I was really looking forward to the evening. Today had been epic: I'd been released from hospital, Tanglewood had transferred twenty thousand into my account with a kind message to say she was sorry for what had happened, and she'd added that Andrew Chamberlain was standing with her during the awful days dealing with the fallout. He had sincere, if conflicted, feelings for their daughter and said the very least he could do was support her. Iona Chamberlain-Turner had also been in touch. She'd visited her cousin in jail. They'd already met when Lisette was hiding in her father's house and Lisette had told Iona part of the truth – enough to make the rector wonder about her relationship to Julie. That was why she'd asked for the DNA test. It seemed to me that the Chamberlains were turning out to be good people after all. Lisette couldn't blame her genes on either side for her terrible life choices.

I put on a short necklace that wouldn't brush against the bandage and checked my handbag for the essentials. Brush, small makeup bag, money, keys, condoms (think positively), and mints. As a last-minute thought, I added a travel toothbrush, just in case.

My phone buzzed. It was a message from Leo.

Really sorry. Can't meet up after all.

That wasn't exactly an adequate explanation.

Is it work?

There was a pause.

No. Something came up. I'm sorry.

I was tempted to heave my phone across the room. Well, damn. It looked like I wasn't going anywhere after all.

Except ...

'Hey, Cory, can you get a last-minute babysitter? How about we go for a girls' night out?'

'Inspector Gorgeous stood you up?'

'He did, the bastard.'

'I'll tell the girls.' Oh Lord, she was summoning the book club. That was serious stuff. 'We can dump – sorry, take – Benji and Leah for a sleepover at Jasmine's.'

Was I ready to face a gang of my girl pals all wanting to hear about my latest adventures? The sky-clad ceremonies, the drug farm, the crazy near-death experiences?

On balance? Yeah. I couldn't think of a better bunch of people with whom to drown my sorrows.

'Boys not aloud?' I asked, gesturing to the sign Benji had made me for my door on my suggestion.

'Exactly. Boys not aloud.'

Chapter 45

Leo

Thirty minutes earlier …

It had been a good day: Julie Dorchester's murder solved, Aaron Barks's death explained, everyone safe. The rest of the material from the blackmail videos still had to be reviewed and the victims who were not yet aware told of their existence, but with Ivy, Maple, Pine, and Oak remanded in custody for other crimes, those charges could be added later. Iona Chamberlain-Turner had been very subdued when Leo had told her that she'd turned up in one of the first videos recovered, but she'd taken comfort from the other evidence that she'd not been responsible for her actions.

'I'll have to tell the bishop – and Jimmy,' she said mournfully. 'But it's a relief, to be honest. It's been hanging over my head since O'Brien taunted me with it. I wish I'd said something sooner … come to you. I don't know why I didn't. I think I was scared I'd kiss both my marriage and my career goodbye.'

Leo could well understand just wanting to forget what felt like a drunken lapse and put it away.

Leo felt the ripple of goodwill in his department as he tidied up his desk. He gave the bonsai a little drink, just enough to tide it over until Monday. For once he had a clear weekend. It was rare for enquiries to tie up this conveniently on a Friday. He was looking forward to making good use of it.

'Have a good weekend, Leo!' called Harry as he left.

It would be nice not to have to think about the detective sergeant until Monday too. Leo walked out to his car and checked his messages. He was worried that maybe Jess wouldn't feel up to an evening out, but he wanted a chance to chat without the case hanging over them. Was inviting her to outdoor drinks in his garden a bad idea seeing as it wasn't exactly a balmy summer's night? But he'd decided that he needed to risk more of himself. Everyone was telling him he was too reserved, too closed off, and he felt that Jess would be a safe person to whom he could risk showing a little more of himself. He could see she had many flaws – didn't everyone? – but her one constant was how much she cared for those around her. She even remained on good terms with her ex. If anyone could be trusted with a glimpse of his back garden, it was her. She'd never use it against him.

He sent her a quick message saying he'd be round to collect her at eight, to which she responded with a smiley face.

Drinks didn't seem like enough. He pulled in to the supermarket car park and did a quick smash-and-grab raid of the ready-meals counter. He could cook but he didn't want to spend hours in the kitchen tonight. If she wanted something to eat, at least he'd have something to offer her. What about a bottle of wine? He looked at the offers and then chose one at full price because he liked the sound of the South African label with its promises of gooseberry and citrus notes. It was not a night for stinting.

It was only as he turned into his drive that he noticed someone sitting in his porch. Jess hadn't come early, had she? No. This woman had dark hair and was huddled in a duffel coat, swathed in a leopard-print scarf. His heart sank. He got out, grabbed his shopping, and walked over.

Dark eyes, so like his own, looked up from the sad bundle that had deposited itself on his doorstep.

'Leo?'

'Mum.'

'I'm in such trouble.'

Steeling himself for what would come next, he reached over her head and opened the door. 'You'd better come in then.'

THE END

Acknowledgements

Thank you to old friends and police officers, Debra and Matt Walker, for helping me with my ongoing queries about police procedures. Also thank you to David Miles, author of *The Land of the White Horse*, an invaluable book about the geoglyph that inspired the story. The book gives a fascinating insight into the archaeology of the site but also the miracle of its survival over 3,000 years and is highly recommended to anyone who wants to solve the puzzle of just what the White Horse might mean. And last but not least, a big thank you to my family for putting up with many little details of our family life sneaking into the book sideways. RIP Goldemort, the family goldfish.